This book is due for return on or before the last date shown below.

8 - SEP 2022

ABOUT THE AUTHOR

S. M. Wilson is obssessed with books – she has read
thousands and written more than fifty. *The Infinity Files* is
her second teen series, channelling her love of all things
sci-fi. She lives with her family on the west coast of
Scotland.

susan-wilson.com
@susanwilsonbook
#InfinityFiles

Also by S. M. Wilson:
The Extinction Trials
The Extinction Trials: Exile
The Extinction Trials: Rebel

THE
INFINITY
FILES

S. M. WILSON

USBORNE

For my three heroes: Kevin, Elliott and Rhys Bain

First published in the UK in 2021 by Usborne Publishing Ltd., Usborne House, 83-85 Saffron Hill, London EC1N 8RT, England. usborne.com

Usborne Verlag, Usborne Publishing Ltd., Prüfeninger Str. 20, 93049 Regensburg , Deutschland, VK Nr. 17560

Text © Susan Wilson, 2021

Cover illustration by Martin Grohs. Copyright © Usborne, 2021.

A CIP catalogue record for this book is available from the British Library.

ISBN 9781474972208   05663/2   JFMAMJJ SOND/21

Printed and bound in Great Britain by CPI Group (UK) Ltd, Croydon, CR0 4YY

CHAPTER ONE

Ash leaned forward, even though she knew it made no difference. The expanse in front of her was still the same. Darkness so wide it almost sucked her in. Tiny lights glimmered around her – stars that were millions of light years away. Behind her lay her home planet, Astoria. But she wasn't interested in that right now.

This was it. The moment she'd waited for. Sixteen years of preparation and study – even when it wasn't the popular thing to do. Sixteen-hundred candidates, whittled down to six hundred, then to sixty. And now there was only one place. One place in the Star Corporation Academy. It was hers. She wasn't going to put a foot, hand or strand of hair wrong. Not when it meant so much to her.

A blue tress of hair floated in front of her eyes. She grabbed it and stuffed it back inside her pilot's helmet with one hand, keeping her other hand on the throttle. There was no gravity in a ship as small as this – it would be considered a waste of energy. The thick harness holding her in her seat was already pinching at her shoulders and the top of her thighs. Tonight, her skin would be rubbed raw.

She waited, slowing her breathing and trying to exercise the thing she struggled with most – patience.

It was so easy to get distracted. People thought that space was dark, just blackness. But up here, there was so much more to see than a blank expanse. If she concentrated, she could see a myriad of colours through the view screen in front of her – streaks of pink and purple, elements of yellow, and a littering of silver strands.

The sun at the centre of their solar system was off to her left. At the edges of her peripheral vision, the three other planets were moving slowly in their orbits. Her face scrunched in a perpetual scowl. Astoria had been at war with Corinez for as long as Ash had been alive – even the sight of the harsh icy planet made the hairs on the back of her neck stand on end. It would be easy to let the feelings overwhelm her after everything she'd lost. All to a war that seemed never-ending.

Five hundred years. That's how long the war had lasted in her solar system. No wonder the reasons behind it seemed blurry – though the effects were not. For her, the war had meant the loss of first her sister, then her mother, then her father. It had meant the bombing of the school in her village, houses reduced to rubble, and people scrambling and digging through the dust. That was the reality for Ash.

She gave an involuntary cough as her body remembered

the clouds of dust sent up from the last blast she'd experienced on Astoria. The ringing in her ears for days, and the huge crater where the village had been. A piece of flying shrapnel had given her the scar on her cheek, which she usually hid behind her hair.

She pushed the memory from her mind. She didn't have room for it right now. All her attention had to be on the here and now.

The green of Hakora and sandy colour of Vallus shimmered in the distance like smudges in the dark. Astoria currently had an uneasy alliance with both of these planets, all three sending candidates to compete for places at the Star Corporation Academy. But that alliance could fade as quickly as the flash of a passing comet.

The Star Corporation Academy had originally been founded as a training academy for the planets allied against Corinez. The shimmering grey metallic sphere hung in the sky like a tiny moon. The defensive forces it provided had been used continually since its foundation – and not just against Corinez. Occasionally there had been attacks from other solar systems – the latest from Resto, trying to plunder resources from their planets.

Ash was determined to become a vital part of those forces. Two more hurdles and then she could proudly wear the red uniform of a Star Corporation fighter pilot and defend her planet against all enemies.

Today was the final pilot test, tomorrow would be the final practical test. She planned to ace both.

The practical test was set to examine their engineering skill and ingenuity under pressure. Last year, an interstellar freight shuttle from Hakora had been damaged in a meteoroid storm, with holes puncturing the hull and some components sucked out into space. The pilot and crew on board had been forced to rebuild the ship using what was left. And it hadn't been much. Their story was one of the most retold and admired, because they'd all survived. Ash was betting credits that the final practical test would involve something similar, like all the candidates being thrown into a room with a random set of components and told to create something to save their lives in space. She'd practised so hard for it that she almost craved it.

Her mind worked in a logical way. Building things and taking them apart again never lost its shine. It had been her favourite way to pass the time, back home on Astoria when the temperature dropped sharply at night and most people didn't want to be outdoors. So it didn't matter what the practical test was – building new relays or landing gears, finding a way to power the engines, repairing the comms system to radio for help, or building an antenna to signal the nearest spacecraft – she would be prepared.

She just had to finish this test first, and it shouldn't be difficult. Her piloting skills were sound. All she needed was a little strategic thinking and she should nail it.

Ash gazed at the view screen, waiting for the test to start – waiting for the battle to commence. This area of space was mined around the edges, owned exclusively by the Star

Corporation Academy and used entirely for their training exercises. All the attacking spacecrafts in the test were controlled remotely from the Academy. The only ships that were actually manned during the test were the ones the cadets were piloting. Her four fellow pilots were out there somewhere. Ezra, Trik, Arona and Castille, all in the distinctive Star Corporation fighters with the bright-green logo on the side. They were all being tested at the same time, and all hoping to come out on top.

She twisted her head from side to side, the clear bubble at the top of the ship giving her an open view of the space around her. A dot appeared to her immediate right. It was almost unnoticeable, but the tiny flicker brought her back to the present with a harsh crash. Ash was ready, spinning her fighter craft around, her fingers poised above the red trigger buttons.

The black test craft seemed to burst from nowhere, directly in front of her. Wormholes were like that – something could appear in literally the blink of an eye. She opened fire, not hesitating for a second. It could have been the wrong move – it could have been a "civilian" ship. But she'd seen this often enough when she'd reviewed every previous test for every previous candidate. And statistics told her the first craft to jump into the final pilot test was most likely to be an "enemy" ship.

White streaked across the darkness in front of her, ending in an explosion of muted yellow as the black craft disappeared. There was no sound – sound didn't carry across space –

but in her head, Ash heard a kind of *pop*. It was weird how her brain just added in sound effects when needed.

She spun her ship around, her heart thudding in her chest. Her hand slid a little on the control lever, sweat coating her palm. She cursed and rubbed her hand on the leg of her dark flight suit. The last thing she wanted was for her hand to slip at a crucial moment. The pilot exam was like a carefully choreographed routine, each test individualized for the participant, pushing them to their absolute limits.

Ash's peripheral vision picked up some other fighter pilots. She frowned. Each ship was identical – a single-seat pilot craft with a standard weapons array and the familiar green logo – so there was no way of identifying who was manning which. She gave a little shiver of excitement – the thought of outperforming Trik, Arona, Ezra and Castille appealed to her competitive edge. She wanted to come out on top. She wanted to be truly the best candidate for the pilot job.

But the other four all wanted the same. Each student was equally committed and equally ruthless. For any of them, getting into the Star Corporation Academy would be life-changing. An opportunity. An opportunity to make a difference. An opportunity to get off the planets they all claimed to love so dearly, but saw no future on. Failure would mean going back to the mines for Castille, the military factory for Trik, the fishing boats for Ezra, and the desert dunes of Astoria for Arona. Ash didn't even want to contemplate her own dusty village.

Her gaze flicked left then right, scanning the darkness for another distortion. There it was. Up to the far right of her vision – the place where she had a tiny blind spot.

If Ash looked at a grid solely with her right eye, four of the small squares would disappear. Part of her retina, near the fovea, had been damaged years ago by one of the explosions caused by the Corinez forces. Most of the time she never noticed. Using both eyes together meant that the tiny loss of vision was almost cancelled out.

Almost, but not quite. The Corporation tested their potential cadets with a scrutiny that seemed over the top. But it was to reveal things like this. This part of the pilot test had been made specifically for Ash – and they meant to pressure anything that could be considered a weak spot.

She yanked the stick towards her, throwing the nose of her fighter upwards as she let out a stream of fire. This time the enemy craft had barely started to materialize from its jump before it disintegrated into a million splinters. For a split second, she saw a flash of red against the pale hull – the familiar circle signalling it as a fighter from Corinez. Too close. She'd been far too close. Her mouth instantly dried as shards of metal shot past her, a few spearing the hull of her fighter.

There was a *ping*. Two orange lights. She glanced at the screen in front of her. Potential hull breach and fuel leakage.

She shifted, the straps of her harness digging in even more as her stomach twisted. The two biggest crises for a fighter pilot. Loss of fuel could leave her floating in space for the rest of her natural life. A hull breach could cause the rest of the outer structure to fracture, or could lead to leaking oxygen – both of which were deadly. If things got to that point, she was sure they would pull her out in time – no pilot had ever died during a Star Corporation assessment – but the test here was for *her* to find a way out of this.

She licked her lips, not taking her eyes from the solar system in front of her.

This was a test.

She had to concentrate. The Star Corporation Academy was watching her now. Waiting to see how she would react to the hull damage.

She noticed one of the other Star Corporation fighters looping around, its green logo clearly visible. It seemed senseless. There was nothing to see except drifting shrapnel from the blast.

Then she spotted it. Her fingers sped across her controls, trying to zoom in on the tiny blot beyond that fighter. Was it another hidden threat, ready to attack? No. She frowned again. A cargo vessel. Generally slow-moving, cargo vessels usually carried either freight or passengers – occasionally both. Unless this was part of the test, under no circumstances should it be in this part of the solar system.

The other fighter hadn't moved. She had no idea what it was doing. It seemed suspended in space, hanging there, watching the struggling cargo vessel.

Two thin streams were currently leaking from her craft – one of oxygen, the other of fuel. But the streams coming from the cargo vessel were much thicker than her own – it was obviously in serious trouble. It was a bigger craft, potentially carrying passengers, as well as crew. It shouldn't be here. Not in this zone.

Expect the unexpected. The thought permeated her brain. One of the instructors had mentioned it on their first day, his mouth quirking into a smile. The Academy must want to see her reactions to this unexpected element. And truth be told, they'd got her – because she'd practised hundreds of scenarios, but none of them had been like this.

Her brain started to rationalize what she was seeing. Maybe they'd combined the two final parts of the test. Maybe she was supposed to help repair the cargo vessel and save it.

Her stomach squirmed. But what if this *wasn't* part of the test? What if this was totally random, and completely out of everyone's control? What if this was *real*?

No.

It couldn't be. Not here. Not now.

She pushed forward with the throttle. The hairs on her body prickled as she flew towards the bigger ship. There was an enormous rent in the side of its metal hull. Cargo vessels had minimal shields. There was a shimmer around the edge of the craft, telling her that right now, it must be diverting all its power to those shields to try and keep the ship together.

The little prickles grew stronger. She lifted one hand to subconsciously rub her arm. Could there actually be *people* inside that craft? Why else would the shields have diverted to the hull? This whole situation was making her distinctly uncomfortable.

Part of Ash's brain was telling her this was all deliberate – a test to play with her mind and her ability to think straight. But something else, a feeling deep inside her gut, was putting her on full alert.

She shot past the fighter, which still hadn't moved. She had no idea who was manning that craft. Maybe they were just as bewildered as she was, and trying to pretend *not* to be. More lights started to flash on her boards. She had to make repairs. She had to pay attention to her own vessel or she would soon need to be rescued herself.

But she couldn't. That horrible gut instinct wouldn't let her. It could just be nerves, but she had a bad feeling about this. She couldn't leave another ship like that, not when it was so damaged. Another light appeared on her control panel – orange. She wasn't going to die quite yet. She only had to *really* worry when the lights were red – but of course by then she might have no time left.

She hit the comms button. Her eyes saw the name on the battered hull. "Cargo vessel *Attila*. What is your condition?"

Her ears were flooded with static and she flinched. She flicked to another channel and tried again.

"Cargo vessel *Attila*, this is Pilot Yang. Give me your status."

Still nothing.

She looked behind her. The clear bubble around her allowed her to see the other fighter now sitting on her tail.

"Fighter, identify yourself and your purpose."

Something resembling a snort came over the comm. The voice that replied was almost mocking. "Guess it's time to go home, Ash. You're leaking like an old pipe in the Carpesian desert."

Ezra. It would be him. Friends or not, in the final test, Trik would likely have ignored her. Castille would probably have spoken first. She wouldn't even have appeared on Arona's radar – the girl was too focused for her own good. But Ezra? He did annoying for a living.

"Are you going to help or not?"

"Not," came the short reply.

"There might be people on that cargo vessel," she hissed.

"There are people on my fighter. Me," he replied.

She heard that clicking noise he always made, right about the time he was about to be most annoying. He was enjoying this.

Ash flicked her switch again and heard something else above the crackle coming from the *Attila*. Something that made panic swell in her chest.

"*Mayday. Mayday. Shields are failing. Request assistance…*"

The rest of the dialogue was lost in a hiss. Ash was sure she'd heard more voices in the background. She responded immediately. "Cargo vessel *Attila*, what assistance do you require?"

She was trying not to freak out, thinking about the capacity of that vessel. Her fighter was tiny. What would she do if they requested emergency transport?

Ash spoke before they had time to answer. "I can tether you. Tow you back to the nearest space port."

"*Negative. There's no time.*"

She struggled to turn again and see behind her, desperately trying to figure how much space there actually was in a single-seat fighter. Could she possibly cram any people in here? Her stomach plummeted as a thought filled her mind. What if there were children on the cargo vessel? Could she squash some kids in behind her?

Her alarms were still sounding. One of the orange lights flicked to red. Too many things were happening at once.

Anger bubbled inside. She'd run a thousand practice scenarios. In every single one she'd been methodical, logical. She'd weighed up complicated situations in less than a few seconds and acted without hesitation.

But none of them had been real.

And that was the difference. This *felt* real.

She could practically hear the heartbeat of the captain of the cargo vessel through the comm. He was a living, breathing person. Practice sessions involved *theory* – not reality. None of the other vessels in the final test should be manned by actual people. The only people in space should be the cadets.

"*Systems failing…*" came the crackle. "*No…time…*"

"How many people do you have on board? Do you have transport technology? I'm a single-seat fighter. I'm not sure how many I can hold."

She couldn't remember any scenario where extra people

had been transported aboard a single-seat fighter. Fear was starting to grip Ash. Her heart missed a few beats inside her chest.

The comm crackled. Most of the words were lost. "...*transporting now...*"

The air shifted in front of her, just above her eyes, as whatever the freighter was beaming over began to materialize.

Her recognition was instant – it was far too small to be a person. A second later a brown package appeared in the air before her face.

"Wh...at?"

The dark space outside lit up as the cargo vessel exploded into a million fragments right next to her. The shockwave pounded off her own smaller craft and sent her rocking and rolling around.

She choked and spluttered, doing her best not to vomit. The fighter was showered with debris and a stuttering voice cut in through the mess.

"T-tethering now."

Her fighter gave a shudder as an emergency tether from Ezra's craft clamped on to her tail and yanked her backwards.

Ezra didn't normally stutter. He sounded as shocked as she was. This was a training exercise. Or it was meant to be. What had just happened?

More debris kept hitting the nose of her fighter as it was pulled away. She winced. Every light on her panel was now red. Her fuel tank was empty – her oxygen tank almost the same. She grabbed for the emergency supply under her seat and clapped the mask to her face. Not that it would be much use for long. Her mind finally started to go into automatic pilot mode. She flicked all power to the shields. The damage to her craft must be extreme. She didn't have the view that Ezra did, but why else would he tether her?

With no gravity to keep it anchored in place, the package bounced off the side of her head. She'd momentarily forgotten about it, in the shock of the explosion. Commander Clay's voice cut across the airwaves.

"Flight Cadet Yang. Prepare for emergency transport."

What? No.

Reality hit. Her craft was too badly damaged. Her test was well and truly over.

She reached out and made a grab for the package. The package that the captain of the *Attila* had thought more important than any life on board his vessel.

None of this was supposed to happen.

Her body twitched as the transporter took hold. The shimmering sensation, like a billion little insects crawling over her skin, started. She automatically sucked in a breath even though it was entirely unnecessary, closed her eyes and prayed.

CHAPTER TWO

Ash thudded onto the hard floor – her body still in the position it had been in, in the seat of the fighter.

The whoosh of the sudden gravity impact, along with the horrible shaking feeling of every molecule in her body reassembling, made her retch. She'd only been transported once before and had vowed then never to let it happen again. Her hands were still clutching the package, but it slipped to the floor as her muscles spasmed.

Ash tried to tell her body to remember to breathe. It was almost like her brain couldn't compute what had just happened.

She lifted her gaze. Three figures in uniform stood behind a control console in the grey room. The three Commanders of the Star Corporation Academy.

She choked on the breath she'd sucked in so hard. These three were hardly ever seen. They were more like a myth than reality. Legends in their own right.

But the three-pronged myth was standing right in front of her.

Commander Clay was the person she'd heard over the comm – at least it had sounded like his voice, the one she'd heard in the many Star Corporation tutorials. He was short and squat, with sandy-coloured hair, his skin having the same bioluminescence as all the residents of Hakora. His brow was creased with worry.

They weren't even looking at her. All of them were looking at the panel at their fingertips.

"Pull him," Commander Trinley said coolly, her dark skin and closely cropped hair glistening in the bright white lights of this drab room. She was so much more petite than Ash had ever imagined, but determination shone through in her steely glare. This was not a woman to ever be questioned.

Commander Anand let out an exasperated sigh. He was tall and lean, his thick dark hair almost hiding his eyes from Ash, but not his larger ears. He was from Vallus, where sound was slightly muted.

Seconds later there was another thud beside her.

All three of the Commanders looked up this time. But none of them looked at Ash, or the crumpled heap beside her. Their eyes were fixed on the wall behind her.

Ash's stomach was still cramping. She clambered onto all fours, still trying to catch her breath. The blue strand of her hair obscured her vision. She clicked the strap on her helmet and let it fall to the floor, then looked beside her.

Ezra. That's who the thud belonged to.

His eyes were wide, his dark hair streaked with flecks of...something. He coughed, trying to catch his breath, then his brown eyes locked on to her gaze.

Something flashed across his face – was it shock, surprise or relief? – before he groaned and clutched his arm. "Ash, I thought you were—" His words cut off. It took her a few seconds to realize there was a dark pool of blood on the floor at his elbow.

Ash moved over next to him. "What the...?"

She didn't finish. There was a thick shard of something sticking out of his chest, near the bottom of his ribs. Her instinct was to pull it out, but what if she made things worse?

"We need some help!" she yelled.

Something flickered to her side. She twisted around and looked up. The wall behind them had an expansive view screen on it – that's what the Commanders were focused on. Against the black background speckled with stars, it showed a small hulk of damaged grey metal with an empty tether line attached that was rippling around in the void of space. The craft looked as if it had ploughed into a piece of floating space junk that drifted nearby. A strip of white was hissing from it.

Ezra's fighter. It had to be.

He'd thought she was dead. The floating space junk must be what was left of her own fighter.

White filled the screen for a few seconds, followed by the same view of space – but this time with no damaged fighter. It had exploded, just like hers. Only one twisted fragment floated on the screen in front of them, its warped structure making Ash catch her breath at the fate they'd both just escaped from.

Ezra made a noise next to her. She turned her head and they locked gazes.

Between them, they'd destroyed two fighters.

Her brain was taking what she knew and what she was seeing, and filling in the blanks. Her own fighter had been damaged by flying debris. If it had exploded while still tethered to Ezra's, she could only imagine the damage that had been done.

He'd tried to save her, and almost killed himself in the process.

She blinked as she staggered to her feet. Her breathing had steadied but her heart rate hadn't.

Final tests didn't end like this. Her gaze caught the package lying abandoned on the floor at her feet. Not a single part of this made sense.

For a few seconds, she actually wondered if Ezra's blood was real – or if this was all some elaborate plan to test her even more. She'd thought she'd known all about the tests. She'd researched enough. But this was just too crazy to be real.

No one had moved since she'd asked for help. Ezra groaned and it pulled her mind back into focus. "Where is the help?" she yelled.

As if in answer to her question, the doors to the transporter room slid open and two medics in green tunics jogged in.

Relief flooded over her. Within seconds they had given Ezra a shot of something and slid him onto a trolley. His head lolled to one side. Ezra's normally luminescent skin had a sickly tone.

That chilled feeling spread over her body again. They were rivals, vying for the one spot. When she'd heard his voice over the comm she'd been annoyed. When he'd mocked her, she'd been angry. Irrational.

But now, seeing him unconscious on the trolley, she realized just how much he'd risked for her. A horrible thought shot through her. Would she have done the same for him? Risked her life, tethering a clearly unstable ship that could blow up at any second? She pushed the thought from her brain, afraid she wouldn't be proud of the answer.

As the door hissed shut behind him, Ash was aware of the silence in the room around her. She pressed her lips together, but she couldn't hold the question in.

"Was it part of the test?" She grabbed for the package. Her hands wouldn't stop shaking. Cold sweat was trickling down her back.

No one answered. There was an exchange of glances between the Commanders.

She wasn't sure where her bravado was coming from. It could only be the adrenaline that was surging through her system, battling with the anxiety building in her chest. "Was it part of the test?" she asked again, as she strode over towards the three Commanders.

Three pairs of eyes were fixed on the package in her hands.

She thudded it down on the console and all of them flinched at her angry action.

"Was this all part of the test?" She flung one arm back towards the large view screen. There were still a few parts of Ezra's fighter floating in sight.

Commander Clay shook his head. His voice was quiet but steady. "No." He didn't offer anything else. He lifted the package, an eyebrow rising for a second as he pulled out something tucked inside. A holocard.

He blinked, but said nothing, putting the package back on the console as he tilted the holocard so each of his fellow Commanders could see it. Neither spoke. But Ash could tell how hard Commander Trinley was trying to keep her face neutral. A tiny tic had appeared at the corner of one eye.

Ash couldn't understand the silence. Panic was roaring in her ears.

"But that cargo vessel, it was damaged. I thought maybe I was supposed to try and help repair it. You've done that before, haven't you? In a test?"

Commander Trinley shot her a look. Ash was babbling. She knew she was babbling, but she couldn't help it. She was starting to realize just how lucky she was to be alive.

She'd never been in a room with the three Commanders before and she didn't know anyone else who had either. She'd spent the last six years of her life hoping and wishing for this chance – the opportunity to impress the people who could actually change the course of her life. All of which meant she should keep her mouth well and truly shut.

But Ash had never really done what she should.

"How did a cargo vessel manage to get inside the testing zone? I thought things like that weren't supposed to happen. And why was it damaged?"

Commander Trinley shot her a look of distaste.

Commander Clay spoke in a measured manner. "The cargo vessel came through an uncharted wormhole. We have no idea how it managed to sustain the damage."

She looked up at Commander Clay. "Then why didn't you launch an immediate rescue mission? Why was I the only ship trying to help?"

Commander Anand's voice was harsh. "There was no time. No time to launch a rescue mission with any hope of success." He pushed his shoulders back. "Cadet Yang. Your concern shouldn't be the cargo vessel. Your concern should be your performance in the test." He gave her a steely glare. "You destroyed your fighter – and you caused another to suffer the same fate." He gave his head a shake. "You had showed such promise, but it's clear that your time in the Academy has been wasted. The protection of our fighters and fleet is our primary aim."

Anguish gripped her chest. She'd failed the test. She'd failed the test she'd spent the last few years studying for. More than that, she'd failed it spectacularly. She had destroyed two fighters. She was going to spend the rest of her life back home on Astoria, stuck in the same dirt-filled village, with no chance of ever leaving. All of a sudden the room felt hot, despite the perfectly constant cool temperature.

The environmental systems regulated temperature, oxygen levels and humidity every ten seconds in all the rooms in the Star Corporation Academy. But knowing this didn't stop Ash tugging at the neck of her flight suit.

"I was thinking about the cargo vessel. There were people on board." She couldn't hide the tremble in her voice. She still didn't know how many lives had been lost out there. "I just wanted to help."

She looked up at the three expressionless faces.

"I acted on instinct. It seemed like the right thing to do."

No one spoke. They didn't even give her a sympathetic glance.

Her stomach twisted in a way it never had before as she saw her future slipping through her fingers, like the shifting sands of the Carpesian desert.

"Report to your quarters, Cadet Yang," said Commander Clay. The words were dismissive but his gaze was locked on his fellow Commanders. She could feel unspoken messages in the air – a whole host of information she wasn't party to, simmering tension she could almost reach out and touch. "Everything about your test is to remain confidential."

As she hesitated, Commander Trinley pressed a button on the console, her voice serious but steady. "Attention, all cadets. Due to unforeseen circumstances, tomorrow's final test has been cancelled. Decisions will now be based on your performances to date. You will all be asked to report to the auditorium shortly for the appointment announcements."

Ash sucked in a breath. She'd never heard of the final test

being cancelled before. Why had they done that? What weren't they telling her? They were deciding, now, who should win the coveted pilot spot?

Commander Trinley met Ash's gaze. "Report to your quarters, Cadet Yang," she repeated.

Ash stared back at the three heads of the Academy, willing them to say something more, willing them to show some kind of emotion about what she'd just witnessed.

But there was nothing.

Yet as Commander Trinley pulled her hand back from the comm…was that a tremble?

The crudely wrapped brown package sat on the console. It took what little self-restraint Ash still had to stop herself sending it flying in frustration.

As she turned and headed out through the door, her eyes caught one final view of the expanse outside. Darkness, broken only by the distant smudge of Corinez. Within a few moments, the debris of all three ships had scattered, floating off somewhere in perpetual motion to travel for thousands of years in the vacuum that was space. It was almost as if nothing had happened at all.

But Ash had been there.

She knew it had happened.

And she wouldn't forget it.

CHAPTER THREE

Ash tried to go to the medic centre to check on Ezra but was readily dismissed by staff who looked down their noses at her. She was only a cadet – and they were definitely low in the pecking order. Although they got to stay at the Academy for sixteen weeks while completing their testing, their access to operational areas was limited.

She hurried along to the mess hall, where the cadets usually gathered. Her heart leaped as she saw Trik, Arona and Castille huddled around one pale grey table.

"Are you guys okay?" She bit her lip for a second. "How did your tests go?"

She'd banded together with these guys as soon as she'd arrived at the Academy. They all had the same goals – to get off their own planets – and the camaraderie between them had grown quickly. Each one of them had been affected by the war, losing family members or friends at some point. All of them had the steel and passion to fight back. It had gelled them together. These guys were her closest rivals. Or, at least, they had been – until she'd blown the final test. The trouble was, they weren't looking so friendly right now…

The others raised their heads in unison. The looks they gave her were far from welcoming. She hadn't been sure how much everyone else would know, or if they would have realized Ezra had been injured. She'd been told to keep everything confidential, but had news leaked out already somehow?

All three of her friends stood up from their chairs. Trik stormed past, his face furious, Arona completely ignored her, her blonde hair swishing in time with her tall lithe body as she stormed away, and Castille just raised his eyebrows.

"Really, Ash? What did you do?" he asked. His thickset muscles were tense, and she could see a tic at the side of his jaw, beneath his slightly large ears.

"What do you mean?"

He shook his head in frustration. "We all got pulled before we had a chance to complete our pilot exam. And from the explosions we saw, it looked like you had something to do with it." He pushed past her then halted, his voice dripping with sarcasm. "You asked, how did the test go? Well, since you've apparently ruined everyone else's, it looks like you should know better than us."

Her heart squeezed. Space was vast and even though they were all tested at the same time, there could have been a chance that the other three pilots had missed everything. It seemed not. And now she was the target for their anger.

But none of them had mentioned Ezra. Did they even know he was injured?

She sagged down into one of the empty chairs. These were the only people she'd considered friends in the sixteen weeks since she'd got here. From their other assessments, she'd known they were her main rivals. But instead of avoiding each other, they'd started to band together. They'd spent their time teasing and taunting each other over results. The rivalry had been real, but it had remained companionable.

Ash had never had a huge circle of friends. After the death of her family, she'd withdrawn. It seemed the safest way. If she didn't love people, she couldn't be distraught when they were gone. But the Star Corporation Academy had given her a sense of family again – something that had been missing in her life and that she'd reluctantly embraced. She'd even wanted to keep in touch with these guys once everything was over and the results revealed. Now it seemed that her performance today could have ruined it all, and she hated the way that burned deep down inside her.

She wiped an errant tear from her eye, willing herself to hold it together. Maybe this was for the best. She'd never been good at friendships. Maybe this was another lesson to be learned in what was easily one of the top ten worst days of her life.

A siren sounded, summoning everyone to the main auditorium, and she filed in with the rest of the cadets. Part of her still held the tiniest hope that maybe things weren't quite as bad as she'd initially thought. Maybe it was all just some kind of bad dream or hallucination. Maybe she'd get to wake up and start this day over again.

As she searched for a seat, her eyes fixed on the dark hair and grey flight suit in the front row.

Ezra.

Her stomach twisted. The room was too packed to get down next to him, but even from here she could see him move and wince a little. They must have patched him up and sent him back out for the announcement ceremony.

Within a few minutes, six hundred other bodies were packed into the tiered seating of the auditorium. There was a hum of expectation in the air. Several of the other cadets shot her envious looks – they obviously hadn't heard about her disaster.

She shifted uncomfortably. Was she about to be humiliated in front of all these people? Most of whom she'd beaten in every assessment.

There were a few disgruntled mutterings about the cancellation of the final test. This had never happened before and it seemed the rest of the room couldn't figure out why it had happened this time. But she could also see some people gossiping excitedly, desperately wondering what was going on.

Part of Ash considered leaving. But part of her was intrigued. What if the Commanders were going to actually explain more about the cargo ship and where it had come from?

She didn't have time to consider any longer. Another

door slid open at the front and the three Commanders walked in, taking their positions on the stage.

There was a simultaneous intake of breath. Most of the other cadets had never been in the presence of the three Commanders. Up until earlier today, neither had Ash.

Now she'd had time to think straight, Ash realized just how big a deal that had been. The Commanders were the figureheads of the Academy. They'd fought in numerous space battles over the years. They regularly advised the allied planets on battle strategy. They didn't only train pilots, they trained engineers, researchers, comms teams. Pilots who'd been trained at the Academy were known for their collegiate flying – almost like synchronized dances in space, even in the most desperate of skirmishes.

They were the best of the best.

And she'd wanted to be one of them.

She'd actually thought she could be.

And now, it had come to this.

Commander Trinley spoke first, her gaze taking in the six-hundred cadets in the room. These were the people who'd made it to the second stage, before the competitors had been whittled down to the final sixty. But at this point, everyone who'd participated in the process was invited to hear the final results.

Ash's mouth was bone dry. Everyone knew there was only one pilot spot. But sometimes there were alternative duties. Some cadets were selected for comms duty. Some for satellite maintenance. Some for engines and design. But none of these alternative paths held any appeal for Ash.

She'd been focused for so long on being a pilot, anything else would just seem like failure.

For the millionth time, she tried to calculate the myriad of possibilities in the room. Had Trik, Arona or Castille aced their assessments? Were they so good that they'd won the pilot spot without needing to go through the final test?

But none of them were acting like that. Trik hadn't shown his normal smug smile, and Castille was flicking his fingers – the sign that usually indicated his nerves. Arona's face was as blank as usual. Did the girl actually have any expressions? Alongside Ezra, they'd been the only ones she'd thought could have a realistic possibility of matching her previous scores.

But, if it wasn't them…who else could it be?

She scanned the room, searching for a few others. Leira, from Vallus. She'd probably been in the top ten. But she had her eyes fixed on the floor and her hands were twisting in her lap. Rebus, from Hakora. His tactical skills were excellent, but his reflexes not quite so good. Maybe he'd been lucky and aced a previous test?

"Cadets. We thank you for your attendance here today, and for all your time and dedication spent during the assessment process for the Star Corporation Academy. We are honoured every term to have thousands of applications. To reach the spots you are in now is indeed an honour in itself. I want each and every one of you to take pride in the fact you made it this far.

"Of course, part of the beauty of being in the assessment

process is the ability to learn about yourselves, to test yourselves to your limits, in mind, body and spirit. I hope you all now feel more confident in your own skills."

Commander Trinley took a deep breath as she looked at the expectant faces, all waiting for her to tell them who had won the ultimate prize. Instead she turned to Commander Anand, with a brief nod to let him speak next.

Ash held in a cry of frustration. How long would this go on? She looked back down towards Ezra. It was almost as if he felt her gaze because, within a few seconds, he turned his head slightly and caught her eye. One hand was across his body, resting at the bottom of his ribcage. Most people in the room wouldn't know why. But she did.

The medic centres could do wonders these days. A sweep of a scanner and instant autorepair was a bit like minor surgery had been a few hundred years ago. The use of the medic autorepair was usually coupled with a whizz of analgesia. But it looked like Ezra hadn't opted for that, not by his stiff and awkward movements. She almost understood. The analgesics usually left someone with a smile pasted on their face and seeming slightly vacant for a few hours. Would Ezra really want to feel like that now, in the moment when all their dreams might be delivered or dashed?

For half a second, she wondered if she should have faked some kind of injury. Maybe being absent for this announcement wouldn't have been such a bad idea.

Commander Anand started speaking. Except, he didn't exactly speak – he boomed.

Once interplanetary space travel had been achieved by their ancestors, the people who'd settled across the four planets in this solar system hadn't all developed identically. Apart from a whole host of different races and religions, there were also fundamental planet-wide differences.

An ancient Vallusian had been the first to chart the subtle changes between the people living on each planet. Hakora was a denser planet, with a slightly stronger gravitational force than the other three in their solar system. That meant people who lived there for prolonged periods became a little shorter, with increased bone density. It was easy to see at a glance that Commander Clay had grown up there. Meanwhile on Vallus the atmosphere was oxygen rich, and sound echo was more muted. Over thousands of years, the people of Vallus had developed slightly bigger ears and naturally spoke at louder levels. For Commander Anand, it seemed a hard habit to break.

"Cadets." A few sat up straighter, startled by the louder voice.

"Thank you for your attendance today. And thank you for your participation in the programme. Our planets continue to be united in war against Corinez, and Resto, in the neighbouring system. We have also had reports of increasing activity around the wormholes between our solar system and the distant U62 system."

There were a few anxious glances. Ash hadn't heard anything about this and, by the looks on other people's faces, neither had they.

The story of the U62 system was one of the most well-told legends that Ash could remember. When Ash had been a kid she'd heard tales that said all life had originated from U62, before damage in the system had made it uninhabitable. At that point, the people of the system had set out through the wormholes, hoping to find somewhere else to live and thrive. Never before had she heard of people returning to the U62 system. It all seemed so strange. Was it possible that travellers from a more distant galaxy had just stumbled upon the wormhole system originating in U62? And were they friends, or foes?

"It is vital in these alarming times that we have the best fleet possible. And it is for that reason that this time around we won't just be recruiting one pilot, we will be recruiting four."

There was a gasp in the room, part of which came from Ash. Maybe her chances weren't as ruined as she'd first thought. Could she at least have made the top four?

"We will also – as in previous cohorts – be recruiting to some supplementary positions. Know that, if we don't recruit you today, we may well recall you in future. Tensions are rising in our galaxy. While we have a fleet that is ready to defend our planets, if situations change, we may need to increase our force at short notice. These are testing times." He paused and let his words hang in the air.

The excitement that had initially been in the room was slowly dying. The cadets were now looking anxious, shifting in their chairs.

War was not unusual in this solar system. Over the last few centuries, Ash's planet Astoria had fought in a variety of battles against all the other planets. Alliances formed and broke down. Wars were even more common between neighbouring solar systems. Refugee ships regularly arrived from other ruined planets, trying to claim land on Astoria, Vallus or Hakora. Most refugees weren't interested in the frozen land of Corinez. For Ash and her fellow cadets, recent tensions suggested that they may imminently face active battle for the first time in their lives.

Commander Clay took over the mantle from Commander Anand. "Circumstances have dictated that our overall final capability test can't be completed this time around. However, we are confident we have enough information to select the best candidates." He lifted his gaze to scan the room. "Now, you all know that the final pilot test is designed individually for each of our cadets. This is to test you at every level, pushing your weaknesses, testing your judgement, reflexes, responses and the ability to think on your feet. Our fighter craft are our most expensive commodity…"

Ash squirmed. This didn't sound good. The pointed reminder felt aimed at her.

"We can only put pilots in them who understand their value."

That was definitely aimed at her. Commander Clay's words seemed to crawl over her, itching her skin, before congregating in a large red sign flashing above her head. Cadets who hadn't looked at her before now seemed to throw glances in her direction.

She hadn't told anyone what had happened. Had Ezra? Had he told the others that she'd wrecked her own fighter and been partly responsible for wrecking his?

Her chest squeezed. She could hear her quickening heartbeat in her ears. Spots appeared in her peripheral vision.

Ash fixed her gaze on the floor, staring at her purple boots and willing the air into her lungs as she counted in her head.

There was a swooshing noise and the door to the right of the Commanders slid open. A stream of people in red flight suits with white helmets tucked under their arms marched in, filling the area behind the Commanders.

The red stream seemed never-ending. More than two hundred current pilots filed in, standing in rows at the front of the auditorium. Ash breathed out slowly, seeing the glint of gold on numerous shoulders. Battle medals. Most of these pilots had already successfully defended their planets.

All of a sudden, there it was. The thing she'd always wanted, right in front of her: to wear the bright red flight suit. To carry the white helmet under her elbow. To lift her head with pride and know that she would be recognized instantly on sight. To soak in the honour and prestige that went along with people knowing just how good you must have been to make it as an Academy pilot.

For a moment, she actually felt sick. An unwelcome tear threatened to spill down her cheek. She swallowed, willing the wetness in her eyes to disappear. There was no one to blame here but herself. It had been *her* actions, *her* decisions out there in space that had brought her to this point.

She'd always felt so self-assured. So prepared. So confident that she would be able to handle things. She'd thought about the daring attack missions. She'd even thought about the deaths. But they had always been enemy deaths – therefore they didn't count.

Today had been different. Today, there had been real, live civilians on that cargo vessel. She wasn't used to the idea of civilians dying in space. It was painful enough to think of them caught up in bombing raids down on the planets.

The last bombing raid she'd seen on Astoria had wiped out her village's market. The one before had taken out a whole row of dwellings. But the first one she could remember was the one imprinted on her brain. It was the one that had hit the village school.

She'd been sick that day and, ironically, she'd been faking. School bored Ash, even at the age of ten. She loved maths and physics but she'd found the teacher took things far too slowly for her. She could learn more at home, taking things apart and creating her own experiments. And that's where she'd been when the bomb had hit.

She'd run to the school along with most of the village, dust clouding her vision and clawing at her throat. As it started to clear a little she could see the pile of rubble. The building hadn't been big, or particularly sturdy. Now it was just a heap of flattened bricks. A heap of bricks that contained Ruhinda, her younger sister.

Ash had no idea how long she and the rest of the villagers had dug. Her mother and father had been distraught. Fingers bled as brick after brick was tossed aside in the hope of finding any sign of life.

In the end, only one adult and five kids had been found alive and pulled from the rubble. None of them had been Ruhinda. The adult and one of the other kids died the next day.

Ash's mother had died a few years later. People claimed it wasn't possible to die of a broken heart, but Ash knew different.

After the attack, Ash had looked at the stars that night and, at age ten, sworn her life wouldn't end in that village. She wouldn't be one of the victims of this interplanetary war that she could barely understand. Not down here. If her life was going to be lost, it would be lost in the stars, as she fought to defend her planet.

She'd only had her father left and he'd been disturbed by her determination to make it to the Star Corporation Academy. He'd already lost two family members and didn't want to lose her too. But in the end, he'd died from the same lung infection, caused by the dusty atmosphere, that affected many of the villagers. The village had been her family after that. And no one had discouraged her will to get out of there.

She sighed as she looked at the ranks of uniformed pilots in front of her. She'd worked so hard and come so far. She couldn't bear the thought of this all slipping through her fingers.

The little light that had been burning away inside her for the last six years flared with persistence. Hope. Everyone had to have hope – even when things seemed desperate.

Commander Clay's voice continued. "Cadets. Our assignments are as follows…"

He did it deliberately. It was notorious every year how long he kept them all waiting. "Uzra Endra, satellite communications."

The cadets in the auditorium applauded as the slightly stunned young guy stood up and walked to the front.

"Arissa Titan, medic centre."

The girl's name seemed ironic – she was tiny and slight framed. Her grin spread from ear to ear as she descended the steps and took her place next to Uzra.

"Petra Mejoz and Lando Rosen, engineering." From opposite sides of the auditorium, two other cadets almost ran down the stairs to join the others.

Ash pressed her lips together. Her dream had always been to be a pilot, but after today's disaster, would engineering really have been so bad? She'd spent her life tinkering with things and seeing how they worked.

"Rudd Aston, astrophysics." A tall, thin boy almost leaped from his seat. He didn't smile once. Ash recognized him. He was probably the smartest guy she'd met. But his coordination had let him down badly in the previous pilot tests. The guy practically had astrophysics stamped on his head.

Her heartbeat was quickening again. They were getting closer, closer to the pilot announcements. There were another few names called for tactical operations, programming and construction.

Then Commander Anand said, "Our first pilot will be…"

Ash closed her eyes and clenched her fists.

"Trik Enliva."

The audience gave a round of applause. Several of the other cadets who came from Hakora, like Trik, let out some cheers.

Trik couldn't hide his grin. He looked surprised and excited all at once. His hands clenched and unclenched as he walked down the stairs, shaking hands with each of the Commanders before giving the briefest of nods and standing next to the red-uniformed pilots. Ash noticed his dark skin glistening with sweat. He'd been worried.

Something unfurled inside of Ash as she noticed Trik's sideways glance at the red flight suits, knowing that today he'd get to put one on. An uncomfortable wave of jealousy. She'd beaten him in every tactical test. Except, most likely, today. But her hands automatically applauded along with everyone else. She knew how much he'd wanted this. He was a good pilot. He deserved to be down there.

Commander Anand continued. His booming voice was starting to give Ash a headache. "Our next pilot is…"

He was enjoying this. He was enjoying the people all left wondering if he'd call their name, no matter how unlikely.

"Arona Rozelle." In the blink of an eye, Arona practically raced down the steps. It was the first time Ash had seen her smile properly.

Her stomach plummeted. Four spaces. Two now gone.

Arona was tall and slim, with a sheet of blonde hair. A perfect poster girl for the next recruitment campaign. She came from one of the desert regions on Astoria. She was the most competitive girl Ash had ever met – except for herself, of course. As Arona reached the Commanders and shook their hands, she regained her signature composure, the smile vanishing from her face, replaced by her usual unreadable expression. She spun around to stand next to the other pilots, her hair swinging out.

Ash was annoyed at the cloud of envy that enveloped her as she watched Arona. As if she knew exactly how Ash was feeling, Arona lifted her long lashes, and her green gaze connected with Ash's.

Ash had expected her to be arrogant. Triumphant. But instead, she gave Ash an imperceptible nod, then averted her gaze.

She hadn't been triumphant. She hadn't punched the air, which is more likely what Ash would have done. All she'd done was smile. Ash felt ashamed of her own feelings. These were people she'd considered friends.

Commander Trinley was now speaking. "Our third pilot is…Castille Pijaz."

The roar was huge. Half of the cadets in the room were from Vallus – the same planet as Castille. Commander Anand had a hint of a smile on his normally sombre face.

Castille's heavy footsteps pounded down the stairs to the side of Ash. Three out of four places gone. One place left. *Only one.*

43

Commander Anand took back over. "And our final pilot will be…"

Silence filled the room. Expectation swelled in the air around her. No one could take their eyes off Commander Anand. Except… There was a tiny flicker in Ash's peripheral vision and she looked downwards. Ezra was looking up at her again, his hand still on his ribs.

His expression was unreadable.

She hated this. She hated how much she despised her fellow candidates right now. Even the guy who had saved her was now her biggest rival.

Her mouth was unbearably dry. Ezra's eyes left hers and he turned back around to face the Commanders. Maybe it would be neither of them. Maybe someone else had risen to the top of the pack. She scanned the room again, desperately trying to figure out who it might be.

Commander Anand seemed to be hanging on the anticipation and expectation in the room, sucking it in for his own pleasure. There was a small clearing of his throat and then he tilted his chin a little higher. "Our last pilot will be Ezra Umbeka."

And just like that, the little light inside Ash flickered and died.

CHAPTER FOUR

It was like having an out of body experience. People around her cheered. Ezra got to his feet and walked slowly over, shaking hands with the Commanders then taking his place next to his fellow crew.

Ash felt numb. Everyone stood up, talking incessantly. The room was a mixture of enthusiasm, with a few tiny twists of disappointment and bitterness. Two out of the four pilots this time around came from Hakora. She could see people scanning the red uniforms and trying to work out the ratio between the three planets. Some people speculated that the Star Corporation Academy tried to keep the ratios even, regardless of the skills of the pilots. But Ash didn't believe that. Not after all she'd seen during the tests. She would have handpicked these people herself.

Commander Trinley held out her arms as she looked at the red-suited pilots with pride. "Fly true and may the stars protect you."

It was like a knife twisting in Ash's gut. She'd always wanted to hear those words from one of the Commanders. But she'd wanted to hear them when *she* was dressed in one of those red flight suits and about to undertake her first mission. Hearing them now was like the final nail in the coffin.

She watched her four friends: wide smiles on their faces as they laughed, with arms around each other. She wanted to go and congratulate them. That was the right thing to do – but they were surrounded by other classmates, and she didn't have the energy to fight her way through the crowd right now.

She could sense eyes on her. People muttering to each other as they glanced in her direction. She could almost read their minds. The girl who had been top of the class had bombed out. Just how bad a pilot must she be?

Ash ignored them, staring at the benches as the people in front filed out, inexplicably slowly.

Astoria. She'd be back there in a matter of hours. She should love her planet with her whole heart, but the thought of going back to the dusty settlement filled her with dread.

What future did she have there? She loved the people, but it wasn't where she wanted to be. She'd spent the last six years looking to the stars, longing to be up among them, wondering about the possibilities and the opportunities. This had been her only chance.

Maybe she'd been too focused on being a pilot. Maybe she should have looked at the bigger picture. Would it really have been so bad to end up as a weapons controller, an engineer, or a comms tech? At least it would still have meant a life in the stars.

Instead, her future had just flickered out like a snuffed flame.

As she finally stood to leave, a hand pressed on her shoulder.

"Ash."

The voice was deep. She spun around. Ezra.

He stood close, his nose just slightly above hers. Ezra wasn't quite as short as his fellow comrades from Hakora. His family had been based on a space station for part of his childhood, so the dense atmosphere of his home planet hadn't affected his bones and stature quite as much.

His skin glistened with sweat. Her hand went automatically to his elbow. "Are you okay? Do you still hurt? Why didn't you take some pain relief?"

He grimaced – every move he made seemed to cause him pain. His face moved into a stiff smile. "I had to be awake enough to listen."

She could sense people looking at them. A staircase in the middle of the main auditorium was hardly a place for a private conversation.

Ash lowered her voice, her eyes darting from side to side. "Does anyone else know what happened?"

Ezra pressed his lips together. "No. I was asked" – he glanced towards the Commanders – "not to mention it."

She lifted her other hand. "Then how are they going to explain your injury?"

He shook his head and gave a wry smile. "Clumsy? Maybe I fell down the stairs. Maybe you should push me in a fit of rage."

Irony dripped from his voice. Again her mind jumped back to that moment in space. The moment that Ezra took a chance on helping her, instead of helping himself.

"Why did you help me?" she whispered. "Why did you do it? You could have got out of there. You wouldn't have been hurt." His hand was still resting subconsciously across the base of his ribs.

Something flashed across his face. Something entirely unfamiliar. He looked ashamed. In all her interactions with Ezra, he'd exuded confidence. Bravado. It was part of the reason he'd annoyed her so much, the reason they'd continually sparked off each other.

He closed his dark eyes for a second. "You didn't hesitate," he said in a voice so quiet that only she could hear. "You moved towards the cargo vessel to help. All those people on board..." His voice drifted off. His eyes opened and fixed on the floor. "I thought it was fake. I thought it was part of the test – that there wouldn't be any real people on board. That the cargo vessel would be remotely piloted, like everything else." His dark eyes met hers with confusion. "How did you know, Ash? How did you know it was real?"

She wasn't quite sure how to answer. She'd asked herself the same question over and over. "I don't know. I keep playing it over again and again in my mind. I wasn't certain, even when I went to help." She screwed up her face. "Maybe just gut instinct? There was something off that I couldn't put my finger on. Something...desperate." She shook her head. "Even afterwards, when we got back – when we were transported out of there – I still didn't *know*, not really."

This time when he looked at her his gaze was steady. "You acted on instinct and so did I. You wanted to save lives and so did I – I wanted to save yours."

Ash held her breath. The tiny hairs on her arms stood on end. "But—"

She didn't know quite what she wanted to say and she didn't get a chance to say it anyway, because Commander Anand's voice carried across the room.

"Cadets. Hurry along. It's time to get our new pilots into training."

He stood behind the podium, watching as the red-suited pilots filed out of the door through which they'd come. Ezra's eyes held Ash's for the briefest of seconds, then he turned and hurried back down the stairs to join them.

Ash's throat felt as if it were closing in on itself as she watched the four grey-suited successful cadets file out after the red.

The lights flashed in the room.

"All unassigned candidates, transport to the outer planets starts in one hour."

And that was it. Her time in the Star Corporation Academy was over.

CHAPTER FIVE

It was amazing how light you could travel. Ash had stuffed everything into the grey holdall they'd given her. She'd only brought a few personal possessions for her sixteen-week stay. All uniforms, clothing and toiletries had been supplied by the Star Corporation Academy.

Her hand traced over the rough surface of the bag. She'd seen these before – admired them even. Other people she'd known had tried out for the Star Corporation Academy. All had failed. Now she would just be another name to add to that list.

She swallowed and glanced around the room she'd stayed in for the last four months. Grey, clinical, with smooth walls, a desk and chair, a screen for studies, and a bed compartment nestled into the wall. All rooms were identical. The only bit of personality she'd managed to impart into the room was her choice of blanket on the bed. She'd gone for a bright orange one, and as a last flash of rebellion she reached out and grabbed it, stuffing it into her bag.

It had been odd at first. This intensely clean environment. She was so used to the dust and sand from Astoria that it had taken some time to get used to not having to sweep the floor every time a door opened. But her favourite part hadn't been the cleanliness of the room. Her favourite part had been the view. She walked over to the round porthole and placed her hand against it, staring out for one last time. For as long as she could remember, she'd stared up at the dark night sky. But here, she could almost touch it – almost reach out and grab a star with her hands.

Of course, she knew how ridiculous that sounded. She understood the physics – the knowledge was embedded within her system. Reaching just one of these stars would take far longer than her lifetime, even with craft capable of travelling faster than light speed, and various wormholes dotted around their solar system. But right now, it felt like she'd never get this close again.

Reach out and grab it, the voice in her head said.

Her hand sagged against the glass. It was over. It was time to leave and she blinked back the tears she still refused to let spill. She turned around and faced the blank grey room. She realized the tears weren't just for *what* she was leaving behind but *who*.

Of course, she'd met people from other planets before – interplanetary travel was relatively common for the wealthy, who made frequent jaunts through the solar system. Some of them even came and "admired" the outer, dusty villages like hers. But she'd never had the chance to make connections and form friendships beyond her home village before. Being here had given her that opportunity. Trik, Ezra, Castille and Arona? Their chats, their teasing – that was one of the biggest things she'd miss. Part of her was happy for their success, but she couldn't pretend the sting of failure didn't hurt. She hadn't even had time to say goodbye. Would they even want to say goodbye to her now? Maybe the exuberance of the results would make them forget about the disaster of the pilot test.

The events of the pilot test might have been a disaster for her, but for the people on the cargo vessel they'd been fatal. Her attempts to help had been futile. She had no idea how many lives had been lost, and for what? Some parcel of junk? She still didn't even know what the package had held. It had been left behind with the Commanders, so she had no idea where it was now. Why had the captain of the cargo ship decided to transport *that* instead of any of the people on board?

The glances between the Commanders had been infuriating. It was clear they knew more than they'd said. But there had been no mention of it at the announcement ceremony and that made her more curious than ever.

She glanced in the mirror, hesitating for only a second before grabbing a transformer wand and, using a few credits, sweeping the brightly-coloured strand of her hair from blue back to boring brown. She didn't want to stand out when she got back home. She just wanted to fade into the background.

Ash shouldered her bag and headed to the door. Others were already filing past on their way to the various shuttle bays and she joined the crowd with a nod of her head to a few individuals. There was no point trying to make conversation now. None of the successful cadets were around, so everyone else was as despondent as her.

The temperature dropped as they headed down to the docking bays, which were buzzing – a whole variety of shuttles were docked, with crew and recruits everywhere. And beyond them, there it was. Space. The great expanse. Visible right in front of her. The wonder of what was out there and all its possibilities hit her again.

Home. At least that's what it felt like to her.

She couldn't explain it, she couldn't even understand it, but she also couldn't ignore the gut instinct deep inside her.

The shuttle she should shortly be boarding was right in front of her, ready to take her back to Astoria.

No.

Not like this. Not until she knew. Not until she understood what had happened today.

Something burned deep inside her. She even smiled as the wild idea took hold in her brain. At this point, what did she actually have to lose?

There was a technician with the name *Turner* stitched across his uniform standing at the side of the dock. She brushed her hand against his arm.

"The Commanders? Where are they now?"

He looked at her in complete confusion.

"Why do you want to know?" he asked.

She pasted a smile on her face. "I want to leave a thank-you gift from the rest of the cadets."

His face was stern and he gave her a suspicious glare. "They'll be in the Board Room."

She blinked. "The Board Room? I'm not sure where—"

"Level Four. Section C," he cut across her, before walking away.

She adjusted the holdall on her shoulder and headed back to the lifts.

The sections were clearly signposted and it only took Ash a few minutes to reach the Board Room. She lifted her hand – steeling herself for what she was about to do – but before she had a chance to knock, the door slid open in front of her.

The three Commanders were sitting at the Board Room table. Commander Trinley arched one dark eyebrow.

"What can we do for you, Cadet Yang?" he enquired.

The element of surprise slightly ruined by the automatic door, Ash fumbled with the holdall, eventually dropping it next to her on the floor. She could feel the adrenaline coursing through her body. She'd never been in the Board Room before. A large oval table stretched in front of her, surrounded by chairs. Behind the Commanders a long window captured the dramatic backdrop of space. But Ash didn't have time to admire the view.

"You can tell me what actually happened out there."

She kept her voice firm, willing herself not to betray her nerves and to keep her anger in check.

Silence.

No one responded.

But her mouth couldn't stop. "I can't – no, I *won't* go back to Astoria without knowing what happened to the people on that shuttle. Why did they appear during my pilot exam? I was the best candidate you had. We all know that. And that cargo ship cost me my pilot spot. But that's not why I'm asking about it. I care more about knowing what happened to those people and why."

As she said the words out loud it occurred to her that they were true. The loss of the opportunity to be a pilot would probably burn for ever. But the facts around the mystery people who had sacrificed themselves for an unknown cause were actually more important to her.

A hint of a smile crossed Commander Trinley's face as she looked at her colleagues. "The attitude could be an issue."

Commander Anand waved a hand. "Not our problem."

Commander Clay finally spoke. "Take a seat, Cadet Yang." His voice had a resigned tone and he waved at the chair on the other side of the table.

Ash sucked in a breath, in an effort to stop herself babbling a hundred other questions as she sat down. Her hands fumbled in her lap, then she stuffed them under her legs. Nerves were finally getting the better of her.

Commander Clay leaned towards her. In the lights of the Board Room and up this close, she noticed for the first time the strands of grey littered through his sandy coloured hair, and the fact that his eyes were actually a pale blue.

"Your timing is fortuitous. We were just about to send for you."

"You were?" The words came out before she had a chance to think. Why were they sending for her?

He gave a slow, thoughtful nod. "You know that we appoint cadets to other roles within the programme?"

Her heart gave a little leap. "Ye…es," she managed to stammer out, even as she realized he seemed to have swerved away from all her questions about the cargo ship.

He exchanged a glance with his colleagues. Commander Anand's brow was deeply wrinkled, his dark hair swept across it. He didn't look happy at all. Was this something they hadn't agreed on?

Commander Clay continued. "As you are aware, your test scores were excellent. Your reaction times, logical processing and engineering skills were all in the top ten per cent." He paused for a second. "Up until today, you were first for piloting."

Her stomach sank again. Those words, *Up until today*.

She couldn't help herself. "Maybe if you give me another chance, let me take the test again, without any other distractions—"

Commander Trinley interrupted. "There are no second chances at the Star Corporation Academy, Cadet Yang. Everyone knows that."

Ash sat back.

She looked from one stern face to the other. She was tired. The last few weeks she'd been like a tightly wound spring, living on her nerves for the entire testing process. Now she felt like she could sleep for three days. She imagined someone pulling a little plug out from the bottom of her heel, and all the tension inside her starting to trickle out, like tightly packed sand. Draining the life out of her.

She didn't want to play games. There were no second chances. "So why were you about to send for me?"

Commander Anand finally deigned to look at her. He sighed, his face grave. "Every so often someone is chosen for a...unique role. One that involves more than the traditional testing routes. We are, of course, asked our opinion, but the decision is taken out of our hands. We weren't expecting someone to be required this time around, but" – his eyes darted sideways to his colleagues – "there's been an unexpected change, and we've been left short-handed."

Ash straightened, trying not to let herself get even a tiny bit hopeful. No matter what they'd said previously, her brain was already telling her that this sounded a lot like a second chance. She felt blindsided. She'd come in here, resigned to her fate of going back to Astoria, but determined to get answers to all her questions before she left. Questions that had so far been ignored. And now this...

Commander Trinley leaned towards her. "This role is different. Most people have never heard of the place we're going to send you."

What? "The job isn't here?" Something shifted inside her.

Ash was ready to accept anything. Anything that meant she wasn't going back to her dusty part of Astoria.

"Tell me what you want me to do," she said, putting her elbows on the table and leaning towards the three Commanders. If they had a role for her, they should be straightforward and explain it.

Commander Trinley pushed her chair out and stood up, her startling white uniform and trim frame outlined against the backdrop of stars behind her. "This is a wonderful opportunity, Cadet Yang. Something you could only dream about." She clasped her hands in front of her chest. "But things are a little unusual. We can't tell you everything right now. You'll find out more when you get there."

"Get where?" Ash tried to keep the edge of impatience out of her voice.

Commander Clay's fingers tapped the table and a star system appeared above them – one that Ash didn't recognize.

He pointed to a small purple-coloured moon. "Your post is here."

Ash blinked, trying to decipher what she was looking at. She stood up and peered at the swirling diagram around her. It showed a variety of small planets circling a very distant sun. Most of them were dark, due to their distance from the light of their central star.

She frowned. In all her studies, she was sure she'd never seen this solar system.

"I'm unfamiliar with this system. Where is it?"

"This is Kobi 12. En route to U62."

Her eyes connected with Commander Clay's. U62 – the ancient abandoned system known only by rumour. "You want me to go there?" She couldn't hide the antagonism in her voice, or her fear.

She frowned.

"Isn't that area virtually…" She searched for the appropriate word, and when she couldn't find it, used the one that had leaped into her head: "Dead?"

Commander Anand let out a sharp cough. "Kobi 12 is a quiet system. There is life there, but only basic organisms. There are no sentient life forms. It's a developing system."

Ash pointed a finger at the dark planets. "Sentient life is never going to survive there. They're too far from the sun." Most of these planets would be dark and freezing, a combination incompatible with virtually any kind of life.

"It's a little-known region," stated Commander Anand.

"I wonder why." The sarcastic comment left her mouth before she had time to think. "What exactly *is* out there?"

Commander Clay got to his feet. "I wonder if we should ask them to reconsider," he said, barely glancing in her direction.

But Commander Trinley turned to face him. "No. The choice has been made. This isn't our decision."

Something crept down Ash's spine, like a slow-moving insect. This all seemed beyond crazy. Who had chosen her, if not the Commanders?

She pointed at the purple moon. "Why?" It seemed a reasonable question to ask. "Why will I be based there?" She wrinkled her nose. "What exactly *does* exist there?"

"A library," said Commander Anand quietly.

"A what?" Her brain searched for the word. She'd heard it before, but couldn't quite put it into context.

More glances were exchanged. "You'll find out when you get there. It's best if you get ready. The journey will take some time."

Her brain was still trying to figure out what she'd been told. *Library.* Was that the dusty old place that one of the elders in her village had mentioned? Didn't it contain something she'd never even seen before – books?

She was shaking her head as she asked the next question. "How long will the journey take?"

Commander Clay pressed a button and a plot appeared on the system in the air in front of her. "About three days," he said. "There are only a few wormholes that can be used, and one area is unsuitable for faster-than-light speed."

"Three days." She blinked and licked her lips. "Three days on a fighter?" Even saying the words aloud made her squirm. There was very little space on a fighter. They were tight and compact. Definitely not made for three days' travel.

Commander Trinley shook her head. "You'll have a little more space than that. You'll use a reconditioned cruiser."

Three days in a reconditioned cruiser. Automatic pilot. A cramped living space slightly smaller than the temporary quarters she'd used here. On the positive side, there was a panel that folded down to provide somewhere to sleep, the ability to pace at least three steps, and somewhere to pee. *Be grateful for the small things.*

She cleared her throat. "So, what exactly do I *do* when I get there?"

Commander Anand retrieved Ash's holdall and thrust it back towards her. "Someone will be waiting to meet you. To introduce you to your new…" He paused for a second. "…and very *important* role. Now, do you have anything else that you need? Because it would be best if you left as soon as possible."

"How long will I be there?" she asked quickly. And how was she supposed to know what she needed?

Commander Trinley spoke solemnly. "This is a permanent position, Cadet Yang. All your needs will be taken care of when you arrive. Don't worry about what to take."

Her stomach twisted with the vagueness of the answers.

Commander Anand's hands settled on her shoulders as he herded her towards the door.

Commander Clay stepped forward and handed her something else. The brown wrapped package. The one from the destroyed cargo ship.

She looked at him in confusion. "For me?"

He gave the briefest nod. "You are to take it with you, but do not open it. That's an order. Things will become clear."

There were so many questions spinning around her head. So many things she still wanted to ask.

"You haven't told me about the shuttle – the people on it. That's why I came here. That's what I wanted to know."

Commander Clay was close enough for her to see a dark rim around those pale blue eyes she'd noticed earlier, and tiny lines around the edges of each eye.

"I know you did, Cadet Yang. But we're not at liberty to tell you. It was…" He closed his eyes for a second. "An unfortunate incident. One I'm sure we all wish had never happened. But it's likely that the person you meet at Kobi 12 will be able to answer some of these questions." He gave her a small smile. "Try and exercise some patience. I know it's a struggle."

There was a flash of red in the corridor beyond the open door. Was that Ezra? Her stomach flipped. They were in their pilot uniforms already? Things seemed to be moving at lightning speed. Should she try and say goodbye? Swallow her pride, and wish them well?

But it was too late. The red flashes had disappeared, and Commander Clay had his arm firmly around her shoulder as he led her down the corridor and into the docking bay.

A new life awaited her. She just wished she had some clue what to expect.

CHAPTER SIX

Before she had time to think, Ash was loaded into the vessel, the automatic pilot was set, and her craft literally catapulted her back out into the stars.

The ship wasn't quite as cramped as she'd imagined. There were two chairs at the control panels, the large pull-down bed at the side and a water closet at the back. There was a small circular table next to a system that could dispense food and water. It certainly wasn't luxury travel, but she could put up with it for three days.

She watched the solar system she knew disappear in the blink of an eye as she passed through the first wormhole.

Now her head really was spinning. Even though she was sitting down, she reached out to press her hand against the wall, to try and steady herself.

It was like speeding through a giant tunnel – light and a myriad of purple and blue streamed past the window, with intermittent flashes of white. Her shoulders were pushed back, her skin stretched on her face.

It took her a few seconds to realize she could still breathe.

How long? How long would this take?

Darn it, why hadn't she asked these kinds of questions?

In the next second the ship seemed to come to an abrupt halt. Blackness surrounded her and she lurched forward, her hand shooting out to the control panel.

She looked at the screen in front of her. She'd been in the wormhole for just over a minute but it had felt longer. The blackness faded, revealing the fact that she was in a brand-new solar system.

Her stomach gave a flip as her eyes tried to focus on the sight in front of her – a vision of space she'd never seen before. An alien sun and planets emerged ahead. A shiver shot down her spine, part excitement, part fear. What had she signed up for?

Ash had always dreamed of flying through space, but the truth was, she'd never imagined going further than her own solar system. This was a sight that even her friends would likely never experience.

She glanced at the star charts. Great. Another four wormholes to go. The trouble with three days of space travel was it gave her too much time to think.

Ash paced up and down the tiny vessel, questions firing in her brain. The three Commanders hadn't really told her anything useful. And it seemed the more she thought, the more her imagination worked overtime. Was this a punishment? She'd been assigned to some far-off outpost she'd never heard of, to do a job that hadn't even been defined. If she'd taken some more time to weigh things up, she might have realized this could be the worst kind of insult. She'd been top of her class – they'd almost told her as much. Right up until that last test, the pilot job had been hers for the taking. But now she was being sent alone to a dead star system at the end of the universe where, as far as she knew, she could be as good as forgotten.

She couldn't work out if she was more confused or annoyed.

By day three, and two more wormholes later, Ash was frustrated and definitely a little stir crazy. The only things to do on this ship were sleep and eat. She closed her eyes and pulled her knees up tight, imagining what Ezra, Castille, Arona and Trik were doing. They'd have been assigned a squadron. Given a fighter of their own. By now, they might already have a call sign.

Part of her body ached at that thought. A call sign. She'd always dreamed of having one, but hadn't allowed herself to consider what it might be. Call signs were usually given by your colleagues, once they'd flown with you for a while. Sometimes you earned one on your first flight. But Ash? She would never find out.

She'd always dreamed of having a nickname, like some of the most well-known Star Corporation pilots. Not all of them were flattering – but that was the risk you took when you followed tradition and let your fellow pilots appoint your call sign. She closed her eyes and smiled for a second as she remembered her favourites. *Riot. Spartan.*

But it wasn't to be, for her. She opened her eyes and stared out of the screen at the latest solar system she was passing through. Most of the planets here were shades of red or brown, speeding past in the blink of an eye. The colour of one pricked her senses and she looked down at the brown lumpy package. It seemed to mock her. Her hands had itched to open it, to try and make sense of any of this. But an order was an order. She'd originally ended up stuffing it into one of the compartments where she couldn't see it any more. Out of sight, out of mind. Except it wasn't really. She still wanted to know what was in the darn thing. So, a few hours ago she'd sat it on the floor and stared at it. There wasn't much else to do around here.

A little *ping* on the control panel warned her it was time to strap in for the next wormhole jump. The colours streamed past her, and the sensation of being pinned to her chair while the skin on her face tried to stretch out any future wrinkles was becoming familiar. She gasped as she pitched forward once more and caught her breath.

It was the last wormhole, thank goodness. But if she ever wanted to go back to Astoria, she'd have to do the whole journey again.

Something in her brain sparked. This job was permanent, but surely she'd be able to travel back and forth between other systems if she wanted to?

Her skin prickled. She should have thought to ask that question before she left. She'd never even had the chance to say goodbye to her fellow cadets. She closed her eyes for a second. The job of a pilot was dangerous. She might never see any of them again. What if this was it for her, alone, on the outer edge of the universe somewhere? As she breathed in, it was like darkness surrounded her, swamping her with nerves and thoughts of loneliness. For the briefest of seconds, her eyes pricked with tears. Castille, Ezra, Arona and Trik could all be lost in the war back home, and would she even know?

The ship gave a shudder that brought her back to reality and she turned to look out the main screen. The automatic pilot had kicked in. *"Coordinates reached. Docking procedure commencing."*

It was weird. She'd never had to touch the controls of this ship once. She wasn't used to being out of control and she wasn't entirely sure she liked it.

She leaned forward, trying to scan this new solar system. There was some random planet in the distance in varying shades of deep purple. There was another far beneath the ship, in hues of navy blue. And orbiting this planet was the moon she was about to dock at.

The moon's atmosphere was every bit as dark as she'd suspected. This whole solar system just seemed…gloomy. Part of the surface of the moon was covered in something resembling ice. There was smoky vapour all around. The screen in front of her stated there was no oxygen in this atmosphere.

She squinted as something emerged through the fog.

Something sleek and silver. The ship adjusted position, not really giving her time to see much else before it slid into place in a docking bay. There was a hiss – the sound of venting. Then the lights above the main door turned green.

She swallowed, her mouth dry. Who was behind this door? Were they expecting her? The only sounds she'd heard so far had been computer-automated. No voices. No welcome message.

She took a deep breath and pressed the button to let the door slide open. There was a hiss, before she took a few steps down from the ship, out into the docking bay. It wasn't the biggest docking bay she'd ever seen. There was only room for a few ships. And it was disturbingly empty. Eerily quiet.

With her holdall over one shoulder and the brown package in one hand, she crossed the hangar floor to the air lock leading into the facility.

The door slid back and she stepped inside and waited. This was normal. It was to stop any weird particles or gases getting to places where they could harm the internal systems – anything she could have carried from her previous destination or picked up along the way. There was a series of beeps and a few more hisses before the lights changed again and the internal door slid open.

Black. The corridor facing her was black. Hardly welcoming. And the air smelled…strange. Ash couldn't quite put her finger on it. She guessed the air was regulated to accommodate oxygen-breathing inhabitants, and to protect whatever lay inside. What was actually in a library, anyhow?

"Hello?" She tilted her head, straining to listen for any reply.

She took a few tentative steps. Small lights appeared ahead of her, automatically illuminating the way. "Hello?" she tried again.

No reply. Creepy. Her skin prickled and one hand automatically started rubbing her arm. Why was it so quiet here?

She took another few steps, following the small lights. As soon as she passed them, they flickered back out.

Her senses felt on overload. The Commanders wouldn't send her somewhere that wasn't safe, but what if something had happened here? Would they even know if this outpost had been attacked?

Her hand went to her hip. She didn't even have a weapon with her. There were some handheld blasters inside the ship, but she hadn't thought to bring them.

Her footsteps echoed as she walked. There was something in the air. Something she hadn't experienced before. A smell of…was it oldness? She inhaled again. She could taste it in her mouth. The mustiness. And the strange thing was, despite her wariness, she liked it.

The passageway was wide and seemed never-ending. It finally curved to the left, taking her into a vast open area. The sense of space was overwhelming after being stuck in the small vessel for the last few days. Her footsteps faltered as the ground changed beneath her feet, from a hard, smooth black surface, to worn grey stone with bumps and grooves.

As she stepped forward, it was like she'd flicked some automatic switch. Her mouth fell open as lights illuminated around her in sequence, one by one, giving Ash a true understanding of the space she was standing in. The lights weren't bright like the ones at the Star Corporation Academy. These resembled ancient flickering torches, sending shadows and orange streaks spilling across the floor and walls.

She held her breath and looked up. Glass. All above her, and around her. She was inside a dome and she could see the stars outside. It was magical. The kind of magical that made her suck in a breath and hold it.

The rest of the vast room, in front and beneath her, seemed like some giant cavern. The lights were still flicking on to either side of her, like a stack of cards falling one by one, the room so huge that they hadn't reached the back yet. It was mesmerizing to watch.

She was standing on what seemed to be a balcony, with stone stairs to both left and right, leading down into the deep vault beneath her. As she put her hand on the cold intricately carved stone, a chill went down her spine. What was this place? And where was everyone?

As the flickering lights gathered pace, the vastness of the vault astounded her. Would she even be able to see the back wall? And she realized that the space was packed. Aisles and aisles of shelves. All holding a wide variety of items.

Some rows held stacks of rectangular slab-like objects in a multitude of colours – like nothing she had ever seen or touched before. Other rows held statues and artefacts. There were suits of armour and jewels glimmering in the lights. Her curiosity got the better of her and she took a few tentative steps down the stone stairs, her palm skimming along the carved handrail.

A library. That was what the Commanders had called this place.

She'd heard the term vaguely before, but never really understood what it meant. A past teacher had referred to a library once as a place where ancient books had been kept. But she'd never seen a book. They were a relic of a distant past. And this place was full of so much more.

She got to the first shelf and reached up a hand to the nearest stack. The item on top was rectangular with a red leather cover, bigger than both her hands put together. As she pulled it down it seemed to flop open and she gasped. This was where the musty smell was coming from. She breathed again, realizing once more how much the strange scent appealed to her. As she tentatively touched the item with her fingertips, she could feel the smoothness of white paper neatly lined with words. At times they looked tiny and Ash had to tilt the item in her hands to let it catch the light. It was a story – the kind of traditional tale her mother and father had told her as a child. The letters and words were familiar but the tone of the language and sentence structure were strange, making it hard to follow. She looked back up. There were stacks and stacks of these, all with a variety of different coloured covers. These were the books her teacher had told her about.

She gently replaced the one in her hands on its shelf and plucked down another. It had a dark brown cover, and this time the language and words were completely unfamiliar. Back home on the consoles, this text would automatically be translated for her – dictated, if she wished it. She sighed for a second, her eyes running down the length of this aisle. It would take her a lifetime to read all these – longer to understand them. She set the book down on a nearby stool.

As she took another few steps, a new sequence of lights started illuminating a path directly in front of her, through the middle of a particular row of artefacts. These treasures were made of precious metals and sparkling stones – crowns, swords and sceptres, all encased in glass. The kind of finery she had heard of in make-believe stories as a child.

Ash walked forward, her hand reaching out, wanting to touch but not daring to.

She stopped in front of a glass case that held a deep-purple crystal, set in the centre of a dark gold crown. As she lifted her shaking hand, the glass dematerialized in front of her. She gasped and jumped back, looking anxiously around.

She could touch it if she wanted to. Ash swallowed, her mouth instantly dry. But did she want to?

There was a deep sound. A laugh. Then a buzz.

The air in front of her shimmered, then changed, and a figure appeared. A hologram. It was a man with a long white beard and equally long hair. Even though he wasn't real, he had an air about him as if he'd been here for ever. There were wrinkles around his eyes, but his forehead was surprisingly smooth. He was dressed in floor-length grey-and-white robes.

He turned to face her. "Report." The command was brief, but she responded without even thinking.

"Cadet Yang, reporting for duty."

The man bowed his head, but she saw his mouth spread into a wide grin. Then he stepped forward and reached out his hand towards her face. A tickle flickered across her cheek. She flinched, her hand going up automatically to the place he'd touched. Holograms couldn't do that. They could interact with people, but they couldn't make physical contact with an object – at least, no hologram she knew of could.

"So, you're my selection," he said as he looked at her in wonder. He gave a nod. "Interesting background. Some hidden petty crime. Top scores in all areas at the Star Corporation, and then…"

He let his words disappear into the air.

She shifted uncomfortably. She'd been sure she'd hidden her supposedly criminal past well – she didn't think the Star Corporation Academy had even picked up on it. Anyway, stealing food when you're starving shouldn't be a crime, as far as she was concerned. But her distraction was only temporary – she was more interested in the rest of his words. "Then…what?"

He held out his hands, his robes swinging around him. "Then, you made a decision that took you between life and death. Put you in the path of destruction." He wrinkled his nose a little. "Very illogical." One eyebrow rose. "Some might even call it stupid. A weakness."

73

She dropped her holdall and the package at her feet, crossing her arms across her chest. "And what would you call it?"

"Humanity." The answer came without hesitation.

It was totally unexpected and took the air straight from her lungs. She'd suspected he was sparring for some kind of fight and would dance around her questions the same way that the Commanders at the Star Corporation Academy had done.

Ash moved her hands to her hips and continued to look around, shaking her head in wonder at the craziness of it all.

"Where and what is this place?" she asked. She tilted her head and looked at him again. "And who, or what, are you?"

He smiled approvingly. "I'm Orius. It's a pleasure to meet you." The hologram held his hand out, as if to shake hers. Could she even do that?

Ash moved her hand towards his, feeling the oddest sensation as her fingers passed into the space where his hand should be.

He pulled it back quickly and laughed. "Stop. That tickles!"

She took a deep breath. She was tired. She was confused. "Orius, where am I? What am I supposed to do here?"

He started to walk down the main path between the shining jewelled artefacts. "So many questions. Young ones are all the same. But never mind, we have time to shape you, to prepare you." He gave a laugh and a throwaway wave of his hand. "Lots of time."

She started walking after him, having to almost run to keep pace. "Shape me for what? Prepare me for what?"

Her eyes were fixed so intently on Orius that she missed the end of a golden spear sticking out onto the pathway, and tumbled to the floor, narrowly avoiding cracking her face on the stone beneath her.

Looking up, she realized that Orius was floating. It had been barely noticeable at first, but now she could see a glimmer of light underneath the space where his feet should be.

He spun back around, his robes whirling out. If they'd been real, a dozen artefacts would have gone flying across the room. "For your new job, of course."

She didn't get up straight away. This was all too crazy for her.

Orius pointed to the artefact nearest her, a chipped varnished pottery jar in a glass display case. "From Dorian. The first evidence of civilization on that planet. It was discovered encased in ice. It seems before Dorian was an ice planet, it was a place with many species, many civilizations. When the Toloreans wanted to settle there, they said there had never been life on that planet. They were wrong."

Her fingers reached out automatically, touching the edge of the glass case as she peered a little closer. How much history was in that little piece of broken pottery?

She flinched as he flicked a hand and a digital screen appeared in the air. It hovered, with text and pictures streaming across it. Her eyes scanned quickly. It was some of the information that Orius had just told her.

Orius smiled. "Museum label. Activates when items are picked up or cases touched. We call them the Infinity Files." He waved his arm over the expanse of the Library. "We have a file on every single item that's held within the Library. Information that might have been lost for centuries is all stored safely here."

She wrinkled her nose and he wagged a finger at her. "The reason it didn't happen before was because I hadn't approved you. Now, I have. Anytime you touch something, the information related to it will appear next to you."

Ash leaned forward, trying to take in what he was saying, her fingers touching the sharp edge of the spear. A tag appeared in the air in front of her, the text moving so quickly that she barely had time to read it all. She couldn't quite work out whether to be more fascinated by the technology or the object. "Why would you have this?" She turned her head to look at the crammed expanse behind her. "What is it all for? What does it mean?"

"Life. As we know it. Little pieces from across the galaxies that signify some specific turning point in time. History, that we can touch." He nodded to the next case, where a glittering blue gem sat perched on a silver cushion. "That is the blue coraporamine that, for seven hundred years, sat in the crown of the ruler of Agrean. This little beauty has caused more wars than any other jewel in the galaxy."

She'd barely touched the gem before its museum tag flickered up alongside her. Ash tried to hide her smile. She could get used to this kind of technology.

He moved further along the row. "The spear you tripped over belonged to Agillas. He led a revolt on U756 that overthrew the ruling government and pulled his people into a technological age." Orius gave a sad kind of smile. "They weren't ready for it, of course, and it led to their downfall and the ultimate destruction of their planet. But that spear apparently hit the heart of the ruler, Helios, and killed him, paving the way for Agillas to take over."

Ash looked down at the sharply tipped spear and moved away from it, not wanting to think of its deadly past.

Her brain was spinning with the myriad of details and the vaguely familiar planet names she had only heard as a child. As she looked around at the packed surroundings, she knew they hadn't even scratched the surface of the stories held captive in this place.

She pushed herself up on to her feet. "But why is all this here?" she asked again.

Orius sighed. It was clear he was becoming weary of her questions. "For safety. For posterity." He touched a crown on a stand nearby. "Some of it will be returned in due course." He raised his fingers in the air. "*Accidentally rediscovered*, of course. When the times of war have finished, and the societies have moved past their arguments." His fingers stroked the crown. "These things don't belong to us. We are only their…" He paused, searching for the word. "Temporary keepers."

Ash blinked. A place that no one had ever heard of, that kept artefacts and antiquities from all over the universe? How could that even be possible?

He kept talking. "Some of these items are the only remnants or memories of civilizations that have destroyed themselves. Tiny reminders that they once existed." Orius walked back and touched the spear with a gentle stroke. He had a sad smile on his face. "Because if we don't keep them and remember, then who will?

"They warn us of lives lost, dangerous decisions, in the hope that we won't make the same mistakes again." He gave a little shrug. "Of course, there are no guarantees."

Orius's manner seemed odd – like this whole place was here for his amusement. It made Ash distinctly uncomfortable. She still had no idea what her role here would be – or if she wanted it.

She shook her head and walked around him. She'd seen dozens of holograms before. They were an integral part of her world. Holograms were frequently used in shops, trading stands, and at any port that delivered safety instructions. But she'd never met one quite so full of personality before – quite so…real.

"How long have you been here?" she asked.

Orius frowned. "Eight hundred…no, nine hundred years."

She stiffened and pointed to the stone floor. "In this place?"

He nodded, and this time it was her turn to frown.

"And what's your job?"

"I'm the Keeper."

"The Keeper," she repeated. Her gaze swept the vault again. This was all getting disturbingly real. Was this her life now?

Alone with a centuries-old hologram, on a forgotten moon? She put her hand to her chest, almost scared to say the words out loud. "And I am?"

He looked at her in surprise. As if it were something she should already know. "Why, you are the Guardian."

The Guardian. A grand title. But she didn't have a single clue what all this really meant. One day she'd been at the Star Corporation Academy, the next she was here – whatever it was called – in a place that was essentially a weird junk shop.

She wrapped her arms over her chest and shut her eyes. Life wasn't fair. She should be donning a red pilot uniform right now and taking her place in one of the fighters to help defend her planet against invading forces. She should be learning strategy, fighting techniques and tactical manoeuvres – not tripping over ancient weapons in a secret far-flung library. This was all a mistake. It was just some kind of horrible mistake. She opened her eyes, ready to speak. But Orius was watching her, waiting.

His wide smile returned and he held out his hands.

"Welcome, Guardian Yang, to the Library at the End of the Universe. Home of the Infinity Files."

CHAPTER SEVEN

"Let's talk," said Orius, gesturing for her to walk back up the stairs.

Ash's head was spinning.

"The Library at the End of the Universe?" She wrinkled her brow. "Doesn't it have another name – a more official name?"

"That is the official name. At least, that's the name I've always known it by – and I've been here a *long* time." He let out a deep laugh that surprised her.

She put her hand on the cool stone banister. "And how long has this place been here?"

He waved a hand carelessly. "In your years? Ten thousand, six hundred and thirty-four years. Do you want the days?"

She swallowed and shook her head.

Orius put his hand to his holographic chest. "I've been here a little longer than some of the other Keepers. Guardians…" He sighed. "I can't seem to keep them."

What did that mean? She wasn't sure she wanted to ask. Ash stifled a yawn. She was still wondering about something the Commanders had said about an "unexpected vacancy", but now didn't seem quite the time to ask.

He hovered alongside her as she climbed the stairs. "Take a seat here," he said, pointing to a grand table with red-velvet chairs on a mezzanine level overlooking the vault. He gave her a quick glance. "Do you need to sleep? Humans…" He looked upwards for a second as if he was scanning some kind of internal file. "I always forget how much sleep they need."

"Don't worry about that. I spent most of my time on the shuttle sleeping – there wasn't much else to do," she said flippantly, trying to figure out what in the world was going on in her life. She licked her lips and held out her hands. "Why here?"

Orius frowned, clearly not quite understanding the question.

"Why is the Library here? In this place?" She looked through the glass dome to the dark expanse outside.

He gave a hint of a smile. "You mean in this forsaken place in the middle of nowhere? Or, as described, at the end of the universe?"

She could hear the humour in his voice and sighed. "There is no end of the universe. At least, not that we know of," she replied. "But yes, it's not exactly the most accessible solar system."

"She gets it."

For a nine-hundred-year-old hologram, he really was quite smart-mouthed.

Her feelings of wonder were starting to get edged out by irritation. "So, it's deliberate," she persisted.

Orius gave her a sharp look. "What you saw down there is only the tip of the proverbial iceberg. You do know what an iceberg is, don't you?"

She nodded, her muscles tensing as he continued.

"Some of the artefacts here are the most valuable – historically, scientifically and financially – in the whole universe; the most important, the most revered…" He slowed down. "The most sought after. Why store them somewhere obvious? In a place with passing traffic? The Library's position was debated long and hard. It's not an easy place to find. And that's exactly the way it's supposed to be."

It's not easy to get back from either, thought Ash.

She licked her dry lips, and a jug of water and a glass materialized in front of her. She'd just poured herself some water and taken a sip when Orius leaned over and clapped something around her wrist.

Ash pulled away instinctively, her other hand wrapping around the cold metal bangle now clamped on her arm. She stared down. It was an odd colour – dark bronze with strange markings. Not grand, exactly, just a little unusual.

Her first instinct was to try and pull it back off. But no matter how much she tugged, the bangle didn't move. It wasn't uncomfortable in any way. But it also wasn't budging.

"Why isn't this coming off? What have you done?"

Orius rolled his eyes and let out an enormous sigh, as if he was growing tired of her already. "It's yours. It blends itself with the Guardian in order to carry out the wishes of the Library."

Mild panic spread across her chest. "What does that mean?" She was still tugging at it, without success.

"It means it will stay on you until you're no longer the Guardian."

There was a buzzing in her ears. That panic in her chest was going nowhere. It felt as if she could breathe in, but not out.

"And how do I get to no longer be the Guardian?"

The words felt garbled, but so was her brain right now.

"You die."

She swayed in her chair. The water she'd just drunk threatened to chuck itself across the stone floor.

She breathed in again, but this time out slowly through her nose. The wave of panic was being replaced rapidly by a wave of anger.

Ash wasn't weak. She never had been.

Now she was who-knows-where in the universe and had just been handed a job that was apparently for life, without consultation.

She wasn't the kind of person to take this lying down.

She straightened her back and stood up, stepping forward. Hologram or not, she would look him in the eye. "Do you want to run that past me again?"

There was a gleam in Orius's projected eyes. "Ah, now we see it."

"See what?" she snapped.

"The grit. The determination. The backbone." The smile spread widely across his face. He turned, waving a finger in the air as he started to walk away. Sometimes it seemed as if he were actually talking to himself. Maybe nine hundred years of existence did that to a hologram. "That, along with your humanity, was the reason you were chosen. Many people have some of the traits we look for – just not usually all of them."

"Stop!" She held up a hand and marched round so she was standing in front of his form again. "I want some straight answers, and I want them now. I've been transported to a place in the middle of nowhere and given a job that I'm not entirely sure I want. I need better answers than this – I need *more* than this."

She stared into his grey eyes and thrust her wrist before his face.

"First, the bangle. What exactly does it do?"

"You're being difficult," sighed Orius.

"You have no idea what difficult is," countered Ash.

Orius shook his head for a second, then looked at her. "Teenagers. Always trouble."

Ash didn't reply, just kept her arm held in front of his face. After the longest time he reached up and pointed. "I'm not supposed to demonstrate. But, as you're being difficult, I'll do it just this once. Let's start with something simple.

Come with me and I'll show you."

She reluctantly followed him into a room away from the main mezzanine.

The first thing she saw was the huge bed – if it could even be called that. It could sleep at least ten people and had a draping canopy above, with pale pink material spilling down the posts at each corner.

She looked around. This room was grander than any she'd ever been in. The Star Corporation Academy had been sleek and smooth; this place was like some kind of ancient palace.

"We'll start with the room," he said. There was a tingle at her wrist. "Put your hand over the bangle," he instructed.

After a moment's hesitation, she did as he said.

He put his hand over hers. "Watch." He smiled.

She felt a little buzz, and the dark room and four-poster canopied bed disappeared. Instead, she was surrounded by a room that was a rainbow of bright colours, with swathes of rich fabric on the walls and a large plumped cushion in the middle of the room replacing the bed. Sprouts of green decorated each corner, as if plants were growing out of the walls. She'd never actually seen colours that bright before, and blinked. It felt as if they were hurting her eyes.

"You can have whatever you want. I opted for a version that I thought might suit you best, but…" He shrugged his shoulders. "Maybe I got it wrong. You can change your room whenever you like. All you have to do is press the bangle and imagine what you want."

There was a second tingle. The room changed again. This

time she sucked in a breath. It was like being underwater. The room was shades of blue and green. Glass surrounded her and an array of sea creatures seemed to be floating just a hand's-breadth away. If she lay on the bed, she could look upwards to a whole world of marine life. It felt tight, claustrophobic. She quickly shook her head.

Another tingle. This time the room was sleek and grey, with no colour at all, mimicking the quarters she'd had in the Star Corporation Academy, except bigger. There was even a window staring out at the stars.

"The only restriction is your imagination," said Orius quietly. "Now, you do it."

He didn't sound quite so tired of her now – as if he was actually a little excited or proud of what he was showing her.

Her hand trembled. She closed her eyes, because it seemed easier that way. There was the slightest tingle, and she opened her eyes again to the room she'd had originally, but with dark red drapes around the bed.

She'd done this?

Orius gave a surprised smile. "Ahh," he said as he looked around approvingly. "You like a little colour."

He glanced at her.

"Now, for clothes. The same rules apply."

She looked down at what she was wearing. It was still the pale-grey uniform from the Star Corporation Academy. Something sparked in her brain. Hadn't the Commanders told her she would find everything she needed here?

She stared down at the bangle, not understanding the science at all. Now she was taking some time, she realized how old it was, the inscriptions worn and slightly battered in places. But just how ancient was it?

"Come on." Orius waved at her, impatience clearly getting the better of him. "We don't have all day. Tell it what you want to wear."

She looked at him as if he was crazy. "What?"

Orius rolled his eyes. "Tell it what you want to wear," he repeated.

She closed her eyes and let the tingle take over. Seconds later, she was dressed in the bright red flight suit of the pilots of the Star Corporation Academy.

Orius raised one eyebrow and she shook her head and closed her eyes again. This time when she opened them she was wearing slim grey trousers, thick boots and a dark red jacket – the same colour as the new drapes on the bed.

"You have a colour preference." Orius nodded to himself.

He didn't mention the pilot suit, but she knew he'd probably stored that knowledge away somewhere, and she silently cursed herself. Ash still wasn't sure what she made of the hologram, who seemed more alive than programmed.

Every hologram she'd met previously had a series of programmed responses and interactions. It was clear right from the start that Orius was much more like a living being than any hologram she'd come across before. But was that level of technology really a surprise when he'd just introduced her to a bangle that could change rooms and clothes?

"Come," he gestured, walking back towards the main Library. "We have work to do."

A tiny part of her rebellious nature wanted to stamp her feet and say no. But the truth was that curiosity was killing her. She wanted to know more. She wanted to know exactly what her purpose here was – and if she agreed with it.

He took her back to the table set high above the Library. "Food is the same." He pointed to its surface. "Whatever you want will appear."

She glanced back down at the bangle and shook her head. "What is this – some kind of magic?"

She closed her eyes, touched the bangle, and a bowl appeared in front of her. She could tell straight away it was filled with her favourite kind of stew from back home on Astoria – exactly what she'd wished for.

Orius laughed. "No, just a technology beyond your years."

She knew instantly that he wasn't referring to her age. "Like you, you mean."

His head turned sideways, acknowledging her comment. He gave the slightest of nods. "You must realize that not every civilization is at the same point of evolution. Some are still developing. Others are just starting to make the first few vital discoveries that will bring them into the technological age." He paused as he moved away from the table and stopped at the top of the Library stairs – she grabbed the bowl of stew and kept eating as he talked. "You must realize that some are far beyond the stage your planet – and in fact your whole solar system – is at. In your role as Guardian, you have to be adaptable. If you visit a civilization at a stage behind yours, you must be careful not to reveal anything, and not to leave anything behind."

She blinked. "Why would I be visiting another civilization?"

Orius gave a soft laugh and gestured towards all the artefacts. "All these things. They didn't just magic their way here. They were collected by a variety of Guardians over the last ten thousand years."

The hairs on her neck stood up. Ten thousand years. Technology to enable the Guardians to do these tasks had been around up to ten thousand years ago. What stage had the planets in her solar system been at then?

The vast scale of what Orius had been trying to explain finally hit home. She only knew about the solar systems that surrounded her own and a little history about a few others that might have been more myth or legend than fact.

"And that's my role now?" Her voice was shaking a little. Fear. Excitement, wonder and a million other questions were flooding through her.

He nodded. "You'll have to visit other planets, other solar systems, all across the universe. Sometimes to retrieve an item, and sometimes to return one."

She nodded as she moved alongside him. But as she looked over the rows of artefacts below, she took a deep breath.

"How many?" she asked, her voice quieter than she would have liked.

Orius turned his head towards her. His hands were on the stone balustrade. They weren't flickering. There was colour and texture to his skin, age lines. He really was the most remarkable hologram she'd ever seen.

His lips were pressed together. She wondered if he was trying to decide whether to answer.

"How many planets? How many solar systems? How many galaxies are actually out there?"

Orius closed his eyes for a second, then he lifted one hand into the air. The top of the dome above them filled with a multitude of swirling galaxies for as far as the eye could see. It was much like the technology that they had at the Star Corporation Academy – only on a much vaster scale.

"How many grains of sand in the Carpesian desert?" he asked.

She blinked. He was using a place from her own planet to try and give her a sense of scale. "Too many to count."

He nodded. "Exactly. The universe is ever expanding. We are only seeing, as they say on Corinez, 'the tip of the iceberg'." He smiled.

The words chilled, even though she'd never visited the icy planet. That was twice he'd mentioned icebergs now.

She leaned forward, still taking in the hugeness of the Library beneath them. "How can you keep track of all the artefacts? How does the Library know what to take and what to give back? How can it possibly know what's crucial and what's not?"

Orius gave a slow nod. "There are a number of people,

across numerous galaxies, who work for the Library." His hand arced in a large circle. "Let me show you how."

He stepped back up the few stairs to where the table was. There was a large empty space to the right of it, and as Orius's hand finished its arc, the air was filled with screens.

Ash gasped and jumped back, bumping into the balustrade.

Her eyes could hardly take in the sight. The screens all hovered in the air, some showing scenes that looked like live action from other planets, some showing data and weird statistics.

Orius turned with a gleam in his eye. "Don't like to leave them here all the time – doesn't fit the aesthetic of the Library."

She was still processing his words as he continued.

"The Library filters information – some might call it a semi-sentient being. It analyses the information received using complex algorithms I couldn't possibly explain. It can predict the rise and fall of civilizations. The statistics tell us which planet or civilization is most likely to be at a crucial point in its existence. When to go in and save an artefact, or when it's a good time to return something."

She wrinkled her nose. "How does it receive the information?"

Orius shrugged. "Remote scans, mainly, but on some planets we have…sources, who feed us information when required." He wiggled his fingers in the air. "It's complicated."

She gulped, trying to take in everything he was telling her. It all sounded like a crazy fantasy story, but inside she could already feel a little fire of excitement about what this job might actually entail.

He pointed towards a circle on the floor near them, directly next to some of the floating screens – she hadn't even noticed it before now. "This is where you need to stand. This is the Proteus circle."

She wrinkled her nose at the name and shook her head. "Proteus? What is that?"

Orius nodded slowly. "You mean who. Another myth and legend from a planet far, far from here. Proteus was apparently a sea god who could change shape and form."

As he said the words, she wrapped her arms around her body, fearing what might come next.

The smile was still on his face. "When you visit other civilizations it won't always be appropriate for you to look like Ash Yang from Astoria. You have to blend in. When you're in the Library the combined force of the bangle and the Proteus circle allows you to transport and change appearance if required." He paused for a second, choosing his words carefully. "Sometimes quite radically."

She was clutching at her own body as a little surge of adrenaline fought its way through. "Oh no. You need to give me more than that."

His grey eyes met hers. "You will take on the appearance of someone local. Their bodies will not always be entirely... Human. Because the universe is not full of Humans. There are thousands of other species out there. And sometimes you will have to inhabit one of their bodies to fit in."

"How does that work exactly?"

He shook his head. "The science is too difficult to explain. Their body becomes yours. Think of it as a second skin."

"And I need to stand on the circle for that to happen?"

He shook his head. "Not always. The bangle has the same abilities on its own. But when you're here, stand on the circle. Less energy required. Makes things simpler."

Ash gave a shudder. "A second skin." She repeated his words with an air of trepidation.

Orius obviously sensed her discomfort. "You are always in control. It's just like wearing a disguise. We've found it safer this way."

"This job is dangerous?"

"It can be."

She stepped forward, peering down at the circle. It was made of metal, with worn letters carved into it that had long since lost their form. In fact, it looked suspiciously like the bangle on her arm. And just as she had that thought, her wrist tingled and her other hand instinctively came over to grab the bangle.

"What happens when I stand there?" Her stomach gave an uncomfortable twist. None of this seemed real.

"You go where you are needed."

"What?" She shook her head. "No way. This is too much. I've just endured three days of space travel to reach this place, jumping through wormholes that stretched my skin and played havoc with my stomach, and you're telling me that I can get to another planet by standing on a circle?"

There was laughter in his eyes. "Pretty much." He didn't wait for her response. "When the Library needs you to undertake a task, you will feel a signal. An artefact may appear next to you, ready to be returned to its place of origin. Or the system will tell you what you need to retrieve. As you stand on the circle, you'll be transported to the designated planet. Your clothes – and maybe skin – will change automatically to ensure you blend in with your surroundings, and you'll be able to understand and speak the native languages."

"Just like that?"

"Technology ten thousand years ahead of your planet's," he reminded her, then gave his head a gentle shake. "Your planet isn't ready for technology like this."

The metal circle beckoned, but she shifted uncomfortably. "It seems large for one person." She tilted her head to the side as she looked at it.

Orius stayed silent for a few moments. "The technology works for more than one person." The words seemed to come out grudgingly.

Ash held up her wrist. "But there's only one bangle?"

Orius nodded. "There's only one bangle," he repeated.

"How do I get back?"

"You just touch the bangle – there's a small ridge to the side, press there and it will automatically bring you back to the Library."

"Only the Library?"

"So many questions," muttered Orius.

It was clear he didn't like her asking so much, but that made her more determined. And she was starting to feel curious about what was out there. Before this journey, she'd only seen one solar system – her own. There had been no opportunity to study or explore on the way here. Now, it seemed like the whole universe was virtually at the tips of her fingers. "So, I stand on the circle, press the ridge on the bangle and get to shoot anywhere, all around the universe, in the blink of an eye?" Anger flashed in Orius's grey eyes. "This isn't some sort of game, Guardian Yang. For some planets, your actions could mean the difference between life and death."

She breathed in, chilled. She hadn't felt snow before, but right now, she imagined this is what it would do to her skin.

"You realize that being Guardian means you have to work to some strict rules, don't you?" He was watching her carefully.

It was weird. She'd been looking after herself for so long that any situation that seemed remotely hostile sent all her defence shields up automatically. Already her brain was asking if this was a trick question – and what would happen if she got it wrong.

She tilted her chin towards Orius, wanting him to tell her exactly what these rules were. But pride made her want to show him that she was bright enough to know.

"Okay, since in my lifetime, I've never heard of the Library, or of the Guardian, or any 'sources', if I had to guess I'd go with: stay unobtrusive; get in, get out; if possible interact with no one; if I can't do that, interact with as few people as possible. Don't do anything memorable. Keep to the task and leave no obvious trace of my actions."

A shadow. That's what they would want her to be. She looked down at her arm, her finger stroking over the bangle. It wasn't pretty, but it was oddly enticing. Yet as she stared at the bangle, her stomach squeezed uncomfortably. Would her life ever be her own again?

The words came from some sense of desperation. "Is this all part of the test?"

A scowl crossed Orius's face and he waved his hand. "Stop obsessing about their test. You failed it. Test over."

The words seemed almost cruel. But before she had a chance to let their weight hit, he put a hand on her shoulder.

The harshness left his face and a twinkle appeared in his eye again. "But you passed mine."

As the bangle tingled on her wrist, he smiled.

"Come, Guardian, it's time to have your first adventure."

CHAPTER EIGHT

Orius pointed to the Proteus circle on the floor.

"Most places you go to, you'll have a…" He paused, searching for the word, then pulled an awkward face. "Friend," he settled on. "Someone who will look out for you. These are the people who are our sources on the individual planets."

Ash's heart was pounding in her chest at the thought of throwing herself into the unknown. "How will I find them?"

Orius shook his head. "Oh, you won't," he said in a throwaway style, "they'll find you."

He met her gaze.

"You'll be able to recognize them, because they'll have some kind of object like yours. It could be a bangle, a ring, a brooch, a medal – their talisman will be made of the same kind of metal that's used in your bangle and the Proteus circle. It allows them to send information to us, but it's not a communication device as such, we can't chat to them.

We send them one signal to let them know a Guardian is on their way. That's it."

"So once I'm there, I'm on my own?"

"Mostly." He pointed to the screens above his head. "I can see you once you reach your destination, but I can't talk to you. I can only monitor the events and hope you succeed."

He gestured towards the circle on the floor.

"One final thing. The bangle, it takes you as close as possible to the place you need to be. But it isn't always exact. It's not powerful enough for pinpoint accuracy. Though we always try our best." He waggled his hand. "Sometimes it's perfect. Sometimes not so perfect. It really all depends on the specific location and how far away the planet is.

"Now step into the circle and I will explain your first mission," said Orius.

Ash nodded and swallowed, her mouth instantly dry. This was it. It was time.

She lifted her foot to step onto the circle and for a second it seemed to hesitate in mid-air, as if it wasn't actually connected to her body. Were her instincts trying to tell her something?

"What's the mission?" she asked warily.

Orius gave a patient smile. "Go on," he encouraged. "It's something simple. Maybe even enjoyable. Something to get you used to your new role."

She pressed her lips together and took that step, standing on the circle. An object appeared before her, hovering just in front of her nose. Ash flinched, then reached out to grab it, but Orius stopped her, handing her a pair of soft gloves. She frowned for a second, then realized they were meant to protect the artefact, so slid them onto her hands before plucking the object from – it seemed – thin air.

This would take a bit of getting used to.

"You're going to Columbia 764," said Orius.

Ash was staring at the object in her hand. It was a stone tablet, firm and heavy, with a row of etchings channelled into its surface.

He handed her a battered-looking leather satchel that she slid over her body. It was big enough to hold the tablet.

A thought shot into her head. "Why do I need to take it – why can't we just transport it into place and let people find it?"

Orius gave a soft smile and a slow nod. "We've learned over the years that many of the pieces are delicate in ways we couldn't imagine. Transporting an object on its own once appears to be acceptable. But transporting it alone more than that can cause irreparable damage. If we transport it with a living being" – he nodded his head at her – "the Guardian, there seems to be some kind of protection for the object. We don't fully understand it, but we have learned to work around it."

Her skin prickled. It was his choice of words – a *living being*. For some reason she'd automatically assumed that all Guardians would have had Human origins. But why should they? Astoria had visitors from other planets and star systems. Ash had seen a whole variety of humanoids who looked entirely different from her, with luminescent skin tones, shorter stature, gills at the side of their necks, or short tentacles around their faces. It was clear that across the universe, Humans had evolved in a variety of ways. But she'd only come across a scattering of completely different species.

The thought of how many species were actually out there, spread across galaxies she'd never even heard of, scared her a little.

"How many Guardians have there been?"

Orius looked thoughtful for a few moments. "Leo Rvunsky, Luna Astrum, Firaz Junz, Oominr, Aldus Dexter, Risti Fereq…the list is endless. We could be here all day if you want me to name all the previous Guardians." He looked her in the eye.

"The list is endless?" she queried. "You get through them that quickly?" She meant it as a half-hearted joke, because she was nervous – *really* nervous – about what she was about to do.

Orius gave her a short stare. "Our Guardian is the heart of our universe. The one person who can try to maintain balance. The selection of a Guardian is never easy. And often, neither are the tasks they are faced with."

She swallowed at the graveness on his face. There was only one thought running through her mind. *No pressure then.*

It took a few moments for Ash to catch her breath. She stared at the tablet in her hands.

"So, this, I'm returning it?"

Orius nodded. "It's time. Centuries ago, Columbia 764 was on the precipice. The landscape of that world was already damaged, almost beyond repair. After years of wars and misunderstandings, the two main populations of the planet had finally agreed to come together to try and save their planet. But there were small factions – splinter groups – who tried to continue the battle. Instead of being the starting point of unity, the tablet, which was their own treaty of working together, became a weapon of war. Rumours began – it was believed that whoever had the tablet could rule the planet. So much was in ruin. The tablet was removed so the residents of the planet could concentrate on their immediate problems, *together*." The last word was emphasized.

Ash wrinkled her brow, but Orius shot her a glance and shook his head.

"But they're past that now. They've had to live with their choices. They've been living in peace, and it's now time to return the tablet to the place it belongs."

Ash looked down at the piece of stone she was holding. It had caused a war? It wasn't so surprising. She'd heard of similar stories – legends even – and often wondered if they were actually true. Now, she had one of those legends in her hands. "Are they really ready to get it back?" She held up the tablet. "Returning it won't cause another war?" She pressed her lips together as she noticed the slight tremble of her hands.

Orius shook his head. "They're ready. We know that. The Library has decreed it." His hand swept outwards. "The objects in the Library aren't ours to keep. When the time is right, they should be returned, otherwise we create an imbalance in the universe, and that could allow civilizations to stagnate.

"Returning artefacts often leads to a step forward. Usually some form of working together." He looked her straight in the eye. "And now, for Columbia 764, the time is right. When you arrive, go to the marketplace to meet your Friend. Luckily today's task is quite a simple one, which should allow you to adjust to your role. Your contact will fill you in on the details of how to return the artefact."

He lowered his head a little.

"Guardian, it's time. Use your bangle."

In an ideal world, Ash would have liked some time to come to terms with everything she'd been told. But she couldn't pretend she wasn't excited at the thought of visiting another world straight away. Her hand closed over the bangle, finding the little ridge and pressing on it. For the briefest of seconds, nothing happened. Then things started to go hazy around her. She'd only been transported a few times, and never liked the sensation – but this was a thousand times worse. It was like every cell in her body objected.

Orius's face disappeared from her line of sight, and even though she barely knew him, the sense of doing this journey on her own was terrifying. She was alone. Again. With no idea when she'd see him next. The Library dematerialized around her, like she was slipping down some enormous slope and everything was just beyond her grasp. There were a few seconds of…nothing. Just nothing.

It was a tiny bit like being in the wormhole. Streams of light flashing past her. A rushing sensation. Her brain and her body being disconnected, along with her fingers and toes. This time, she could feel the electrical charges in the air around her. She could hear the beat of her heart and ringing in her ears.

Then there was a brightness. A new world started to shift into focus. Buildings. Colour. A strange sensation in the air.

Her reaction was instinctual, just like before. As her body started to materialize into place, her legs immediately spasmed, collapsing beneath her, and she retched.

CHAPTER NINE

She stayed like that for a few minutes; hands pressed on the ground to steady herself, her stomach tumbling over and over. Every muscle in her body tingled, as if every nerve fibre in her body was reconnecting.

Please don't let it be like this every time.

When she straightened up, the first thing Ash noticed was the clothes she was wearing. Her hands brushed against the loose fabric. Shades of blue, baggy trousers with a wide tunic over the top and some kind of sash around her waist.

As her eyes adjusted, she realized that blue was the overwhelming colour around her, and the air seemed strange. Denser than normal. The light felt a little different too. She took a few deep breaths and started coughing.

There were lots of buildings, most only a few storeys tall. Her hand touched the wall next to her – she'd been transported into an alleyway, enclosed on both sides. In front of her was a bustling street.

It took a few moments for the paralysing fear to leave her chest. This was it. She was here. What was this place called? Columbia 764. She didn't even know what galaxy it was in. What had she been thinking, letting herself be transported to a distant planet, with so little information or preparation? Excitement had got the better of her. But it was too late to worry now.

She stood for a few moments, watching figures passing across the alleyway. A lot of them seemed Human, or at least humanoid, and there was a definite style – most people were dressed similarly to herself. But the biggest fascination was that there was also another life form among the Humans. Lizard people. It was the only way she could think to describe them. Green scales showed at the parts of their bodies that weren't covered. They had clawed hands. Clothes that allowed their tails to glide along the ground. Deep ridges on their heads, and narrowed eyes. The lizard people were slightly larger than their Human counterparts, with equal numbers dispersed among the crowd.

For Ash, it was an amazing sight. She'd only ever seen a few other life forms, who had, on occasion, visited her home planet. Now she was surrounded by a whole different species. Or two different species. The humanoid people looked like her, but she didn't know for sure they were identical. This was wonderful. Amazing! All of a sudden she was struck by just how far she'd travelled. There was a whole universe out here for her to explore.

Ash glanced down as she slid the tablet into her satchel.

The transport didn't seem to have harmed it. Her feet moved automatically to the opening in the alley, taking her out into the bustling streets – the ground slightly spongy under her feet.

She walked in the direction that most other people seemed to be walking, hoping it would take her to the marketplace. It was much busier here than her home village on Astoria. She glanced around, trying to work out what felt odd – beyond materializing on a planet she never even knew existed. The people seemed friendly enough, and the marketplace wasn't hard to find. There was a whole array of stalls set up in a square just ahead. She kept her head low as she slipped through the crowd, glancing sideways at the variety of items for sale. Some of them she recognized, others she didn't.

Green was everywhere. Plants were everywhere, growing up the sides of buildings, in between the market stalls, and in a variety of pots that seemed to line the streets. Her hand lifted to brush the nearest one – a tree, growing small fruits from its branches.

She'd never seen food growing like this before – her own planet was so dusty and barren, and the space station she'd just come from was stark and grey. Being surrounded by this much green life, and trees that grew food, was astonishing.

She was so focused on the strange tree that she didn't notice a small child in front of her and stumbled over her own feet as she tried to avoid running into them, her hands automatically moving to cradle the bag at her hip.

She landed on her other side and froze, praying she'd not done any damage to the tablet inside her satchel. She slid the bag round as she sat up, lifting the leather flap and searching for any sign of a break.

The child had disappeared into the crowd, which parted around her, but a man stepped forward, holding out his hand towards Ash. She looked up at him and then glanced beyond, directly upwards, and her heart almost stopped in her chest.

Glass. Where the sky should be was a vast expanse of curved glass.

She hadn't noticed it at first, but it was clear this whole settlement was under some kind of dome. Except there weren't stars on the other side of this dome. There was water.

"Miss?" The man was still holding out his hand, waiting for her to grab it so he could help her up.

But her eyes were fixed on the view above, taking in the expanse of water and sea life. More wonder. There were small oceans and seas on Astoria but Ash hadn't lived anywhere near them. As she watched, an array of different coloured fishes swam past the glass – none of them recognizable. The vibrant colours were beautiful. What else was out there? She wasn't even under the centre of the dome, as the part she could see definitely sloped upwards. It was far, far above her, but how had she not noticed straight away? No wonder the light had felt different.

For a few seconds, her chest was tight with panic as a million thoughts flooded her head. What if it leaked? What if this place wasn't safe?

The material of someone's tunic brushed her arm as they walked past. It jolted her senses and she looked up into the eyes of the man who was waiting for her. His hand was slightly shaking now and he had deep furrows in his brow. It was clear he was wondering what was wrong with her.

It seemed as though he'd spoken her language – even though she knew that was highly unlikely. Orius had told her she would be able to understand and speak the language of the planet she landed on – like the disguise and the clothing, the Library took care of that. Whatever had happened to her during the transport had worked effectively and she'd never been so grateful.

She reached out quickly and grabbed his hand, allowing him to pull her to her feet. "Sorry," she said swiftly, "I felt a little dizzy there."

The man's brow relaxed and he nodded understandingly. "Ah, all better now?" His hand rested reassuringly against her back, as if she might fall once again. But she was quick to nod.

"Yes, thank you so much."

She moved away through the crowd with nimble steps, anxious to find a place to gather her thoughts. What kind of world was this?

The market led on to an open area with wooden benches and a whole host of carts selling food. She settled at one and spent a few moments watching the crowd as she caught her breath. Ash smiled. She was in a whole new world – a whole new culture. She might only be here for a short period of time, but why shouldn't she try to learn more about this world and its people?

She leaned on the table, the satchel safely stowed on her lap as she watched. Part of her wondered what the language sounded like. Thanks to her universal translator she'd never know, but she still felt thirsty for that knowledge. Her hand brushed against her tunic and she felt something in the pocket. She reached in and pulled it out. Some kind of coin. It seemed the Library thought of everything.

She watched, curiously, as a large queue formed in front of one of the stalls, half humanoid people, half lizard people. The atmosphere was friendly. Welcoming. This world seemed to belong to the two species equally. It was an interesting dynamic. Would any of the civilizations in her solar system be able to share a planet like that?

All the customers came away carrying a dark-green drink. Ash bit her bottom lip and then joined the line.

A few minutes later she sat back down at her bench and placed the drink on the table, staring at the dark-green liquid cautiously. She gave it a sniff, then lifted the drink to take a small sip. A shudder stole down her spine at the slightly salty assault.

"Takes a bit of getting used to."

The voice startled her, as a figure slid onto the bench on the opposite side of the table, extending a hand. And, yes, it was a hand. Or close enough. Instead of fingernails, those were definitely claws.

Ash held her breath as she looked up into the lizard-like

face. It appeared to be female. She couldn't help but stare at the small dark-green scales and brown ridges that adorned the cheeks and forehead. The eyes and lips were similar to her own, but she noticed lines around both, along with slightly thinner, more worn scales. This female was older than her.

"First time?" The hand was still extended to her. Twice, in the last twenty minutes. She would really have to get better at this, and stop acting like some dazed rookie.

She tried not to show any hesitation on her face as she grasped the proffered hand. The scales were bumpy and cool against her palm.

"Amara," said the woman – because that's the only way Ash could think of her. She shot Ash a smile that revealed eye-teeth longer than a Human's. Ash tried not to stare, but it was *hard*.

"A-ash," she stuttered in return.

Amara shook her head. "You mean, 'Guardian'. That's how you should introduce yourself now."

Ash picked up the green liquid and gulped thirstily. She didn't like it at all, but right now, she needed a distraction. How did this woman know who she was?

The confusion on her face must have shown because Amara's expression changed. "You are the Guardian, aren't you?"

Her eyes swept up and down Ash's form.

"Bit younger than I expected." She took a little longer then said slowly, "First person I've ever met who's not from

Columbia 764." She tilted her head. "I thought you might look a little…different."

Ash straightened her shoulders. "I am the Guardian," she said with more confidence than she actually felt. "I take it you're a…" She couldn't quite bring herself to say the word "Friend". It didn't seem natural in this weirdest of situations. "The person who's supposed to help me."

The words came out prickly. She wasn't quite sure why she felt so defensive. She was in an unknown galaxy, on an unknown planet. She could do with a friend right now.

Friend. The word sent a memory of Ezra, Trik, Arona and Castille into her head. She wondered how they were getting on, and what they would make of what was happening to her now. Part of her longed to talk to someone she knew about all this. To try and still the crazy thoughts that were circulating in her brain. But the truth was, apart from Orius, she had no one. The realization made her stomach twist in an uncomfortable way.

Amara looked at her in amusement. If she'd had eyebrows, Ash was sure they would be raised right now.

"I guess you could call me that." Amara's voice had a teasing edge. "Or, you could just call me your Friend." She touched a little badge on her clothing. It glinted in the light. Metal, matching the bangle. Amara was indeed her Friend.

Relief flooded over Ash. She pulled at her tunic. "Orius told me that if I don't fit in with the civilizations on the planets I visit, my appearance will be altered. But…" She looked around – half of these inhabitants were definitely Human. "I guess they didn't need to change me much this time."

Amara looked almost disappointed. "You're normally Human?"

Ash nodded.

"Hmm. I knew you would look either Human or Callean, but I thought I might actually be meeting someone I consider alien." She shrugged. "Never mind."

Ash leaned forward and lowered her voice. "What is this place? Are we actually under the sea?"

Something flashed through Amara's eyes. A hint of annoyance, or indignance perhaps. Ash had caused offence without meaning to.

"This is home," she said sharply. Her gaze drifted upwards. "And yes, we're under the sea. Have been for generations."

"Why?" Ash couldn't help herself.

Amara's face tightened. "Habitats were destroyed by the wars between the Humans and us Calleans, which lasted hundreds of years. Eventually the safest place on this planet was under the oceans." Her hand waved. "The air above is toxic, and is expected to be that way for many more generations. The land? It won't be able to sustain anything for longer than that. We have an age-old expression: you reap what you sow."

She shook her head.

"The seeds we sowed led to the partial destruction of our planet. The deterioration was rapid. These domes were constructed quickly, as the only way for us all to survive." The words had raced out of her mouth, and she took a few seconds before finally adding, "And several of them have failed."

A pang of fear dashed through Ash's chest. Her gaze shot upwards, as if she half expected to see a spiderweb of cracks appear in the glass high above her head.

Amara's cool hand touched hers and she jumped. "Not this one. It's safe. Has been for hundreds of years. Repairs are constant. But it keeps us alive." She gave a little sigh. "There are seven hundred thousand of these domes, protecting the entire population of Columbia 764. Occasionally there's bickering. Things can be tense. We realize now that the damage our ancestors did will take longer than expected to fix. There will be generations on this planet who never see the sky, or breathe the air above." She rested her hand on her chest. "Me included."

Ash sat still, wondering how that would feel. Guilt surged through her. She'd been desperate to get away from her own dusty village, desperate to have a life with a different view. But how would she feel at the thought of never, ever being able to go outside again? Space was different. Going outside meant death. But everybody living and working in space came from somewhere, had their own home planet they could go back to. A place where they could breathe the air. Life on Columbia 764 had changed for ever.

She watched the youngsters, both Human and Callean, playing in the market. They would never feel the sun on their faces, or the rain on their cheeks, or even the wind in their hair. How would she feel if it were her?

The tone of Amara's voice changed, breaking Ash from her thoughts. "Do you have the tablet?"

Ash nodded, her hand going to the satchel on her lap.

Amara's lips twitched, her voice barely a whisper. "Good. We should go. We need to head to the ancient museum. If you leave it there, it will be found quickly." There was a hint of reverence in her voice. She glanced at the table. "Bring your drink."

Ash stood up, her hand hesitating above the cup. "What is it?" she finally asked.

Amara smiled. "I'll tell you later. Come on. The museum will be closed right now. Which is just as well – we can't go in the normal way."

CHAPTER TEN

Ash followed Amara, threading her way through the crowded streets. The town was busy and cramped. It was totally different from her own dusty village. The houses back home were a lot shabbier than the ones here, yet the streets were wide and the landscape stretched out as far as the eye could see. But she hadn't lived in a dome under the sea.

The houses here were elegant but stacked closely together. The few facts she knew started tumbling around in her brain. If the other domes had failed, had this one had to take more people in, or had they all died? And what about the increasing population? Was the dome equipped to deal with a naturally occurring increase over the years?

There were so many questions Ash wanted to ask. The breathable oxygen. Food supplies. Drinkable water. She was so curious. The list was endless.

Amara slowed slightly in front of her and Ash followed

suit. A large yellow building appeared ahead, with a wide arched doorway. There were words carved above in a language Ash couldn't read. Although the bangle allowed her to hear and speak alien languages, written alien words were a mystery to her.

Amara glanced over her shoulder and reached back, grabbing Ash's hand and pulling her around to the back of the building.

The narrow rear entrance was shaded, away from the busy streets. There was a large silver lock on the door. Amara sighed, and gave it a little shake, as if she hoped it would come away in her hands. "They sometimes don't secure it well," she muttered.

Ash reached over and gave it a shake too, leaning forward when nothing happened, to see if she could figure out how the mechanism worked.

The bangle on her wrist sent a buzz of warmth up her arm and she jumped in shock.

"What is it?" whispered Amara anxiously, glancing over her shoulder to check no one was approaching.

Ash rubbed the skin around her wrist. "I'm not sure," she said.

She stared at the bangle for a few seconds, before lifting her hand towards the lock again.

Again, she gave a small jump as the warmth seemed to spiral around her wrist.

"What's happening?" asked Amara, as she stared at the bracelet too.

"I have no idea," said Ash. She gave Amara a shrug. "I'm new at all this."

She bit her lip for a second then lifted the bangle and let it come into contact with the metal lock. There was a wave of intense heat, followed by a hiss, then a click, and the door creaked open.

Amara opened her mouth in shock, her expression rapidly turning into a smile of admiration. "Your bangle can do that?"

Ash rubbed her wrist again. The heat had disappeared just as quickly as it had arrived. "Apparently," she murmured in wonder.

She took a quick look round to make sure there was no one watching them, but the back street was empty.

"Ready?" Amara whispered.

"It's my first mission. I don't want to make a mess of this," Ash whispered in reply, suddenly nervous.

"You won't," Amara reassured her. "But we have to be careful. We can't get discovered doing this." She put her hand on Ash's wrist. "If people found out about the Library, not everyone would believe it's a force for good."

Ash blinked but didn't speak. Those kind of thoughts hadn't actually occurred to her. But it was true, the Library seemed to be immensely powerful and those who knew about it might wonder about its actions.

Thank goodness she had Amara here to keep her on track. On her own? She might have carried on blundering around, attracting all sorts of dangerous attention.

Amara disappeared through the door silently and Ash followed, her eyes taking a few seconds to adjust.

The air inside was still. Drier. Amara's nose twitched, as if it were uncomfortable for her. The museum was darker than outside, the dim lights illuminating a few pieces that were sealed behind glass. Ash stepped forward to look.

Now that she'd experienced the Library, the artefacts behind the glass didn't seem quite so strange. More stones. Scrolls with writing similar to the lettering above the door – the same lettering that was on the tablet. Jewels. An odd piece of metal that looked like some sort of technology.

As they walked quietly among the exhibits, Ash's hands were drawn to the satchel. One hand slipped inside to touch the tablet. It was still there. Not broken.

"Show me," Amara whispered in her ear.

Ash glanced around her, then stepped a little further back into the shadows and slipped on the soft gloves Orius had given her.

She gently eased the tablet from the satchel, holding it firmly between her gloved hands. Amara's eyes became moist as she gazed at it. It seemed that just seeing the legendary artefact was having an impact on her, and crying wasn't only a Human trait.

Amara's hands trembled as she held them over the tablet, then she pulled them back, as if she realized she shouldn't touch it. Instead, she came around behind Ash, and read the letters on the tablet over her shoulder. Her hand went to her mouth and she let out a strange noise.

Ash turned to her. "What? What is it? What does it say?"

It took a few moments for Amara to find the words. "It's the founding tablet. I thought it was a legend."

She held one trembling hand above it, her long green finger extended.

"*All are free. All are equal. Our populations shall live in harmonious institute, whether above the land, or underneath it. The planet shall be shared. And the damage done shall be restored. For one. For all.*"

There was a melodic tone to her words, as if they had been repeated frequently, and for years.

"You know it," Ash whispered. "You've said it before. How can you do that if you've never seen the tablet?"

Amara pulled her shaking hand back. "Like I said, legend. Every child learns this. It's the treaty between" – she paused then looked at Ash directly and gestured with her hand – "you and me."

She gave a gentle smile and pointed to some of the exhibits in the museum.

"A thousand years ago, we didn't live like this. Humans and Calleans lived separately. Most of that time was spent fighting. When the atmosphere was ruined, and the lands partially flooded, it was the first time we had to learn to work together. The treaty was the first step in those plans."

Ash stared in wonder at the object in her hand, trying to keep herself steady. She looked towards some of the other exhibits. Traditional-style weapons. Old paintings.

An intricately designed machine. All capturing a moment in time on this planet, Columbia 764.

"Why was it removed?"

"There were warring factions. People believed whoever held the tablet could rule the planet. The treaty had just been established – had barely had a chance for the elements to become embedded." She lowered her head for a second. "There was an explosion in the first dome. Humans and Calleans died. It led to riots. All reason was lost.

"When the treaty was declared missing, each side blamed the other. It had become a talisman to hold in front of an army, not a set of words for unity. But when it was thought to be lost for good, things seemed to calm down. Reason returned. And words were remembered. Humans and Calleans started to work together again – just the way they were supposed to."

Ash pressed her lips together. Part of her wanted to stuff the tablet back into her satchel and take it back to the Library. How did anyone know it was truly the right time to return this? What if it just started wars again?

"How can this be right?" Her voice broke a little as she said the words. She was starting to feel overcome with nerves, and responsibility. Was she really qualified for this job? What if she made a wrong decision or did something stupid? Something that caused death and destruction to another planet? In an instant, her sliver of confidence had vanished.

Amara put her hand to her chest. "My generation have

never known war. Have never known fighting between our species. It's as alien to us" – she smiled and looked upwards – "as someone from the stars."

Her hand closed over Ash's wrist.

"This, this will only bring us joy." Her smile was wide. Her words reassuring.

A part of Ash's brain was still whispering a million questions to her. Questions she couldn't possibly answer. But Amara lived on this planet, she knew her people. Ash had to trust her.

She peered out into the museum space.

"Where should we leave it?" she whispered.

There was a carved stone table in the middle of the room, protected by glass. It was flat and secure. Someplace the tablet couldn't slip from, or go unnoticed. Amara pointed towards it. "We'll need to be quick. The museum is due to open again in a few moments."

Ash nodded, pulling the tablet's cloth covering from her satchel, setting it down on the glass and flattening it out, before laying the tablet on top of it.

Both of Amara's hands went to her chest for a few seconds. Ash could see it in her face – that second of trying to capture the feeling and lock it away somewhere in her brain.

"This is the greatest moment in my life," Amara murmured, with tears in her eyes. "I'll never forget that you did this."

The warm feeling was instant, spreading through Ash's chest and stomach. Was this what being the Guardian would always be like? The sensation of doing something intrinsically good?

She touched Amara's arm. "And I'm honoured that you're the first official Friend I've met in my role as Guardian."

A gentle humming sounded down the corridor. They glanced at each other and retreated into the shadows near another exit.

A woman wearing a kind of uniform appeared. She was drifting between the exhibits, an old-style melody sounding from her closed lips.

Ash held her breath, her fists clenched at her sides. Every part of her wished for something good. She'd blindly followed instructions. She'd transported to an unfamiliar world, with an object she knew little about. She almost felt as if she'd fallen into one of the stories her father used to tell her at night, when she was in bed and longing to fall asleep. He'd tell her fantastical tales about travelling to other planets and living in strange places, along with vivid descriptions of the imagined people who lived there and the exciting lives they all had. Everything about this experience had an unreal quality to it.

Yet she knew she really was here. In whatever "here" Columbia 764 was. She could tell by the tinge of blue-and-green light around her, and the heavier atmosphere in every breath she took.

There was a kind of strangled sound. Then a voice: "No. No, it can't be."

Amara gripped her arm, her clawed nails pinching Ash's skin.

"Desi, Roara, Honi, come here now! Come and see what's here!" The voice was full of both incredulity and joy. The shout was followed by a whisper. "Tell me I'm not losing my mind."

Ash and Amara pushed back further into the dark corner as other bodies rushed into the room, followed by a tour guide, with a group of schoolchildren behind them – a mix of both Humans and Calleans.

Within seconds the excitement became palpable.

"It can't be!"

"I think it is."

"Careful, don't touch it."

"But we'll have to move it. We have to protect it."

"Contact the governors. They'll want to know about this."

"There'll need to be a proclamation."

Amara's grasp tightened on her arm and she pulled Ash towards one of the exits. They could still hear the voices inside.

"Where did this come from?"

"Who could have left this here?"

Anxiety was rising in Ash's chest. She was supposed to slip in and slip out. She couldn't afford to be found out as the person who'd brought the relic back. Orius had been clear. No questions about the Library. It wasn't to be revealed. The existence of it was a closely guarded secret.

She glanced nervously over her shoulder as they pushed out through the exit. "What if they come looking for me?"

Amara shook her head, guiding Ash with quick steps back

through the streets to the marketplace. "Sit down," she gestured.

"Shouldn't I just go?" asked Ash, her hand itching to press the thick bangle on her wrist.

"Where's the fun in that?" asked Amara. "Don't you want to see the effect of what you've just done?"

Ash's skin prickled. Amara was smiling. She didn't look like she thought anything bad was about to happen. Ash slid warily onto the bench opposite. Her mouth was dry again and her heart was galloping inside her chest.

But this was her first mission as Guardian of the Library. She wanted to know everything. And there was no denying that Orius seemed reluctant to share information with her. So why shouldn't she relish the fact she was on a whole new planet, in an unknown part of the universe, with a population she would likely never see again?

Her thoughts flew back to her sister Ruhinda. A child who'd always been thirsty for knowledge and would have loved the opportunity Ash had right now. Ruhinda would never get this chance, and Ash was determined to do this on her behalf. Shouldn't she learn something from every place she went?

She rolled her shoulders back, curiosity and enthusiasm washing over her, and grinned at Amara. "Sure, why not?"

Four hours later, she'd learned exactly how the Humans and Calleans on Columbia 764 celebrated. The market square was packed. Word of the tablet's return had spread fast. First there were rumours and whispers, quickly followed by an official announcement and the biggest party Ash had ever seen. All the other domes had been notified. Drinks were flowing, and these weren't the green kind from earlier – these were filled with something that made your legs weak and head swim, a bit like the cheap alcohol they brewed back at home.

In the dark waters outside the dome, flashing lights kept shooting past.

Amara nudged her and explained: "Corpereans. Luminescent fish. They're excitable little characters. Or maybe not so little. A trail of food will have been released into the waters to bring them closer to the dome."

Raucous music was blaring from one of the streets nearby. Amara turned towards the sound; people were dancing at the other end of the marketplace. Her head started to move in time with the rhythm. Ash could tell she wanted to go and join in.

"We haven't had much to celebrate for a while," she said to Ash. "The tablet? It's come at just the right time. It will pull the residents of the domes together. Help them remember the end goal. Stop them fighting among themselves about trading resources and rising populations within the domes." She extended her arms wide. "It will help us remember that there's a whole wide world out there – one worth fighting for."

Her hands rested on Ash's shoulders.

"Thank you. Thank you for doing this." She leaned forward and kissed Ash's cheek, her skin cold next to Ash's, which was flushed with the effects of the alcohol-like substance.

Ash watched as Amara danced off into the crowd, her hands waving high above her head. It only took a second for a loud cheer to erupt as Amara was hugged by those who were obviously her family and friends, and they continued to celebrate together.

Ash smiled as she ducked into a side street, finding a dark doorway to hide herself in.

This had been good. This had been right.

The right thing, at the right time.

She'd been so nervous about coming here, wondering exactly what she was getting herself into. But if this was the role of the Guardian – returning artefacts to bring people together, or taking artefacts to stop wars – all of a sudden it seemed like such a good opportunity. Something special. Something to learn from.

She'd gone from failure to protector…a huge leap, in less than a few days.

And with that last thought, she reached over for the bangle on her wrist, and pressed.

CHAPTER ELEVEN

Life had changed. Life had changed completely and each job taught Ash that little more. Seven jumps. That's how many she'd done now.

Last time she'd jumped, she'd landed on a planet where no one had looked remotely humanoid. And, it had turned out, neither did she. Again, the Library had merged her, moulded her to fit with her new surroundings. She'd put out what she'd thought was one foot to move and landed flat on her face. The population of this planet didn't walk. They flew.

The sensation of flying had been more than strange. Telling a temporary body to flap its wings, then attempting to steer herself to her destination had been the steepest learning curve so far.

She'd almost crashed into one of the huge trees, where a whole variety of dwellings were interspersed among the branches. Thankfully the return of the artefact – an ancient bone belonging to a being like the one she'd been inhabiting

– had been relatively easy, as she'd been able to clutch it in her beak. Another weird sensation.

Pressing her bangle again, with a wing tip instead of fingers, had been a feat for some kind of contortionist, but in the end she'd managed and landed back on the Library floor, where Orius had been waiting for her with laughter in his eyes.

"Oh, very funny," she'd said as she'd stood up, brushing off her loose cream clothing, and stamping her feet on the floor to make sure they were real. "Next time, give me a heads-up, would you?"

Orius had laughed. "We have a wonderful universe filled with a variety of species. Often there is a species close enough to Humans to use as a default. But occasionally that doesn't happen and we have to go with whatever species is indigenous to the planet."

She'd nodded as she kept stamping her feet. "I get it, but, like I said, give me a heads-up next time?"

Orius had drifted off, disappearing among the stacks in the Library and Ash had sighed. She'd wandered back through to her room and collapsed onto the comfortable bed, her hand brushing over the soft cream material that had become her uniform for working in the Library.

It wasn't the first time he'd tested her initiative. When she'd arrived back from Columbia 764, she'd immediately asked why he hadn't told her the bangle could open doors.

"Can it?" he'd said with an unconvincing air of innocence, before letting out a low laugh and shrugging. "Just checking that you can think on your feet," he said. "But it won't work everywhere. Remember that."

Sometimes there were days between jobs, at other times it seemed like she'd barely managed to make it back before she had to leave again. But with each jump she'd become more and more confident with the role she'd been given.

She'd seen a whole series of other planets, all at a variety of developmental stages. Temptation was everywhere, whether it was to spy on some of the newer technology or to leave something behind that might hurry some of the more primitive civilizations along. She had to keep repeating Orius's mantra in her head. *Don't interfere. Don't interfere.* It seemed ridiculous though, when from the second she appeared on a new world, that was *exactly* what she was doing.

Ash had been to a planet where the inhabitants were still burning fires for heat and building ornate stone temples. Another where land was scarce and the people lived in cities in the clouds – her Friend there, Rudy, had been the leader of one of the gangs in the city. That had been an interesting experience – her heart had been in her mouth most of the time she'd been there. Rudy didn't try to hide the danger around them, but the cheeky glint in his eye had given her some reassurance that she was protected in his company.

She'd experienced near-riots in one jump, where the population was in panic mode over a new discovery – part of a spaceship from another planet – that they just weren't ready to cope with. Ash had been tasked with removing it for their own good, but it had been tricky to transport back, as the metallic flap had been almost as big as Ash. She'd managed it, though, and the large flap now sat at the end of one of the rows in the Library. Aron, the maintenance man who'd been her Friend on that mission, had been one of the most excitable characters she'd ever met. Even though she'd only been with him for two days, she kind of missed him.

And she still missed Amara from Columbia 764. They'd had a connection. Amara had been a little protective towards her – probably because she realized it was Ash's first mission. But it had meant Ash's first experience of a Friend on another world had been a good one. Was there a possibility that a Guardian could jump back to places – to visit previous Friends as a way of keeping their life from feeling so lonely?

She stretched out on her bed. The one thing she couldn't escape from was the fact she didn't have anyone to share this with. To talk through what she'd seen – the good and the bad. To discuss the experiences which were opening her eyes on a daily basis and helping her to realize that no civilization would ever be perfect.

Orius didn't see the wonder she did in these new worlds. That was understandable. He'd been here for nine hundred years and nothing seemed new to him. But it made her feel all the more isolated.

As she closed her eyes, Amara crept into her thoughts again. The expression on her Friend's face when she'd seen her family and friends during the celebrations on Columbia 764. The pang of loneliness that had shot through Ash's body as she'd watched.

She sat bolt upright on the bed and stared down at the bangle.

Orius had never said she could only use it for Library business. He'd actually never said that at all.

In theory, she could imagine any place in the universe, press the bangle and…go.

Faces swum into her mind: Trik, Arona, Castille, but most of all Ezra.

She tried to work out how long she'd actually been gone. It was hard. Between the endless days in the Library and the jumps to other planets, she had no idea of the actual star date. Was it a few weeks since she'd left the Academy – or more than a month?

Ash stood up. Orius was nowhere in sight. She wasn't going to speak to him. She wasn't asking permission. He'd likely say no, and as Guardian, she had to have some say over her own life. This was something she could do on her own. Now, before she had a chance to think about it too much and change her mind. All she wanted was some contact – some chance at a normal conversation.

She grabbed her bangle, strode to the Proteus circle, smiled, and pressed.

CHAPTER TWELVE

Every part of Ash's body was tingling. She could feel it. She could feel every cell in her body rematerialize back into…her. It was still the oddest feeling ever.

This was the first time she'd chosen to jump on her own, without some kind of initiation from the Library. It felt kind of rebellious but also gave her the feeling she was taking back some control over her life.

She automatically gulped in a breath and choked on the air, resulting in an awkward coughing fit.

She heard a voice, but it seemed far away, kind of tinny.

"Ash? Is that you?" Ezra's voice had an edge of panic attached to it, as if he couldn't quite believe what he was seeing.

It took her eyes a few seconds to adjust.

It was dark, which meant it was night-time on the space station. Not that a space station ever slept. But they did attempt to keep some kind of cycle to assist the circadian rhythms of the people on board.

Ash's body hadn't stopped tingling. She looked down. A grey flight suit. Thankfully the Library had known not to give her someone else's identity – probably because she was already established here.

Ezra's voice sounded again, closer this time. "Ash?" His hand reached towards her just as her stomach lurched.

As her eyes adjusted, she realized she'd landed in his room. Awkward. She dived towards the hand basin.

A few seconds later Ash felt his hands brush her neck as he pulled the hair back from her face, letting her concentrate on vomiting. She ignored the weird thought of how personal that seemed, and waited for her stomach to finally settle back down. What if all her cells hadn't gone back to the right places? Maybe her stomach was now in another part of her body.

She'd thought she was actually getting used to transporting. Apparently not. She had this kind of reaction every, single, time.

Ash grimaced as Ezra pushed a towel into her hand and she used it to wipe her face. She sighed in relief and straightened up, turning to face him.

"Sorry," she started, then abruptly stopped.

Ezra was wearing a red flight suit. Of course he was. He was a pilot now. But somehow the sight felt like a punch to the gut. His uniform was slightly dishevelled and he looked tired, as if he'd just collapsed into his bed without getting changed. She couldn't help but look down at her own grey suit and still sense that overwhelming rush of failure –

in spite of everything she'd experienced since.

She stared up at his face for a few moments. His sandy coloured hair, his dark eyes and his slightly blue-tinged skin. All people from Hakora had a kind of luminescence to their skin tone.

Last time the two of them had been this close had been just after Ezra had earned the final pilot's place and Ash had crashed and burned out of the Academy – at least, that's what they'd both thought.

His voice cut through her thoughts. "Where did you come from? Where did you go? I came to say goodbye, and no one knew where you were. I thought you'd just gone back to Astoria."

She shook her head. Her body was starting to feel like her own again. She held up her wrist so he could see her bangle.

"This is how I got here."

The furrows in his brow deepened and he lifted his hand to her arm. "Ash, are you feeling okay?"

It was clear he thought she was crazy.

Ash shook her head and walked over to his bed, sitting down on the edge of it. As she sat down, she realized his mattress was just as hard as the one she'd had, and smiled.

She waited for him as he took a few hesitant steps before sitting down beside her, then she turned to face him.

"How are you? How are your injuries? Did they heal okay?"

His hand went to the bottom of his ribs. He gave a slow nod, along with a curious look. "It's been a few months.

My ribs have healed. It's almost like nothing ever happened. The med bays can do almost everything these days."

A few months? Ash tried not to let the surprise show on her face. She nodded, pressing her lips together as she thought about how to tell him where she'd been. No matter what she said, she *would* sound crazy.

"After the announcement, I went to the Board Room," she began. "Once I got there, the three Commanders told me I'd been assigned another role."

Ezra frowned. She could see him thinking. "I thought everyone got assigned their roles in the auditorium."

She nodded. "So did I. But this?" She paused for a second. "It was different." Her fingers stroked the metal of the bangle. "I got sent in a shuttle to a place far away – a Library – the Library at the End of the Universe."

He tilted his head to one side, as if he was trying to see if she had some bump to her head, but Ash kept talking.

"It took three days to get there and it's full of..." She held up her hands. "All this *stuff*."

She was getting too excited. Words were failing her.

"Stuff? What kind of stuff?" he asked. "And, a Library? Do they even exist any more?"

She shook her head again, yet couldn't help but smile. "You know what a Library is?"

He half shrugged. "I've heard of them. Seen old images."

She reached out and grabbed the material of his flight suit, pulling him towards her as if it might help him listen. "That's just it. Half of it is old, ancient even, some of it I don't even understand – I've never seen anything like it before." She licked her lips. "And the Library? It's probably bigger than this whole Academy. They call the artefacts held there, and the information held on them, the Infinity Files. Some of it is lost information from bygone civilizations. Some of the items will be returned. Some will just be held and kept for ever. The last memories of distant pasts."

"What?" His brow wrinkled. "I don't understand. This all sounds…crazy. A place at the end of the universe? What are you supposed to do there?" His frown deepened. "And why would the Commanders send you there when things are so desperate here?"

"The Library. It's full of artefacts, all retrieved from planets across the universe at some kind of crisis point. Some of the artefacts I give back. But sometimes I go to a place and retrieve something new."

She could tell from the expression on his face that he didn't believe a word of any of this.

Ash released his flight suit from her grasp and held out her hands. "The Library, it's like it has some kind of omniscience. It cares for the universe, trying to protect the different species – from themselves, mainly."

Ezra shook his head. "But why? And what is this place? Who's in charge of a place like that? Why does no one know about it?"

"That's just it. There's a hologram there. He calls himself the Keeper. And he calls me the Guardian. He says the Library has been there for more years than I can count. I'm not quite sure who is in charge. Orius says there's lots of people throughout the universe who contribute to what happens. I've met some of them on the planets I've been sent to."

"Orius?"

"The hologram." She held up her bangle. "This can transport me to any place in the universe." She let out a laugh. "I know it sounds incredible. I know it sounds ridiculous. But I've done it. It's how I got back here. And I've transported to places all across the universe – most of which I couldn't even show you on any of the star charts you have here. I've been to planets where they live under the sea, places with species I don't even know the names of. Each place more wonderful than the next."

"With a bangle?" Ezra's voice had an unbelieving tone. She didn't blame him. The more she said out loud, the more ridiculous it all seemed.

She took a deep breath. "I know how it sounds. But it's true. And I had to tell someone." She gave him a sad kind of smile. "Try living it and having no one to talk to about it. No one to tell about the amazing things you've seen, and the people you've met."

She looked around at the grey walls and felt a pang inside. It was odd. She'd thought this place was what she wanted. And while she might wish the bangle had put her in a red flight suit when she materialized here, it seemed oddly fitting it had chosen the colour worn by most of the cadets. Unobtrusive. A colour that wouldn't be noticed and merely blended into the background.

Ezra wasn't looking at her as if she was completely crazy any more. He was looking thoughtful. There was a smudge on his face, right at his cheekbone, and her hand lifted automatically to wipe it off.

"Didn't wash your face this morning?" she joked. As she said the words, a little ripple ran down her spine. He was tired. He had dark circles under his eyes. Lines around them. She hadn't noticed at first because she'd been so overwhelmed by the transport and seeing him again. "What happened?" she whispered.

He shook his head and didn't try to hide the shadows in his eyes. "Dogfight. Three days in a row. Corinez are angry about something. They seem to have some way of refuelling that means they can stay in the air longer than us. Our squadron had to come to the command centre to refuel and they chased us back and bombed the landing bay."

Ash let out a gasp. "What about Trik, Arona and Castille?"

Ezra gave a limp smile. "They're all okay. But my landing gears were hit. It made for a bumpy finish."

A horrible weight was pressing down on her chest. She'd only ever attempted that manoeuvre in a simulator and managed to kill herself on all but two occasions. She knew just how hard it was.

Her instinct was to throw her arms around his neck, but something about his manner made her press her elbows into her sides to stop herself.

She tried to smile. "So you've ruined two fighters now? You must be popular around here."

He shook his head. "No, this one isn't a write-off. It can be repaired." His gaze met hers. "Being a one-canner is bad enough. I've only just got my pilot's wings." His face was serious and his voice quietened. "Being a two-canner would send me straight back to Hakora." He closed his eyes for a few seconds. "As it is, I have three days' leave."

Ash winced. She might only have been at the Star Corporation Academy for a short period of time, but she knew how it operated. She could only imagine the meeting with his squadron leader, or maybe even with the Commanders. Asking the details right now just didn't seem appropriate.

Her bangle tingled, giving her such a fright that she started. A few seconds later Orius materialized in front of them both.

She hadn't even known he could do that. She'd kind of imagined he was bound to the Library in some way – but apparently not. Orius's nose wrinkled as he took in his surroundings. It was clearly a look of disdain.

Ezra jumped to his feet beside her, his hand automatically going to his side. She realized instantly he was going for his weapon. Now he was a pilot, he would carry one. Her hand closed over his, stilling his actions.

"This is Orius." She swallowed. "The Keeper of the Library."

Ezra's eyes widened as he stared at Orius. His mouth moved as if to speak, but nothing came out.

The hologram's nose twitched and he frowned.

"Guardian Yang, you're needed." The words came out clipped. The bangle tingled again.

"What is it this time?"

Orius narrowed his gaze. "You're going to Tallux 5. You have to retrieve the Mirinex Crown."

He clicked his fingers and an image appeared in the air next to him. The crown had a heavy, thick base, with delicate filigree work in an intricate pattern and large blue stones woven throughout. A few weeks ago Ash would have been stunned, but the Library was full of beautiful crowns. She heard Ezra suck in his breath, and wondered whether it was because of the crown itself, or the technology he was witnessing.

"You really should have told me if you were leaving the Library," Orius added with a sniff.

"Why?" she asked. "Am I some kind of prisoner?" Ash folded her arms across her chest. Daring him to reply.

"Of course not," he said quickly.

"Good," she replied even quicker. "Now, why do I need to retrieve this crown?" she asked.

She kind of wanted to say the word "steal", because that's exactly what she'd be doing. And she also didn't want Orius to think he could give her some kind of telling-off for leaving the Library in front of Ezra. She'd done a number of missions now as Guardian of the Library. She wasn't a clueless rookie any more and this job came with a huge degree of responsibility. She wasn't about to let him get any more snarky than he already was.

Orius stared at her, as if he didn't want to answer the question. He looked pointedly at Ezra – as if he shouldn't be there – apparently forgetting that he'd been the one to materialize into Ezra's quarters uninvited.

Ash placed her hand on Ezra's arm. "This is my friend, Ezra Umbeka. A pilot from Hakora."

Orius made a noise – one that meant he was clearly uninterested. Ash's temper flared. They weren't in the Library now. These were her friend's quarters. The least she expected was for Orius to show a few manners.

"There's little time for this, Ash," Orius muttered impatiently. "There's been a change of circumstance on Tallux 5. Time is of the essence."

Ash's hand closed around Ezra's more firmly. "Then we should go," she replied. Something flashed through her brain. That rekindling of camaraderie. Being around someone who was familiar, along with a flash of potential excitement. She spoke quickly. "And this time, Ezra will be coming with me."

Two heads shot around to look at her, one holographic, one Human.

Ezra's eyes were wide.

"You have three days' leave, don't you?" she asked.

He nodded. "But—"

"But nothing," she interrupted.

"No," said Orius, with a tinge of panic. "He can't go with you."

"Why not?" Ash kept her voice steady. She put her free hand to her chest. "I'm the Guardian. Surely I get to decide if someone comes with me?"

Orius looked momentarily stunned – as if no one had actually asked him this before. "This is very…unusual," he stammered.

"Is it? Well, why don't we just see how it goes? Let's call it a trial run for me recruiting a Friend of my own."

Orius blinked.

Ash took the cue to keep talking. "What do I need to know about the crown and Tallux 5?"

"Their continents have been warring for months. Things have reached a critical stage. The Mirinex Crown has to be removed."

"What's so special about the Mirinex Crown?"

"Nothing," Orius said quickly, then hesitated for just a second too long. "Or maybe something that we don't quite understand."

Ash tilted her head. "What do you mean?"

"Does someone want to tell me why a strange old guy has turned up in my room? Is this a dream? Or am I just plain crazy?" Ezra's voice interrupted them both. He prodded Ash's arm. "Nope. You're definitely here." His brow wrinkled and he looked back at Orius. "Who are you again?"

Ash sighed. "I told you, he's the Keeper of the Library – you know, the place where I work now?"

Ezra held her gaze for a few moments as if he was trying to take all this in. "And he's a…" It looked like Ezra was trying to decide on the word. "A…hologram?"

Orius let out a loud sigh and Ash smiled. "Yes, he's a hologram."

Ezra gave a slow nod, looking from one to the other.

"Can I continue?" Orius asked, then waved his hand without waiting for an answer. "The legend of the Mirinex Crown on Tallux 5 goes back hundreds of years. The Library hears of similar legends from all across the universe, when people believe that an artefact – in this case, the Mirinex Crown – has special powers. It's said that whoever holds the crown will have the power to take an army across the land unchallenged. Conquer the whole planet.

"Tallux 5 is on the brink of war." Orius lifted his head and met her gaze. "An army which carries the Mirinex Crown before it…is invincible."

For a few seconds Ash could swear she felt a cold chill sweep over her body. "But that isn't really true, is it?"

Orius waited the longest moment before answering. He lifted his clenched hand to his chest. "But what is truth? Isn't truth just really what a person believes, in here?"

Ash leaned back against the wall in Ezra's room.

"And I thought I was the crazy one," muttered Ezra.

Was Orius being coy because Ezra was here, or did he actually not believe in the legend at all? It wasn't exactly an answer. But she was getting used to this kind of behaviour. She was beginning to wonder whether Orius didn't give her straight answers deliberately because he wanted her to find out things for herself.

She straightened back up. "Where will it be?"

Orius narrowed his gaze, aiming it at Ezra. "It will be in the safe of a palace. Likely in one of the underground rooms.

Security will be in place. It will be tricky to retrieve, but, as always, you'll have help. Burovski, your official Friend on Tallux 5, is primed. He's waiting for you to appear and will brief you on your identity."

Orius leaned forward and held out something towards Ash.

"What is it?" she asked.

"It will help with the safe when you get there."

Ash looked at the small flat circle in her hand and shrugged, unzipping her grey flight suit and tucking it inside her top.

The hologram flickered. "It would be better at such an important time if you weren't" – his nose pinched – "*distracted*."

Ezra straightened up, his shoulders pushing back. It seemed that telling him he was a distraction was enough to help him decide to come along. He turned to face Ash, staring down at the bangle on her wrist. "You promise me this thing works?"

She nodded and smiled. "Can't promise you won't be sick though."

"Sickness I can handle. Dematerializing into molecules that might never reform? Not so much."

Ash's eyes gleamed. "Better hold on tight then."

Both of them were ignoring Orius – it was like he wasn't even in the room any more. He gave an impatient kind of snort. "If you're going to transport another person, then you have to be touching." He flicked his disapproving gaze to Ezra. "Closely."

She stood in front of Ezra. "Okay then, put your hands around my waist," she said over her shoulder to him.

He took a tentative step forward and slowly slid his hands around her waist until they were clasped in front of her stomach. She put one hand over the other, grabbing hold of the bangle.

"Ready?" she asked. Ash was still smiling. She couldn't help it.

She was excited, maybe she was even showing off a little at the thought of taking Ezra to another world, another planet, another life. She'd seen so many weird and wonderful things over the last few months and she wanted him to have a taste of that too. She wanted him to see that even though she'd longed for his life as a pilot, hers wasn't too shabby, as it turned out.

"Ready," he said, taking a breath.

"Then let's go."

CHAPTER THIRTEEN

The world slid into place around them in a bumpy, jolting kind of way. The clip-clop noises were unfamiliar, as was the darkness and the cramped feel.

Ash's first reaction was to retch. No surprise there. Her second reaction was to reach up one hand to steady herself. She was sitting on some kind of cushioned seat within a strange enclosed space, which was shuddering all around her. Ezra was directly opposite her on a similar seat. Her hands touched something soft at her side that partly covered the vibrating wall. Heavy velvet drapes, she realized, at the same time as she heard Ezra retch. His hands were flung out wildly, before his head found a gap in the drapes that led to the outside world.

A thought struck Ash: were they travelling in some kind of moving box?

As Ezra pushed the drapes aside, the first thing that hit them both was the cold.

The second was the white.

For as far as the eye could see, everything was white.

Snow. Something she'd never seen in real life before. She'd seen it on monitors back home, reports from other planets, and she'd always imagined it would be cold. But *this* cold?

"What...?" gasped Ezra, his retching instantly stopping in his shock. His eyes were wide. He lifted one hand. "Ash, what's happened to you? What's happened to your face?"

She put both hands to her face. It took her a second to realize what he meant. He looked totally shocked.

"Oh," she realized. "When I transport, I sometimes change appearance – like a disguise. I guess in this case I've taken on the appearance of someone else." She felt her face again, a little worried. "Why? Do I look terrible?"

Ezra shook his head, still apparently in shock. "No. Just... different. Your hair is longer and lighter than before, your face a little thinner." He put his hands up to his own face. "Have I changed?"

She smiled and shook her head. "No, you're still Ezra. Only your clothes have changed."

Ash shivered. She looked down, trying to work out what she was wearing now they had some light. Her chest was tight. It only took a few seconds to work out why. Something was holding her in place, strapped around her waist, stomach and chest, stopping her from taking a proper deep breath. She pulled at the front of herself, trying to work out what it was. Panic started to grip her.

It was a dress. Something she never wore – even back on

her home planet. But no dress on her home planet had ever looked as constrictive as this thing. Before she had time to think about it much more, she heard that strange noise again and the jostling stopped.

A man appeared at the side of the compartment, pulling back the drapes completely. He was dressed in grey: a fur-lined hat with gold embellishments on his head and a thick coat up to his neck. It took her a few seconds to realize that Ezra was wearing something similar, just in a different colour. Dark blue trimmed with red. Was this some kind of military uniform?

As she breathed in the cold air, she realized the stranger was wearing a medal that glinted on his chest. A medal made of the same metal as her bangle and the Proteus circle.

Her eyes blinked at the bright white light reflecting from the snow. The man bowed his head.

"Czarina, is something troubling you?" From his bowed position, one heavy eyebrow cocked towards her. His eyes were gleaming.

He knew. He knew who she was.

She blinked again. "Just...the noise," she stammered.

His head bowed again. "Apologies, the horses are finding the weather tough. We are only a few minutes from the palace. Can we continue?" He lowered his voice completely. "Lucky landing. I thought I was going to have to pull you out of the snow and pretend you'd stopped and wandered off for a minute." He eyed Ezra carefully. "Wasn't expecting two. But don't worry, I'll think of something."

Another man pulled up next to them on what she assumed was a horse. She'd never seen one before but that's what her Friend had just referred to the creatures as. Four legs, elegant heads with thick hair, and long tails – the creature reared backwards on two legs, nearly tossing the man onto the thick snow surrounding them. Both the man and the horse were staring at them, their eyes wide.

The grey-coated officer turned and shouted at them gruffly, gesturing them to move on.

Of course. This carriage must have been empty before. Now, it had two occupants who had, apparently, appeared out of thin air.

There was a slight nod from the officer. "Burovski," he said gruffly. "We shall talk later." He shot Ezra another inquisitive look, then dropped the drapes, leaving them in complete darkness again.

Ezra leaned back against the cold seat as if he was trying to take everything in. "Where have you just brought me?"

Ash gave him a half-smile. "Tallux 5, to retrieve the Mirinex Crown." She lifted up a corner of the drapes at her own side of the compartment and shivered. "And it seems that Tallux 5 has snow."

The carriage stopped a short while later, in the early part of the afternoon. It became clear that they were part of a large procession of carriages, with everyone unloading at the main door of what looked to be the palace. It was a long and

149

drawn-out process, made worse by the frigid air.

The palace almost seemed to grow out of the snowy ground. White and grey glistening stone towered above them, topped by a golden dome. The main entranceway was grand, with a white set of steps leading up to the biggest doors that Ash had ever seen. She ran her eyes along the length of the building. It seemed almost as big as the Star Corporation Academy.

Burovski appeared at the carriage door, holding out his hand to help her step down.

Getting out of the carriage was harder than she'd imagined. First, she had to gather up her voluminous skirts in her hands – well, one hand, since Burovski intended to grasp the other. Then Ezra slid a thick red cape over her shoulders, which she struggled to pull around her.

In the end, she ignored Burovski's hand, grabbed her skirts with both hands and just jumped. The ground underneath her had been swept clear of snow, but that didn't stop her slipping and sliding. Burovski grabbed her elbow sharply, which resulted in a brief gasp from the man who was standing at the top of the palace steps.

Ash stiffened. She had to stay in character – whatever character it was that they'd allocated to her.

Burovski immediately lifted his hands, stepping backwards and away from her. "Apologies, Czarina," he said quietly. It was like he read her mind. "It seems the Library has given you the appearance of the Czarina of Meduvlok." He gave a hint of a smile. "An interesting choice. People tend to take your orders, and you don't suffer fools. Intelligent, and confident. The role is all yours. Play it," he said encouragingly.

Ezra jumped down beside her, his sturdy boots making him more sure-footed than her own stupid shoes. She hadn't even seen them yet but she could already feel them pinching. And what was it with this darn dress? How could anyone with a modicum of sense wear something this big, flouncy and impractical?

She shot Burovski what she hoped was an in-character look of disgust, waving one hand and muttering darkly before starting up the steps to the palace. But Burovski's eyes were fixed on Ezra.

The man at the entranceway bowed his head.

"Czarina."

She swept past, desperate to get away from the biting cold. But inside, the palace was just as chilly.

A uniformed member of staff approached her.

"Czarina, can I take you to your rooms?" He glanced at Ezra, obviously wondering who he was.

Ash tilted her chin indignantly. "This is Ezra Umbeka, my personal guard. He must be stationed in the rooms next to me."

Another member of staff approached. She watched the exchange of confused glances. "Of course," muttered the first man. "We'll see to it immediately."

Ash gave a grateful nod as her stomach gave a few flips. All of a sudden she was wondering just how wise it had been to bring Ezra along. Chances were, she'd just made things more complicated for herself. Worse than that – she'd done about as good a job of preparing him as Orius had for her.

She had to get better at this. For both their sakes.

One hour later, Ash was deposited in a set of rooms like nothing she'd ever seen before. A maid helped her settle in and then bobbed a curtsey before departing. A fire was blazing, giving off an impressive amount of heat. Ash walked over to it immediately, her hands outstretched. As she stood there for a few minutes, the warmth started to penetrate her cold fingers and arms.

Her room was enormous, with eight long windows complete with ice outside, and a little inside too. The bed was bigger even than the one she had back at the Library, covered in pale-green satin sheets and matching woollen blankets. The surrounding furniture was solid but opulent dark wood, decorated with hand-painted figures and gilt edges. A giant intricate light, made from what seemed like a million glass pieces, hovered in the air above her. She ran her hand round the arm of one of the chairs sitting next to the window. The fabric was velvety in texture. Inviting.

She'd never seen a place like this – not even in her imagination. Part of her wished that back outside the drapes had been pulled back sooner so she could have seen the full view of the palace as they'd approached.

Each new planet opened her eyes wider to the possibilities

and variations of the universe. Had the people on her planet ever lived in opulence like this? She couldn't imagine it – surely there would be some trace if they had?

But Astoria *was* familiar with space travel, while there wasn't any obvious technology around here that made her think Tallux 5 was that advanced. Not every civilization had made it into space yet, she knew. Her room was gradually warming as the fire roared in the hearth, but the fact was, the rest of the palace was cold. If they hadn't mastered basic temperature control here yet, surely they couldn't possibly have reached the stars.

Orius had told her that whatever talisman the Friends owned, it allowed them to send information back and receive a message about the arrival of the Guardian. That item might be the most technologically advanced on this planet.

She stood at the window, hands on her hips, staring out at the snowy landscape and wondering how she could possibly find her way around this palace to track down the Mirinex Crown. She could see people arriving in carriages all the time, and a multitude of servants. As in her own solar system back home, there were a whole variety of skin tones, and everyone looked Human.

There was a gentle knock on the door. A few seconds later, Ezra stepped inside.

His uniform jacket was open, his face still full of amazement.

"Where have you brought us?" He glanced back into the corridor outside and closed the door firmly behind him.

He took a step towards her then stopped, staring at the voluminous pile on the bed.

Ash laughed. "Yes, that apparently is one dress. I had to get someone to help me out of it. That, and what they wear underneath." She pointed to a strange contraption on the bed. "It seems in Tallux 5 women wear strange underthings that make your waist tiny and mean you can't actually breathe. They must be crazy – and there's not a single thing in that trunk that can be worn for comfort."

Ezra smiled. "So you decided just to make do?"

She looked down. She had one blanket knotted around her waist, and another around her shoulders. "Well, yeah, I still have some things on under here. It's just the restrictive thing I've taken off. I have to breathe for a bit." She smiled and sat down on one of the purple velvet chairs positioned by the window.

Ezra moved closer to her. In the afternoon sun from outside she realized that the bioluminescent factors in his skin, which were only vaguely noticeable in space, seemed much more apparent here. There was almost a reflective quality. He sat down in the seat next to her, taking a few seconds to run his hand over the fabric.

She reached over and touched his cheek, remembering the other people she'd glimpsed since she'd got here. A whole variety of different skin colours, but none that looked like Ezra's. The Library had turned her into a whole different species before. Why hadn't it adjusted Ezra's skin tone?

He'd frozen when her fingers touched his face. "What is it?"

"I think we should stay inside," she whispered. In the dimmer lights of the palace, his skin tone wasn't as noticeable.

Her stomach churned. She'd wanted to bring him along, assuming he'd have the same protections that she did. He appeared to understand the language – and she had no idea how the Library managed that. But maybe Ash's actions had endangered her friend's life? Was that why Burovski's eyes had been fixed on Ezra for the few moments when they'd been outside?

Ezra gave her a gentle smile. "Have you seen outside? I have no intention of stepping back out there even for a second."

There was another knock at the door and Burovski appeared.

"Guardian," he murmured in a quiet voice.

She gave a silent nod of her head, looking at the guards at the end of the corridor, and gestured for him to come inside.

The maid who'd helped her out of her dress had yet to reappear with any more comfortable clothing, so Ash excused herself for a few moments and struggled her way back into the uncomfortable gown – this time without the tight contraption – in case she had chance to explore the rest of the palace.

Burovski moved across the room quickly and laid a textured piece of paper out on the table in front of them both. He pulled a small pencil from his pocket and started to sketch. Both Ezra and Ash leaned closer to watch.

"The best time for you to take the crown will be tomorrow night, when the Count is holding a grand ball. You need to familiarize yourself with the palace," he said gruffly. His hands flew over the page, sketching certain rooms. He pointed at corridors, stairways, alcoves and all the rooms surrounding the main ballroom. "The Mirinex Crown has been moved on multiple occasions. They never keep it in the same place, or even in the same palace, for long. That's why you couldn't go directly to its location. It was too big a risk. I could have told the Library it was in one place and meanwhile they could have moved it to another."

She gave Burovski a smile. "I think you overestimate just how good the Library is at setting me down in a precise location. Today, with the carriage? I can assure you, that was just pure luck."

He let out a low laugh, then gave her a look. "Maybe you bring luck with you from the stars."

It seemed a wistful thing for such a burly man to say and she gave him a gracious nod. "Maybe."

He pointed back at the drawing. "The guards who've gone off duty were bribed, and they've revealed that the safe containing the Mirinex Crown is near the back of the palace. I don't know its exact location, but it's in the Century room, which is well away from the ballroom and always guarded."

Ash wrinkled her nose. "Then how will I get in?"

Burovski shook his head. "We'll need to think of some kind of distraction."

She shifted on her chair a little uncomfortably. That didn't sound exactly reassuring. She tried to think logically.

All she had to do was get in the room and open the safe. Once she had her hands on the Mirinex Crown, her only requirement was to press the bangle and get back to the Library. It wasn't like she had to duck and dive and find a way back out.

Burovski gave her a curious look. "Our main problem is the safe. I don't know the combination. I've made some quiet enquiries. It seems that only the Count knows the number."

"If we don't know the combination, how will you get in?" Ezra asked.

Ash's hand settled at her waist, just beneath where she'd tucked the small flat disc from Orius in her underwear. "Don't worry about that. I've got it covered."

From the way Ezra was looking at her she knew he understood. He'd been there when Orius had handed over the disc. His brow furrowed a little – as if he wondered why she wasn't telling Burovski.

But Ash said nothing. She wrinkled her nose again. "But the Count, who is he exactly? And just how rich is he, that he owns a palace like this?" Before Burovski could answer she shook her head again. "And how does this nobility thing work here? How am I a Czarina, and he is a Count? We don't have anything like this at all where I'm from."

She could see another flash of curiosity in Burovski's eyes. It was clear he wanted to ask about where she lived, but she knew she couldn't really tell him. Another rule of being a Guardian. Don't reveal too much about yourself. Don't put the Friends in danger. Telling him about the disc might put him in more danger.

She was still getting her head around the Friend concept. Orius's details were sketchy at best. It seemed that in every planet across the universe there was a designated Friend. Most of them would never meet the Guardian in their lifetime. Hundreds or thousands of years could pass before a Guardian had to return to a planet. So for most Friends, the role was passed down through families, from generation to generation, along with their individual talisman.

Burovski had seemed gruff to begin with, but the man had a twinkle in his eye. He had no reason to trust her. He didn't know her at all. But the title of Guardian seemed to bestow automatic trust and obedience from every Friend she came into contact with. It was good. It was helpful. But it was also unsettling.

Was she really worthy of this status?

"Guardian." She jerked as Burovski brushed his fingers next to hers.

"Sorry." She shook her head and gave him her full attention.

His face changed to a soft smile. "As I was saying…"

She straightened her shoulders as he continued. "While we are all part of the same continent, there are a myriad of principalities. You are the Czarina of Meduvlok. Rarely seen, barely known."

He held out his hands.

"Here, we are in the Principality of Rejula, and Count

Stani rules this land. He's merciless. His reputation precedes him. He's been known to kill competitors on the spot. Count Stani is rumoured to have massacred a rival family in their sleep, and, when one trader proclaimed he hadn't been paid, the man vanished without a trace." Burovski raised one eyebrow. "And while he currently only rules Rejula, he actually wants to rule a whole lot more."

"He does?"

Burovski nodded. "And he won't let anyone or anything stand in his way. The ball tomorrow night is centred on him getting as many of his allies and rivals as possible in one place at one time."

Ash took a careful breath. "That doesn't sound particularly safe."

"It's not. But don't worry. I'll keep my eye on you. Once the dancing starts you'll have a chance to sneak out and retrieve the crown."

"But why does he want all these people under one roof?" Ash questioned.

She was part alarmed, and part intrigued. Nothing really made sense to her. But how could it? She was being spirited into a world for a few days, and then back out again. There wasn't time to even begin to understand the wider picture, and that bothered her. As if there was something she wasn't quite putting her finger on. The Library told her what it thought she needed to know – or at least Orius did. But did it know everything? She wasn't entirely sure it always could. Count Stani sounded like a formidable character. One she would really have liked an entire back history on.

"The enemy of my enemy is my friend," she said softly.

Ezra gave her a curious glance.

"What?" Burovski's head shot up.

"Nothing." She shook her head quickly. "Just something I've heard before."

He moved on, obviously not giving too much thought to her words.

"One of the maids will be in shortly. With some clothing you may find more suitable." His eyes skimmed over her bouffant dress.

"I already asked…" she began, then stopped when she caught his gaze. "Where will you be able to find something?"

He shrugged. "I brought a range of attire in the trunks."

"How did you know what to bring?"

One eyebrow quirked. "I didn't – not really. I guessed. I was simply informed the Guardian was female and your age. I had about two hours before the carriage procession set off to acquire whatever I could in a variety of sizes and styles. The maids are sorting through it as we speak." He waved a hand. "I made an excuse that there had been a mix-up with the trunks as it was clear that some of the dresses were too large, and some too small. I'm sure we'll have something suitable for a Czarina that you can wear for tonight and tomorrow."

She gave a grateful nod. "Thank you for your assistance with all this. I hope I haven't compromised your safety."

Burovski let out a low laugh. "What? By mysteriously appearing in a previously empty carriage? I might have told one soldier he was drunk, and another that the cold had addled his mind."

"Thank you," she said, "I appreciate it."

"You're the Guardian." He gave a dip of his head. "It's my honour to serve you."

The medal on his chest glinted in the light and curiosity spurred her on. "How long have you been a Friend?"

"All my life." The answer came out quickly. "My father was one before me, and his father before him."

"But you've never met a Guardian before?"

He shook his head. "Before now, there's never been a need." He looked outside the window. "But, as changes were happening on Tallux 5, I knew it was time to notify the Library that things had reached a crucial stage." A wave of sadness swept his face. "I do not wish my comrades to be at war. But thanks to Count Stani, things have accelerated at a rapid pace."

After a few seconds he straightened his gait, his stricter face falling back into place. "Guardian, I will leave you to your plans," he said, walking briskly to the door and shutting it behind him, leaving Ash with the drawing still in front of her and Ezra by her side. She ran her fingers over the paper. It was something that was seldom used in her world now. Technology had made it obsolete.

There were mountains of paper in the Library – ancient scrolls and texts. She was still getting used to the touch and smell of them. This paper was a little rougher than others, as if the process here wasn't quite as refined.

She was conscious that Ezra was watching her.

"Everything okay?" she asked him.

He gave an almost smile and half shook his head as he looked around. "These rooms are enormous. I could fit the quarters of five cadets in the room they've given me next door. Yours? They're even more ridiculous. Why would anyone need a room this size?"

She shook her head. "Maybe they've given us these rooms because of who I'm supposed to be? A Czarina from a distant part of the land that very few people have actually set eyes on." She looked back down at the plans. "So, it sounds like the grand ball tomorrow night should give us time to steal the Mirinex Crown while the palace is full and most of the staff distracted."

"Won't it be more dangerous if there's more people about?"

She shrugged. "I don't know this place at all – or its politics. But it is easier to get lost in a crowd. As long as I find my way to the correct part of the palace, I should be able to get into the safe using Orius's gadget. The security measures here can't be that elaborate – they don't have the technology."

Ezra gave a little nod. "I guess as your personal bodyguard, I should be able to ask some questions. Not specifically about the safe, but about the security around here, general access."

She raised an eyebrow. "Are you getting into the spirit of things, Ezra?"

He was quiet for a few moments then gave her a resigned smile. "Let's just call it a welcome distraction. The war at home is…challenging, all-consuming. Even though I've been put off-duty for three days, I won't be missed. No one will come looking for me, because every other person I know from the station will be behind the controls of a fighter."

She shivered – and not because of the temperature, the room was actually becoming quite comfortable. It was the thought of the people she'd trained with actually being out there, fighting, on a daily basis.

"How bad are things?"

Ezra looked away and stared out at the white landscape. "I wonder what it's actually like to live in a place like this," he murmured.

She touched his arm again, trying to pull him back to the here and now, hoping that he might actually answer her question.

But his gaze was fixed steadily on the horizon. "This is what it must look like on Corinez, right?" He turned to her. "Can you imagine living on the ice planet?"

Ash took a deep breath and stared out at the stark landscape in front of them. Her mind flooded with a million thoughts, before she gave a slow nod. "It's almost the exact opposite of Astoria," she whispered.

He shook his head this time. "I saw one of them, Ash, *really* saw one of them, when we were fighting in space. I'd never got that close to another craft before. But they look just like you and me – the Corinezians. Only angrier. More bitter. Her bitterness seemed to reach across the stars and grab me."

"Her?" Ash's voice trembled.

"She was just the same as us." His gaze met hers again. "The people of Corinez have always been strangers. But this time I saw a face. A Human, fighting for the survival of her planet."

The shiver across Ash's skin was real. Even a bit terrifying. They hardly knew anything about the population of Corinez, back home. Just that they were the enemy.

"Orius said we were here to stop a war," said Ezra, his voice sounding a little distant. "It's horrible to think that beyond the war we're always fighting there's just...more wars." He shook his head for a second and looked down. "You've no idea the things I've seen in the last few weeks. The things I've done." His voice broke a little and Ash tightened her grip on his arm.

For months she'd been lost in the bubble of the Library and the role she had there. She'd been so busy seeing other planets and experiencing other cultures that she'd barely thought about the war back home. Now Ezra had answered the question she'd asked, and she could see the pain it had cost him.

No matter how much time she spent in the Library, Astoria would always be Ash's home.

Their eyes connected and she saw him take a deep breath. "I can't stop the war in our system, but maybe we can stop a war for other people." His chin tilted upwards. "That would be good. That would be worthwhile. Even if they don't know it's happening."

"We don't know where the safe is yet."

Ezra stood up, blocking the light for a few seconds, his frame filling her view. He gave the briefest nod of his head. "Let me see what I can find out."

And before she had a chance to say anything else, he turned and walked out.

Ash sat for a few moments, contemplating what she'd left behind and what lay ahead. She hardly even noticed when the maid silently entered the room and started laying dresses on the bed. Ash pushed the paper into a drawer at the desk she was sitting at. It wouldn't do to let the maid see her with a layout of the palace.

"Did you find everything?" she asked the maid conversationally, trying not to reveal that she'd never set eyes on any of these clothes before. Subterfuge and plausibility were skills she'd had to acquire quickly in her role as Guardian.

The maid gave a polite nod. Ash could tell from the expression on her face that she was a bit bewildered. It suddenly struck Ash that palace staff might already be gossiping about her. She'd entertained two different men in her room. Somehow she knew that didn't quite fit with the rules of being as unobtrusive as possible.

She gave a little sigh. Too late now.

"Czarina, would you like to select your dress for this evening, and for the ball tomorrow?"

Ash stood up. There were so many dresses on the bed now, despite the fact she knew that many more had already been discarded. Just how many trunks did a Czarina travel with?

She ran her eyes over the mounds of beautiful fabrics on the bed. Dark red, gold, rich green, pale pink, ice blue, plum and purple. The dresses were all full-length, and full-skirted. Some were lace-trimmed, some had embroidery or beading, and there was a variety of sweetheart and square necklines.

Ash had never worn clothes like these. Back in her village on Astoria they would be cumbersome and unnecessary. Ash had spent her life wearing baggy trousers and tops. To be honest she wasn't entirely sure she wanted to squeeze herself into these dresses for the next two days, but there was no other option.

She pointed to an emerald green dress trimmed with black lace. "I'll wear that for dinner tonight." She paused for a few seconds then pointed to the plum-coloured dress with beads around the neckline. "And this one for the ball tomorrow night."

"Beautiful choices." The maid nodded as she lifted both dresses from the pile and started to shake them out. "I'll get them ready."

Ash walked back over to the window. The ice had melted from both the inside and the outside of the glass, leaving a clear view of the sun dipping in the sky outside. Glimmers of purple and pink streaked across the white snow on the landscape, giving an almost magical glow.

It was beautiful, but Ash shivered. There still something that didn't sit quite right in her mind, and she just couldn't work out what it was.

Burovski appeared to be a solid companion. He'd filled her in on the crucial details. But everything still felt like half a story. And she couldn't shake the ominous sense of doom that surrounded her in this isolated winter palace. She'd yet to meet Count Stani and she could only hope that her presence as a Czarina would be convincing.

If not, she might have put both friends, Burovski and Ezra, in danger.

CHAPTER FOURTEEN

It was late by the time dinner was served. It seemed that the Count had been waiting for a few of his final guests to arrive.

Ezra escorted Ash down to the grand dining room. He was wearing the navy uniform again, trimmed with red and gold. His eyes widened as she stepped outside her room in the dark-green dress.

"Wow. Bit of a change from the usual, isn't it?"

She smiled. "Yeah, but between you and me, there's no way I can eat much dinner. I feel like I'm welded into this thing." She tapped her stomach with one hand. "I can't imagine a life where this is what you have to wear every day. I can't get my head around the fact that the sexes on this planet don't seem quite so equal. I feel like some kind of decoration dressed like this. Do you think I would create a scandal if I decided to wear your uniform instead?"

He laughed. "And I thought we were trying to fit in and be unobtrusive…"

She tugged at the dress again. "Yes, but that's annoying."

Ezra nodded. "I hadn't imagined a life where civilizations weren't at the same stage we are. There's virtually no technology here at all." He gave his head a gentle shake. "The normal transport is – what did they call them – a horse? And carriage." His face changed. "I feel stupid. Just because all the planets in our solar system are at more or less the same stage – galactic war – I just assumed every other planet in the universe was the same." He lifted a hand and ran his fingers through his hair. "And now, when I think about it, I know that's ridiculous."

Ash smiled at him. "That's what I used to think too. After all, every other time we meet a new species or race, it's because they've made it into space, and somehow into our solar system. It doesn't seem quite so stupid when you think about it like that."

The cold of the palace was starting to sweep around her. She'd spent the last few hours cocooned in her room with a blazing fire. But the corridors here were vast, with nothing to heat them, and lit by something that seemed like a cross between a candle and an oil-burning lamp. The light was fair, but certainly not bright, and for that she was glad. It meant no one would have reason to pick up on Ezra's slightly unusual colouring.

As they walked down the corridor, Ezra kept his voice low. "This all seems like some kind of weird dream. It doesn't feel real at all. This is your life now?"

"I guess so. I'm still getting used to it."

"But this is what you'll do – for ever?" There was worry on his face and her heart squeezed, because she had worry inside too – there just hadn't been a chance to talk about it to anyone.

"I don't know much about the history of the other Guardians." She shot him a sideways glance. "I do know that not all have been Human."

His footsteps stumbled. He turned towards her. "Really?"

She nodded. "We only know about our corner of the universe. We know there are other species. I've met some already. For all we know, Humans might be in a minority across other galaxies. Maybe because of planetary conditions and climates, other planets will have evolved differently."

"You mean, with species who don't just want to fight, destroy and kill like Humans?" There was pain in his voice and she gripped his arm a little tighter.

"But we don't want to do that, not really."

He met her gaze. "Maybe not before. But when someone has almost killed you – blown you out of space – and you've seen their face, seen the expression in their eyes, it changes you. It makes you want to exact revenge. When you fly over the place you lived and see the homes of people you love and grew up with disintegrated into nothing, and know you can chase down the fighter that did that, you do it, Ash. You do it without thinking."

His hands were clenched into fists and Ash was doing her best to ignore that horrible feeling in the pit of her stomach. Ezra's words were sparking memories. Pictures of her own village; the devastation, the dust and the screams.

It was the reason she'd wanted to be a pilot. She'd been focused on exacting revenge. For a while, it had been all she had focused on, but now the idea made her uncomfortable, and hearing it from a friend's lips made her even more uneasy.

They turned the corner and both sucked in a breath as they reached the dining room. It was giant and the table was set for more than two hundred people.

Ash gave Ezra a quick glance as they were approached by a uniformed member of staff.

"Czarina, let me show you to your seat." He gave Ezra a dismissive glance, as if he should stay at the doorway.

Ash stepped forward. "Is there a place for my personal bodyguard?"

The staff member drew backwards, a look of confusion on his face. "Your bodyguard can stand behind you, Czarina, like all the bodyguards do."

She shook her head. "Not good enough. There have been attempts on my life – including poisonings. I insist he sits with me. He has to check my food." She tilted her head in a manner she knew was authoritative.

The staff member cast an anxious glass across the room.

Ash continued, "I'm sure that Count Stani would wish to ensure the safety of all his guests."

The man bowed his head for a second, then quickly shouted instructions to a few others, who immediately started shuffling name tags near the end of the table. The few guests already seated looked around in amusement.

Ash walked confidently to the further end of the room, taking her seat at the table and letting Ezra slide in next to her. He gave her a dubious glance. "Quick thinking, but you do realize I'm going to have to eat half of your dinner now?"

She gave him a private grin. "And we have no idea what that might be."

He let out a low groan.

Ash sent out a private thanks for the seating plan. At least now she would know the names of those around her and not have to feign forgetfulness.

It only took a few moments for the majority of the other guests to arrive.

Ash hadn't left her room since she'd got here, and she dipped her head towards Ezra's ear. "Where are all these people staying?"

"You have no idea just how big this place is," he murmured. "I did some exploring this afternoon. It's massive. So many levels, so many wings. The number of rooms seemed endless. Some had guards positioned outside."

He glanced down the massive table. Some of the guests had guards standing directly behind them, just like the member of staff had suggested Ezra should.

Ash felt a tiny wave of panic. Had she been totally out of character by asking for Ezra to sit beside her? But her panic calmed as she realized the whole table was scattered with men in uniform. With this many guests, most people would have no idea who Ezra was, or what his role was.

The noise in the room was rising, even though most of

the guests were talking quietly. The edge of cold had disappeared from the room too, as it filled with bodies.

A man near the entrance door stamped a large staff on the floor.

"Count Stani," he announced at the top of his voice.

Ash stifled a smile. Everything here was so grand.

The Count entered. He was an older man, dressed in a black uniform, with a curled moustache and grey hair. He barely glanced around the room before taking a seat at the head of the table. There were at least twenty places between her and the Count.

Ash sat quietly for a few moments, nodding to the people around her. The guests on the other side of the wide table were too far away to talk to comfortably, and the woman to her left, whose name appeared to be Sophia Vasa, was already chatting happily with her neighbour.

It only took a few minutes for Ash to realize that the further away from the Count you were seated, the less important the guest. She smiled to herself. Perfect. This would help her stay completely under the radar.

Get in. Grab the crown. Get out.

As the first course was set down in front of them – some kind of meaty soup – Sophia started talking to her.

"Czarina, it's a pleasure to meet you. You must have had such a long journey from Meduvlok."

As Ash automatically reached for her spoon, Ezra gently touched her hand. "Czarina, allow me."

He lifted his own spoon and tasted her soup.

She'd forgotten. She'd completely forgotten her own cover story. Ezra gave a nod of his head towards Sophia. "The journey was long, it took nearly six days. We were glad to finally arrive."

There was a momentary pause from Sophia, as if she was wondering who this man was. Ash nodded her head. "Allow me to introduce Ezra Umbeka – he travelled with me from Meduvlok." She spoke with more confidence than she felt – Ezra had just saved her twice in a row, because Ash had no idea how long it would take to travel between Meduvlok and here. She shot Sophia a smile. "I've been the victim of a number of threats, a few attempted poisonings. Ezra keeps me safe."

She hadn't actually introduced him as her bodyguard – as she somehow knew that wouldn't meet with Sophia's approval. Her introduction had been woolly, but it seemed to have worked – Sophia stared at her soup, then smiled while giving a nervous shiver.

Ash picked up her own spoon and tasted the soup. It was…odd. Salty. Not particularly warm. It wasn't the best thing she'd ever tasted, but it wasn't the worst either.

By the time she was halfway through, Sophia was filling her in on all the people around the table. After the first five minutes, the names of people and principalities all seemed to smudge into one. It sounded like some elaborate game; each time a piece moved, a countermove was deployed. Alliances had been built and destroyed so many times that Ash couldn't keep track.

"How many alliances does Meduvlok currently have?"

The soup bowl had been removed and replaced with a plate of foodstuffs that were mostly indistinguishable to Ash. She gave Ezra a teasing smile, as he had to test everything first.

"Don't touch the purple stuff," he whispered in a tone so low only she could hear it.

She gave a nod and turned back to Sophia. "I'm not at liberty to talk about the alliances of Meduvlok right now," she said grandly. "We are at a crucial point in negotiations. Until things are finalized, I'd like to keep matters secret."

A flash of annoyance flickered through Sophia's eyes. But Ash wasn't sorry. It was the easiest get-out clause for her. She had no idea what the names of the principalities surrounding Meduvlok were, and no clue whether they were at war or peace. It wouldn't do to make mistakes.

Sophia lowered her head and whispered. "Have you heard the rumour?"

"Which one?" Ash smiled conspiratorially.

Sophia glanced to the head of the table, where the Count was holding court. "The one about the Count having the Mirinex Crown? I'm starting to wonder if it may be true…"

Ash froze. She was going to have serious words with Orius when this was all over. She had no idea that the fact the Mirinex Crown was here was supposed to be a secret. Since Orius had told them, she'd assumed it was common knowledge.

Just as she thought she was getting used to this job, it turned out she still had so much to learn.

She choked back a little of the food in her throat. "What makes you say that?"

"This," said Sophie, gesturing down the table with her fingers. "The mysterious invitations. Was it really an invitation, or a demand that we all attend? I mean, you've attended. Rumour about you is that you never leave Meduvlok."

Ash gave her a hard stare. "And what else have you heard?" This woman was beginning to strike her as rude. Back home, Ash would have told her exactly what she thought of her. But was that really the way a Czarina would act? Something told her no.

"Just that the Count has major plans. We all know the rumours about the Mirinex Crown. If Count Stani has it, who knows what he could do? We already know he's amassed an army. With the Mirinex Crown, he could march through every principality until he ruled the entire land."

She gave a visible shiver.

"And you know the rest of the stories about him. He's a cruel man. Every time he's conquered a principality his first rule has been to slaughter the royal household."

Ash gulped. She could easily vomit all over her expensive green dress. Why would a Czarina accept an invitation from a man who was likely to try and seize her lands at some point, and then kill her?

But she wasn't the Czarina. She was only pretending

to be, which meant the real Czarina – the one who never left her principality – was probably a whole lot safer than she was.

Ash set down her knife and fork. "Maybe Count Stani isn't the only one amassing an army," she said in her most authoritative tone.

What am I doing? The voice in her head was screaming at her. She was getting caught up in something that was none of her business. She was supposed to fulfil her task without drawing any attention.

Sophia's chin just about bounced off the table. She looked quickly from side to side, as if checking to see if anyone was listening. "You shouldn't say something like that," she whispered. "There are spies everywhere. You don't want Count Stani to see you as a threat. If he really has the crown, he will be unstoppable."

"It's only a crown," said Ash crossly. She was getting tired of all this. She lived in a land with technology that would probably be seen as magic to the people in this room. There was no way a crown held any mysterious powers.

Sophia put her hand up to her mouth, her eyes wide. "You shouldn't say such things."

"Why not? A crown is purely for decoration. It's not a weapon. It's not a force. It's simple metal and sometimes gems. There's no magic in it. No power. Maybe it's time to forget about the Mirinex Crown and start looking at the people in charge of our principalities." She glanced down the table to where Count Stani sat. There was an arrogance about the man, along with a hardness in his eyes. "Maybe we should just call them what they are – tyrants."

Sophia jerked her glass, tipping deep red liquid across the table, which pooled back towards her skirts. She stood up, her chair landing on the floor behind her, muttered an apology and fled from the room.

Her exit from the room took longer than Sophia would probably have liked, as she struggled with her heavy ornate dress, and every guest turned to stare at her.

"Go you, Ash," murmured Ezra. "You managed to upset the only guest who was actually talking to us. Don't you want to get a bit more information about this place?"

One of the servants rushed over, picked up the chair and started blotting at the mess on the table.

Count Stani stood up, narrowing his gaze as he glared down the length of the table.

"Czarina," he barked. "What is the problem?"

For a few seconds, Ash froze. He knew her. Well, he thought he did. There were probably more than two hundred people in this room, all with name tags, but this man who'd never met her before knew exactly who she was supposed to be. Somehow that wasn't a comfort. He'd definitely never met Ash before, but she didn't know if he'd ever actually met the Czarina.

She wondered how the true Czarina would act. Knowing that she never left her principality made Ash think she was some kind of recluse or scared young woman.

But Ash could never play that part. Right now *she* was

the Czarina. And Ash Yang had never shied away from a bully.

She lifted her chin and stared back at the Count with the indifference she thought he deserved. "I think you'll find I have no problems, Count Stani." Her words came out cold as the ice on the outside of the windows.

Everything stopped. People stopped whispering, their conversations forgotten. Forks froze in mid-air and glasses never reached the lips they were intended for.

Even though he was twenty places away from her, she could practically feel his glare burn her skin. But Ash didn't quiver. Not for a second.

The whole room was watching.

"Ms Vasa seems upset—" he started to say.

"Ms Vasa's upset is her own concern. Not mine." She cut him dead, ignoring the sharp intake of breath from across the table.

Ezra's hand moved under the table, settling on the mounds of skirts above her thigh and gripping her tightly. She wasn't sure if he was telling her to stop, or to keep up the act.

The Count bristled. She could practically see rage emanate from his every pore. She was showing him up in front of his guests. But she wasn't sorry. He probably expected her to scuttle from the room like Sophia had.

Ash was not that person.

"You offend me, Czarina." The words sent a chill down Ash's spine.

She moved one hand under the table and put it over Ezra's. Whether he'd meant to offer support or not seemed irrelevant. Right now, she needed something to hang on to.

"And you offend me, Count Stani. How dare you blame me for the actions of another guest?" She let the question hang in the air between them, and the other two hundred guests.

All she was doing was calling him out on his behaviour. He was attempting to belittle her to the rest of the company. Part of her wondered again why he had asked all these people here. No one really knew. They'd all apparently just responded to a rather mysterious invitation. Maybe some had been intrigued, and maybe some had been afraid to refuse. But Ash wasn't in either of those categories.

Burovski had mentioned that Stani was trying to get all his allies and rivals under one roof. Her suspicions of his reasons for this ran deep. This palace, in the middle of nowhere, didn't seem like the safest place on the planet. It seemed *isolated*. Dangerously isolated.

She released Ezra's hand and stood up straight and tall, giving what she hoped was an air of both distaste and anger.

"My journey was long today, and I am tired. Too tired to tolerate slights and insults."

Before she had quite finished, the serving staff appeared, desserts in hand, oblivious of the events currently unfolding in the dining room.

Ash took the opportunity to look down at the plates held in one of the serving girl's hands.

She gave the Count a hard look and a sardonic smile.

"And it seems that your desserts are not to my standards or my tastes." She gathered her annoying skirts in her hands and nodded politely to the other guests. "Good evening."

She ignored the gaze of the Count, keeping her shoulders back as she strode from the room. She could hear footsteps, and knew that Ezra was right at her shoulder.

As she sharply turned the corner beyond the room, she was confronted by a large grey figure. Her haste and momentum carried her smack into the chest of Burovski.

He raised an exasperated eyebrow at her.

"Well done, Guardian. You've just made yourself a walking target. Tell me this is part of the plan? Because if not…" He let his voice tail off.

She could see the gleam in his eye. He was partly amused by what he'd clearly witnessed from the shadows somewhere.

Ash jumped as a door slammed and an uncomfortable blast of cold air skittered over her skin.

The momentary bravado she had felt started to fade. Count Stani and his bullying manner had pushed every wrong button in her. He clearly had an agenda. He had the crown, and was amassing an army. Whatever she believed about the true power of the crown, the man had an air of danger around him. She could practically feel it spark in the air. Ash could guess what a man like him was capable of.

She'd witnessed too many atrocities back home on Astoria, probably committed by people very like Count Stani. In her head, the rulers on Corinez had the same kind of mindset and drive to conquer and kill. This might not be *her* planet, but if she could do anything at all to stop him, she wouldn't hesitate.

Her mind focused a little – remembering the faces in the room during the exchange. She hadn't allowed herself to concentrate on them at the time, but now she recalled the looks of shock and horror. A few of contempt. And a few of what she hoped was solidarity.

Somewhere in this land was a young Czarina who barely left her principality. Had Ash's actions tonight just made Meduvlok Count Stani's first target for his army?

She fingered the bangle nervously on her wrist. What had she just done?

CHAPTER FIFTEEN

The bed was comfortable, and the fire had burned for most of the night. When it had died to embers and a maid had appeared to replenish it, Ash had leaped from her bed in fright. The screams of the maid had caused Ezra to come bursting through her door. He was only half-dressed, which had caused yet another scream from the maid.

By the time Ash's heart had stopped racing in her chest, as she realized someone wasn't actually trying to kill her, she and Ezra had been struck by a completely inappropriate attack of the giggles. To the horror of the maid, they had dissolved into laughter that probably disturbed the sleep of other guests just as much as the screams had.

Ash sagged back down onto the bed, relieved, as Ezra collapsed into one of the velvet-covered chairs. The maid gave a panicked look towards the fire that she was obviously supposed to restack, but Ash waved her away.

"Don't worry."

The maid backed out of the room.

Ezra was only wearing his trousers. He gave a shiver and kneeled down next to the fire, throwing some wood onto it and creating a backlash of temporary smoke. He choked and spluttered, and then laughed again.

"You bring me to the best places, Ash."

She grabbed one of the blankets from her bed and walked over, putting it around his shoulders.

"In less than twenty-four hours we'll be out of here. The ball will be underway, Burovski's distraction will happen and we'll be able to sneak away and find the Mirinex Crown." She held up her wrist with the bangle. "At that point all I have to do is press the button, and send us both back to the Library." She kneeled down next to him. "Think of what we've learned while we're here, experiencing a world completely different from our own. We've travelled in a carriage pulled by horses. We've seen first-hand the politics at work in this land. We've tasted some strange food. We've even had the chance to see snow."

Ezra frowned. "And will anything I've learned here help me when I'm the only pilot in the sky, facing off against three Corinez ships? Or when some cocky Corinez pilot blows my landing gears and laughs, while leaving me for dead?"

She'd missed it. She'd missed it all. The fact that back home the war was ramping up. That people she knew were now piloting those fighter crafts. That Ezra, Trik, Arona and Castille were now coming back after those battles, tired, drained and with traumatic images that would never leave them. Maybe even with physical injuries – that is, if they got back at all.

Even though they were in front of the fire, she could see the tiny hairs on Ezra's arm rising. This wasn't the cold. It was memories.

She wrapped her arms around him from behind and hugged into his back. "Maybe you don't have to go back. Maybe you can stay at the Library with me. You could help me. You could—"

He was already shaking his head. He separated her hands, which had been grasped in front of him, and turned around to face her. "I need to go back. You know I need to go back."

She took a deep breath. She could see a world of pain in his eyes. Had any of Ezra's family back home been hurt? She'd never asked him about family, in case he, in turn, asked about hers.

Parts of her twisted inside, because she understood again. He'd mentioned the growing war before, but she was too busy getting caught up in visiting other worlds, in learning, in experiencing, to take the time to think about it.

Thinking about back home meant revisiting the past. Her mum, dad and sister. The no-hope village. The dust so thick she could barely breathe. The tightness in her chest every time she heard the sound of approaching fighters. Hiding in the darkness, huddled under her bed and wondering which one of her neighbours or friends would die this time.

Months and years of plotting revenge. Practising piloting an imaginary fighter, and pressing the buttons to fire the guns.

The thoughts left her feeling hollow, and guilty.

She hadn't answered, and Ezra gave her shoulder a squeeze as he stood up and made his way back to the purple chair. He propped his legs up on a nearby table. "I'll sleep here. You upset a lot of people tonight. Safety in numbers."

The logs in the fire spat and crackled, and Ash gave a little nod, crawling back across her bed and under the covers.

She looked up at the draped canopy above her head. This bed was similar to her one back in the Library, but a million miles away from the bed she'd slept on at the Star Corporation Academy. Everything there had been minimalist. There wasn't room for junk in space.

This room seemed crammed with furniture. She watched as Ezra shuffled, trying to make himself more comfortable in the chair. She flung him a pillow from the bed. "Try this."

He grabbed it and tucked it by one of the arms of the chair. "Better," he murmured, his eyes already closed.

Just as she thought he'd fallen asleep she heard a quiet voice.

"Ash?"

"Yeah?"

"Tomorrow evening we need to be entirely focused on the crown."

"Absolutely," she agreed.

"But how about we take a tiny bit of time to have some fun first? Before everything gets deadly serious."

She almost sat back up. "What did you have in mind?"

"Oh," his voice had a lazy kind of drawl, "I thought that might be obvious. In a few hours, we hit the snow."

She smiled at the hint of mischief in his voice as she snuggled down under the covers.

CHAPTER SIXTEEN

The palace was bustling with staff. Ash had watched a whole host of new arrivals through her window since sunrise. It seemed that in order to have a ball, the staff numbers had to double.

The maid had brought a breakfast of sorts to her room, but had hardly looked at her. Ash wondered if that was because of what happened in the middle of the night, or if she'd heard of the Czarina's behaviour in the dining room.

Ash didn't really care either way. Today, she needed a chance to explore, to get a feel for the layout of the place, so she could complete her task easily tonight.

Ezra appeared at the door wearing a thick hat, coat and scarf.

"Ready to face the snow?"

She pulled down the scarf that was wrapped around her face so she could talk. "Better get out of here soon or I'll suffocate."

He laughed and gestured to the open door. "After you."

Several other guests looked at them curiously as they walked past. "I guess they're used to the snow," said Ezra. "We'll probably look odd to them for going outside, but this is our one opportunity, we've got to take it. Because we just landed in the carriage, I didn't really get a chance to get a feel for this place from the outside. If we scope it out now, it might be easier to find our way around tonight."

There was a hint of excitement on his face. It warmed her. This was what she'd wanted for him – to see somewhere else in the universe. To be curious. To look for another experience. To see that there was life beyond the brutal one they'd both been trained for. Later tonight she'd press that bangle on her wrist and send them both back to the Library, then Ezra back to the space station. Back to fighting in a war that seemed never-ending. How could it be wrong for him to take a bit of time off to see some snow?

She walked quickly alongside her friend. He seemed to have memorized some of the layout of the palace already. "How do you know where to go?" she asked.

"I told you yesterday, I went for a look around."

Ash tried to remember the drawing that Burovski had given her. They were skirting around the edge of the ballroom. The Century room couldn't be too far away.

She tugged at Ezra's sleeve. "I think we might be near the room…"

They turned a corner and met a group of uniformed men. "This area is off limits for guests," said one gruffly. "You'll have to go back the other way."

Her eyes focused on one thing. These guards had weapons. Guns of some description. Nothing like the weapons they had back home.

Ezra bowed his head and grabbed Ash's hand. "Of course. No problem."

He pulled her back in the opposite direction, through a myriad of corridors that seemed smaller than the others.

"Where are we going?"

"Out the back through the servants' entrance."

She shot him a smile. "I guess you have been busy." She glanced over her shoulder, thinking back to the other corridor. "Burovski told me the room was always guarded. I guess I didn't think there'd be quite so many guards. They'll be a problem tonight. How will he get rid of them?"

Ezra took her down a flight of stairs and through some more narrow corridors, finally reaching a door that he pushed open.

The bright whiteness made her blink again, just like it had yesterday.

"That," he said as he squeezed her hand, "is something we can think about later. We can plan. We can meet with Burovski. This is all going to get serious really quickly. For this hour? Let's just experience snow. This is probably going to be the only time in our lives that we'll see it."

It didn't take long to realize that the style of clothes on Tallux 5 wasn't really suitable for the weather.

They'd only walked a little way from the palace and into a walled garden, before Ash's boots were soaked through and the bottom of her skirts were dragging her down. She kicked at the snow with her feet. "I wish I could take this stupid dress off. It's ridiculous! How can anyone function in these things?"

Ezra laughed and shook his head, bending down and taking off one of his thick gloves. He pressed his hand into the snow, and shuddered for a second, before pulling off his other glove and gathering the snow between both hands.

It was easy for him – he was wearing trousers. He didn't have skirts to deal with. But after a few seconds of delay, Ash joined him – bending down, pulling off her gloves and putting her hands in the snow.

"Yikes!"

Ezra laughed. "Yeah, it's cold, isn't it?" It was clear he was fascinated by the snow. He held a small blob in the palm of his hand and watched it slowly melt. He moulded other heaps into shapes, poking and prodding them.

Ash copied him, even though her hands were chilled and her body was starting to shiver. It only took Ezra a few seconds to flick some of the snow at her. It landed on her nose.

"Hey!" she yelled, grabbing a handful and throwing it at him. But she'd been too quick, it disintegrated mid-flight.

Ezra wasn't so unprepared. He grabbed one of the mounds he'd made and threw it straight at her. It hit her square in the chest and Ash tipped backwards, lying flat in the snow.

Coldness immediately started to seep through the thick coat she wore, getting into the space at the back of her neck. She stared straight upwards at the almost identically white sky. There was hardly any hint of blue.

Ezra appeared above her, looking sheepish and blocking her view. "Sorry." He pulled a face. "Didn't realize snow could have quite that much impact." He did look sorry, but his shoulders were moving slightly, holding a laugh in.

He held out a hand to help her up.

"No problem," said Ash, holding up her soaking arm towards him. "You learn something new every day."

As his cold fingers closed around hers, she yanked him with all her might, sending him splatting into the snow right next to her.

Now she laughed, arching her back and then thumping her hands and legs into the snow around her, sending it up in clouds.

Ezra made a grimacing sound and pulled his face out of the snow, leaning on his elbows and shaking his head. He looked down at his clothes. "Well, guess I'm soaked now," he said as he flipped around and mimicked her position in the snow.

She leaned up and looked at the palace, trying to figure out where everything was. "You were right. It does help to see it from the outside too. Looking at the drawing didn't feel real. Now I'm here, I can picture where all the rooms are, where the corridors lead. What each of those windows are."

Ezra nodded as he brushed some of the snow off himself.

"You ready for this tonight? It could be dangerous."

She didn't want to tell him about the little feeling of dread creeping around her stomach. This mission felt much more risky than any of her previous ones. She'd looked into Count Stani's eyes. She'd seen the ruthless expression on his face. She didn't want to find out what he was truly capable of.

"As dangerous as snow?" she quipped. "I guess we know why the rest of the guests don't go outside."

He nodded. "Snow must lose its pleasure when you have to see it every day."

She opened her mouth to speak and then stopped. Their light-hearted mood had kind of evaporated, and it was bringing her back to more serious thoughts. Corinez. As she cast a glance at Ezra's face, she realized he was mirroring her thoughts. Neither of their planets ever had snow. It was a completely new phenomenon to them. But not to the people of Corinez.

"How cold do you think it is here?" Ezra asked hoarsely.

"You mean, is it as cold as Corinez?"

He slapped one hand down in the snow. "Yeah, maybe."

She sat up, squirming as some snow slid down her back. "I don't think so. I think it's colder – much colder than this."

Ezra sat up too, dusting some of the snow off his jacket. "Then how do they survive? How do they grow food? How do they generate heat?"

"I have no idea." How *had* the Corinez people survived all these years? What must it be like to live there? Ash scowled, distracted by her soaked skirts, which were tangled around her legs and allowing the coldness to seep through to her very bones. She couldn't get them free to stand up, and muttered an expletive. Ezra stood up next to her, planting his feet firmly on the ground.

He smiled as he held out his hand. "Okay, so I've learned. Let me help."

She sighed and reached out and grabbed his hand, letting him pull her up.

The skirts were like a giant weight around her. There were just so many of them. Walking was like trudging through mud. "Maybe this wasn't such a good idea," she muttered.

Ezra pulled his jacket from his back. It was clear that the cold had soaked him through too. "Let's get back. Dry off." He looked up at the palace.

There was still plenty of activity at the back. Crates of food were being carried inside. Servants were bustling to and fro. A few people glanced in their direction, wrinkling their noses in curiosity and disapproval.

Ash looked up at the rows and rows of windows. She could see a few flickers at the windowpanes, likely more disapproving glares.

An uncomfortable shiver snuck down her spine. Would a Czarina really go running around in the snow? This might not have been the best idea they'd ever had.

"We need to make a plan for tonight – what are we going to do about those guards? Do you really think Burovski's distraction will make them leave their posts?"

Ezra nodded. "Let's dry off and find Burovski. He might already have an idea. Bottom line, we can't get into that room, we can't get the crown." He shot her a look. "And neither of us will be going home."

CHAPTER SEVENTEEN

The trouble with plans was the more you thought about them, the more flaws you began to spot.

Ash tugged at the dark plum gown she'd chosen to wear for the ball. She'd actually wanted to dress as a maid, but Burovski had put her off the idea. Apparently someone had snuck into Count Stani's palace recently, disguised as a servant, trying to carry a tray of some kind into the Century room. Their illusion had no substance and they'd apparently been shot on the spot, their body dragged down the corridor, leaving a trail of blood as a message to anyone else with similar ideas.

Servants were banned from that corridor now. And Ash wasn't in a hurry to get shot.

It felt entirely possible that the maid had pushed her into a smaller-sized corset. Before, she couldn't breathe. Now, she felt as if she couldn't move *or* breathe.

Her hair was twisted up in first a braid, then a bun.

She longed for a shade of blue, or even a vibrant pink. Dark brown was so boring. What was a Czarina supposed to look like anyhow?

Ezra appeared at the door, dressed again in his uniform. She was jealous. At least he could breathe and move.

"Ready?"

"As I'll ever be." She didn't want to admit to the fluttering in her stomach. Ash Yang didn't do nerves. At least, none she admitted to.

She picked up the ornate gold and red-stone necklace that Burovski had dropped off earlier and fastened it around her throat. Apparently the Czarina was renowned for having beautiful jewels, so something extra was required. He'd glanced at her bangle and shook his head. "You should hide that one, it's not grand enough."

She'd put her hand over the bangle. "I need it close at hand," she'd said protectively, gripped by panic at the very thought of not having a way back to the Library, and knowing she had no way of removing it anyway.

She'd slid a red ring that matched the necklace onto her finger, even though it was a little loose, hoping it would distract from the bangle. That would have to be enough.

"Will I do?" she asked Ezra as she held out her hands.

He nodded. "Oh, you'll do. Let's just hope you don't have to run in that dress."

She looked down at the huge skirts. "Well, every dress is as big as this one. There wasn't anything smaller. So, I guess I just need to live with it." She swished the skirts.

"I can last another few hours, I think."

It was odd. These dresses were so far out of her comfort zone, but there had actually been a fun part of wearing them. It was like nothing she'd ever worn before – and nothing she would wear in her normal life.

As she approached the door, she could hear the noise from downstairs drifting up towards them. Voices. Bustle. Excitement.

They took a few steps down the corridor and she could feel a buzz in the air.

A number of other guests were making their way down the various corridors, all emerging onto a balcony with a set of curved stairs on either side leading down to the main door.

The door was wide open, the cold air rushing in, along with a few new guests who had obviously elected not to stay beforehand. The staff took their overcoats and cloaks, directing all the guests towards the ballroom.

Ash hadn't paid attention to the preparations today – her brain had been so consumed with running over the plans for tonight. The strange-styled lanterns that lined the corridors and rooms seemed to have multiplied exponentially, meaning the previously dim lighting was a bit brighter than before.

A group of people were playing music at the end of the ballroom. Tables were scattered around the room, adorned with glasses full of different coloured liquids. The drapes at the myriad of windows were still open, but a variety of coloured cloths had been pulled across them, bathing the ballroom in an array of magical colours lit by the setting sun.

The ballroom was already crowded, with a few people dancing in a gentile kind of way. Ezra nudged her. "It seems that everyone here shows up on time."

Ash looked from side to side. "They do. I'd say that I've never been to a party where everyone arrived on time, but the truth is, I've never really been to a party at all."

Ezra couldn't hide the surprised expression on his face. "You've never been to a real party before?"

She gave a small shrug. "There was never much to celebrate, where I lived. We sometimes had gatherings in other family houses at night, but I would never have called it a party." She stopped walking and picked up her skirts, which were already beginning to annoy her. "And I've certainly never been to a ball."

He nodded. "Yeah, neither have I."

They moved to a position close to one of the walls, a spot where they could watch without being too obvious.

After a few moments Ezra muttered under his breath, "Does this seem like a ball to you, or more like some kind of political game?"

Ash knew exactly what he meant. There was a strange, tense atmosphere in the ballroom. It was busy, and people were moving freely around, but every now and then, there was a small gathering with angry glances from side to side. The Count seemed to be holding court and giving orders to a variety of other guests, some of which weren't well received.

A few people walked away angrily. Others gathered in separate areas of the ballroom, talking in hushed voices.

"Oh, to have a bit of technology where we could actually hear what they're saying," sighed Ash.

She lifted a glass from a passing silver tray. The liquid was a strange kind of purple. "Might as well give some of these a try. We'll need to wait a bit longer before Burovski puts his distraction into effect." Her stomach was clenched in knots. What would happen if she couldn't get the crown? What happened if they were caught in the act of taking it? She hadn't even asked Orius that question, because there hadn't been time.

But if things went wrong, surely it would be okay just to grab Ezra and get out of there?

It was almost like Ezra could sense how tense she was. "Finish your drink and we'll find our own distraction for a while. Think you can dance like that?"

She screwed up her face as she watched the people facing each other on the dance floor, with their hands on each other's shoulders and moving in a slow, lilting fashion. "Probably, but there's also a high chance of me treading on your toes."

He held out one hand towards her. "I'll take it. We need the distraction." He smiled at her and she took a quick look around the room. There was no chance of them making their move until the guards were distracted. Until then, she might as well try and enjoy her first ball.

Ezra moved much more easily than Ash did. His body

seemed to fall into the rhythm, while she started stiff and jerkily. The music style changed, becoming quicker, and the people around them started spinning around together in time to the upbeat tune. Ezra was laughing now, not caring that she trampled over his toes. His arms changed position so he was guiding her around the floor, taking the lead as he spun her round and round.

Her skirts bounced and the room blurred as she circled. It was fun. It was exhilarating. Everything that lay ahead tonight didn't matter right now. She just wanted five minutes to forget about everything else – to forget about being the Guardian and all the responsibilities that came with it.

She saw a woman frown as she watched them. Of course. Ezra was her personal bodyguard. She probably shouldn't be dancing with him. But right now, she didn't care.

Someone tapped Ezra on the shoulder and murmured something in his ear. Before she had a chance to think about it, a stranger stepped into Ezra's place. As she looked around she realized that everyone on the dance floor had changed partners. The man was older, with a greying beard, but he laughed and joked as he spun her around. He even gave an occasional yelp as she stepped on his toes.

For a few seconds the music slowed and the men swapped positions again. Her new partner was a younger man, maybe in his mid-twenties. His gaze narrowed as he stared at her for a moment. He lifted his hands to hold her, but she froze. The feelings she got from him weren't good. He made her instantly uneasy.

The gentleman bowed his head a little – but not in a respectful way.

"Czarina."

Apparently her body couldn't unfreeze, and he noticed as the music started. She had no idea who this guy was, but it was clear he might know her.

Was his behaviour because of last night? She shouldn't have caused that scene. She should have kept a low profile – just like she was supposed to.

The man started moving to the music and she willed her body to relax a little. She could do this. It would only be a matter of minutes before they would swap partners again. At that point she would make an excuse and find Ezra.

But the man kept his eyes firmly on her, never moving them from her face. Eventually he tilted his head to one side. "Forgive me, Czarina," he said, "but the scar on your face. It's remarkable. It seems to have completely disappeared."

Her feet stumbled and she let go of him to grab her skirts and stop herself falling. A scar? The Czarina from Meduvlok had a scar on her face? Since when? If the Library had known this, it would have been replicated when she transported. Burovski hadn't said a word.

Then it struck her. She wasn't sure that Burovski really knew the Czarina. Not personally. She'd taken it for granted that no one actually knew the Czarina because she was such a recluse. But maybe that was why – because she had a scar on her face.

All these thoughts raced through Ash's brain. Whoever this guy was, he had completely unnerved her.

She gave him a cold glance. That felt like something a Czarina would do – particularly when a man had remarked on something so personal. "It's amazing what medicine can do these days," she said smartly, and then she turned to walk away.

But the man caught her arm. He pulled her so close to him that she could smell the liquor on his breath. "There's something off about you."

She tried to wrench her arm free, but his grip was much firmer than she'd realized. People were still dancing around them and she could see a few sets of eyes looking over. Ash was no weak-ass girl. She'd never let a guy in her life get a grip on her like this. Anyone who'd ever got that close uninvited had received a knee to the groin or been tossed over her shoulder.

She had to will herself to stop her instinctive reaction. In this environment, on this planet, those movements would be shocking for a woman in her supposed position – particularly in the middle of a crowded ballroom. Ash needed to get the crown and get out of here. She kept repeating that in her head, to stop herself punching this obnoxious guy in the face.

As a couple spun past, she caught Ezra's eye. It only took him a few seconds to realize something was wrong and he dropped his arms from his dance partner and started to move through the many people on the ballroom floor.

No. She didn't need help. Throwing this guy to the ground might attract too much attention, but she could still get rid of him.

She lifted her other hand and grabbed hold of the smallest finger that was gripping her arm. With all her might she twisted and wrenched it completely backwards. Even among all the background noise she heard a satisfying crack, followed by a muffled yelp from her dance partner. "Don't ever put your hands on me," she said through gritted teeth. "Come near me again, and I'll break more than your finger."

Once more she turned to leave, but this time he put a foot firmly down on her skirts as he grasped his injured hand. "Your cheek – it seems a remarkable recovery, *Czarina*?"

It was the way he said the word. Questioning. Like he knew. He knew she wasn't who she was supposed to be. Ash grabbed at her skirts, tugging with all her might. There was a rip, but she couldn't care less. She'd pulled herself free just as Ezra appeared at her side.

She held her head high, her jaw tight. "Let's get out of here."

Ezra glanced towards the guy, who had a mocking expression on his face now, then he took Ash's elbow and they threaded through the crowd.

They reached the corridor outside the ballroom a minute later. There were a number of guests milling around outside, and Ezra kept walking till they reached a room with a door that was a little ajar. He pushed it open, led her inside, then closed it quietly behind them.

A library. Ezra had brought them into a library. How ironic.

Ash sagged against the door.

Dark wood surrounded them. Uniform, brown books filled the shelves, and there was a desk and several hard-backed chairs. Lamps cast a dim light around them.

Ezra rounded on her. "Want to tell me what just happened?"

She squeezed her eyes closed for a moment. "That guy – I don't even know his name – but I think I'm supposed to. I think he knows the Czarina." She reached one hand up to her cheek. "He asked me what happened to my cheek. To the scar."

"What scar?"

"Exactly." She shook her head again. "The Library takes care of the details. It puts me in the body and the clothes I should be in." Her hand was still cupping her cheek. "But how could it miss a detail so important?"

Ezra started pacing. "How sure are you the Czarina has a scar? Maybe he was just trying to smoke you out. Maybe something else we've done made him suspicious."

Ash groaned. "Like playing outside in the snow, fighting with the host at dinner, and dancing with my bodyguard?" She was starting to feel guilty. As if she'd put this mission at risk.

Maybe Orius and the Library had been wrong to select her as the Guardian.

Recognition seemed to dawn on Ezra's face and he sagged

down into the nearest chair. "I keep forgetting that this is real life – for the people here at least. It still seems like some kind of crazy dream." He leaned his arm on the desk. "I thought that man had hurt you."

"I've never needed a guy to rescue me, and I wasn't about to start now!" She spat the words out and Ezra just looked at her. *Really* looked at her.

And she realized how much of an idiot she'd just been.

When she'd been in trouble in space, Ezra had been the one to come and help her. Okay, he might not have officially rescued her – the Commanders had done that – but the intent had definitely been there.

Ash rubbed at her arm. "I wonder if the bruises will transfer when we go back," she said. It seemed easier than saying sorry.

She looked down. Even in the dim light she could see the bottom of her dress was torn. Ash let out a long, slow breath from her lips.

"Why do I feel as if all this is going to go horribly wrong?"

"What happens if you go back without the crown?"

She straightened her spine and walked across the room, sitting in the chair next to Ezra. "To be honest, that's never happened before. Whatever I've been sent to return, or take, I've always managed to succeed." She pressed her lips together. "And I guess it's not about me. It's about them. The people here. You know that Orius said that there are rumours – a legend – about the crown that people believe. Count

Stani already appears like a tyrant. What kind of ruler would he be if he tried to conquer all the principalities?"

Ezra gave a visible shiver. "I'll be glad to get out of here."

She nodded. "We need to find Burovski. I want to get this done. We need to shorten the timescale." She had an edge to her voice now. "What if that guy from the ballroom tells everyone I'm not the true Czarina?"

Ezra stood up. "What would he gain by doing that? And who else in the room actually knows the Czarina? Who can testify that you're not her?"

Ash was kneading her hands in her lap. "I'm not sure. But still, if he speaks to the Count then they might come looking for me. Try and hunt me down." She stared at the rows of books. "I'm supposed to be inconspicuous. Get in, get out." As she said the words out loud, she felt a wave of failure wash over her.

When she'd brought Ezra here, she'd wanted him to have fun. To see a new world and get a taste of a different life. But not like this. Everything about this situation seemed wrong.

Ezra's hand appeared on her shoulder. "Then let's do that," he said quietly, but with a determined edge. "Get in, get out."

She licked her dry lips and nodded. This was the first time being Guardian had gone wrong for her. What bothered her most was that she didn't really understand what the consequences would be if she didn't succeed.

Ash stood up and smoothed down her rumpled skirts. "You're right. Let's find Burovski. Let's get this plan started."

She walked over to the door and reached out her hand to pull it open.

Just as the sound of gunfire started.

CHAPTER EIGHTEEN

Ash's hand froze in mid-air as Ezra pulled her backwards. She shook her head and frowned.

"Is *this* Burovski's distraction?" Now she was confused.

"It doesn't sound too close," replied Ezra. He cracked the door open. The palace had erupted into chaos. People were running screaming from the ballroom. Or, at least, they were trying to. Once the guests reached the main corridor, they spotted the men coming through the main entrance, who were carrying guns, and turned back the way they had come, causing confusion and panic.

One of the men with a gun fired it directly at the ceiling. Plaster rained down on heads, and women screamed.

Ezra turned to Ash, his face grave. "This can't be the distraction. It just can't be."

"It'll do though," said Ash as she gathered her skirts in her hands. "Let's go."

They ducked out of the library door and turned right,

heading down the corridors towards the Century room. It wasn't only the guests who were panicking, the serving staff were too. Indiscriminate shots were being fired. But it was difficult to determine where they were all coming from.

Ezra grabbed Ash's hand as they ran down a corridor. She was so glad he had scoped this place out earlier. He seemed to remember the way along the many corridors. A few of the guards she'd noticed earlier pushed past them, heading in the opposite direction. Her heart leaped. Maybe, in the chaos, the Century room would be free to access?

As they turned the next corner, they ran straight into Burovski. It was the first time Ash had seen him without his thick coat on. He was only wearing his grey military uniform. Gun in hand, he gestured them behind him.

"Move!"

She grabbed his arm. "Was this you? Is this the distraction?"

He pulled back from her. "What? Of course not. This is real. This is an invasion. I have a bad feeling. Now go, go quickly." He gave her a quick push, then turned and ran along the corridor, towards the gunshots.

Ash's heart was racing. Burovski had been good to her. She didn't want him to place himself in danger.

Ezra yanked her arm. "Come on. Let's get the crown, before whoever's shooting the gun gets there first."

They sped through the maze of corridors, ducking back when they saw armed soldiers approaching along one. Ash and Ezra flattened themselves against the wall, praying the soldiers would go in a different direction. When they did, they raced on.

There was a body lying in one corridor. Both of their footsteps slowed. Ash vaguely recognized the man on the floor. She was sure he was a Count from one of the other principalities. He was crumpled on the carpet, blood smeared down the wall next to him.

She bent down and felt at his neck, shaking her head at Ezra. "No pulse." She could see the flash of fear in Ezra's eyes; she recognized it because she felt it too.

Of course, being a pilot meant that places would get bombed and people would get killed. She'd always known it. But this? Shooting someone at close range with one of those old-style weapons? This was different. This was ugly. This was more real than she wanted.

"Who did this? And why?"

Ezra bent down, putting his hands either side of her waist and tugging her upwards. "I have no idea. But there's nothing we can do. Let's go, before whoever did this comes back."

Ash wanted to wait. It seemed wrong to leave the man's body there, like some discarded, unimportant piece of rubbish. But the sounds of shots and screams were getting closer.

She took a deep breath and willed the sight of the man's body out of her head. She had a job to do. A job that was beginning to seem more important by the second.

They rounded the corner to where the Century room was situated. The door was closed but there were no guards in sight.

"Yes!" whispered Ezra as he pushed open the door and they both dashed inside.

Ash stood for a moment with her back to the door. The Century room was elaborate. The furnishings were pristine, the wood carved and dark-stained. There were a few shelves of books and a huge desk, with leather stretched across it.

"Where's the safe?" Ezra's voice was blunt. He was right. There was no time to admire the scenery.

Her head flicked from side to side. She started pacing, looking across the shelves and pulling out a few books. Ezra got down on his hands and knees and started looking about the floor and under the desk. The safe had to be big enough to hold a crown, so surely it couldn't be that hard to find?

There was no safe. She couldn't find the safe.

If there was no safe, there was no crown.

Ash hated to panic. Shots sounded, closer this time. Then there were some shouts. She was sure she recognized Count Stani's voice.

They had to pick up the pace.

Ezra was still on the floor. "Why do you think we're being attacked?" he asked.

She was now pressing the wooden panels on the walls, desperate to try and find some trace of a safe. "I guess we're not the only ones who want the crown. It must be soldiers from another principality. *We're* not being attacked. Count Stani is. And have you met the man? No wonder people are ready to shoot him. He's a megalomaniac."

She glanced down at her feet, where Ezra still was.

"Anything?"

He shook his head. "It doesn't feel right. Something feels off about all this."

She stopped for a second. He was right. Something about this *did* feel off. It had right from the beginning. But before she could say anything, Ezra's face changed. He sat up on his knees, his hands rubbing the rug beneath him.

"I've got it."

He shoved the desk, moving the rug that was under it. As the rug rumpled upwards, a dark panel in the floorboards was revealed.

"How did you know?" she asked.

Ezra rubbed his knees. "I thought it was odd that the rug was partially under the desk. Most people don't want expensive rugs marked by heavy furniture. Plus, I could feel something under my knees."

Ash bent down. There was a small metal loop. She didn't wait – there wasn't time. She slid her finger into the loop and tugged hard.

It took two hands and sore shoulders before the panel came free.

She stumbled backwards as Ezra leaned forward to look in.

Darkness. Complete and utter darkness. Ezra reached a tentative hand down. "There's a ladder, or steps, or something. Let me see." He swung his legs into the darkness.

Ash felt her insides twist. They had no idea what was down there. They weren't even entirely sure if the safe was there.

She should be doing this. She had no right to put her friend in danger like this. She put a hand on his shoulder. "No. Let me."

Ezra looked up at her in confusion. "Why?"

She didn't have time to spill all her fears. "Because I'm the Guardian."

He blinked. It was as if he could read exactly what was in her thoughts without her saying the words out loud. He held out his hand towards her. "Let's do it together."

She couldn't pretend she wasn't relieved as she put her hand in his.

In her copious skirts she fumbled down the ladder after him, pretending not to notice when he attempted to help by holding some of them out of the way for her.

She jumped down, her eyes trying to get used to the dark.

The immediate lack of space was apparent. This wasn't some fancy tunnel system. This was literally a cupboard underground. There was some light streaming in from above but it wasn't enough to see well by.

"You take one side, I'll take the other," said Ezra.

They stood back to back, hands feeling along the walls. It only took a few seconds for her fingers to fumble over a large cold box, halfway up.

It had to be what they were looking for. "I think I've got it. It's set into the wall."

Ezra spun around, his hands touching hers as he felt the safe too. She located a large dial at the front that clicked and spun as she touched it.

Ezra groaned. "We can't see to spin the dial, even if we knew the code. Any ideas?"

Her fingers were still spinning the dial, listening to the series of clicks.

"Want to guess a code?" he asked again.

Ash leaned in next to him. "I have something." She stuck her hand inside the top of her dress and pulled out a small grey circle. "Remember?" She pressed the disc against the safe. "I'm hoping this means we don't need a code."

Shots fired somewhere close by. They both jumped.

"Why is the Century room unguarded?" The voice was instantly recognizable: Count Stani. "Fools! We have to protect the crown."

There was noise above. Pounding feet in the distance.

Ash's eyes widened as the dial on the safe started to whirr round on its own. She didn't know which way to look. Her mouth was dry, her heart missing a few beats. This couldn't be happening.

Before she had a chance to think, Ezra jumped up, fumbling around and then pulling the panel closed above them.

She gasped just as footsteps rushed into the room above. She automatically looked up. Through a gap in the panel she could see dark-coloured uniform trousers.

"We've killed some of the leaders – but not all. In the chaos a few of them have disappeared," one of the guards reported.

Ash's body froze. In the darkness she exchanged an

anxious glance with Ezra. He was shaking his head and pressing a finger to his lips. "I don't think I managed to get the rug back in place," he whispered in her ear.

"How are they going to get out? We've covered all the exits," said someone else above.

There was distant yelling – it had to be out in the corridors. "Of course there would be chaos," Count Stani spat. "They're running for their lives. Not that it will make any difference." His voice was chilling. Cold, a bit manic.

Ash turned back to the wall. The safe door was now ajar and she could see a glint of something inside. Whatever the piece of technology was that Orius had given them, it seemed to have worked.

Ash nudged Ezra. "Look," she hissed. "The crown. We can grab it."

"Are you crazy?" He mouthed the words at her.

His eyes were wide and he bent to her ear, his lips brushing against her as he whispered. "People are shooting guns out there. This is a coup, Ash. We're not supposed to be in the middle of this. Orius didn't send you here to get yourself killed." Even though he was whispering, his voice was full of anger and tension. "The people out there – they're getting slaughtered. For nothing – for a crown."

"Wait!" Count Stani's voice was loud, dripping with suspicion. "The rug, someone's moved it. Someone's been in here! Open the panel!"

A shot fired through the wood above them, splintering into the wall next to Ash.

She let out a tiny yelp as the panel was yanked open, giving her a glimpse of Stani's furious face. "You!" he yelled as she fumbled to grab the crown. Even as she moved, she knew it was pointless – and then, as her hands touched the crown, she felt something like a low-grade electric shock.

Arms reached down to grab first her, and then Ezra, depositing them both in crumpled heaps on the ground between the desk and the gap in floor. The crown was clutched to her chest but there was no chance for her to grab for Ezra and use the bangle. Plus, she was momentarily distracted by the strange buzzing feeling flowing through her from the crown.

"Did you like it down there, Czarina?" hissed Stani, spit flying from his mouth. "Think you can take my crown? Well, let's see how much you like it in there when I throw you back down and you have a lifetime to rot."

His hand reached out for the crown as bedlam erupted in the room. Shots came out of nowhere. The guards yelled at each other, one of them slumping to the ground near the door, clearly hit.

Stani bent down and grabbed the slumped guard's gun, keeping one in each hand. "Who dares to fire at us? Kill them, kill them now!"

There was more noise outside, like a charge.

Ezra tried to grab Ash and yank her behind the desk. It was the only place to take cover. But the crown was heavier than she'd expected, and her already-torn dress caught at the edge of the desk.

Ezra managed to get firmly behind the desk, but she still couldn't get a hold of both him and the crown at once to use the bangle and get them out of there. Her panic and frustration were almost overwhelming.

She pressed the crown close to her chest, absorbing the buzz, as she turned around. Shots were still being fired. She had little or no cover here.

With horror, she realized that Count Stani had part of her torn skirt in his hand, trapping her in place, his gun outstretched towards her face.

She gave the smallest shake of her head – a sign to Ezra to stay exactly where he was. If she got them out of here, she was taking her friend straight back to the Star Corporation Academy. This was supposed to have been fun, but at this point she wasn't even sure that either of them would survive. It was all her fault. She'd got smart. She'd got cocky. She pressed her lips together. If they got out of this, she promised herself she would do better.

Count Stani's face was pale, his eyes darker than ever. "You little snake. I knew the rumours about you were lies."

He waved his gun as he stepped forward.

"You, the hidden Czarina, who never leaves her castle. Who refuses to see anyone. Lies! All lies. You've been plotting for years, haven't you?"

He was furious. He was irrational. And he had that menace in his eyes. This man would do anything to get what he wanted.

"I didn't plot anything, Count Stani. This is your doing,

not mine. Wasn't this what you planned? Invite all your rivals, get them all under one roof, and once they're here, attack?" She gestured to the guard on the floor. "I heard your men. I heard them say they'd shot some of the leaders. What kind of a man are you? One that traps people in your palace, then hunts them down? Is that the only way you could think to defeat everyone – by pretending to be hospitable, then killing them as they sat at your table?" She kept her voice even and calm, then jumped as he fired a shot into the wall directly behind her head. Ash's ear felt warm, as if the bullet had barely missed her.

"Give me the crown!" he yelled. This time his voice had a different edge to it, as if he was losing it entirely. "Ivan Remizov came to me earlier. He insisted you were an imposter." He tilted his head to one side. "Where is your scar, Czarina?"

Ash could feel a bead of sweat trickle down her spine. What would happen if he fired as she pressed the bangle on her wrist? Would the bullet travel with her, and still kill her? But of course, she couldn't press the bangle. Not without holding on to Ezra.

She'd only been at the Star Corporation Academy for a short time, but the rules of never leaving someone behind were imprinted in her brain – just like they were in Ezra's. She could never press the bangle without having her hands on him, and right now she wasn't sure she could make the move without getting shot first.

Something about Ash's fear sent her into clear Czarina

mode. She had to play the part better than ever. "Ivan Remizov is a liar. A poor excuse of a man who I would never receive in my castle. You are a fool to have him in yours."

The two guards in the doorway were still firing out into the corridor. Shots blasted into the door frame in return. It was clear that some of the guests were fighting back.

"Yow!" yelled one of the guards, sliding down the wall with large splinters of wood embedded in his skin and eyes. The other guard threw a nervous glance over his shoulder towards the Count.

"We're outnumbered. Where are the reinforcements? We need to go now!" he shouted.

But the Count didn't seem to hear him. He was so focused on Ash. "Give me the crown. It is mine."

She gulped and looked downwards. The crown was already causing her arms to ache. The base was heavy, thick gold, but the top was gorgeous. Just like the holo picture Orius had shown them – intricately woven delicate gold work, decorated with beautifully set jewels. Only a master craftsman could have created something this beautiful. But had they created it for people to die over?

There was something else about the crown. She couldn't ignore the buzz in her arms. She wasn't quite sure how she could ever describe it, but from the second she'd taken hold of the Mirinex Crown, it was like having some kind of low-level electrical charge run through her. A kind of force. She'd heard the legend, and she hadn't believed it for a second.

But there was definitely something there – even if she couldn't get her head around it.

There was no way a man like Count Stani could be allowed to lead an army with this crown at the head of it. Legend or no legend, the man was crazy. He didn't just want to rule. He wanted to dictate. No person living in a land ruled by him could be safe.

The last guard was getting nervous. After one final look, he ducked out the door. The sound of his running footsteps was overwhelmed by more shots. The Count didn't even seem to notice.

Two seconds later Burovski appeared at the door, gun in hand.

He marched straight in. His face was bright red, sweat running down his temples.

"Drop it now, it's over, Stani," he said.

At the sound of Burovski's voice, Ezra climbed out from behind the desk. But Stani's gun still pointed at Ash. She didn't want to move.

Stani let out a manic kind of laugh. "What do you mean 'It's over', Burovski? This is only the beginning." He turned a little towards his rival.

Burovski's hand was steady. "I mean that you've taken things too far. Other principalities heard about your plot. It seems they put their own plans in place to stop you." Burovski met Ash's gaze and her heart fell. He was bluffing. This was a bluff.

Stani threw back his head and laughed. "You can't stop me.

No one can. I have the Mirinex Crown. I will lead my army all across this nation and crumple every principality who is fool enough to stand against me."

His gun was still pointed at Ash, but it was the first time she realized that his madness might work in her favour.

"You can't rule this land, Stani. You're just not clever enough," she said mockingly.

Burovski and Ezra both threw her shocked looks.

She kept talking. "After all, you didn't realize you had an imposter in your midst."

Stani's gaze narrowed.

She bowed her head slightly towards him as she deliberately smirked. "Ash Yang. I'm afraid – or not – that the real Czarina wasn't fool enough to accept your invitation. She obviously realized what a complete, untrustworthy slimeball you are. The scar thing?" She raised one hand to her cheek. "Your friend Ivan might have got this entirely right. Truth is, I don't know. And I don't really care. I only had one reason for coming here."

The frown on Stani's face deepened. "What are you talking about?"

She couldn't work out if he was more mad or confused.

"The crown. I'm here for the crown, Stani."

Burovski was looking at her as if he couldn't quite believe what she was doing. Ezra's eyes were focused completely on Stani's gun.

Stani shook his head and laughed again, looking at her as if she was the mad one. "You? A little thing like you thinks she can take my crown? I don't care who you are or where you come from. The Mirinex Crown is mine."

Ash took a step around the edge of the desk. "But maybe you *should* care who I am, and where I come from. I'm not from here, Stani. I'm not from Tallux 5."

As she continued talking, Burovski started to move a little closer to Stani.

"I don't come from your planet at all. I come from another solar system in a galaxy far, far away."

Burovski was nearly close enough now, close enough to either knock the gun from Stani's hand, or to push him completely to one side. All she had to do was keep the Count's eyes firmly on her. Distraction was the key.

It was clear Ezra was agitated. His hands were held like claws, his body rigid. She knew he wanted to do something, but she prayed he'd stay put.

Stani leaned towards her a little. "You, crazy lady, are as captive here as everyone else, unless you haven't noticed. No one is getting out of here alive. Your friend behind me included."

Stani whipped around so quickly, Ash barely had time to take a breath.

"Go!" yelled Burovski.

Both guns fired – then one was skittering across the floor as Burovski flew backwards. One bullet must have hit the ceiling, because plaster showered around them.

Ezra moved over next to Ash. He tugged the crown from her hands and put it on her head. The weight made her

223

wobble. He'd realized she couldn't hold on to him and operate the bangle while clutching the crown. "Do it," he said through gritted teeth, moving behind her to the position they'd been in the last time they transported, both hands on her waist.

They both raised their heads to the sight of Stani wrestling towards his gun again and Burovski leaning back against the wall, wheezing, with blood running down the front of his chest.

Ash's eyes met his. Her hand was poised above her wrist.

But she couldn't do it. She couldn't leave – not while Burovski was injured.

His dark eyes stayed on hers. He was in pain, it was clear. The colour had drained from his face. Her stomach clenched and as he breathed in there was a distinct gurgle.

Stani was still wrestling about the floor towards the gun, clutching at his shoulder. There was blood between his fingers. He was obviously injured, but in another few seconds he would reach it.

Her chest was tight. She couldn't actually suck a breath in.

Burovski gave her a nod and hissed, "Guardian. Go, or this will all have been for nothing."

Ezra's hands were anchored on her hips, keeping her firmly in place. She didn't want to leave. She didn't. But Stani had planned this. He planned to kill everyone in this palace. Even if a few guests had rebelled, it wouldn't be enough. Not with the palace surrounded and every exit covered.

She knew that. She did. If he got the gun and shot at her, then he would get the crown. He could trample over every person in this land. How many lives would be lost? How many people would suffer?

A tear slid down her cheek as she kept her eyes fixed firmly on Burovski. "I'm sorry," she mouthed as she pressed the ridge on the bangle on her wrist.

As the world disintegrated around her, she heard his words rasp out. "My honour to serve."

And then Tallux 5 was gone.

CHAPTER NINETEEN

She'd meant to transport them back to the Star Corporation Academy, but somehow they ended up back at the Library. A glass wall blanketed by stars appeared in front of her, just as her legs seemed to lose their strength.

Ezra guided Ash over to a chair and she sagged down, her hand still on the bangle.

"Burovski," was all she could say.

Orius appeared in front of them, watching carefully. It was a few moments before he spoke.

"You succeeded," he said softly, with a nod of approval.

Ash gave an involuntary shiver. It all felt too much. She put her hands up to her head and lifted the Mirinex Crown carefully from her head.

The tears were still falling. Her hands were shaking. The crown still had that buzz, that quality she couldn't identify.

She looked up at Orius. "Have you any idea what happened? Have you any idea what it took to get this crown?

How many lives were lost?" Her voice was trembling with emotion. It felt like everything had spun out of control.

Of course he knew. He would have watched everything unfold from back here at the Library.

Orius's hands reached out and took the crown from hers. She still didn't really understand how a hologram could do that.

"What about Burovski?" she demanded. "Is he okay? Is he dead or alive? If he hadn't helped us, we would never have got away."

Orius stood silent for a few moments. He seemed to choose his words carefully. "Sometimes lives are lost. The crown had to be seized. If it hadn't been, thousands more would have died."

Ash shook with sudden fury. "You knew? You knew this would happen? Why would you send me there – to get stuck in the middle of all that?"

Ezra cut her off. "Ash could have been killed. Did you think of that before you sent her to Tallux 5?"

Orius looked at them both. "There is always an element of danger in being the Guardian. The Library's job is to save lives – not to sacrifice them. But the universe is a big place. We don't have the power to stop time. We don't have the power to time-travel backwards to stop wrong turns being taken. When we hear of imminent trouble – something that we know we could possibly prevent – then we try to do something about it."

She understood the wisdom of his words. She could

remember the faces of the people she'd met on Tallux 5. The maid who'd been assigned to her, the doorman. Sophia Vasa from dinner. They were all part of a population that Stani had intended to conquer and control. What kind of life would they have been destined for if she hadn't fulfilled her duties?

"I didn't want to leave," she said quietly. "I almost didn't return with the crown."

Orius moved in front of her. He gave her a sympathetic look. His hand touched her shoulder. She could feel it. She could.

"But as the Guardian you made the right decision. You saw the bigger picture. Just like we knew you would, Ash."

The way he said those words sent prickles over her skin. The expectation. The pressure. The responsibility.

Was he remembering her actions when she'd risked herself to rescue the crew of the freighter? She suspected he was. He'd already told her that decision was part of the reason she was here.

She looked at the crown again, her curiosity piqued that this one item had caused so much strife. "The crown. What kind of power does it have?"

Ezra shot her a bewildered glance. But she shook her head and put her hand to her chest. "I felt something when I held it. I felt something that I couldn't explain."

"It's just a crown," said Orius quietly as he moved away. "Anything you've heard is only part of the legend. You know that."

She could see something in his eyes. A hint of something. Tallux 5 hadn't been as technologically advanced as her own world. But there were other worlds in the universe that were more advanced still. Was it possible that the Mirinex Crown had originated from somewhere else?

Ezra touched her arm. "Ash, I need to go home." His face was tired, with dark circles under his eyes.

"I'm so sorry, Ezra. None of this was what I thought it would be."

He looked at her for a long time. "You have a big job, Ash. Harder than anyone's. I don't envy you. I don't envy you at all."

She felt a pang in her heart at those words. An emptiness inside her. Despite the wonder of the Library, it still left her feeling lonely at times. And after today, could she really keep doing this?

She gave a gentle nod of her head. "I'll take you home."

He moved beside her, but this time didn't walk around and hold her waist. This time he stood in front of her and put an arm on either shoulder. "I believe in you, Ash," he said as she twisted the bangle.

They appeared in the middle of Ezra's room. Bland. Grey. Absolutely no clutter. For the first time she wondered if he'd brought anything here from his home on Hakora. Anything to remind him of the people he'd left behind.

After two days together, and everything he'd seen, she wasn't quite sure how to say goodbye. But Ezra seemed more relaxed than Ash was. He was back in his normal clothes, and he kicked off his boots and walked over to the bed, flopping on top of it. His stomach gave a loud growl and he groaned, smacking a hand over his belly. "I don't think I'll ever recover from that food," he said.

She gave him a half-smile. They weren't going to talk about it. They weren't going to talk about what had happened. That whole other world, and the horrors they'd experienced.

In a way she was glad. She wasn't quite sure what to say, and talking about Burovski was likely to make her cry.

"Will I see you again?" he asked.

She hesitated, not quite sure what to say. She'd put her friend at risk and that had never been her intention. "I hope so," she whispered.

He gave a gentle nod of his head.

"Goodnight, Ezra," she said as she closed her hand over her wrist.

"Goodnight, Ash," he repeated as she pressed the ridge on the bangle and he disappeared from her sight.

CHAPTER TWENTY

For a few days Ash drifted around the Library in a kind of numb state. She had so many questions. But Orius seemed to be steering clear of her. Whether he knew she needed some time to think things over, or whether he just didn't want to answer any of her questions, she wasn't sure.

The Mirinex Crown had appeared in among the artefacts. It was one of the few that was behind glass. That made her curious. But not enough to demand answers. It was likely there would be objects in the Library that were more advanced than anything she'd seen before, objects she would never understand.

She'd changed the decor of her room again, this time to resemble the scenery of Amara's world. Instead of looking at stars outside, she was looking at fish. Somehow being in an imaginary bubble under the sea was less intimidating than being in a real bubble at the end of the universe.

She'd asked the food station for something different,

something sweet, and was currently eating a bizarrely coloured cake. The taste was strangely compelling – not like anything she'd experienced before. She carried the food out to the table overlooking the Library. Orius appeared in a seat on the other side.

"Oh, you're alive." She shrugged as she kept eating, then smiled. "Well, not technically alive, but you know what I mean. Where have you been?"

"About," he said casually.

Ash licked her lips and put down her spoon. "We need to talk about something serious."

She could tell he wanted to sigh. "Is that wise? I thought you needed some headspace. Being the Guardian is hard, Ash. It's not for the faint-hearted. Sometimes you have to make decisions that are tougher than anything you've done before. Tougher situations than most other people will ever have to deal with."

She put her head on one hand. "I get that, Orius, and I still don't know if this is for me. But that's not what I want to talk to you about."

"It's not?" He seemed surprised. He'd obviously steeled himself for some long and drawn-out debate about the work of the Library.

She shook her head. "No. It's not." She picked up the spoon again and started playing with it. "Something went wrong on Tallux 5."

"Ash…"

She held up her hand. "The *Library* got something wrong."

Orius waved a hand. "The Library never gets anything wrong."

"Well, this time it did." She kept her voice firm. "My face. The Czarina of Meduvlok apparently has a scar on her face. When I got to Tallux 5, it wasn't there. I had no scar. And one of the other guests noticed. It nearly blew my cover."

Orius had pushed himself up from the table. "No, no. That can't be right." He started to hover back and forth. If he'd been Human, he would have been pacing.

"It is right. At least I think it is. I made up a story about medical technology being wonderful these days. But the guy stared right at my cheek, asking about my scar. He *knew* I was an imposter. How does that happen, Orius? The Library transports me, changes my clothes, sometimes my appearance. What happened this time that meant the scar was missed?"

Orius was still hovering backwards and forwards, muttering under his breath. "This can't be right. It can't be. This has never happened before."

Ash rocked back on her heels. She couldn't let this go. It was important. "Well, it happened this time. Why wouldn't the Library know that the Czarina has a scar?"

He was still muttering. "It does. It knows everything."

"But it can't. Or, at least, I hope it doesn't. Because…if it knowingly sent me there without the scar, what does that mean?"

She pushed herself up and started walking, unconsciously mimicking Orius's pacing.

"Are the Guardians just seen as disposable? Is that it? If I'd died down there, I'd just be replaced, right?" A horrible creeping sensation trickled down her spine. "How long have the other Guardians lasted?"

She pulled her tunic from her skin. All of a sudden, Ash was flushed with heat.

"Or maybe the 'Library'" – she lifted her fingers – "has decided I'm not too good at this job. Maybe that's the reason it didn't give me the scar. Was I sent down there to be conveniently dispatched – allowing you the chance to move on to the next Guardian?" Her voice had risen with her words, leaving her practically shouting by the end.

Orius whirled around, his face aghast. "No, Ash. No, absolutely not. That would never happen." He shook his head frantically. "Never."

She stepped up to him. "But it did."

Somewhere nearby there was an ancient clock ticking. The noise was amplified by the cavernous space of the Library, echoing around them. They stared at each other. Orius's eyes filled with tears.

It was something she'd never imagined a hologram could do.

"I would *never* allow one of the Guardians to be deliberately put in danger."

"But every mission has an element of danger," Ash said simply, quoting Orius's own words back at him. "Of course they do. They just don't usually have people firing guns at them."

She took a few moments.

"I want to know."

Orius gave her a look as if he wasn't quite sure what she meant. Did she want to know if the Library had made a mistake, or if it had deliberately got things wrong?

She pressed her lips together for a second. Those would be the obvious choices, but they weren't the most important to her. She chose her words carefully.

"I want to know what happened to Burovski. I want to know about Tallux 5. I want to know what happens to the people there. I want to know the consequences of the actions I took on behalf of the Library."

Silence. More clock ticking.

Orius spoke slowly. "It's an unusual request."

She put her hand on her hips. "Maybe your other Guardians acted like mindless pawns of the Library, but I won't. It's non-negotiable. If you don't tell me what I want to know, I'll leave."

Orius gave a small nod of his head. "I understand," he said.

And then he vanished.

He was gone for four days.

And Ash felt as if she'd counted the seconds.

She could have disappeared at any point. All she had to do was press the bangle and wish herself somewhere. But the most obvious place to go was back to Ezra, and he needed time right now. They both did.

Her bangle hadn't tingled. The Library hadn't tried to send Ash anywhere. And she wasn't sure she would have gone. Not until she had some answers to her questions.

Ash spent her days in the depths of the Library. She read ancient scrolls, translating the words. It was much harder than she'd ever imagined and she had to find her way around the Library's technology to do it. She examined broken pottery that had been pieced together. She admired precious jewels, and wondered over strange items that were obviously considered important in some worlds. A twisted kind of branch that looked as if it was from some ancient tree, carved with tiny symbols. A smooth, pale vase that changed colour every time Ash touched it. Ash thought the colours corresponded to her mood. Green when she was curious. Purple when she was growing frustrated. And black when she was tempted to throw it on the floor. She read all the accompanying museum tags, fascinated by some of the facts she was discovering.

Then she moved upstairs. Waved her hands to pull down all the screens Orius used. Watched feeds. Scanned other planets. Ash had always had a head for science and engineering. It didn't take her long to realize how some things worked. She could see reports of civil unrest in some places; riots, disturbances. It seemed that half the universe wanted to fight each other, and all the time the Library ran algorithms to calculate risk.

She grew impatient, even though she tried to hide it. Questions were constantly forming in her mind. She knew that every world was at a different stage of development. But the majority of artefacts in the Library seemed old, ancient even. Where were all the modern-day artefacts? Were all the more developed worlds past the stage where they needed interventions? Somehow she knew that couldn't possibly be true.

She ran her hand across one of the glass cases near the back of the Library. What about the previous Guardians? Didn't they keep any records of who they were, and what they'd done? She was curious about those who'd gone before her. Did any of them have the same kind of doubts that she was having?

As her fingers smudged the glass she realized that any records about the Library itself wouldn't be on paper, they'd be digital. The technology that the Library had access to was way beyond what she'd ever been exposed to before – she only had to look at Orius to know that was true. So how did she access technology that she didn't even know how to work?

She sat down in a large red chair. It faced out towards the bottom of the glass dome and the space outside. From here she had a perfect view of the stars in this part of the solar system.

Ash had never really considered shades of black before, but as she lifted her feet up onto one of the nearby stools, she could see them right in front of her. Blacks, greys and glimmers of darkest purple all seemed to decorate the view before her eyes. In lots of ways it was beautiful.

She had no idea how long she watched, but eventually her back ached and she pulled her feet back down. Her heel caught something under the chair and she bent down for a look.

It only took a few seconds for the flicker of recognition to hit. The brown package. The one that had been transported to her, back in the fighter.

What? She shook her head as she tugged it out from under the chair. Everything in the Library was catalogued. How could Orius have forgotten about this? How could she? The momentum of working as the Guardian had pushed it from her mind.

There was rope around the thick brown material. She undid the knots and pulled the fabric back, then tilted her head and stared.

She didn't even know what she was looking at.

It looked like part of some machine – triangular in shape. But a machine that she'd never seen before. The metal was light, but strong. It was perfectly smooth, with no dents or marks. In the middle was a giant kind of crystal. It was rough, with particles inside, and although mainly clear there was a tinge of green.

The only thing she knew for sure was that she didn't have a single clue what this was for. Her breath caught somewhere in her throat. Had this been worth that doomed crew dying over? She carefully rewrapped it and sat the parcel on the table. She'd talk to Orius about it later. If he ever showed himself again.

Ash walked back through the Library and got ready for bed. She'd only just slid under the covers when Orius materialized in her room.

"Hey," she said. "Boundaries!"

Orius nodded.

"Apologies, Guardian, but I thought you might want to talk."

"Four days, Orius. That's how long you've been gone."

If it were entirely possible, he looked tired. "I know." He moved, perching at the edge of her bed.

She was surprised. Of course there was no indent on the bed – how could there be from a hologram? It was just the fact he'd made that movement that surprised her. Sitting at the edge of her bed seemed personal. Orius had never behaved like this before.

"I know how long I've been gone, Ash. It took longer than I expected to try and get some of the answers you asked for." He shifted a little. "The Library is no longer receiving direct reports from Tallux 5."

Her heart gave a twist in her chest. She couldn't breathe. It was clear what was coming next. "But you know what happened there after I left?"

His grey eyes met hers. "I…do." The words seemed to take an age to come out.

She sat, hands on the soft blanket, telling herself not to drum her fingers in impatience. It took all her self-control.

His voice was deep. "I'm sorry, Ash, but Burovski died, along with a number of other Counts and Czars who were head of some of the other principalities."

Tears sprang to her eyes. She'd known it. She'd known from the paleness of Burovski's skin and the wheezing in his chest. But that didn't mean she hadn't hoped for a miracle.

Orius continued. "Overall, one hundred and seven people were killed that night."

"That many?"

He nodded again. "Count Stani is now imprisoned. He was injured, but not badly. He will be held for trial in each of the principalities across Tallux 5. Many have their own justice system."

There was an implication in the way Orius said those words. Somehow she knew Count Stani wouldn't live for long.

"So taking the crown has made a difference?" She couldn't hide the anxiety in her voice.

Orius nodded. "It has. Stani would have murdered everyone in the palace that night, and then marched through every principality, brandishing the crown and claiming all land as his own. He would have been ruthless. Anyone who challenged him would have died. And most people would have believed him invincible because of the crown.

"Can you imagine what kind of ruler he would have been, and what kind of suffering the people on Tallux 5 would have endured?"

Ash took a long, slow breath as a shiver went down her spine. For the most part, she hoped her imagination couldn't stretch that far into darkness.

"What about the Czarina?" she asked. "What about her scar?"

Orius lowered his head. "Ah. Yes. It turns out the Czarina does have a significant scar. It was caused by an intruder in her castle. She killed him in a sword fight, but was left with a large scar on her left cheek. This happened a few weeks before you arrived."

"Why didn't we know about it? Why did Ivan Remizov know something that the Library missed?"

Orius sighed. "It's a good question. A reasonable question that took a long time to get a reasonable answer for."

She just gave him a look.

"There had been no contact with the Czarina. She was known as a recluse. Our Friends on Tallux 5 had already decided she would be a good role to occupy. They hadn't paid as much attention as our Friends normally do. It was an error." His voice was grave and he didn't quite meet her eye. "It was an error on the part of the Library. One that hasn't been made before. And you were right, Ash." Now he did lift his head and meet her eye. "It could have cost you your life."

She let the words hang in the air between them. When she'd got here she'd been in awe of everything. It had all seemed unbelievable – an absolute power beyond her understanding – and out of her reach.

"So the Library makes mistakes," she said steadily. It was a statement, not a question.

She could see the wrestling going on in Orius's head right now. He wanted to say no. He wanted to make excuses. But he was wise enough to know that wouldn't wash with her.

"So it seems." He stood up from the bed. "You are my responsibility. I will put every measure in place to make sure that doesn't happen again."

Ash knew he would. She also knew that he couldn't guarantee her safety. She didn't respond. She didn't feel as if she could.

His head tilted slightly. "It seems that our recluse Czarina has surprised everyone."

His words intrigued her. "How so?" She leaned forward.

"As soon as she heard about the coup, she travelled for three days. She arrived with her own army. She made alliances along the way. Apparently there had already been negotiations in process. She was angry. A number of people she had written agreements with were slaughtered by Count Stani. She's announced she feels a duty to the citizens of those principalities and that she will protect them."

Ash stared at him. "You mean she's taking over."

"Perhaps. The Czarina has a fierce heart. A good business mind. But she's fair. With Count Stani, she will be ruthless. For everyone else?" He gave a slow, approving nod. "She will prove to be a good leader. The people of Tallux 5 will prosper under her guidance."

Ash leaned back against her pillows. "And she can do all that without the Mirinex Crown?"

Orius kept his face neutral. "Of course." Then a small smile teased at the edges of his lips. "She reminds me of someone else that I know, but I can't imagine who."

Ash rubbed one eye; she was tired. "The Czarina?" she asked. "The whole time I played her, no one ever called me anything other than Czarina. What is her name?"

Orius smiled. "Her name? Why it's beautiful, and I imagine her name will become one of legend on Tallux 5. Her name is Anastasia."

"Anastasia," Ash repeated. "That's a nice name. A strong name." She kept smiling. "I have a feeling that's the kind of name that could be legendary on more than one planet." She sighed. "I have to sleep now, but thank you, Orius. Thank you for finding out what I wanted to know."

They exchanged a glance of understanding, before Ash pulled up the covers and Orius vanished.

CHAPTER TWENTY-ONE

Ash was in the midst of a dream. She was battling, pilot against pilot. Everything was going perfectly. She had the other fighter lined up in her sights. She could take them.

And then she caught a glimpse of green scales. Amara. The other pilot was Amara. Her heart missed a few beats. There was no way she could fire at Amara. She considered her a friend. Her brain swam with confusion. Why would Amara be in a fighter – firing on her?

She didn't have a chance to find out. Her arm was tingling and a voice was breaking into her thoughts.

"Ash!" Orius was standing next to her bed. His voice was anxious. "Ash. Wake up. You're needed."

She sat bolt upright.

"You need to go," he said, immediately turning away with a sweep of his robes.

Ash was still fuzzy. Orius had never woken her up like this before. Of course – the tingling of her arm wasn't because she'd fallen asleep on it, it was the bangle. She rubbed her wrist for a few seconds, then swung her legs out of bed. Orius hadn't even waited for her. Did that mean she didn't have time to get washed and dressed?

She padded through to the Library in her bare feet.

Orius was standing next to the Proteus circle on the floor. In front of them he'd already pulled up a holo image. But instead of showing her the artefact – like it normally did – this time the image was of a map.

"What's going on, Orius? What's the big emergency?"

Orius did his best to look aloof, but she could see the traces of anxiety in his face.

"This time is different. This time we're sending you to a planet that's more advanced than any you've visited before."

She held out her hands. "Why are you showing me a map? Why aren't you showing me what I'm taking, or returning?"

Orius waved his hand for a second and the map vanished, replaced with a real-life view of another land. Ash sucked in a breath. "Where is this?"

"This is U62."

Ash spluttered. "But it can't be." She lifted her hand up as if she could actually touch the world in front of her. "It's… dead." At least that's what she'd always been told. Her skin prickled.

She couldn't take her eyes away from the sight. There were large grey metal buildings, with blue glass. The place was spotless, with paths and bridges covered in clear glass between the buildings. The place certainly wasn't dead – in fact, it was bustling with life.

Or was it life? She peered closer. Some of the figures moving looked like Humans and others looked like some kind of android. The landscape was sleek. Manufactured. She thought back to her own planet and half-smiled. It looked as if dust wasn't a remote possibility on U62.

But the smile left her as confusion reigned.

"How is this possible? We were told U62 was destroyed millennia ago, and the population left through wormholes to find safe havens. How can there possibly still be people there?"

Orius's gaze drifted, as if he was contemplating a suitable answer. He pressed his lips together – a strange action for a hologram. Finally he spoke.

"It seems that things in U62 are not what was expected. The Library hasn't monitored that part of the universe for a long time. We saw no need. As far as we knew, life didn't exist there. But electrical activity was picked up on U62, followed by rapid technological development, which allowed the Library to shadow and monitor activity." He slowed down. "Recent events have led us to believe that U62 requires an intervention."

She narrowed her gaze. "An intervention?" This sounded different. This didn't sound like stealing something or returning it.

"The fundamentals are the same. As Guardian, you're required to visit U62. We need you to enter one of their facilities and" – he hesitated – "remove and destroy some information that they hold."

"What?"

Orius waved his hand to reveal the map again. "The bangle can't take you directly in or out. There's some kind of protection around the building and the immediate area outside. Which also means that I will be unable to monitor your mission from here. And this time, we don't have a Friend in place, as such. We've not been able to infiltrate U62 for long enough to ensure loyalty. We have, however, gained knowledge that something significant has happened."

"What?" Ash put her hands on her hips. This all sounded muddled and imprecise.

"A source has let us know that the scientists on U62 are close to a breakthrough. This breakthrough, while it may be significant for their planet, could cause problems for others."

"So you're asking me to do what, exactly?"

"We need you to infiltrate their technology and use a virus to destroy their files."

She shook her head. "This doesn't sound like something the Guardian of the Library should do."

Orius took a long, slow, fake breath. "It is...unusual, I admit. But U62 has always been a difficult planet. They've destroyed and rebuilt their own world twice already, both times with great losses."

"But this is different," Ash argued. "You told me not to interfere with natural development. Isn't that exactly what

247

this is? You're trying to prevent another planet becoming even more technologically advanced than it already is. What gives the Library the right to decide that?"

Orius gave her a long, hard look. "Because if they are left alone, and develop this technology, they could use it to destroy other planets."

Ash started walking backwards and forwards. "But won't this just be a delay tactic? Surely they will go on to develop this technology anyway?"

Orius gave a slow nod. "You're right. They could. But the virus that destroys their files will also destroy other systems. It is highly unlikely they will have the capacity to prioritize these systems over the others. It will be years before they are at this stage again."

Ash felt as if a sharp cool breeze had just blown through the Library – even though she knew it was impossible. "You said they're developing technology that could destroy other planets. A weapon. They're making a weapon?"

Orius held her gaze. "I'm not at liberty to tell you that. I can only say that what they have planned could affect every other solar system that they have access to via the wormhole system. For that reason, it's imperative that you succeed."

She could practically see the electricity sizzling in the air between them.

"Let me get this straight, you're sending me somewhere on a planet that, until a few moments ago, I thought was an uninhabited wasteland. Without backup. Not only that, but the planet's inhabitants are *so* evolved that they have beautiful buildings, a thriving population, technology more advanced than I've ever seen and are just about to take an even further step in their evolution?" She folded her arms across her chest. "Oh, Orius, what could *possibly* go wrong?"

Orius had the good grace to look embarrassed.

Ash kept going. "I'm starting to get mad. I'm starting to think you acquire a Guardian and manage to get them killed within a few months. Is that what happens? You told me stories about some Guardians being here for years, but I don't believe you. Not at this rate anyhow."

"Ash," he said quietly. "We need you to do this."

She bit her bottom lip and stared down at her still-bare feet. She didn't want to admit the fear that was sweeping around her body right now. She waited. She waited quite a while, and when she finally looked up at Orius through only half-opened lids, she sighed. "I take it you need me to leave right now?"

He gave a tight-faced nod. The layout appeared before her eyes again. Orius pointed her through the map.

"This is the building. You should be able to enter here, cross through the security points with a card you'll be given and then move through to the control room and find this workstation. Once there, your hand will activate the computer system. Technology is a little different in U62. The only way to activate a station is with individual DNA – it's scanned through your skin. Once activated, the station will flash green." An image flashed up before her. "You'll take the place of one of the Humans who work there." He paused for a second. "But not all of them are entirely Human."

Ash wrinkled her nose, but before she even had the chance to ask what that meant, Orius continued.

"Some of the Humans have android parts. Replacements for weak bones or joints. There are gravity issues on U62." Orius held up something else. "Give me your hand."

Ash frowned and held out her hand. He swiped something over it. "The virus is in your genes now. All you have to do is scan your hand at the correct target station and wait a few moments for it to work."

"A different station? And how do I get access to that?"

"You have to access the command centre, where security will be heightened. It looks after the most important systems." He showed her another room layout, with one computer highlighted in red. "This is the one you need access to. You'll have to stay at your assigned station in the control room until the signal for break time. You should have your chance to move when you return – half of the other staff will be gone."

She stared down at her hand. There was nothing on it. Nothing at all. She had a strong urge to wipe it on the soft nightwear she was wearing. She looked back up at Orius. "How will I know it has worked?"

He gave a soft laugh. "Oh, don't worry. You'll know."

She shook her head for a second. "And if I can't get access to the command centre straight away, is there someplace safe I can stay before trying again?"

A worried look flashed across Orius's face. "Well – yes." He pulled up another schematic. "Take the internal train system to here. You have use of a room if required." He hesitated. "But, Ash, try and do this as quickly as possible. You're impersonating someone who has been…indisposed… for one day. An overnight stay…could be dangerous."

She looked up at him. "For me, or for them?"

"For the rest of the universe."

Ash breathed slowly. "How good is your intel?"

Orius wrinkled his brow. "What do you mean?"

Ash straightened up. "I mean, last time, the Library let me down. How reliable is the information you're giving me?"

"It's just been verified."

"Verified by a contact on U62 who you can't even term a Friend?"

"Perhaps."

That was a yes then.

"Get in, get out," said Orius steadily.

"Get in, get out," Ash repeated.

"Your timing will be crucial. Wait for the first bell before you enter. It signifies the shift change. The card will gain you entry to a number of points. You shouldn't be noticed. And, Guardian," Orius added, "you know U62 is more advanced than your own planet. There may be temptation. You may be tempted to try and find out more, learn how some of their technology works. Don't do it."

She ran her fingers through her hair. "Don't worry, Orius,

I'll be too busy getting in and getting out to take notice of anything else." She was doing her best to ignore the thrumming in her veins. If she didn't acknowledge the fact she was actually scared, then she didn't need to address it.

Something pinged in her brain. "When I get back, we need to talk."

Orius's eyebrow rose. "We do?"

"We do." She nodded as she stepped onto the Proteus circle.

"Wish me luck," she said, not joking in the least, as she pressed the bangle and let the world around her vanish.

CHAPTER TWENTY-TWO

Everything was smooth and shiny. The whole place. Everything.

Ash was wearing a grey-and-blue uniform. Dark shoes on her feet. Her hair was black and in a short bob. It was already annoying her, scratching at the edges of her cheeks and irritating the back of her neck. Who would have hair this length?

Her stomach twisted, her eyes scanning around her, as if she expected someone to jump out at any moment and guess who she was. It didn't matter that the idea was ridiculous. She just had a bad feeling about this whole place.

Ash was next to some kind of transport. Every so often the doors on a cylinder slid open and people walked out.

But were they people? There were definitely some who seemed Human, but the biggest percentage of the population around her were some kind of androids. They walked and interacted entirely like the Humans, but they had smooth steel and glass faces, with a blue visor where their eyes should be. They wore clothes, but their arms were metallic too. Most were similarly dressed, but a few had individual traits. Red shoes. A flash of colour on their uniform. A pair of gloves.

Ash took a little time to orientate herself to her surroundings. No sand. No grass. Nothing green. If this planet had ever been fertile, it didn't look like it was now. Maybe they had no need for growth? Maybe life had evolved in a different way here.

She took a breath and started walking towards the building she'd been directed to. The card was in her hand. She just prayed it would actually work.

People and androids walked past, their heads nodding politely at each other. There were some gathered together, having conversations. She couldn't quite work out what the status system was here. Did the Humans work for the androids, the androids work for the Humans, or were they all equal?

It was fascinating. Part of her wanted to stay and find out. Part of her felt she needed to know more, to try and ensure her own safety here. She bent over for a second, pretending to fix her shoe as she tried to get a better feel for the place.

Ash was terrified. She couldn't pretend that she wasn't. The previous missions hadn't felt quite as dangerous as this one. This was something the Library had never attempted before – and it wasn't like she had any real backup. There was no Friend here.

Orius's words echoed in her ears. *Wait for the first bell. You shouldn't be noticed.*

It wasn't exactly reassuring.

There was some kind of statue in the middle of the square that she had to cross. It was definitely a man. She paused to take a moment and look. *Aldus Dexter. Founder of Organis Technologies.* He was an ordinary looking guy but the positioning of the statue was odd. He was leaning forward and pointing somewhere. What exactly did that mean?

As she turned away, something stopped her dead. The name. Aldus Dexter. There was a ring of familiarity about it.

She searched her memory, trying to remember where she'd heard it before. He wasn't from her village – she'd known everyone there for years. She couldn't remember him from the Star Corporation Academy – either as a candidate or as a teacher or a member of the crew. She frowned, sure she'd seen or heard the name somewhere.

As she stood staring at the statue, the first bell sounded. It was loud and clear. Within a few moments a huge wave of Humans and androids started streaming through the doors of the main building just across the square. The science lab. It was exactly where Orius had told her it would be.

Ash joined the line of workers waiting to get in. Her uniform matched those around her. She was dressed inconspicuously – so why did she feel as if she stuck out like a sore thumb?

She kept her head tilted downwards but her eyes alert as she scanned in using the pass Orius had given her, along with the rest of them. The barrier opened routinely and Ash breathed a sigh of relief.

With a quick glance from side to side, she tried to familiarize herself with the layout, picturing the diagram Orius had shown her. Left, right and right again. Several of the androids nodded politely at her as she passed them.

She reached the entrance to the control room.

For the first time there was no one else about. She took a deep breath and stared down at the palm of her hand. This should be her entrance key to both the control room and the computer at her workstation.

She needed this to work. She needed it to work so badly.

She lifted her head. There were bound to be cameras about – if Ash lingered for too long she'd be noticed. She lifted her hand, ignoring her trembling fingers, and pressed them against the flat panel, giving it a few seconds to read.

It should go green.

Nothing happened.

Then the machine flashed, giving off a little buzz. It seemed to be reading her palm again. Her heart was beating frantically. She didn't even know what would happen on U62 if she was found to be an imposter. What was the punishment system here?

She could feel the scanner checking her hand again as she stood there. She looked up and pasted a blank expression on her face. *Work. Work. Work.*

There was a buzz, and the control room door opened. It was all she could do not to rush inside and sag against the door. But the room beyond was full of figures – Human and android – working calmly and quietly.

She let the metal door close behind her – heard the hiss of the lock sealing.

Her eyes scanned the room, trying to figure out where her station was. It wasn't as simple as it had looked on the diagram. There were two stations side by side, both empty, and she wasn't sure which one might be hers.

Everyone else had their heads down. There was a weird kind of tension about the place. She noticed they had something small in their ears – a device that Orius had explained, which linked the brain of the user to the computer. In order to carry out a function at that terminal, the user just had to think about it. Luckily that seemed to be occupying everyone's attention.

She looked around the control room. It was much bigger than she'd first expected. The section she was in was only a small part of it. The whole area was nearly as big as the holding bay for the fighter craft at the Academy.

Ash threaded her way between the stations and desks to the two empty ones, hesitating at one, before sitting at the other. The android next to her looked up. "Is your terminal downloading again?"

She painted a smile on her face, as she slid over to the chair nearest the android. "No, at least I think not. We'll soon see." She tapped her back. "Bad back, you know, Humans."

A smile appeared on the android's steel and glass face. It looked odd with her blue, flickering gaze. This android had blonde hair, the style mimicking the short black bob that Ash had. She shrugged her metallic shoulders at Ash. "You should go to the tech centre. I'm sure they can replace whatever part you need."

Ash gave her a weak smile. She turned towards the screen in front of her and put her hands to the console while her brain whirred round and round.

Replacement part? The android had said it so easily. As if it was the norm. She stared down at her body, tempted to head to the bathroom and strip all her clothes off to ensure she was actually Human. Orius had warned her…

The screen in front of her sprung to life at the wave of her hand. She slipped the sensor in her ear and could hear a whole range of instructions. For the first few moments she followed them, playing her part in whatever was going on here.

The instructions were complicated, and she had to concentrate to get the computer to follow her thoughts. Part of her was suspicious, hoping it could only hear the thoughts and commands related to the work she was assigned. But no alarms sounded, marking her out as a traitor in their midst, so after a few moments she began to relax a little.

She seemed to be monitoring lots of different systems. Her curiosity was piqued. Ash wanted to know what was actually happening here. If she was going to do something to sabotage this control centre, surely she should take the time to find out the basic systems? Despite Orius's words of warning.

Ash couldn't help how she was. She'd always been naturally curious about everything. Even now, there were a hundred things she wanted to know about this world.

Get in, get out, reverberated in her brain.

She had to stay focused on the Guardian's role. Complete her task. So most importantly, where was the top-security room?

She tried to stay calm and look relaxed in the completely foreign environment. She was just a little cog in a wheel. It was an expression a teacher at school had told her about years ago and she liked it. Everybody was important. Everybody had their part to play.

She started to get the hang of the screen in front of her. And then it vanished and changed to another.

She kept in her groan of frustration as she realized that the same had happened to the android next to her. She lowered her head for a second and realized the android was wearing yellow sneakers with *Azla* written on the side. Was that her name?

Ash was supposed to know her. She didn't want to mess up and call her by the wrong name. That would be the biggest giveaway yet. She filed it for possible future use and concentrated back on her screen.

After an hour she realized the screens were on a cycle. The first was linked with hydroponics. She was controlling and monitoring a system that was growing food sources somewhere underground. As soon as she'd realized that, the screen changed again. The calculations for this one were more difficult, but Ash recognized them instantly.

This was a star chart. She was monitoring an area of space. Tracking pieces of space junk across the sky and watching for any activity. She had no idea where this part of space was. As far as she knew, the area around U62 had been abandoned for more than a thousand years. Everyone thought U62 was a dead planet. There was occasional wormhole activity that was monitored by several other planets in the nearest solar systems, but they were still light years away.

Just as she was familiarizing herself with the system, the screen changed again. It took a few moments to work out what she was supposed to be doing. She straightened in her chair. This was part of a factory system. Now she was confused. It was a production line.

The android next to her stood up and went to walk away, glancing at Ash's screen. "Lucky you, you're on the arms today. I got spine. Maybe I should make you one?" A smile appeared on her glass face as she laughed at her own unfunny joke and then disappeared through the myriad of stations.

Ash froze. Manufacturing. She was manufacturing the android parts. For some reason it sent a chill down her spine.

She could see the production line on her screen. She could watch as each component was slotted into place. She could see the electrical charges being sent into each part. It seemed these androids could make their own energy supplies. She watched as one part was deemed imperfect and tossed off the line to a recycle bench, and the whole process began again. An alarm showed on the top right of her screen. Her accuracy had dropped to ninety-five per cent. It seemed that a defective part was a big deal.

She swallowed and concentrated. There. She halted the line by issuing a command from her brain. Her whole screen went red and people around her glanced over. She breathed steadily. An android – she could only assume they must be some kind of supervisor – glided over towards her. She shot a smile over her shoulder and pointed at the screen. "The arm here is off by a two per cent angle. The component parts aren't being slotted in perfectly. I'm just correcting it."

The supervisor remained silent, watching until the mistake was corrected. "Good job," it finally said, before drifting away again.

The red glow cleared from the screen and Ash took a few deep breaths. It seemed that any error in the system was noted straight away. That couldn't be good news for what she was planning.

How long would the break time last? Did this mean there was a bigger chance of her being noticed if she didn't get back to her station in time?

She got back to work, but her head couldn't make sense of this at all. One minute she was monitoring hydroponic systems, next minute space, then android parts. This was crazy.

All of a sudden, she realized what was happening. The cog in the wheel idea was right. They didn't let one person – Human or android – be in charge of a single whole system, because then they might have a full understanding of its function. By only letting them be in charge of a few screens at a time, no one could ever really see the bigger picture.

Clever. And a little bit scary.

What was the bigger picture here?

The place seemed…odd. It was nothing to do with the Humans and androids living harmoniously together – she'd already seen two species live together on Amara's planet. This was different. The vibe here was weird. She could see general conversations taking place. But it wasn't the usual atmosphere in a workplace. There was no relaxation. Everyone seemed on edge.

It didn't help that she still hadn't figured out where the terminal was that could destroy the entire system.

She sighed and looked around. The screen in front of her right now didn't require much input. Ash had no idea how long the shifts lasted here. She decided to have a quick look about. She stood up, arching her back, with her hands at her waist. Then she started slowly sauntering between the workstations, trying to take a note of what was on each screen. There were several screens she didn't recognize at all.

"What's wrong, Ruby?" asked a dark-skinned guy sitting at one of the consoles, in a low voice.

Ruby. Was that her name? She kind of liked that one. "Taking a walk," she said, pushing her hands into her back again for dramatic effect. "My back is aching."

"Why haven't you just gotten a replacement part? You know you don't need to put up with that."

There it was again. The Humans on U62 could obviously

replace their own parts. Maybe part of this body had already been replaced? That thought made her distinctly uncomfortable.

The guy pulled up his trouser leg. "Best new ankle around. No scars. Wouldn't even know it was there. It only took ten minutes. Can't imagine why you put up with any kind of pain." He glanced over her shoulder. "Anyhow, they catch you slacking, or your rate goes down, they'll ask questions. You know that. Why risk it?"

A sensation of unease crept over her. She didn't like the implication in those words. She gave a casual shrug. "You know me. I have a good work rate. A few minutes walking won't do any harm."

Just at that moment an orange alarm sounded. The guy put his head down automatically. "It'll be Darim," he mumbled.

Three supervisors appeared out of nowhere, surrounding a Human with big dark eyes. The guy gave a few muffled yelps as he was pulled from his seat.

"No! It's not my fault. It's the system, it's malfunctioning."

One of the supervisors – all android – looked at him coldly.

"Darim Quates, you've been warned about your productivity before. Please vacate your seat and report to the admin block."

"No!" he yelled again. "I won't. You can't make me."

But it seemed they could. He was frogmarched from the room and along a grey corridor, out of sight.

"Guess we won't see him again," said the other guy quietly.

"What do you mean?" asked Ash.

The guy looked at her as if she was stupid. "Aldus doesn't like inefficiency, does he? Darim will be down the salt mines before you know it, along with all the malfunctioning androids."

Aldus? That was the name on the statue outside.

There were so many questions she wanted to ask right now. But how could she do that without giving herself away? She gave a nod of her head and moved back through the workstations, towards her own desk. As she walked, she caught sight of a side door with a purple panel next to it. No other door had a security panel like this. Her heartbeat quickened a little. Was that the command centre she was looking for?

Ash sat back down in her chair and started checking her screens, all the while keeping an eye on the door she'd spotted.

An alarm sounded and around half the people and androids in the room stood up, heading towards an exit. She was still giving commands in her head when the whole screen flashed: *Mandatory break time.*

She sat for a few minutes, still watching the room. The door she'd spotted opened and the yellow-shoed android came out and threaded her way back to her station. She glanced at Ash in surprise.

"Shouldn't you be on your break?" Whether her name was Azla or not, that's what Ash was calling her in her head.

There was something in her tone that made Ash stand automatically. "Sure. Was just finishing something off," she said as she moved towards the grey door that everyone else had exited through.

It seemed like androids ate just like Humans did. Ash had no idea how that worked, but she joined the same queue and took some food that looked reasonably appetizing. It was beyond frustrating though. She hated waiting. But Orius had given her instructions to make her move when she returned from the break, and she intended to follow them exactly. This place had a dangerous enough air without taking chances.

She noticed again that noise was minimal in here. There was no raucous laughter at a joke or funny story. Most people weren't talking – just eating. A few androids and Humans did have conversations, but they were low-voiced interactions and none were close enough to Ash for her to figure out what was being said.

She tugged at the collar of her uniform. This room was warmer than the other. There was a dispenser for fluids and she filled a canteen to the top, drained it, then refilled it. She'd take it back with her.

The alarm sounded again and everyone stood at the same time. Ash hurried to stand too, following the rest as they dumped their food containers and filed back into the control room. As she scanned her hand for re-entry an alarm went off again.

Some kind of sentry guard appeared. "Ruby Cole, you are in violation of code 369, please step out of the line."

She could feel her face drain of colour. A few others looked at her and shook their heads. The guard continued. "This is your third violation in three months. One credit will be removed from your quota."

Ash was trying to hide the panic she could feel gripping her body. "Ruby Cole, please place violation code 369 in the waste disposal unit."

What? The only thing she was holding was the canteen of water. She dropped it into the waste disposal.

The guard nodded. "Please rejoin the queue."

Beads of sweat were forming on her forehead. That was it? Water? She joined the queue and scanned her hand again, half-expecting the alarm to sound louder and declare her an intruder. But it didn't. This time she was free to pass.

Her heart was still racing as she stepped back into the control room. A quick glance told her that no one else had brought fluids back inside. They clearly weren't allowed. She should have known that. This was a room full of computer systems that seemed to control every part of U62. It wasn't really such a jump that water wasn't allowed in here.

She was cursing herself. She should have realized. She should have known. Then a smile curved at her lips. She might have been responsible for the last violation, but she hadn't been responsible for the two before. Ruby Cole had managed that herself. Not for the first time, Ash wished she'd actually had a chance to meet the person she was currently imitating.

As she sat down at her computer station again she noticed her android colleague was still in position. She narrowed her gaze and took in the rest of the room. Yes, it appeared that it was normal for half the workers to go for a scheduled break together. The ones who'd all been on a break with

Ash had returned, the rest were walking out the exits.

She waited a few moments. "What were you doing in the other lab?" she asked Azla, in what she hoped was a conversational manner.

If it were possible for an android to scowl, that's exactly what Azla did.

"I have duties," came the curt reply.

Ash gave a nod and tried not to smile. That was nothing like the friendly response she'd received earlier. She leaned her head on one hand and crossed her legs, turning to face Azla. "Really? What duties? Fill me in."

Azla was concentrating on her screen, her blue gaze flickering rapidly, sending instructions to more than one system at a time.

"Don't you have a scheduled break?" Ash went on.

Azla's head turned in her direction. "I have duties," she replied again, just as her screen showed the orange message that Ash's had before: *Mandatory break.*

Ash tapped her fingers on her desk. "I'm pretty sure if you don't go it's a violation," she said cheerily. It might be a guess, but she was sure she was right.

It was a weird sensation for Ash. Maybe it was something to do with being the Guardian, but just like on a few occasions back when she'd been on Tallux 5, she felt a wave of confidence. She was sure this was the right path – the right thing to do.

She could see Azla tense, as if a shiver was going through her android systems. She made an exasperated noise and

267

pressed her hands on her own desk before standing and walking towards the exit.

Ash smiled and waited five minutes before glancing around the room to make sure no one was watching. Everyone was too busy, focused on their own terminals. She slid over to Darim Quates's now empty station and flicked through the screens. Nothing significant.

But she could make that happen. She picked up Darim's discarded earpiece and stuck it in her own ear. It took seconds to make a choice. She adjusted something in the watering systems that Darim had been responsible for, turning the rate up as high as possible, before sliding quickly back to her own station before the alarms sounded.

She rubbed her palms against her uniform as she looked at the door at the other side of the room. She couldn't help but smile. Any second now…

She swallowed. She would kill for a drink of water right now.

The orange alarms sounded. Heads turned towards Darim's empty station. Ash let out a long slow breath, got to her feet and walked swiftly to the pale grey door while everyone was distracted.

She held out her hand over the scanner. A few seconds later the door slid open, and Ash stepped inside while everyone was looking in the other direction.

CHAPTER TWENTY-THREE

The room was empty of people, with an eerie purple glow coming from the computer screens adorning every surface.

In here, each screen was devoted to a single system instead of scrolling through them all, so Ash could see the monitoring stations around the planet, the full array of hydroponics with projected outputs, water systems, defence capabilities, android production and numerous other systems.

She scanned the room, looking for the station where all she needed to do was place her hand to it and wait for the virus to take effect.

Except…she couldn't find it.

She screwed up her face. She could remember the diagram that Orius had shown her exactly. Except, this room didn't look like that.

Not at all.

She eyed the bangle on her wrist, wishing it would work so she could jump back and ask some questions. But Orius had told her this place had some kind of protection around it. Jumping from here wasn't an option.

There was a noise to her side. She noticed another door – the sound was coming from behind it. She'd thought there was only one – and she was too far away from the one she'd entered through to get back to it now. She ducked down, hiding beneath a desk and crouching in the far corner.

The door swung open and a man walked in. He was surrounded by a group of guards and followed by a few women in uniforms Ash didn't recognize.

The man started talking in a loud voice. "We're ready. Schedule the celebrations for tonight. By tomorrow, our plans will be in place. U62 will be unstoppable. We'll be able to conquer every other solar system in the universe. The final piece of the jigsaw puzzle is here." He turned to one of the women, and as she turned Ash let out a silent gasp. She was half Human, half android. Her face had been partially replaced by metal and glass. One of her hands was also android and flew across a nearby screen. She bowed her head to the man.

"Aldus, the final calculations will be inputted tonight. Our system will be ready." She smiled, which looked odd as only half of her face moved.

Was this man Aldus Dexter?

Ash squinted a little, trying to see through the gap between the smooth metal desks. Yes, this guy looked exactly like the statue outside. How odd. Statues were usually made of people who were long dead. She hadn't imagined that the guy named outside was still alive. He must have an ego bigger than the average megalomaniac.

But something still bugged her about his name. She hadn't quite managed to put her finger on where she knew it from.

Everyone seemed to jump to attention around him. He gave orders constantly:

"Check the systems again. There must be a glitch somewhere."

"Lu, the incident from earlier, send the worker to the salt mines."

"I'm not happy with the rate from hydroponic lab four. Tell the scientist I want answers."

"Assign more stations to the monitoring of space sector 480. I don't want any late surprises."

No one questioned Aldus Dexter, and everyone seemed to want to please him.

Ash wondered if her breathing was too loud. The last thing she wanted was to be caught here by this man. But hiding under the desk was giving her a whole lot of insight that she needed. She'd always valued having a Friend on her visits to new planets – but she'd never realized just how vital they were before today.

There'd been a whole list of questions she'd wanted to ask Azla. But all of them would have made it seem like the real Ruby had experienced some kind of head injury. This Guardian stuff was even trickier without backup.

The two women in uniform sat down at one of the terminals and started inputting data. Ash grimaced. Was she ever going to get out of here?

There was a ping at another station and Aldus walked over to scan it. "Culzean, check the environmental systems. Check the Kronos crystal is functioning as it should. There's been a shift in the tectonic plates. It's minimal, but important." He muttered furiously under his breath. "I didn't pull this planet out of an ice age for it to catapult back in there."

Even from her restricted vantage point, Ash saw a few members of the staff exchange anxious glances. "The Kronos crystal replacement isn't ready yet. It won't be ready for another few months. If the current one isn't functioning..."

"Enough!" Aldus slammed his hand down on one of the countertops. "Don't remind me that our alternative was stolen! I don't need to hear that again." He moved slowly in a circle, pointing his finger at everyone in the room. "If I find out that anyone here was involved..." He let the words hang in the air.

"All those found responsible so far have been dealt with. Their replacements have been screened. From tomorrow, new scanners will be installed. There will be no mistakes. There will be no espionage. My plans will not be put on hold, for any reason." He was so angry that saliva was spitting from his mouth.

It was then Ash realized where she'd heard the name before. Aldus Dexter. It was one of the names that Orius had used. One of the names of previous Guardians.

A chill spread over her body. She stared downwards at her bangle – the bangle that Orius had told her stayed on a Guardian until they died.

But if Aldus Dexter was here – with no bangle – then Orius had lied to her.

Part of her wanted to storm out from under the desk and start yelling and asking questions. But part of her could see the kind of man that Aldus Dexter was.

He wouldn't hesitate to get rid of an irritation like her.

Five minutes' experience was enough to know the guy was clearly a megalomaniac, even worse than Count Stani on Tallux 5. This guy wasn't just talking about taking over a planet, he wanted to take over the universe. But she was intrigued by his comments about turning U62 from an ice-age planet into what it presently was. She'd had no idea something like that was even possible.

The two women at the stations were speaking in low voices. "The crystal isn't anywhere near the growth it should be. We should check on it."

One leaned closer to her screen. "I know the calculations show all the components are there…" She shook her head. "But something seems wrong."

The other woman side-eyed her. "Well, if something is missing, you can tell him. Not me."

The first woman made some kind of *hrmph* sound. "We'll flip for it."

They shot each other a smile, finished up at their stations

and left, leaving the screen showing the last readout they'd been discussing.

Ash was frozen. She was looking at the component on the screen through a gap between the desks. It was achingly familiar, with its triangular shape – just like the device she'd seen in the Library – and every tiny hair stood up on the back of her neck. She closed her eyes and put her head down onto her knees, which were pulled up to her chest. "This cannot be happening," she whispered.

This had to be a bad dream. It had to be. This was every worst-case scenario in one:

A Guardian who was supposedly dead, reinventing himself on a ravaged planet that he'd found some magical way of pulling out of an ice age.

A calculation that would allow this forgotten planet to create a weapon that could help them take over the rest of the universe.

A component she'd seen before. That she'd touched before. That was currently lying under a chair somewhere in the Library, uncatalogued…

Ash had always thought that her dream job might make her sick to her stomach – that she'd be a fighter pilot and being sick would be an occupational hazard. She hadn't for a second realized just how much the Guardian role would make her want to lose her lunch.

She fixed on the screen again. It showed the component and how it fitted into a bigger device. She tried her best to memorize all she could see.

There was some more ranting and raving by Aldus, before he stormed out the door, his entourage rushing after him.

Ash couldn't help it. Her brain was too full to think about safety. She flew out from under the desk, her feet carrying her automatically to the screen with – what did they call it? – the Kronos component on it.

Part of her prayed she was wrong, but as her eyes ran over it, her heart sank. It was completely identical to the item that was wrapped in brown cloth in the Library.

The item that had been transported to her fighter.

The thing that people had lost their lives over because it was so important.

She rubbed her arms. The chill wouldn't leave her body. It seemed to have taken up permanent residence there as little pieces slotted into place in her head.

The damaged freighter must have come from U62 – but why had it been coming to her system? Why would anyone in her solar system need technology like that…

The thought died in her brain. *Corinez.*

Corinez had been in an ice age for as long as Ash had been alive. She had no idea how it had happened. All she knew was it had caused a war – a war that was still ongoing in her lifetime.

Her hand reached out and hovered above the screen. Was the item in the Library the cause of the war?

People at home didn't talk about Corinez much. The ice planet. The planet that continually bombed and fired upon her village. The planet that had caused first her sister to die, then her mother, and eventually her father. It was difficult to put a death down to a broken heart, but Ash had always known that both her mother and father's bodies had deteriorated after the death of their youngest daughter. No parent should outlive their child. It was like someone had flicked a switch on their immune systems and both had just given up. And could Ash blame them?

She rocked back on her heels. Her hand was shaking. This was it. She was alone in the room – she should just go and put her hand on all these stations, trying each one until the virus finally worked.

She knew she had to. She couldn't let someone like Aldus develop a weapon system that would make him a threat to the entire universe.

But there was also no reason that she couldn't find out the answers to the questions that she had, while she was here.

She had friends currently fighting in a war over an ice planet. An ice planet that hadn't always been an ice planet. If the thieves had brought the device from U62, had they been trying to take it to Corinez?

Ash stared at the far door – the one they'd all left through. She could follow them, see if she could find out more.

She bit her bottom lip and stepped over to the nearest console, placing her hand on the scanning panel.

Nothing.

She tried again. Nothing.

Someone would come back here soon. She'd have to leave.

Orius had assured her that all she had to do to implant the virus was scan her hand on the correct computer. But he'd often been reluctant to tell her everything. Like the fact that Aldus had been a Guardian. Had he been trying to protect her from the truth? Had he forgotten he'd told her Aldus's name?

Or maybe he really had no idea that Aldus was here. After all, the Library hadn't known about U62's reinvigoration until just recently. Maybe they didn't know who the lynchpin was.

Ash was systematic, working her way around the room. Still nothing. She'd got about two-thirds of the way and was cursing Orius and his outdated diagram when the door she'd entered through buzzed open.

Azla walked in. The android stopped cold when she saw Ash.

"What are you doing in here?" she asked.

"Same as you," said Ash smartly. "Working."

It was almost as if calculations were going on in Azla's head. She watched as Ash switched on the next workstation, scanning her hand, waiting a few seconds, then moving along to the next.

"That doesn't look like working to me," Azla replied. "It looks like you're doing something you shouldn't be."

Ash narrowed her gaze as she kept going. She hadn't quite expected snark from an android. "I guess we've both been given different instructions." She stuck a sarcastic smile on her face. "You do your job, and I'll do mine."

Azla took a few quick steps closer, her metallic hand

closing down on top of Ash's open palm in the scanner. The movement was smooth, but the weight pressing down on Ash's hand made her blink and stopped her in her tracks.

Azla's glass face was almost against hers. "What exactly are you doing?"

Something sparked into Ash's brain. "I'm testing their new DNA scanning software. Obviously, they couldn't ask you to do that."

She could swear she could hear an old-fashioned clock tick somewhere as the seconds eked past. Azla leaned forward a bit, putting even more weight on Ash's hand. Ash was sure she heard a quiet crunch, before Azla slowly peeled her hand back.

"They haven't made an announcement." She kept her blue flashing gaze straight on Ash.

"It's being introduced from tomorrow. They needed a Human to test the systems in here. I was asked while you were on your break." She straightened, denying the desire to grab her crushed hand and rub it. She honestly couldn't remember the last time she'd felt pain like it.

Ash moved onto the next station, placing her smarting hand on the scanner and waiting for it to start. This time there was a beep. She jumped, because she'd kept her gaze on Azla and her watchful stare.

"You should press your hand down properly," said Azla with a taunting tone. "You can't even test the systems adequately."

She knew exactly why her palm print hadn't read properly.

278

Her palm didn't want to lie flat now. It was curled up against the pain, and Orius hadn't activated both her hands, only one. He'd had no reason to do both.

Ash waited a second, straightening her palm in mid-air. The effort made her hand tremble, and she pressed her lips together to stop from crying out. As soon as she was sure it was in the right position, she placed it on the scanner.

Nothing.

She didn't even lift her gaze. "What is it you said you were doing in here, Azla?" she asked as she gritted her teeth and moved on to the next station.

Azla ignored her and walked over to the stations in the middle of the room, one hand flying across the keys while the other slid a card into one of the entry points.

There was a pause at Ash's machine. Almost like a hiccup. She pressed her hand down a little firmer, ignoring the pain shooting up her arm. In the bottom left-hand corner of the screen a tiny emblem appeared. A green circle – only partly shaded. As she watched, the shading started to move round.

The virus was uploading.

CHAPTER TWENTY-FOUR

Ash was holding her breath, waiting for the circle to complete.

It was excruciating.

Her eyes drifted to Azla, who was completely focused on her task, whatever it was.

There was an almost inaudible *ping*. The circle was complete. Ash pulled her hand back.

"Finished here." Her voice came out in a sing-song manner and she cringed.

Azla's glass face lifted from the screen. "You aren't doing DNA testing."

Ash's skin prickled. "Yes, I am," she said with a confidence she didn't actually feel. "You just don't have the clearance to know that." She spun away. "But I'm finished now. I'm going to give them my report."

She'd almost made it to the door with her hand outstretched when she felt a sharp yank from behind.

"No," spat Azla, "you're not."

The screens around them went blank. The security lock on the door made a hissing sound and opened slightly. Next second, the lights above them blinked.

Quick as a flash, Ash turned to Azla. "What did you do?" she yelled, trying to distract her, before grabbing for the door and hurrying back out into the larger control room. The lights were blinking in here too. Several supervisors scurried about. Some operators looked in confusion at their screens, while others stood up, shaking their heads. All Ash could think about right now was the fact that Orius had told her the bangle wouldn't work inside the building, due to some kind of shielding. Right now she just wanted to get out of here.

"No," shouted one guy, his seat flying out as he jumped to his feet. His hands hammered against the keys. "What's wrong on the production line? This will affect my percentage!" He held up both hands and yelled, "I didn't tell it to do that. What's going on?" before realizing that hardly anyone was paying him any attention.

A small stream of smoke started coming out of one of the android's necks. Ash tried to slip through the rest of the people in the large control room, heading towards the exit. She could see a few guards beyond the glass screens, but they looked just as confused as everyone else.

The lights in the room switched to flashing amber and an electronic voice came over the intercom system. "All personnel, shut down all systems. Emergency protocols in place. Control centre will go into lockdown."

Ash didn't like the sound of that.

"Stop her!" came the shout. She didn't need to turn around to know who it was.

Azla was standing at the door between both control rooms, her arm outstretched and a metal finger pointing at Ash.

Ash didn't hesitate. "Stop her!" she yelled back. "What's she doing in the inner control room? She doesn't have clearance. Where are the guards? Get the guards!"

Ash ran to the main entrance and exit, waving her hands and gesturing for the guards to come in. "We need help in here. Someone unauthorized has been in the control centre."

There was momentary confusion. Azla stepped away from the high security room and started pushing her way towards Ash. She was strong. Several of her counterparts were shoved to the floor, while others were thrown clear across the room.

The guards were looking frantically from one to another. Ash could tell that their earpieces weren't telling them anything. "Get her!" she urged, as Azla surged towards her.

The guards nodded and simultaneously moved forwards. As soon as they took their first few steps, Ash ducked behind them and out the security doors. The corridors were filled with people and androids. Most of them were headed for the exits. It was like everyone had heard the lockdown announcement and immediately panicked.

Ash's thighs were burning. She was resisting the urge that was surging through every part of her body and telling her to run. Even among all this chaos she didn't want to do anything that drew attention to her.

The main doors were straight ahead. She let herself be carried along by the rest of the exiting crowd.

There were some muffled shouts behind her. She kept speed-walking, trying to get lost among the bodies around her.

The shouts continued. Another alarm sounded over the top of the other one: "*Seal the building. All exits to be secured.*"

Ash could hear her heartbeat thudding in her ears as she pushed through the barrier at the front of the building. Dark glass was sliding over the clear glass ahead of her.

Stuff it, she thought as she broke into a sprint. She didn't care who was watching her. If she didn't get out of this building, she couldn't transport back home.

People were streaming from the building, from every exit. She wasn't the only person who was running. Even some of the androids had adopted a weird half-run, half-walk method.

The alarms were audible outside too. People from other buildings were standing on the street with worried expressions on their faces.

Ash kept moving, heading towards a strange kind of circular train stop. She wanted to get away, to get out of sight. But there was nowhere close to duck into. Every doorway was filled with people watching the exodus from the control building.

As she reached the bottom of the steps to the train stop,

there came an ear-piercing shriek. She dropped and covered her ears, wincing at the noise. It was an instantaneous reaction. The noise was so bad her body seemed frozen, all its focus on trying to protect itself from the noise. She squinted across the crowd. Every Human appeared to be doing the same as her. Every android was frozen.

Then she saw something. A flash of yellow.

Yellow sneakers.

Surrounded by black-uniformed guards.

Oh no.

The shriek continued as the guards fanned out. They were scanning the crowd, looking at the hundreds of figures that were crouched near the ground, holding their ears.

Ash tried to weigh up her options. She was just another person in uniform with a bad hairdo. She wasn't particularly distinguishable from any of the other people clutching their ears right now. But should she actually run? How far away from the building did she have to be for the bangle to work? Orius hadn't been precise in his information – probably because he didn't know.

The Guardian wasn't supposed to make themselves known to anyone on the planets they visited, apart from their Friend. Transporting in front of a whole crowd of people would probably get her into a whole host of trouble. But if she could pull her hands from her ears right now, that's exactly what she would do.

She could hear another noise. An approaching transport. The doors were only open for a few seconds at a time. She could make a dash for it. But her concentration was shot. She couldn't take her hands away from her ears. The noise was just too intense, too powerful.

There was another flurry of activity behind her. Her pursuers were close now. Aldus Dexter was with them, she realized – his face was bright red. She could see him screaming and shouting, even though she couldn't hear what he was saying over the siren. Why wasn't the noise disabling him?

In among the melee, something occurred to her. She'd looked at him and assumed he was Human. But she didn't know that for sure. Orius had told her that not all the Guardians were Human. So what did that make Aldus Dexter?

Her eyes were scanning around her frantically. The androids were frozen. The Humans were all incapacitated. But maybe she could run with her hands still over her ears. Once she reached an empty carriage, she could transport. It could work. It *would* work. Anything to get away from here.

But as the silver cylinder of the transport system approached, her legs spasmed. She could feel the muscles in her thighs jerk. One minute she was close to the ground, the next she was standing upright.

No. This couldn't be right. With her hands still over her ears she glanced quickly from side to side. There were others like her. Their faces confused as their bodies stood up unintentionally. It was like she didn't have control of her own body.

She tried to bend her legs to crouch again, but her body wouldn't obey. What was happening?

As if in answer, the siren cut out.

The silence seemed loud and she swayed on her feet.

This couldn't be happening.

Fear was all around her. She felt like a target as Aldus started moving through the people now standing. Ash tried to lift one foot, gritting her teeth with effort. But her foot wouldn't move. It *couldn't* move. It seemed rooted to the spot.

There was nothing else for it. She'd done what she'd been tasked to do. She would just have to transport in full view of the surrounding crowd.

Her bangle gleamed and she reached for it…except, she didn't.

It was like her joints were under someone else's control. Her elbow, her shoulder wouldn't let her reach over and grab her other wrist.

This was madness. Crazy.

She wasn't even watching Aldus now. She was too busy focusing on what was happening inside her own body. A body that wouldn't do as it was told. No matter how much she gritted her teeth and willed her arm to move, it just wouldn't.

Her breath caught in her throat. The guards had dispersed among the "stuck" people and androids.

Azla was walking rapidly among the crowd, trying to find her. From the determined way that her head moved from side to side, Ash knew it wouldn't take long.

But Aldus was almost sauntering through the crowd. The redness in his face was dying down. He was talking now, laughing even. As if everything had changed to the thrill of the chase.

Ash felt her heart turn cold as dread crept over her like the virus she'd just dispersed.

He held out his hands and laughed. "Guardian, where are you? I know you're here somewhere."

CHAPTER TWENTY-FIVE

Ash was cursing herself for every mistake she'd made since she'd got here. She should have paid more attention to Azla. She should have grabbed her bangle as soon as she'd exited the building. She should have tried to get into the inner control room earlier.

Anything that meant she wouldn't have ended up here, under the radar of a madman.

Aldus was still walking slowly among the people frozen to the spot. He was talking loudly as he glanced over each person.

"I wonder who you might be. What lies the Library will have told you. Do you feel righteous? Do you feel good? Or are you confused by your missions?"

He ran his finger along the cheek of a woman standing in a uniform similar to Ash's. She looked terrified. But she wasn't the one he was looking for, and Aldus sauntered on past.

Azla was at the other side of the square, discarding people quickly with one glance.

Aldus kept moving closer. "What have you done to my systems? How dare you enter my paradise, my sanctuary? Have you any idea how long it took to create my own world?"

The more he spoke, the madder he sounded.

"I took this shell, this husk of a planet, with a population of only a few hundred left, and made it into something great. Something beautiful." He held up his hands to the pristine buildings, then pointed at his statue. He laughed again and moved over next to it, mimicking the position of the statue.

It was the eeriest thing, seeing statue Aldus and real-life Aldus next to each other. She squeezed her eyes closed for a second – it was the one thing her body would actually let her do – and tried not to let the image imprint on her brain.

"Have you worked out yet why you can't move?" He sounded gleeful. "I suppose you think you're Human. But you're not. At least, not fully."

Azla's words echoed through Ash's brain from earlier. The ones about getting a new part. It was like all the blood in her veins turned cold.

"Humans," Aldus laughed again. "As if they could survive on my terraforming planet. They were weak. Fallible. My new android beings were superior. More efficient. As for the others? We created replacement parts for the Humans to try and keep them up to par with their counterparts. I only kept them around me for fun, really. Not for any useful function." He kept moving. "And now? Your replacement parts have been told to freeze. To stop functioning. Until I restart them again, of course. Because I can do that – tell the parts when and where to stop functioning. It's quite ingenious really."

Ash stared down at her skin. How did the parts get in? How did they get out? Azla had implied she could go and get a replacement part for her back in a matter of minutes. Ash shuddered. Was that really how things were here?

Anger pricked at her. Why had the Library let U62 slip under their radar? They should have known about this kind of thing. Warned her that the body she'd be in might have parts that weren't under her control. It seemed like a pretty vital piece of information.

Yellow flashed to her side. Azla was getting closer by the second. Aldus too.

She tried to keep her gaze straight ahead, hoping that she wouldn't draw any attention to herself. But a few seconds later Azla stepped right in front of her.

"Ruby," she said with a smile on her face. Her tone changed. "I've got her."

Ash could sense that everyone who could move their heads did, to take a good look at her. It seemed that remaining inconspicuous was out the window.

"Well, well, well, Guardian. I would say it's a pleasure to meet you. But it isn't, not really." Aldus's eyes were a strange shade of blue, his skin waxy. Ash tilted her head – it was the only part of her body she could move right now. His hair seemed even stranger, as if every strand had been individually implanted and was not quite where it should be. It didn't have the flow of normal hair. It seemed there was something that Aldus hadn't quite perfected. It was the first good sign that she'd had.

He lifted up her arm, staring at the bangle. "Well, this brings back memories."

"You're supposed to be dead."

He grinned. "I am, aren't I? What a pity. Guess I'm not." He tugged at Ash's hair. "Well, I know your real name isn't Ruby. So what is it?"

"Ash."

He tilted his head to the side. "I suspect you're quite young. I also suspect you're Human."

"And I suspect that you're not," she countered quickly.

Aldus nodded. "I'm Anterrean. A far superior race." Of course. She'd learned about them in her studies at the Library.

"I know exactly who the Anterreans are. You live for eight hundred years. That's still pretty fast to terraform a planet – particularly one that's in an ice age."

"I can do it in much less time than that," he said with a wave of his hand. He stepped closer, as if examining her face could tell him something he wanted to know. He had a strange look in his eyes. "What planet are you from, Ash?" He said her name as if it caused distaste.

She did her best to straighten her shoulders. "Why?"

"I'm just wondering what tiny part of the universe you come from. What little speck you think is important."

She didn't answer. She wasn't about to give this guy his next target. "Why are you doing this?"

Aldus gave her an incredulous look. "Are you younger than I think? Guardians are usually carefully selected for a range of skills." It was clear he was trying to insult her.

"What happened to you then?"

A slow smile appeared across his face. "Feisty. Hmmm. Orius won't like that."

"He does actually. I'm pretty sure I'm his favourite."

This time Aldus's gaze narrowed for the briefest of seconds, then he shook his head and held out his hands again. "The Library. An archaic, redundant structure. Flawed in so many ways." He started pacing, as if he were talking to himself. "But it opened a world of possibilities to me. It gave me the opportunity to access new technologies, to adapt things to my needs. To gain riches from one planet, and to help cause destruction in another.

"All part of my master plan. I sowed seeds. I gained contacts – and respect, because I was the Guardian. And when I returned sometime later, they remembered me." His smile widened. "It made things easier, when I wanted to borrow equipment and transport. When I had already ensured I had unlimited wealth and resources."

"What a disappointment you must have been."

"Me?" Aldus put his hands to his chest. "Oh no. Not me. Didn't Orius tell you? I died in a tragic accident and had to be replaced by numerous…" He looked Ash up and down. "…less able models."

"You're evil," said Ash. She didn't care that her feet were still rooted to the ground and her arm wouldn't do a thing it was told. "I have no idea why you got picked as a Guardian. You're shallow, self-obsessed and power-mad. I'm glad I planted a virus. I'm glad I've planted a virus that's destroyed all your systems. I'm glad Orius sent me. I'm glad they discovered what was going on here. I wouldn't be at all surprised if they closed down all the wormholes that leave from U62 and leave you here, in your own tiny part of the solar system where you can't annoy anyone else."

Aldus made a snort. "Oh, look at you. You're all excitable. You're all that" – he held his hands up in the air, moving his fingers as if searching for a word – "*young* way. The way I was when I first started as Guardian." He rolled his eyes. "Oh, don't worry. It'll pass. You'll get jaded, or bored, just like I did."

He looked her up and down again.

"I give you…hmmm…a hundred years." He snapped his fingers. "Oh no, you're Human, you won't live that long." He raised his eyebrows. "But maybe you want to think about that. Look at the body you have now. It could last a whole lot longer than your own." He put his hand to his chin. "Maybe we can negotiate?"

Ash didn't even get a chance to answer. Aldus obviously liked the sound of his own voice.

"Yes, maybe we should. It could prove useful having a Guardian in my pocket." He looked her up and down again, and she couldn't even try to hide how repulsed she was by his gaze. "But do I really need you?" he mused. "After all, it wasn't that hard to corrupt the Library systems. I doubt that old fool Orius has even worked things out yet." He looked at her again. "But you could still be an advantage."

Anger flooded through Ash. Corrupt the Library systems? What did he mean? She spoke through barely parted lips. "This Guardian has a mind of her own. This Guardian will never be in your pocket. This Guardian will do whatever she can to ensure that you don't get to hurt a single other person." She shot him her best smile. "Let's just call it my new mission."

She could see the colour rising in Aldus's cheeks again. He was getting angry. Perfect.

"How dare you speak to me like that? You insignificant little Human!"

She widened her eyes at him, deliberately trying to bait him, praying that the instincts that told her to do this wouldn't be wrong. Even though he had control of parts of her body, even though he was telling them not to move right now, there must still be some Human left in her.

"Why? Does no one challenge you here, Aldus? Does no one tell you that you're wrong? Have you programmed everyone to agree with you? Where's the fun in that? Respect and leadership should be earned." She looked over at the statue and laughed. "As for that, I bet you ordered it yourself. How pathetic, to commission your own statue."

Aldus whipped around; he was only centimetres from her face. She was trying to curl her toes inside her boots, any tiny movement to give her hope, but she was failing miserably.

"You pathetic creature," he hissed, "it's about time you learned some manners."

He pulled back his hands and shoved her with all his might. As her feet left the ground, it was as if a thousand little lights went on around her. Her muscles spasmed again, released from their frozen state. Her taut arms automatically stretched out to try and brace her body against the fall.

A Human, instinctual act.

But Ash wasn't interested in breaking her fall. She yanked her arms back in to her chest, folding one hand around her wrist and pressing firmly.

Leaving U62 far behind.

CHAPTER TWENTY-SIX

S he landed heavily on the Library floor, her face smashing down onto the Proteus circle.

For a few seconds Ash didn't move. Her body had reverted to the foetal position. She was curled up, her legs tight against her chest and her arms wrapped around herself. It felt safe. Insular.

"Ash."

She felt someone shaking her shoulder, and long cool fingers pulling back the hair that was stuck fast to her neck with sweat. She shouldn't feel that. Orius was a hologram. How could she feel that?

This time an arm slid around her waist, attempting to help her up. "What happened? Are you hurt? Are you injured?" The questions came thick and fast, laced with genuine concern.

She looked down. The transportation had reverted her into the original red-and-grey uniform she'd chosen for her regular attire when she'd got here. She rubbed her hands self-consciously up and down the material, then pulled up the leg of the uniform, checking her skin and feeling her bones. Making sure nothing felt different. Then she did the same with her arms.

She was sitting now, and she felt Orius lift her up, helping her over to a large comfortable chair. Seconds later she had a blanket over her, and a mug pressed into her hands.

Ash couldn't stop shaking. She didn't even feel particularly cold, but it was like her body had gone into meltdown.

Orius sat down next to her and didn't speak. He seemed to know she needed some time to compute what had just happened.

She sipped at whatever was in the mug. It was warm and tasted kind of herbal, in a calming sort of way. Her breathing slowed, her heart stopped racing inside her chest. The sharp pains in her muscles started to fade to a dull ache.

Finally, she let herself relax back into the chair. She wanted to close her eyes, go to sleep, and forget all about the nightmare that had just happened.

But she needed to report back. So, after a few minutes, she let her eyes open again and looked at Orius. He'd never looked so old. She'd always thought that it seemed normal for the Keeper of Library to appear as an older figure. But now, the circles under his eyes seemed so dark they were purple, the lines across his forehead deeper than ever.

"We need to talk," she said softly.

Orius lifted his head. He'd been lost in his own world. She wondered what that was like. He didn't interject.

"Tell me about Aldus Dexter," she said.

Orius visibly recoiled. "W-what?"

"Aldus Dexter. Tell me what you know about him."

Confusion was written all across the hologram's face. "He was a Guardian, several hundred years ago. He was an Anterrean – the first of his race to be a Guardian. We expected him to be here for a long time, but his time in the Library was cut short."

"Okay, you've told me the short version. The factual part. Tell me about the person. Who was he? How did he act? How did you find him?"

Orius shifted uncomfortably. "I don't normally discuss previous Guardians." He said it as if it were some kind of imperial decree. But Ash wasn't about to accept that.

"Would it help if I told you that it was Aldus Dexter who has brought U62 back to life? Would it help if I told you that he controls every single aspect of life on that planet? That he has plans to conquer what he knows of the universe, and that he stole technology in his role as Guardian and faked his own death?"

She didn't mean for it all to come out that way, but once she started, she just couldn't stop.

Orius stood up quickly, shaking his head. "No, it can't be. Aldus died. There was an accident – an explosion on the planet he was visiting." He pointed to the bangle on Ash's wrist. "There have been another two Guardians between you and him. If Aldus were still alive, you couldn't have the bangle."

"Well, I do." She held it aloft. "But I nearly didn't. He trapped me. I uploaded the virus but didn't quite make the getaway I wanted. He came after me with his androids and guards. It seems that the Humans who are left on U62 have multiple replacement parts – the body I was in included. It meant that Aldus could control any part of me."

She shifted in her chair.

"You told me I didn't have a designated Friend on U62. You had information, and you weren't sure how reliable it was? Well, every single living thing on that planet is controlled by Aldus Dexter. He's incredibly dangerous."

It was clear that Orius was horrified by this news. "I must talk to the people of the Library. I must let them know about Aldus, about his plans. His intentions."

Ash set down her cup and pulled the blanket back. Her legs were finally beginning to feel like her own again. "We're not done. Come with me."

With shaky steps she led Orius down through the Library, snaking through exhibits until she reached the back. She stared out at the dark space dotted with glimmers of light in front of her. She'd wondered if she would ever see this again. She couldn't pretend she wasn't relieved, but part of it also made her sad, because she knew what came next.

She walked over to the table and chair near the domed glass. The brown package was sitting on top. With a sigh, she pulled the rope from around it and let the sacking fall open.

Part of her had hoped it would look different this time.

But no. It was exactly as she'd remembered. The metal light, but strong. Perfectly smooth with no dents or marks. In the middle, a giant kind of rough crystal with particles inside.

She ran her hand over it, as if proving to herself it was still there, and it was what she'd recognized on U62.

"Tell me why this hasn't been catalogued yet, Orius," she said. She couldn't help the weary tone in her voice.

Orius looked bewildered. "It should have been. But there are lots of items that haven't been fully processed." He swept the air with one hand. "It happens more often than we'd like."

"Try again." She kept her voice perfectly steady.

"I don't know what you mean," he said in a wary tone that told her everything she didn't want to know.

"How long have you been the Keeper here, Orius?"

He wasn't looking at her now. His eyes were fixed on the gallery of stars right above their heads. He knew. He knew exactly where this was going.

"A long time," he said in his best throwaway voice.

"Aldus told me that he'd corrupted the Library systems. That he'd managed to steal things," she said steadily.

"What? No!" Orius seemed shell-shocked.

She picked up the item with both hands and turned so she could face Orius. "I'm going to talk now. I'm going to tell you exactly what I think, and you are going to listen." She took a deep breath. "I think you might have guessed, but I know exactly what this is."

His gaze was back on her now, but she could see a flash of wariness in his eyes. His voice was steady. "What is it?"

"This is a Kronos device. It's the item I was sent here with. The item that was transported to my ship from the failing freighter. A freighter full of people who thought this was worth dying over. I didn't know who they were, or where they came from. I didn't know why they headed to my solar system, but I do now."

Her fingers traced over the green-tinged stone before she set the item down on the table.

"I want to be angry. I want to scream and shout." She held out her hands. "Because I feel as if something really wrong has happened here."

Orius flinched; she could see him automatically switching on every defence mechanism. But Ash wasn't going to let him talk his way out of this.

"This was stolen from Aldus Dexter, and I wonder if he stole it from somewhere else first."

Orius was watching her carefully.

"I wonder if it was stolen from a planet a bit closer to my home."

Orius shifted slightly. She'd been playing guessing games, hoping that she might be wrong. Because none of this had made sense in her head, not until now. Not until she'd connected the parts.

And connecting the parts was heartbreaking.

All those people. All those years of war. All those lives lost – for what?

That one tiny movement by Orius told her more than she really wanted to know.

Ash bowed her head and closed her eyes. She was the Guardian of the Library. It felt like she'd only just got here. And now, she would have to decide if she wanted to stay.

She pushed her hands down on the table and breathed in long and slow, opening up her chest. She was taking the space that she needed to decide what must come next.

She'd never fully understood why she'd been chosen, but she didn't really care why any more.

It would be easy to hide here. To jump to other worlds, live other people's lives, follow instructions, no questions asked. But that wasn't who she was.

She lifted her head and turned to face Orius. "It's time for the truth."

He didn't speak.

"Aldus Dexter used this device to take a planet out of an ice age and make it something much more habitable. I'm going to ask one question, Orius, and I expect an honest answer. Was a Kronos device stolen from Corinez?"

There was the longest silence.

Finally, Orius glanced towards the stars. He was visibly shaking. "I don't know," he whispered.

It was like red mist descending around her. She'd tried so hard to keep her temper and rage under control. But now? It was in danger of brimming over.

Ash kept her voice steady. "You brought me to this place. You impressed me with its technology. You let me think that the Library knew everything. Had control of everything. That it was an all-seeing entity that worked for the greater good of the universe and its inhabitants."

She took a deep breath. Now, she couldn't hide the emotion in her voice.

"I've risked my life for this place on more than one occasion. And now, I'm questioning everything I've done. Who gives the Library the right to decide what happens next – to decide the fate of everyone in the universe? I've met one of your previous Guardians. The guy is clearly nuts." She threw up her hands. "So, whoever makes the decisions around here – I've got no faith in them. No trust in them at all.

"The Library has been corrupted once. Who says it's not corrupted now?" She looked at Orius and her voice broke as she said the words. "That *you're* not corrupted now."

Now she'd started she couldn't stop.

"As for this? A device that has the ability to take a planet out of an ice age? Or put a planet into one?" She shook her head. "What happened back on Corinez? Why are they at war with us? I've never stopped to ask the question before. It was before my time. But you can bet your life I'm asking that question now."

All her emotions threatened to overwhelm her. She'd trusted Orius. She'd believed everything he'd told her. She didn't even understand how Aldus had managed to corrupt the systems here – had he just messed with the cataloguing system to allow his thefts to go unnoticed, or had he done much, much more? Could she trust anything?

"You don't even get it, do you? You don't even understand." Her face was up next to Orius's. For the first time, he was the tiniest bit fuzzy – but she didn't have time to think about that. "I hate them. I *hate* them." She was spitting now and she just didn't care. "They bombed my village. They killed my sister. Maybe the bombs didn't hit my mum and dad, but they might as well have."

She reached out towards him, gasping in frustration as her fingers snapped through thin air.

"I know that this is wrong. Stealing something from a planet is morally and ethically wrong; stealing something that can send that planet into an ice age is practically murder. Made all the worse by the fact that your Guardian, *your* Guardian was likely the cause of this, with his crazy, egomaniacal mind. And just so we're clear, I don't just blame him. I blame you. I blame you, Orius, you and the Library, for the fact I'm an orphan. I blame you for the fact my sister died in the ruins of her school. I blame you for the fact that my mother died of a broken heart, and so did my father a few years later. My family – all casualties of war." She leaned forward and hissed in his face. "A war we should never have been part of."

She thumped her hand down next to the Kronos device.

"How would I feel if I lived on a planet that knew a way to keep itself out of an ice age? How would I feel if one day the device that did that was stolen, and me and the rest of my planet were left on the brink of extinction? I'd want revenge. Of course I would. And who would I blame? The people nearest. I would assume that someone from a nearby planet had discovered our secret, and stolen the device. Would I bomb them? Of course I would. Because I'd want their planet to be every bit as damaged as mine." She let her words trail off, leaving Orius watching her with terrified eyes.

Ash drew herself up to her full height.

"Well, I'm Guardian now. And I get to decide what happens next." She picked up the Kronos device. "This goes back. This goes back to the planet it was taken from. How long does it take for a planet to go from an ice age to something more liveable? I don't know. But I guess I'm about to find out."

"Are you sure that's the right decision?" asked Orius quietly. "Your one decision is just the same as a small stone dropping in the ocean. The ripples you will cause will travel far and wide – you can have no way of knowing the full impact of your actions."

"I'm not interested in your analogies, Orius. You let this happen. You caused a planet to freeze when you selected Aldus Dexter as Guardian. When you let him flash around this universe, allowing his brain to swell in his stupid head while you poured power into his hands. When he started to get ideas and make plans that would affect other people in this universe. When he played dead and you bought it.

"You obviously didn't investigate enough – or was the Library just glad to be rid of him? I bet he'd given plenty of signs that he was as mad as he currently is. Did you ignore it when he stole a Kronos device from one planet and allowed ninety per cent of the living things on that planet to die – all so he could be master on a dead planet elsewhere? All so he could build his own universe." She shook her head fiercely. "Oh no, you don't get to do the old 'ripple in the water effect' with me." She put her finger to her chest. "I, I might be a pebble, but you lot? You weren't even a boulder – you were an entire mountain!"

She shook her head.

"When I first got here, I was blinded by the glamour and mystery of this place. But my overall thought was that it was essentially good. Good. I thought it was safe. But now? Now, I just don't know. What is the role of the Keeper of the Library? To not notice when someone deliberately tampers with the function of the Library? To let that go unnoticed and uncorrected for years? And if your selection processes are still as bad as they've always been, then you've hit the jackpot with me as Guardian. Because I won't let this happen. I won't do this. I won't be part of a place that I feel has no integrity, that can let something like this happen." She stood almost nose to nose with Orius. "The Library is entirely responsible for all of this!"

Ash grabbed the Kronos device to her chest and marched away. She was leaving. She had to. She had friends currently fighting in a war and there was a chance she could stop it.

She had no idea who the leader was on Corinez, but surely someone there would listen? If she told them what she'd discovered, and what she was bringing back to them, surely that would create a chance for peace in their part of the solar system?

Orius was shouting after her, but she was too angry to listen. The Library had let her down. It had given an illusion of grandeur, of safety, of infallibility.

Right now? She didn't care if she never set foot in the place again.

CHAPTER TWENTY-SEVEN

All the anger that had previously consumed Ash had nowhere to go.

By the time she was almost at her room, it had formulated a plan in her head.

This place had been corrupted. How could she be sure any of the decisions the Library now made were sound? Who was the Library to decide what artefacts were saved, and which were left behind?

Something sparked in her brain. What would happen if she ended all this?

What would happen if the Library didn't exist any more?

The seed of the idea sprouted instantly into a giant beanstalk. That would be the perfect solution. The logical solution. Destroy the place that had allowed a war to take place. That hadn't even noticed it had been corrupted.

Give it the solution it deserved.

Her breathing hitched for a few minutes as the crows of

doubt started to circle. She was acting on impulse. She knew that. But this place had done wrong. So, so wrong. Thousands of people had died. She couldn't, wouldn't, be a bystander.

But the Library had also been a force for good. Deep down, she knew that. But Ash felt so blindsided by her own experiences.

She had to ensure that nothing like what had already happened in her solar system – to her family, her people – could happen again.

Was destroying this place really the right thing to do? She folded her hands across her body, trying to stop her own trembling. First of all, she should find a way to return the Kronos device to Corinez. She should find a way to right the wrong that had been done there.

One second she was walking back to her room to grab a few things, the next she was lying on her back, still clutching the Kronos device and looking straight up, the noise of a blast ringing in her ears, the breath punched from her lungs.

She took a few seconds to figure out what had happened.

The second blast hit to her right, sending a display case of artefacts spilling all across the floor.

"What?"

Orius blinked into existence next to her. "The Library, it's under attack."

She stayed on the floor as a third blast reverberated around her. Her hair came loose and she started choking on a cloud of dust.

Something had just disintegrated. That couldn't be good. "Under attack from who?"

Orius shuddered. "A whole host of fighters from U62. They're led by Aldus Dexter."

"He's here?" She couldn't believe it. She'd just barely got away from him. "How did he get here so quickly?"

Orius lifted his hands. "He has technology beyond your own."

"But the virus – the virus was supposed to stop him."

Orius gave a gentle shake of his head. "The virus was designed to stop the plans for his Kronos device by knocking out a number of his systems. Apparently it hasn't disabled his space-travel capabilities."

She ducked as another blast hit the Library, and raised her eyebrows at Orius. "Seems like he means it. Guess he didn't take too kindly to the Library planting a virus."

Orius grabbed hold of her arm. "Ash, you need to defend the Library. You need to stop this attack. You need to save it."

She yanked her arm away. "Are you crazy? This might be the best thing that could happen. Maybe the universe doesn't need a Library – a place like this. Maybe destroying it is the right move."

A fighter appeared in the dark space above them and started raining down an array of blasts.

Another cabinet near them collapsed. Although the glass dome was still intact – for now – each blast was sending dangerous reverberations around the place, like an earthquake.

The spear that had belonged to Agillas on U756 rolled past her. Ash made an instinctive grab for it. Seconds later something else crashed down next to her.

There was a glint. The blue coraporamine that had sat in the crown of the ruler of Agrean and caused a seven-hundred-year war. History she'd only recently learned but that was imprinted on her brain. These planets had been destroyed. They didn't exist any more. And these artefacts were all that was left. All that was left to tell the story of planets that had sent themselves into extinction.

Something tugged at her heartstrings. Weren't there lessons to be learned from these places? Lessons that could stop other civilizations facing the same fate.

"Ash, please, I need you. The Library needs you." Orius was up close to her. His form was shimmering, as if whatever powered the hologram had been damaged.

"How can you expect me to help?" She glanced over her shoulder, trying to catch a glimpse of the fighters. "I'm not even sure this place should exist."

His mouth was only centimetres from her face. He was cowering next to her as if he was scared of the blasts from the attack above. Orius had always seemed far too close to life for a computer-generated being. Even now, he was acting as though his life depended on what happened next. And maybe it did.

He closed his hand over hers, touching the golden spear. "But if we let everything be destroyed, what do we have left?" he asked her. "How do we remember those who have no planet left to speak of? Shouldn't we carry their voices, their dreams, their lives?"

Tears sprang to Ash's eyes. "But who cared to carry the voices of my family? Who cared to carry the voices of the people of Corinez?"

"But they're still there, Ash." Orius pushed a finger towards her chest. "In here. In you. And in the people that are left in Corinez. Those voices aren't lost. Yet. And we can't let them be."

There was another crash, and then a much louder blast, sending a bolt of flames across the room.

"The scrolls," yelled Orius, "the texts!"

He got up to run and Ash found herself running alongside him, reaching the row of shelves where all the scrolls, books and texts were kept. She started tossing them as far away as possible from the flames, the Kronos device still held in her other arm.

"GO!" Orius yelled at her. "Get help."

She didn't understand. "How can I get help? How am I supposed to defend this place?"

Orius thrust some more books in her direction. "We have fighter craft underneath the Library. They've been there for decades. An ancient type of protection that we never really thought we'd have to use. Go, go get your friends. You'll need help to fly them."

Ash stumbled to find words. "Y-you have fighters?"

She thought she knew this place. She thought she'd examined every part of it. But it seemed that there were areas she hadn't even reached yet.

Ash had so many questions, so many thoughts, but as the Mirinex Crown shimmered and disintegrated in front of her, she realized that she just didn't have the time.

She looked down at the bangle on her wrist, then glanced back to Orius. She could read so much in that old face – the regret, the passion, the commitment.

As another blast impacted the glass dome next to her, she wondered just how much power the Library's shields needed. It was a question she'd never needed to ask, but the fact that artefacts were already being destroyed by the shock waves told her enough for now.

She ran back to her room and grabbed a backpack, pushing the Kronos device inside, wrapped in its thick cloth. She kept running, heading down the stairs and into the depths of the Library, shoving the bag under a shelf full of books. Aldus was coming for this. To take it or destroy it. She didn't even wait to catch her breath before she ran back up the stairs.

It was time.

She put one hand out to Orius. "I'll be back," she said as she slid her hand around her opposite wrist and pressed.

CHAPTER TWENTY-EIGHT

The place was in complete darkness. It was night-time here.

She leaned against the wall for a few moments, catching her breath and getting her bearings. She smiled as she realized where she was. Buckets, mops, supplies and tools. Ash looked down at the bangle and shook her head. Sometimes it seemed to transport her to the precise place she wanted. Others? Seemed to be a little more random.

She pushed open the door of the supply closet and climbed the three flights of stairs to the crew accommodation. It only took a few minutes to reach Ezra's door. It slid open easily, with a little beep.

He was sleeping peacefully in bed. The noise hadn't woken him. She hesitated, wondering how to make her presence known without scaring the living daylights out of him. But time was of the essence. Ash didn't have time to be nice.

She ran over and shook him by the shoulder.

"Ezra, wake up. I need you."

There was a grunt, a shake of his head and then he attempted to roll over to his other side.

"Ezra!" This time she shouted and his eyes bolted open. She kneeled in front of his bed. "Wake up, I need you. I need you right now. Get dressed. I'm going to wake Trik, Castille and Arona."

"Ash?" He was still half-asleep as he swung his legs from the bed and rubbed his eyes. "What in the blazes…?"

"Get dressed," she flung over her shoulder as she ducked out his door.

Seven minutes later she had herded Trik, Arona and Castille back into Ezra's room. Trik was still zipping his flight suit, Castille's hair was sticking up in every direction, and Arona was shaking her head.

"Where did you say you came from again?" she muttered. They all looked completely confused.

"Guys, I'm sorry, and I don't have much time to explain. The place where I work now – the Library – it's under attack. It's under attack by a guy who used to do the job that I do now." She took another breath. "He's a bad guy. He's done some terrible things… I will tell you all about that later. But right now, I need you all. I need you all to help me defend the Library."

"Am I dreaming?" Castille asked out loud.

"More like a nightmare," Trik muttered.

Arona's brow had creased in a frown. "What do you mean, under attack?"

"I mean 'under attack' – it's being fired on by fighters. We think they're from U62. They mean to destroy the Library and all the artefacts inside."

"Wait." Castille held up one hand. "U62 is only a legend. It's dead. We don't even know if it was ever really alive. The idea that life started there is just a kids' story."

Ash stepped forward. "Let's pretend it's not a kids' story. Let's imagine that it's very much alive, and has a whole fighter fleet led by some kind of madman. Will you come and help me? I'm the Guardian. I have to protect the Library."

"The what?" asked Castille.

Ash put her hand to her chest. "I'm the Guardian of the Library. It's my job to protect the Library and all the artefacts in it." Beneath her own panic she felt a sense of ownership and responsibility. The Library really did feel like hers.

"How far away is it?" asked Arona. "How quickly can we get there?"

Ash bit her bottom lip. "Yeah, about that. I have fighters at the Library you can use. And to get there? You'll have to take a bit of a leap of faith."

Ezra stepped forward. He hadn't spoken up until now. He'd listened. "Do you think you can do it?" He looked at his colleagues. "For us all?"

She nodded. "There is no think. I just have to. I have no choice. Now, please. Will you come, will you help me? We were rivals, but I think we were also friends. There's no other pilots I know like you guys. No other people I think can help me fight this battle."

Part of Ash's brain was screaming at the irony of all this. An hour ago she was contemplating destroying the Library herself. Now, she was pleading with her friends to risk their lives saving it.

But watching those artefacts fall and shatter, knowing that memories of civilizations could be lost for ever – that had made her gut churn in a way she couldn't live with. She wasn't happy about what had happened. She didn't know if she wanted to be the Guardian any more. But those were all problems she could solve later. Right now, she had to save the Library. And save her solar system. And she couldn't do one without first doing the other. The Kronos device was back at the Library. She just had to pray it was still in one piece.

"A fight? Well, yeah, I'm in," said Trik. He ran his hand over his dense cropped hair. It was the shortest she'd ever seen it. It suited him.

"Any opportunity for more flight time is a win for me," said Castille. He was flicking his fingers again. The sign she knew meant he was either excited or nervous – or maybe both. The tips of his larger ears stuck out from his untamed hair.

Arona gave a nod, even though her arms were folded across her chest. "As long as I get an explanation later," she said. It didn't matter that she'd only had a few minutes to get ready. She looked as smooth and composed as ever, her hair sleeked back in its signature long ponytail.

Ash nodded and turned to Ezra. "And you?"

He shrugged. "How come you manage to complicate everything?"

"It's the friends I keep." She smiled as she looked at them all. "Okay, so this is going to sound a little crazy, but, everyone, grab the person next to you."

CHAPTER TWENTY-NINE

A few seconds later all five of them materialized on the Proteus circle in the Library. Several pieces of furniture were lying on their sides and the whole place was shuddering under the continuing attack.

Castille was first to stand up straight. He took one look around. "Trashed the place already, girl?"

"Still tidier than your room," she shot back. "Everyone okay?"

Ezra gave a nod, Trik had his hand over his mouth, and Arona looked a little shaky.

Orius chose that moment to emerge in front of them.

"Good, you're here. The shields are starting to fail. Let me show you to the fighters."

For a second her friends were stunned. Then Arona gave a smile and a nod, Castille kept looking around, and Trik stared hard – as if he wanted to somehow take Orius apart and try to understand how he existed.

Ash held out her hands. "This is Orius, the Keeper of the Library. Orius, meet the rest of my friends. Trik, Castille and Arona. You already know Ezra."

Orius gave the briefest of nods and led them down a dark corridor that Ash hadn't even known existed. It seemed to run under the base of the Library.

They entered a wide dock. The whole place had a strange air. There seemed to be something ancient about it. And yet the technology was more advanced than anything else that Ash had seen. Though there were similarities to the Star Corporation Academy – the dock had an obvious force field in place that shimmered and shifted momentarily, keeping them safe from the dark space and stars beyond – a window to what lay outside.

There were nine fighters in dock. With a wave of his hand, Orius lit up the whole docking bay, and the lights on the fighters came on simultaneously.

"Will we even know how to fly these?" asked Arona. Then she paused and turned back as she ran her finger through a thick coating of dust. "Are they even space-worthy?"

"They're instinctual," said Orius quickly. "Don't worry, you'll get the hang of it."

Ash swallowed as all four of her friends turned to look at her. Somehow she didn't think it wise to tell them she had no idea what Orius meant, or that she had all the same questions herself.

"Let's go," she said, marching with what she hoped was some kind of confidence towards the furthest fighter.

"Wait." Orius raised his arm for a second, then scanned something over Ash's hand.

She felt the buzz instantly and rubbed her hand against her leg.

"What was that?"

"Healing technology." He raised his eyebrow. "You never told me Azla had broken your hand back on U62." A red scan appeared in the air at the side of his head, and she understood that her transport had alerted him to it. She'd been too wound up when she'd arrived back from U62 to mention it, or to let him treat her.

The confused faces around her were full of questions, but Ash shook her head. "Later, I promise. Let's go, everyone."

The cockpit of her chosen fighter opened as she approached, and stairs emerged out of the side of the machine for her to climb up, then promptly disappeared again once she'd embarked.

As her body relaxed into the seat, the harness strapped itself into place. A few seconds later, the seat seemed to move, adjusting position, then moulding around her body.

She didn't have her own pilot helmet, but one was sitting on the floor near her feet. It was bright red and she pulled it on and clipped it in place.

The panels around her were lit. Tracking systems. Fuel. Oxygen. Orientation. Comms. Targeting. Weapons.

The throttle and joystick were right at her fingertips. One button flashed orange. *Engine start-up.*

She flicked the switch at her helmet. "Are we good?"

She spoke hoping that someone, somewhere would answer.

"If this is old, I'm not sure I can handle the new," said Arona's sarky tone.

"Me either," added Castille.

"Let's fly these babies," said Trik.

"Any idea what we're facing yet?" asked Ezra.

"Not sure," admitted Ash. "But I'm pretty sure their technology will at least match ours."

"Then it's time for a fair fight," said Trik, just as an enemy blast exploded near the entrance to the docking bay. "Looks like that's our signal. Ready to go?"

"Ready," came the simultaneous replies.

"Then let's get out there." Trik let out some kind of catcall as he throttled his fighter out into space.

The rest were on his tail, shooting out into the blackness to meet whatever lay outside.

The acceleration thrust pushed Ash backwards into her seat as her craft dived out of the docking bay after them, making her catch her breath. She guided her fighter back around, facing the Library and the scene in front of her.

She'd never actually seen the Library properly from space before.

As her fighter positioned itself she sucked in a breath. There, sitting like some graceful beacon in the dark, was the glass dome of the Library, set on its small purple moon, with the great desolate planet it orbited in the far distance. Vapour and fog surrounded it, giving it a mysterious edge. The bottom part of the Library was smooth silver, and there was a slight tremor around the glass – the shielding that was gradually failing.

But the most spectacular feature of all was the fact you could see inside. As her craft floated in space before it, she felt like she could reach inside and grab some of the artefacts. They seemed that close.

The sky lit up to her right.

"Bandit on your right," came a voice. Trik.

A quick succession of voices and commands now filled her ears. Rook. Viper. Razor. Punk. Call signs. They all had call signs. The honour she'd always wanted. That she'd always craved. And she'd no idea what any of them meant. She'd missed the camaraderie and funny stories that had evolved into their nicknames.

As she banked to her left and fixed her eyes on her tactical screen to check the number and position of the enemy fighters, her vision went a little fuzzy. No. She reached a hand up to wipe her eyes. There was no time for sentimentality. Not when it looked like an endless stream of narrow, pointed, bronze enemy fighters were streaming through a far-off wormhole she hadn't even known existed.

"What do we call Ash?" Ezra's voice cut across the comm.

"Oh yeah, our girl doesn't have a call sign," said Castille.

"Shouldn't it be Guardian?" asked Arona. "Makes most sense."

Ash's skin prickled. Call signs were notoriously dragged out of thin air. Not always complimentary. But did she really want Guardian to be her call sign?

"How many bogeys you all getting?" asked Castille.

"I'm getting forty," said Trik, obviously keeping his eyes halfway between the sky and his screens.

"I think there's more," said Arona. "I think they're hiding behind that other moon. The one that fired at the dock seems to have headed that way."

"There's more damage to the other side of the Library," said Ezra, who'd obviously taken another look. "Not sure how much strength is in those shields, but if that glass shatters…" He left the words there. The rest of them knew exactly what he meant.

Ash swallowed. Everyone was talking at once. Trying to keep ahead of the situation. They didn't have time for her to decide on some random call sign.

"Call me Ink."

"What?" came one reply.

"It's home. It's where I'm from. Let's keep things simple. It's just a shortened version of my village name, Inkosata."

"Fine." It was Ezra's voice that replied first. "Okay, Ink, you're with me. Let's engage with our friends."

There was barely time for any planning. By the time they'd made it around to the other side of the Library, the U62 fighters were in attack formation.

"Let's go!" yelled Ezra as his fighter banked to the left of the oncoming enemy.

Ash banked right, letting rip with an onslaught of blasts. The fighter was similar to the technology on U62. It was her brain commands that gave it instructions. And she could work in unison with the fighter, letting it analyse things on her behalf as she reacted to what was happening in the sky around her. Her first few blasts lit up the sky around the enemy fighters, but then the range adjusted and the next blast clipped one of the fighter's wings, sending it spinning across space. She was really getting a feel for this. The second blast made contact with what she assumed was the fuel tank of another fighter, because it disappeared in a fiery explosion.

Her breath caught in her throat. She'd just killed someone. Another person, flying a ship just like she was. Shots fired to her bow brought her back to reality, as her sensors showed that her shields had absorbed the impact but lost some of their strength. It was survival of the fittest out here. She couldn't let herself be distracted again.

Part of her was a bag of nerves. These guys had all flown in combat together. They trusted each other. They had each other's backs. Ash hadn't flown in combat at all – only in the same tests that they all had. Would they trust her? Or were they all currently remembering the fact that she'd had to be transported out of her last fighter before it exploded? It wasn't a good memory.

But the more she flew, the more she realized Orius hadn't been kidding when he'd said these ships were "instinctual". This felt like a true partnership.

"These things are amazing!" came a shout through the comm. Trik.

"Right back at you, Punk." It was clear the team were experiencing the same effects that she was. Ezra's voice sounded elated.

"Watch your six, Razor." It was Arona. She was out of sight, around the other side of the Library.

"I'm on it, Viper," came Trik's voice again. "They can't even see me coming. Where have you been hiding these things, Ink? I can't believe you had fighters like this and you didn't even tell us."

Neither can I. Trik's voice was joking, but as Ash manoeuvred about the sky she could easily feel how smooth these fighters were compared to ones back home. These could be the difference between winning a battle and losing.

Part of her was angry at Orius for not telling her about them, but part of her understood. Just how tempted would she have been? To take one and leave, or to steal them for her friends to help the war back home.

"Careful, Punk," she warned. "There's a good chance their fighters are just as advanced as these."

The comm crackled and a loud expletive came across the waves. It was Arona. "There's eight of them coming at me. Attack formation, at least one's locked on."

The fire from the enemy fighters was continuous, both at them and at the Library. But they were managing to manoeuvre in the sky to avoid a large percentage of the shots. The enemy fighters weren't quite as instinctive as theirs were. Maybe they were manned by androids? Androids who were programmed. It made sense. Technology was everything to

Aldus. He would assume androids could perform better than Humans. He was wrong.

Ezra was still firing rapidly at a retreating fighter, then he picked off another that was firing on the Library. Ash pulled her craft up, moving over the top of the dome to the battlefield opposite. Her heart almost stopped.

It didn't matter how advanced their craft were. There was no mistaking the standard attack formation, spread out like a giant bird with wings fanning across the sky. One locked on to Arona, and the other locked on to Trik. His voice came across the comm at the same time as Ash emerged: "Me too, Viper. We've got to outmanoeuvre these guys."

Castille was coming in from the side, firing blindly at the large attack formation, but he was too far away to make a real impact.

Before Ash had a chance to shout any instructions, Arona's craft disappeared.

Just clean disappeared before her eyes.

"What the…"

The voice was Ezra's – he'd just pulled up alongside her.

Castille was panicking. "Rook, what happened? Is she gone? Did Viper take a hit?"

"Negative," Ezra replied. "At least I don't think so."

Ash scanned her weapons, looking for something more substantial. There wasn't time for questions. She found what she thought she needed, targeted and fired.

She watched the sky as proton torpedoes found their marks. The enemy ships hadn't had time to lose their attack formation, and their close proximity meant that the torpedo only had to hit one craft for the outgoing explosion to cause maximum damage to its counterparts.

Castille's stunned voice came over the comm. "Ink, what was that?"

She was having trouble breathing. She'd just killed eight people. Or eight androids. She had no idea who was piloting the U62 ships. Did it matter? Wasn't each a form of life?

"Press the red button, Razor," she breathed. "I think it's proton torpedoes."

Something moved in her vision. Her brain was still focused somewhere on Arona and the actions she'd just taken. The rest of them had battle experience. The rest of them had likely already killed, and lost colleagues. Ash hadn't. She was a space-battle novice and none of this felt good.

Not the way she'd imagined. Not the way her stomach had clenched in excitement and terror as a child, thinking of how she could finally be a fighter pilot and destroy the enemy. She'd thought it would spark joy.

But it didn't. Nothing close.

The image in the corner of her vision blinked again then appeared fully.

Another fighter. She turned her craft around automatically then stopped.

Arona?

There was a squeal in her ears. "Don't push the red button, press the green one!" It was Arona.

"What?" Four voices started speaking simultaneously.

Ash, Ezra and Castille positioned themselves around the Library, strategically moving near the second attack formation. This one was double the size of the previous one. Sixteen craft. Out to destroy their five.

Ash turned her head towards the silver fighter in the sky. "Arona? What happened? Where did you go?"

Arona let out another squeal. "These things are magic! I panicked a bit and hit the green button. It's a jump drive."

"A what?" Ash stared down at the innocuous green button at the tips of her fingers.

"Come and catch me, guys!" yelled Trik. Two seconds later he disappeared before their eyes, leaving the second attack formation that had been closing in on him left in the space before them, like target practice.

Castille, Ezra and Ash automatically opened fire. This time there was no need for torpedoes. Ezra clipped the wing of one fighter, sending it spinning into another. The enemy fighters lit up like a firework show.

But there were more to take their place. The battle raged on.

"I've taken damage," shouted Arona. "Shields down to fifty per cent."

Castille made a grunting sound. "I'm out of proton torpedoes."

"We can do this, guys!" shouted Trik, trying to keep their enthusiasm up.

Ash's craft rocked as a shot hit it. The red button on her panel flashed. Her shields were down to thirty per cent. She spun her craft around to return fire. A fuel light flashed on as she used the last of her proton torpedoes. "Go!" she yelled, feeling the reverberation through her hands and arms as she fired.

"Ink," Ezra shouted, "bank left."

She moved without hesitation as the remains of an enemy fighter exploded into the space she'd just been occupying. She could see inside the torn-open bronze shell. Strapped into the seat was the silver glint of metal – the remains of an android. Her breathing stuttered. The ship would have hit her, and probably killed the last of her shields. Space junk could be more dangerous than some of the weapons out here.

"Th…anks," she breathed into the comm.

Ezra came up alongside her ship and gave her a thumbs up.

The space around them had quietened.

The last enemy ship hesitated for a few moments before firing off a few random shots at the Library then beating a hasty retreat.

Trik appeared again midway between them and the remaining fighter.

"Let it go!" shouted Ash, suddenly struck by some kind of regret over killing whatever was inside. Azla's face flashed into her brain. She might have been an android, but she had personality. She had life.

She could sense his fingers above the trigger in his cockpit. "Leave it. It might give its friends a message not to come back."

"Wouldn't it send a better message if *none* of them went back?" said Castille.

He was probably right. But Ash just couldn't watch the last retreating ship being blown out of the sky. It seemed ruthless and unnecessary.

"Let's make sure none of them *can* come back." The voice was Ezra's.

His ship was positioned facing the gate that held the wormhole steady.

Ash's heart missed a few beats. "Are you saying what I think you're saying?"

Four voices sounded over the comm. "Yes." It was unanimous.

The wormhole. They were going to collapse the wormhole.

"Do we even have enough firepower?" Ash asked.

"There's only one way to find out," said Arona. "Flick back the cover on your stick. There's a switch to arm a super-torpedo."

Castille gave a little noise. "And I thought I was all out…"

Her gaze flickered back to the Library. They'd followed the last enemy craft to the entrance of the wormhole and her engineer brain could tell the Library was far enough away not to be harmed by the hole collapsing.

"Take up positions," she said hoarsely.

Her eyes got a little fuzzy as her fellow cadets lined up alongside her. There was only originally supposed to be one pilot from their class. Now, they all got to do this together.

She licked her lips and lifted her head. "Ready? Three, two, one…"

The black sky lit up. Spirals of yellow and orange light

emanated from the space in front of them. It looked like some kind of spinning supernova. But they all knew what it really was. The space collapsing and folding in on itself.

All five ships were pushed back by the momentum from the blast. What was left of their shields was just enough to protect them.

One moment there was the colourful collapsing spiral. The next moment, there was nothing. Not a single sign that anything had existed there.

For a few seconds, there was only silence as they all hung in space, contemplating what had just happened.

"You gotta give us these ships for back home," Trik joked, breaking the silence. It was just as well. Ash didn't want to think too hard about all this. Would a collapsing wormhole be enough to truly stop Aldus? She had to hope that it would.

"Hey," Castille cut in. "We could just jump home in them, couldn't we? Where did you guys jump to anyways?"

There was a loud clearing of someone's throat. Arona spoke first. "That's just it. I'm not actually sure. Because I'm not really familiar with the controls or navigations, I couldn't read where I was. All I know is, one press made me jump, another made me come back."

"Me too," said Trik, sounding a little less enthusiastic than before. "You gotta explain these things a bit better, Ash. We could do some *serious* damage in these."

Ash's stomach was churning. It was like being torn down the middle. These ships could make a difference to the battle back home. But the technology was way beyond her and her solar system's expertise. She shouldn't have it. She shouldn't even have seen it. That's why Orius hadn't told her about the ships.

She only knew about them now because the Library had been under attack. Desperate times called for desperate measures. But she'd just asked her friends for help and they'd come and put their lives on the line for her. How could she explain this?

"Let's get back to the docking bay. We can talk there."

She flew over the dome of the Library, her insides twisting at the carnage inside. There were a few visible spots of damage on the outside too. She had no idea how they could be fixed, or even *if* they could be fixed. It was all beyond her range of expertise.

The ships virtually self-docked, their landings all smooth and coordinated. The cockpits slid open, the steps in the sides of the fighters materialized once again, and they all climbed down into the docking bay.

Orius was nowhere in sight.

Ash bit her lip. "Thank you. Thank you all. I could never have defended this place by myself."

Castille was still staring open-mouthed at the row of fighters. "They don't look like much initially, but all those features? We've got a winning attack squadron. We just need some details. Come on, Ash." He looked around at the smooth walls of the docking bay. "There must be some kind of control panel somewhere. Instructions. Even a manual. Anything that tells us how these beauties work."

She shook her head. "I don't have a clue. I don't think I

was even supposed to see these, or know that they were here. Anything that's more technologically advanced than our current world – I'm not supposed to use it for my own purposes. It would be an unfair advantage."

Trik spun around. "An unfair advantage? An unfair advantage of not dying? Not being bombed to death by the crazy Corinezians?"

He was angry. And she got it. She understood. He'd every right to be angry.

"I'm sorry." She held out her hands. "I don't make the rules. But…there's something else I need to tell you all."

Arona folded her arms across her chest like she knew this wasn't going to be good. "What?"

"The war. The bombings. I think…I think that Corinez might have a very good reason for acting the way they do."

Trik stepped up and put both hands on her head, turning it one way, and then the other.

She batted his hands away. "What? Stop it."

He raised his eyebrows. "I'm checking to see if someone's hit you on the head, because you're talking crazy."

"I know it sounds that way, but the things I've learned here have been just like that – a bit crazy. Corinez wasn't always an ice planet. It was made that way when something was stolen from it."

They were all staring at her now, confusion and disbelief written on their faces.

Ezra stepped forward. "Do you have it?" He didn't need to specify what.

She pressed her lips together and nodded. "I need to come back. I need to come back and try to return it. Try to stop this war before any more people die."

Castille narrowed his gaze. "But what about this place? Don't you have a job to do here?"

She wasn't quite sure how to answer that. She took a deep breath. "This is more important. This isn't a mission that's been assigned to me by the Library. I'm choosing to do this. This is about my home, my people. And it's about a war between four planets that I might have a tiny chance of stopping. That's got to come first." She took a deep breath and continued, "And I think the Library has played a part in all this. I think it made a mistake in not putting all the pieces of this puzzle together – in not realizing exactly what Aldus was up to." She put her hand on her chest. "But I'm Guardian now. And if I can find an opportunity to fix any of this? I will."

No one spoke. Everyone just looked at her for the longest time. Eventually Castille turned and started walking back towards the door of the docking bay. After a few moments Arona turned and followed him. She didn't look happy.

Trik paused the longest. "I'd still rather fly home," he said, looking longingly at the ships.

Ash put her hand on his shoulder. "I know," she said simply.

Upstairs, the Library was in chaos. Artefacts were everywhere, along with drifts of smoke and dust. Orius materialized in front of them, making Castille start. He waved

335

his hand, and screens appeared in the air in front of him. They watched as he scanned them, turning his head to meet their gazes.

"The wormhole is definitely closed. It looks like U62 managed to send those fighters out before every single one of their systems crashed. They have no way of sending more anytime soon. For now, it looks like we're safe from them. Thank you."

Ezra gave Ash a look of relief.

Orius headed into the middle of two demolished rows, and began picking things up from the ground.

Arona put her hands on the stone balustrade. "Where will you start?"

Ash gave a slow nod. "The artefact that was stolen is down there. I need to find it. I need to give it back."

Right now it would be like finding a needle in a haystack. She had no idea where to start her search. Almost every set of shelving or unit had collapsed onto the floor. The whole area was littered with scrolls, books, vases, glints of gold and shards of metal or glass. She'd always known the place was crammed, but seeing the entire contents of the Library on the floor in front of her was daunting.

"Come on," she said. "Let me send you guys back. I'll follow as soon as I find it."

"You're not coming back with us?" Ezra was right next to her.

She shook her head. "I can send you back another way. Come with me."

Ash walked them over to the large metal circle on the floor. "Stand on this together."

Castille shot her a suspicious glance as he peered at the circle.

"Why, what does it do?"

"If you stand on it, you'll find out."

She waited for them to position themselves on the circle. Ezra was last, like he didn't actually want to leave. Ash touched his arm as she glanced back at the disarray in the Library. Somehow the sight of Orius on his hands and knees in among the artefacts was tugging at heartstrings she'd forgotten she had.

"I'll be as quick as I can."

He joined the others and she gave them a sad smile. "Thank you all again for coming. I appreciate it more than you can ever know. And I'll join you soon to stop this war."

Arona gave her the most minimal of nods and Ash put her foot at the edge of the Proteus circle and pressed her bangle, thinking clearly of the Star Corporation Academy.

They vanished in the blink of an eye.

And Ash swallowed, as the emptiness around her threatened to invade every part of her. They'd done it. Her friends had helped her stop Aldus's plan and save the Library. It had been terrifying. But what came next was even more so.

She was the only one who could try to put an end to this war. She had to fix this. She had to. For all their sakes.

CHAPTER THIRTY

Ash picked her way through the remnants of some of the most precious pieces of the universe.

"You're leaving." Orius's voice was flat; he didn't even lift his head to look at her.

She kneeled down next to him.

"I'm going to right a wrong. After that…" She licked her lips. "I'll consider my position."

Now Orius did lift his head. He looked even more worn than ever before. But he didn't speak, he just fixed his grey eyes on her.

"My friends saved the Library – or part of it – today," she said, then paused. "I thought I wanted to see this place destroyed. I thought I wanted it finished, gone." Her heart was twisting in her chest and tears brimmed in her eyes. She couldn't believe how attached she'd become to this place, despite her earlier rage.

Now she was containing her anger, she could take a

breath and think rationally.

The damage around her actually made her stomach ache. She picked up a piece of red clay pottery. Even though it was broken, the museum tag flickered up alongside it, causing tears to well in her eyes. It had been part of an ancient statue from a planet that had long since been destroyed. She traced her finger around the edge of it and pressed it to her chest, trying to remember as much as she could about the culture, the belief systems, and the people who had once lived there, now their last remnant was gone too.

"So much work," she whispered.

The air still had an aroma of burned paper. She didn't even want to see the damage in the row where the scrolls were housed.

Orius was still watching her.

Ash started picking her way through the piles, stopping to lift vases and jewels that were still intact, laying them carefully to one side. She kneeled on the floor, sliding books from underneath broken shelving and stacking them gently on top of one another. A scroll perished as soon as she touched it – already damaged by the heat from nearby flames, it disintegrated into tiny fragments.

There was another heap of scrolls nearby. They seemed to have escaped the heat damage, and she moved them off to one side, brushing dust from their delicate surfaces.

The search continued for hours. Ash tried to find some patience – treating the artefacts with the respect they deserved, and picking up broken pieces and grouping them together in the hope they could be salvaged somehow.

From a pile of rubble she saw the familiar edge of her backpack. Her heart jumped and she stumbled over and pulled it out, tugging at the opening and sliding out the wrapped Kronos device. It still had the rough material around it and she drew it back. The device was in one piece, the crystal in the middle undamaged.

She still wasn't sure what came next. Was this really the last time she'd be in the Library, or would she come back?

"I have to go, Orius. I can't let the actions of a previous Guardian ruin the lives of millions." She shook her head. "I know this place is a mess, but I have to prioritize the people I love."

She looked him in the eye.

"What can you tell me about Corinez?"

Orius sighed and shook his head. "Last time the Library had information on Corinez was before their ice age. Five hundred years ago. We've had no contact with them since then. No way to scan them, no way to access any technology they might still have. Nothing. It looks like Aldus did something to the Library to hide Corinez from our systems."

Ash nodded and pressed her lips together. She was stepping into the dark on an ice-age planet.

Orius's voice cracked. "Will you come back?" he asked.

She clasped the Kronos device to her chest and reached for her bangle. "I don't know," she said as she pressed it.

CHAPTER THIRTY-ONE

After she transported, Ash found herself in darkness. At first she thought she might have made a mistake. She'd wanted to transport to the Star Corporation Academy. There, she could talk to someone, maybe even one of the Commanders, and ask for a fighter or a shuttle – anything that could take her down to Corinez.

Transporting directly to Corinez would be madness. She didn't know the planet at all – it was all just one icy wilderness to her. She had no idea how or where the residents lived. She had no idea who was in charge. If she wanted this to work, Ash would have to use a skill she didn't normally enlist – careful planning.

The ground moved underneath her feet, tossing her to one side and into a wall. She rubbed her shoulder as she straightened herself.

Lights flashed, revealing that she was in a corridor.

She put her hand to the wall to steady herself, then

frowned. The smooth wall was familiar, as was the logo beneath her fingertips. This was definitely the Star Corporation Academy. There was another shift, this time followed by a not too far off explosion. Her senses went to high alert.

The Academy was under attack.

Almost simultaneously the emergency lighting pinged on around her. It took her eyes a few seconds to adjust.

Then something else struck her. Where was everyone?

Low smoke drifted at one end of the corridor. She checked the wall again. Level two. The staff quarters were on the floor above. She stumbled along to the end of the corridor and the emergency stairs, gripping the rail tightly as she climbed them. It felt like every few seconds the station lurched to either side.

She yanked open the heavy door at the top of the stairs. Alarms were blaring on this level. This felt more like it. Figures were dashing around. She made a grab at a few.

"Have you seen Ezra? Trik? Arona? Castille? Any of the last flight class?"

She was met with shaking heads and annoyed glances. Several people stared at the unwieldy package in her arms. She couldn't exactly hide it anywhere.

Ash kept going. The smoke up here was thicker. She checked the staff quarters for Arona, Trik, Ezra. All were empty. Castille's room was further along, and she closed her hand over her mouth as she tried to reach it.

Part way along another hit made her fall to her knees. Something flashed in front of her. There was a scream.

A back-draught of flames. Then everything in front of her was sucked outside. Out, into the vacuum of space.

It was less than a second. That's how good the systems were here. A force field had zapped into place across the corridor. It was shimmering, transparent. Through it, Ash could see the blasted end of someone's quarters. Part of a metal bed still gripped to the wall. There was a huge hole where the outer wall of the station had been. The metal twisted in every direction from the blast.

Panic gripped her chest. What if someone had been sleeping in that bed? One minute fast asleep, the next sucked out into space.

She shivered, then shook her head. No. No one could have slept through the barrage of shock waves that had been reverberating through the station. Everyone must be on high alert right now. Every team member would be at their battle stations.

She glanced at the number outside the door. It wasn't Castille's. It wasn't his. She had to assume he was safe.

Ash turned and headed back the way she had come. The smoke was getting thicker, filling the air with noxious, choking fumes.

She covered her face as she ran down the steps as quickly as she could. Orange lights were flashing as she headed down the corridor that took her to the heart of the action. The shuttle bay and tactical control room were all in this part of the station.

Her eyes were streaming. Part of her brain was wondering

why the air filtration system hadn't kicked in, hadn't automatically sucked all the oxygen out of the place the smoke was coming from. Anything to prevent the chance of a fire spreading.

Unless...

Her heart fell in her chest as she turned the corner to the shuttle bay. A crashed fighter lay like a tangled, sprawled mess halfway off one of the landing pods. People were running everywhere. Technicians were trying to manually fight the flames. Ash could see the unconscious pilot slumped in their seat.

She shoved the Kronos device into a half-full backpack she retrieved from the floor, leaving it there, and ran straight at the fighter. It could be one of her friends in there.

The flames were shooting towards the ceiling. The technicians blasting them with smotherfoam were being driven backwards. As she ran, she could hear the crackle of the fire against the metal. The temperature was driving others backwards. She looked around for something to grab, finding an engineering blanket to shield her from the worst of the heat.

The steps for the fighter hadn't even managed to be rolled alongside. "Cover me!" yelled Ash to the technicians. She kept her hands and head tightly hidden behind the blanket and grabbed the steps, pushing them over.

There was a *skoosh* next to her as the mustard-coloured foam headed in her direction. She held her breath, knowing that for the next few seconds inhaling would be impossible.

The steps clanged against the side of the fighter and Ash ran up them, keeping her hand behind the blanket as she hit the external release for the cockpit.

It made a defunct kind of sound. "Give me something I can use to get in here!" she called to the crew behind her.

She thumped against the glass of the cockpit, which had taken on a kind of warped structure, making visibility poor. From beneath the rim of the pilot's helmet she could see a swathe of blonde hair. Arona. This was Arona.

Ash had transported them here just over an hour ago. What had they come back to?

There was a loud suction noise. "Crew!" came the shout.

The crew around her dropped instantly to the ground. Another fighter was landing. That should never happen – not while crew were still on the pads. It was extremely dangerous. But the whole place seemed to be in chaos right now.

One of the crew hung back for a few seconds, to press an iron bar into Ash's hand. She pushed one end into the small gap that had appeared near the door where the cockpit glass had warped, and used her whole body weight to try and lever it free.

The flames were still flickering on the far side of the fighter – clearly fanned by the other one landing. "Help me!" Ash yelled to the guys beneath her.

One of them, a stocky man, grabbed a piece of discarded metal from those strewn around them and jumped up alongside her, mimicking her actions. His added weight gave them enough leverage, and there was a soft release of air as they burst the seal around the cockpit.

"Arona," Ash gasped, leaning forward to grab her friend's face. She'd barely had a chance to even tilt Arona's chin upwards, catching a fleeting sight of a jagged cut across her cheek and eye, before the man knocked her sideways with his hips.

"Move." He reached in, slashed the safety harness with a knife and yanked Arona from the seat.

Ezra appeared at the bottom of the ladder. "Is she okay?" His face was deathly pale.

Ezra. It was Ezra who had landed next to them.

The technician had flung Arona over his shoulder as he descended the steps. "Let's go, people," he shouted as he ran to the side of the landing hangar.

Ash heard the sizzle to her right. It was the sound of something igniting within the engine of Arona's fighter.

She'd never seen so many crew move so quickly.

Ezra caught the material at her shoulder and yanked her with him. She didn't have time to catch her breath before he flung them both behind some storage containers and the fighter lit up.

The blast shield went down on the tactical control room, cutting it off from view. Arona was on the ground in front of Ash, the technician bent over her.

"I can't wake her up," he murmured. "We need to get her to the medical bay."

One of the other technicians shook his head. "Part of it's gone. The injured are in the corridors."

Gone. The medical bay. The place that Ezra had been taken after he'd been injured. Dr Nero, Nurse Ratmizr, Medic Batz. Were any of them still alive? The words stuck in Ash's throat. She didn't want to ask them out loud.

Ezra stepped forward, pushing others out of his way. His hand rested on Arona's undamaged cheek. "Arona? Arona? Can you hear me? Wake up. You're back. You're safe."

Her eyelids flickered for a few seconds, but didn't open.

Another crew member hurried over, his voice low. "They've set up an emergency medical bay along the corridor. Let's take her there." His voice dropped even lower. "But I don't think anywhere is safe. Not while this attack continues."

Ash stood as the heavy crew member picked up Arona easily. Her gaze caught the full view of Ezra's fighter. It wasn't the usual one that they'd trained in. It was an X32. Bigger, less manoeuvrable. One side had clearly caught the impact of the blast of the other exploding shuttle, but the other? She took a few steps to see it and winced. There was a deep rent in the far side of the fighter, making her wonder how the fuel tank was still intact. Or maybe it wasn't? Was that why Ezra had landed so hurriedly?

She turned towards him – wanting to ask him what had happened – but he was walking alongside Arona, worry written all over his face.

She took a few breaths. She hadn't thought. She'd just acted. But her actions meant that somewhere in among the debris strewn around the landing bay was the Kronos device.

347

The device that could actually stop the war they were in the middle of.

She started picking her way through the twisted shards of metal in the hangar, kicking pieces aside and lifting others. A few times she was shouted at by other crew when another fighter was coming in to land, having to scurry to the side and wait until it was clear to move again. Finally, she found the device – with some of the sacking and the backpack singed – next to one of the containers.

She glanced up to the tactical control room. The blast shield had been pulled back again and she could glimpse at least one of the Commanders in there.

She had to speak to someone. She had to find a way to Corinez before this whole station and all the people on it were destroyed.

Ash threaded her way through the busy crew members and up the stairs. The tactical room had a secure entrance, but when she knocked sharply the door was opened.

"Yes?" A woman she didn't recognize blocked her view.

"I need to speak to the Commander."

"And you are?" The unfamiliar eyes looked her up and down. Of course. Her grey-and-red flight suit didn't match any of the uniforms here. The woman was trying to place her designation. Ash's brain flooded with answers, desperately trying to decide how to answer. Ash? Cadet? Visitor?

She straightened her shoulders. "Tell the Commanders the Guardian needs to speak to them."

The woman's brow creased in a frown, her head gave the

briefest shake as she made to close the door. She clearly thought Ash was crazy. "Commander Trinley is busy."

Ash jammed her foot in the door. "Not too busy for me." Her heart jumped a beat. The woman had only mentioned one Commander. Ash didn't want to consider what that meant. She kept her voice steady but clipped. "Tell the Commander that the Guardian needs to talk to them. Tell her we need to talk about Corinez." She wasn't about to take no for an answer.

The woman scowled. "Hold on." She shouted something muffled over her shoulder, then a few moments later stared hard at Ash as she reluctantly opened the door. "Come in."

The tactical room was in a quiet kind of chaos. Commander Trinley was dressed in her usual white, her dark skin beaded with sweat as she leaned over one of the star charts and monitored the fighters in the space around the Star Corporation Academy base.

"Comms," she said sharply. "Report."

"We've lost another seven fighters. Four confirmed fatalities. Three over Corinez. I can't get comms on those pilots. Squadron Seven is in trouble. They're outflanked and taking heavy damage."

"Send Squadron Six to assist," said the Commander sharply.

"Squadron Six are depleted. Two have damage to radios. One fighter is returning to base because of engine failure."

"Send them anyway."

Ash's stomach clenched. These didn't sound like tactical

349

decisions, these sounded like desperate measures. Commander Trinley looked up at her. She gave the briefest dip of her head. "Guardian, you can see we're under pressure. Talk quickly."

Ash was stunned. It was the nod of the head, the accord she'd just been shown. She hadn't expected it. Not from a Commander. Her eyes scanned the rest of the room. No one else was paying her any attention – no one was interested in what she had to say. Everyone was too busy doing their own job and defending the station.

She moved quickly, closer to the Commander. Seeing the space battle playing out live in front of her was terrifying. Fighters were shown as tiny bright sparks. White and blue. She could only assume that the blue ones were the Corinez fighters. As she watched, one of the white sparks flickered and faded.

Just like that.

A life lost.

The Commander flinched. She cared. She cared about every single person out there. This must be killing her.

Her dark eyes looked up into Ash's for a second.

There it was. The hurt. The responsibility. The effort. Ash was conscious that Commander Anand and Commander Clay should be in this room too. But she couldn't form the question to ask about their absence. She didn't want to hear the possible answer.

"Talk."

So she did. "I discovered something. I discovered this." She uncovered the Kronos device in her arms.

Commander Trinley looked thoroughly confused. Ash couldn't pretend she wasn't relieved. After the corruption in the Library she couldn't help but wonder who she could actually trust. Especially since the Commanders had sent her off with the package containing the device in the first place. Knowing that Commander Trinley clearly had no idea what this device was, or what it could do, filled her with relief.

"I have reason to believe that this – a Kronos device – was stolen from Corinez five hundred years ago. The removal of this device caused the planet to move into an ice age, doubtless causing numerous deaths across their population. I think" – she took a long breath – "the war was caused because they believe that one of their neighbouring planets carried out the theft that more or less caused the destruction of their planet."

Commander Trinley's eyes widened, her jaw slackened. "Wh…at?" she muttered, her head giving the smallest shake. Her tense body sagged and she gripped the side of the console. "I've never heard any of this. Communications were cut off with Corinez more than one hundred years ago. The whole time I've been in the post, we've never heard from them at all. I was under the belief that they started this war when they attacked the other three planets in the system."

Her eyes fixed back on the screen of flickering sparks. For a few moments all the Commander did was breathe.

When her gaze shifted back to Ash she looked shattered. "How sure are you?"

Ash wanted to tell her she wasn't sure at all. Some of this was guesswork. But the look of devastation on Commander Trinley's face told her it wasn't wise to say that out loud. Not right now.

She couldn't hide the way her words shook as she spoke. "Sure enough that I'm here, now, to ask for transport to Corinez. To ask for a chance to speak to them. To ask for a chance to end this war."

There was an almighty explosion, debris flying everywhere again. People were thrown from their chairs in the tactical room. "What's happened to our shields?" yelled Commander Trinley.

"Fifteen per cent," answered the technician directly to her left.

There was no need for a command. Someone flicked a switch. "All crew resources to shields. Priority one."

Ash didn't need anyone to tell her that those shields wouldn't improve anytime soon. The only way they could be down at that level was if they'd been hit by prolonged and sustained damage.

"What about the fleet?" she asked as she stepped alongside the Commander.

"What fleet?" The Commander's voice was so low it was barely audible. But the answer was only for Ash. Seconds later she started shouting commands to others in the room. "Damage report. I want a casualty list."

She looked up at Ash again. "I'm not sure what we have left that's in a flyable condition."

"Ezra. Give me Ezra's ship. I know it's damaged, but it will be good enough to get me to the surface of Corinez." She couldn't use the bangle. She had absolutely no idea about the planet, or where any of the areas of civilization would be, so the chances were she'd transport herself into a dense area of snow where she would rapidly freeze to death. At least with a fighter she could fly over the ground, get a feel for the landscape, and scope out possible sites where the inhabitants might stay.

The Commander pulled up a screen. It was a map of the planet. She pulled a face. "There's so much we don't know. We think there are living areas here, here and here." She pointed with her finger at places on the map. "We also think there could be the equivalent of military bases here and here. But we can't be sure of anything. This information could be wrong."

"A name. I need a name."

The Commander shook her head. "Years ago, before I even qualified as a pilot, there was talk of a military leader on Corinez. But the woman was more like a legend – I don't even know if she was real."

"Give me her name. It's somewhere to start."

"Aurora Damocles."

Ash nodded. "Thank you," she said, trying to keep the emotion from her voice. This station was on its last legs. They both knew that. It was unlikely she would see Commander Trinley again – because if she knew one thing about this woman, it was that she wouldn't abandon ship.

"Commander." The voice came from their right. "We've lost contact with another fighter. They went down over Corinez. It's Trik Enliva."

Pain speared through Ash. A few hours ago he'd been flying with her, laughing and joking. He'd asked for the fighters from the Library. If she'd let her friends take those, would Trik be missing? Would Arona be injured?

If Trik had survived the crash he wouldn't last long in the current climate of Corinez. Ash didn't hesitate. "I'm taking Ezra's ship. Send the last known coordinates of Trik to the comm."

"Guardian?" Commander Trinley's voice was calm.

Ash spun back around. "Yes?"

"Fly true and may the stars protect you."

The words she'd always wanted to hear as a pilot. Tears pricked at her eyes. "Thank you." She dipped her head in return as she hurried to the door.

The docking bay was in chaos outside. The smoke had reduced but the number of injured in the nearby corridor had increased tenfold. It seemed that other parts of the station were rapidly becoming unsustainable. Ash could see a few trolleys in the corridor ahead, and she dashed forward, hoping to catch a glimpse of Arona.

Her friend's blonde hair was distinguishable from a distance. Her pilot helmet had been removed and there was a red streak across Arona's hair and cheek. One of the medics was checking her.

"How is she?" Ash pushed past some crew members

struggling by with their arms laden. Ezra was standing at the foot of the trolley, his face grim.

The medic looked up. "No change. She's not regained consciousness. And we don't have our med bay to assess her properly." He held up a few of the portable equipment monitors. "These aren't enough."

Ash looked down. Arona was one of the most determined and single-minded people she'd ever met. She'd fought every step of the way for her place in the Academy. Now, Ash would have to leave her. Leave her behind in a space station that was under attack with no real defences left. She fought back the panic as she glanced at all the people around her. She had to leave all of them behind to a fate that right now could be written in the stars.

She blinked back tears. "I need to go," she whispered to Arona as she reached down to brush a strand of bloody hair from her face. "I'm sorry," she whispered.

"Where are you going?" Ezra asked.

The words stuck somewhere in her mouth. "I need to go down to C…Corinez."

"You can't go down there! You have no idea what it's like out there. Our fighters are no match for theirs. Not even close. You won't last five minutes."

A tear slid down her cheek. "It doesn't matter if it's hopeless, Ezra. I have to try. I'm the Guardian. That's why I'm here." She shook her head and started down the corridor to the landing bay. She couldn't argue with him. Not here. Not now.

But Ezra was angry. He wouldn't leave it. He followed her

down the busy corridor, shouldering people out of the way. "What do you think you can do? Are you crazy? Did Orius tell you to do this?"

He kept going as she emerged out onto the landing bay.

"And why do you want to fly? Why don't you just use your thing? Press it. Do it that way. Otherwise you'll just be target practice in the sky! In case you haven't noticed, we don't have the kind of fighters that you do."

He reached forward, making a grab for her wrist, but she batted him away as she spun around. She could hear the stress in his voice. She couldn't blame him. Right now, she *did* wish she'd ignored all the morals and ethics of exposing people to technology they weren't ready for, and just brought one of the other fighters with her. She couldn't believe things had escalated so quickly in the last hour.

"How can I transport to a place that no one – not even the Library – can tell me about? You know as well as I do, it's an ice planet. Do I just twist and hope for the best? Or do I use my brains, and do a fly-over? Do I look for the place where I think there might be a military base, where I might actually have a chance to talk to who I need to?" She shook her head and lowered her gaze. "And Trik's down there. Do you think in the midst of this battle anyone has time to look for a downed flyer?"

Ezra flinched. Of course, he'd had no idea about Trik. His hands were shaking with rage. He was so angry right now he probably couldn't think straight. He'd gone from one space battle to another. He'd been under fire. He'd almost died out there himself. He'd seen his colleague Arona injured, and now he knew his other friend could be trapped on Corinez. She watched as he tempered his anger, his hands going from fists, to claws, to fists again. When he looked up, his jaw still had a tremor in it.

"I'm coming with you."

"What? No." She knew how much danger she would be in out there. She had no intention of taking anyone with her.

Ezra flung his hand towards the tactical room. "Where do you think I want to die, Ash? On a space station, where I can't do anything to help? Or on a mission above a planet that I still think are the enemy? Because from where I'm standing it looks like I'm going to die somewhere today. None of us are feeling lucky right now."

Ash ducked as a stray blast struck the area above her head.

The shields must have failed around the landing bay.

Her eyes darted to Ezra's ship. It was one of the bigger fighters – it might not have much manoeuvrability, but it had room for them both.

"If we're going to go, let's go before the landing bay is destroyed," he said, striding towards the fighter.

She wanted to tell him no. But any minute now this place could go up like a giant space bomb.

Ash scrambled over to the fighter, noticing the roughly welded panel where the large rent in the side had been. They must just have mended it. Would that even hold?

As the canopy closed over the top of them and she strapped herself in, she didn't even have time to think about it.

Together, Ash and Ezra blasted from the space station out into a floating debris field, and as they pulled away, the area behind them lit up.

CHAPTER THIRTY-TWO

Ash had always been aware of the four planets in her solar system. From her school years she'd looked at a drawing of the black sky with four circles orbiting around a sun. The kids' pictures had never been entirely accurate, but they'd been good enough. Vallus, the sandy planet, was always depicted in shades of yellow and brown. Hakora was always shown as green and blue. Astoria – her own planet – was a mixture of different reddish land masses and vast oceans. And Corinez was always shown as completely white. The ice planet.

She'd spent her life looking at that white planet and focusing all her rage on it.

Now, as they shot away from the violence in the space around them, Ash felt swamped with guilt. She'd never asked questions. She'd never demanded answers. It seemed that those around her had never asked questions either. Were they all just too wrapped up in the immediacy of the next attack to think about what had happened in the past? She'd accepted they were at war with Corinez and that the people of Corinez were the enemy. They were bad.

Or were they?

Ezra banked the fighter to the right to avoid some remnant of a destroyed craft. There were dual controls on this craft and Ash wasn't sure which were the primary. This could get ugly. The last thing she wanted to do on her way to a potential peace mission was shoot down more ships.

"Wanna tell me what this is about – what that is?" He rolled his eyes in the direction of the package that was behind her seat.

She positioned her hands on her own controls. "Remember I told you how something got transported over to me on the pilot test?"

He frowned. "Well, yeah. But what's that got to do with anything?"

"Okay, so I didn't know what it was. Then the three Commanders sent it with me when they put me on the shuttle to the Library, and I still didn't know what it was. I got to the Library, gave it to Orius, and then…everything else happened and I forgot to ask questions."

"Is this a quiz? Because I'm going to fail. Are you finally telling me what it is you've got?"

She nodded and bit her lip. "Turns out I know what it is. It's from Corinez – at least I'm pretty sure it is."

Ezra wrinkled his nose and threw a glance at it. "How can something like that be so important?"

She took a deep breath. "I think this is the device that was stolen from Corinez that made it slip into an ice age."

A blast erupted in the sky next to them and Ezra yanked at the control lever as another scattering of explosions littered around them.

Ash twisted her head, trying to get a better look behind them. But there was no time – one of their own fighters appeared, showering their pursuer with fire.

"Whoopee!" came the recognizable shout over the comm.

Ezra and Ash exchanged glances. "Castille," they said together.

"Thanks, partner," Ezra said automatically into the comm, as Ash's stomach twisted and turned. That was someone's child, brother, sister, parent who had died in the sky next to them.

"Anytime!" yelled Castille as he turned his fighter and headed back into the thick of the fighting.

Ezra cursed under his breath and banged his hand against the console. "Stupid, slow," he growled.

She knew exactly what he meant. This ship didn't have the manoeuvrability of the one-man fighters. "Why are you in an X32?"

He shrugged. "Most ships are beyond repair at this point – and you've seen what's going on. There's no time to fix anything properly. I just fly whatever I can."

Ash could spot a number of other fighters in the sky. Her stomach twisted. Even from here she could recognize that there wasn't a single fighter squadron intact.

Before she would have had the same mentality as Castille – us against them. But now? It felt like she was questioning every decision she'd ever made.

She took over the controls as they moved further and further away from the fighting.

They flew in silence, each of them focusing on the white planet in front of them. It was so easy to think of it as that: the White Planet. A planet covered in snow and ice that looked cold, heartless and virtually uninhabitable.

But as they grew closer, the planet started to take shape.

They dropped out of space and into the atmosphere.

White turned into mountains and deep ravines. Now they had a better view, Ash could see smudges of blue against the thick ice fields. Every now and then, there would be another tiny smudge of...something. A blip on the landscape that didn't look quite right.

She checked the coordinates Commander Trinley had given her. The fighter was close to where they thought one of the rebel bases could be. She'd chosen this one deliberately, because it was also close to the last known coordinates of Trik's fighter.

"Start scanning for signs of Trik," she said as she pressed her nose up against the glass.

"Could he land in this?" asked Ezra. "I mean, does the snow here have firm ground underneath it?"

She shook her head. "We can't possibly know. But no emergency beacon has been activated from his fighter. So we just need to look." *And cross our fingers*, she wanted to add.

Ezra's face was grim. They both knew what wasn't being said out loud. A ship that had no emergency beacon signalling had usually disintegrated into pieces so small the beacon didn't exist any more. It often meant things were hopeless.

But Ash wasn't ready to let go of an Academy mate so easily. If Trik was down there, in that winter wasteland, how could he possibly survive for more than a few hours?

They had to look. They had to try.

Ezra moved in a pattern, sweeping the landscape around the coordinates, keeping the fighter low so it wouldn't trigger radar signals. They were lucky they weren't already under attack, but it was likely the dogfight in the sky near the space station was keeping everyone busy.

They swept one way, then the other. There was nothing distinguishable about this landscape. No obvious military constructions. "Do you think they live underground?" Ezra asked, his nose wrinkling as he kept scanning.

Everything was just white to Ash. It all started to blur into one. Maybe this was hopeless. Maybe she'd left her colleagues behind to die, while she'd hopped off on some wishful mission that would never come to anything.

"There!" Ezra pointed and thrust their controller forward.

"Where?" Ash's heartbeat quickened as she leaned forward in her seat, scanning to pick out what it was he had seen.

Her stomach rolled. A grey patch in among the white. It was further away than they'd expected, on the absolute outer edge of the area they were scanning.

They'd already covered this area. But last time, it had been her eyes that had been looking in this direction – not Ezra's. The grey patch must have been lost in her blind spot.

"Oh no," she whispered, partly at the guilt of having missed the debris, and partly at the sight emerging in front of them.

As Ezra hovered lower, snow flurried up around them. Pieces of wing and engine were scattered around. "I'm going to land," Ezra said. "Hold on."

For a few seconds they were surrounded by snow, whiting out the cockpit glass. Ash's stomach clenched, waiting for the landing gear to find some kind of purchase on the unknown land beneath them. A few moments later there was a reassuring shudder.

Ezra leaned forward and released the cockpit hood, letting in an icy blast. There were no steps for them to descend so they both scrambled along the wing, jumping into the snow underneath.

"Oooph!" Ash landed in snow up to her thighs, suddenly realizing just how cold it was. For a second she flashbacked to Tallux 5. Despite everything else that had happened there, they'd had some fun moments in the snow.

Now though, there was no time for fun and they hadn't really thought to dress for the climate. There hadn't been a chance. The package landed in the snow next to her. It was much deeper here than it had been on Tallux 5.

The debris of Trik's fighter was scattered around in metal shards of all sizes. "There!" she yelled.

A little ahead there was a tiny flash of red. The seats in those fighters were red. Ezra tried to run, but ended up wading unsteadily through the snow. Ash tried to follow. Walking in thigh-high snow was much tougher than it looked.

By the time they got closer to the chair, they could see it was turned on its side and partly submerged in the snow. Ash wasn't sure she wanted to walk around to the front, but Ezra didn't hesitate.

He kneeled down as best as he could in the snow, his arms moving wildly as he tried to sweep some of it away.

Ash moved around. It was Trik. Still strapped into his pilot seat, his helmet still on his head.

"Wait!" she yelled as Ezra went to yank the helmet free. She moved right up beside him and slid her hands around Trik's neck. "Okay, do it now. Be gentle."

Ezra lifted the visor then placed his hands on either side of the helmet, giving it a wiggle, then easing it off Trik's head.

Trik's eyes were closed. Ash reached out and touched him and noticed for the first time that the rest of his body was shivering.

"We have to try and get him moving. Get some heat into him. Who knows how long he's been lying here. Help me."

She released the harness on his pilot seat and tried to wrestle his arms out. Because the seat was sideways it was easy to get the top arm free, but the one underneath proved more difficult. She reached right down, digging her face into the snow and spluttering it back out while she wriggled his arm out of the strap.

Ezra helped her, pulling Trik from the seat and into his arms, talking to him the whole time. "Come on, Trik. Wake up."

"Give me a sec," said Ash. She patted Trik down, making sure there were no obvious broken bones, then went around his other side, so she could sling one of his arms across her shoulders.

"I think everything seems okay." She looked out across the white landscape. "But where can we take him?"

Ezra looked around too. "The only place is back to the fighter. At least we can get him out of the wind."

Ash's hands were freezing already. She reached over and touched Trik's cheek for a second and he winced. "Trik? Try and wake up. We're going to move you – get you out of this snow."

For a few seconds his eyelids flickered, then they finally fluttered open. His face was completely screwed up, as if he couldn't quite remember what had happened, or understand what he was seeing.

"Ezra?" he muttered as he gave his head a shake. "Ash?" He pulled back. "What the…"

Ash leaned closer and patted her hand against his chest. "Yeah, it's me. We came to rescue you. Didn't want you freezing to death out here."

She pulled him a little closer to her hip, hoping that some of her own warmth would flow through his shaking body. He was clearly still groggy. His forehead creased. "Where…

am I?" His body sagged a bit again.

Ezra hoisted him back up. "You crash-landed on Corinez."

"I did?" He looked completely blank. "Darn it, which one of those creeps shot me down? I'll get them. I'll get them next time."

Ezra gave a wry laugh. "You don't exactly have much of a ship left. And we need to get off this frozen pit before we all freeze to death. Let's do that first, eh?"

They stumbled through the snow. Trik's legs dragged at first, and then started to take a little weight. It was tougher than Ash had ever imagined. She could barely lift her own legs, let alone support her friend. Trik was no lightweight. The cold wind was biting at her skin, cutting through the flight suit she was wearing. The snow had got inside her boots, so every step was a squelch, feeling heavier and heavier than the one before. It didn't help that snow had soaked through the legs of the suit, weighing her down even more. Were they ever going to reach the fighter?

Every muscle in Ash's body ached. She was shivering now too, desperately hoping to get back inside the fighter and pull the cockpit down, so they could at least avoid freezing while they decided what to do next. It would be a tight fit, but right now she didn't care.

Ezra was struggling too. Their heavy breaths were clouding the air around them. "Whose idea was this?" he muttered.

"Yours," she said. "I was always coming, you just came along for the ride."

"You think you could have landed in this snow?" he

challenged, but there was an edge of laughter in his voice.

"I know I did," Trik cut in sarcastically and they all stopped for a few seconds, laughing and catching their breath.

This was what she'd missed. She hadn't even been that good at it. But the camaraderie, the companionship, was still there between the people she'd trained with. It had made her heart swell when they'd all been in the sky defending the Library.

Because being the Guardian was lonely. Waking up every day in that giant bed and wandering aisles and aisles of ancient artefacts, with only a hologram for company, didn't do anything for the soul. Eating dinner alone every night had made Ash lose her appetite. Sometimes all she wanted was a vacant "Hello" or a nod in a corridor. Anything to let her know that other people were breathing the same air she was. That she wasn't entirely alone.

Her eyes were starting to adjust to the glare that came off the bright white snow. For the most part it was dazzling. But now, the landscape was starting to look a bit more unusual. Lumpy in an odd sort of way.

"Ezra…" she started to say.

But the words strangled in her throat as everything happened at once.

In unison, a dozen shapes emerged from the snow – some rising up only a few paces away.

Men and women, dressed in thick white layers, with white paste smeared across their faces. The snow just seemed to fall off them, as if now they had decided to rise, it didn't dare stay on their bodies. They formed a circle around Trik, Ezra and Ash. They looked like terrifying ice warriors, waiting for their prey.

All had weapons strapped across their chests.

"I guess the fighter's a no then," said Ezra in a voice so low she barely heard it.

It was the last thing she remembered before everything went black.

CHAPTER THIRTY-THREE

Ash was shivering. But her body was confused, because this room was warm. Was there somewhere warm on Corinez?

Ash tried to lift her head but the room swam and her head pounded.

"Yeow," she murmured as she put her head back down on the hard surface.

"Ash?" A hand landed on her shoulder and gave her a shake.

She winced. It didn't matter that they hadn't touched her head, the shake was enough to make it pound even more.

She snuck a hand through her hair. There was a large egg-sized lump at the back of her skull. No wonder her head hurt.

She blinked. The room was lit by a pale-blue glow. Ash sat up and immediately felt a wave of nausea. She dipped her head down and put it between her knees.

flying preferences and settings. It also came with a string of command codes that allowed the ship to be identified by its pilot. Pass codes for docking procedures, safe flight paths through war zones – basically all the information that an enemy fighter would need to fly right into a space station unchallenged.

Ezra shook his head. "There wasn't time to configure things. My own ship was damaged – they gave me the first ship they could find. Everything on it was unlocked."

"Oh no." She sagged back against the hard wall behind her. The Star Corporation Academy was already in bad shape. Now? They'd just signed its death warrant.

"Yeah," said Trik. "Great rescue, guys."

Now she understood why he was so mad. At least his fighter had shattered into indistinguishable pieces. Theirs? It would give the Corinezians everything they needed to know.

Fear struck into her bones and she looked about quickly, ignoring the searing pains in her head. "Where's the Kronos device?"

"You mean this?" Trik kicked at something beneath the bench he was sitting on. "They haven't even looked at it. They were too interested in the ship. They just searched us for weapons and threw us in here."

She let out a sigh of relief and stood up, crossing the room in a few steps and picking the package from the ground.

"What is it anyway?" asked Trik.

"It might just be the thing that saves us all."

Ash pounded on the door.

"I need to speak to Aurora Damocles! I need to speak to her now!"

For a few minutes there was silence, then there was a grinding noise as if something was being slid back from the door.

The door opened and two heavily armed guards stared at her. They had dark, deep-set eyes contrasting with their extremely pale skin.

"Take me to Aurora Damocles. I need to speak to her."

They looked at her suspiciously. "How do you know Aurora?"

"I have a message for her." She'd deliberately not answered the question in the hope they wouldn't notice, but it didn't work.

"She doesn't speak to strangers." One of the guards started to close the door again.

"She'll speak to me."

He raised his eyebrow.

"I have a peace message for her."

The guards looked at each other and laughed. "Peace? We're about to conquer all three of your measly planets. There won't be peace. We don't need it. We don't want it."

"Are you sure? Are you sure that Aurora won't want to speak to me? What if I tell you I have something that could help your planet, something to get you out of this ice age?"

One of the guards leaned in so quickly she didn't have time to react. He grabbed her and pulled her right up to his face. "What are you talking about?"

Ezra jumped forward. "Get off her," he yelled, swinging at the guy.

The other guard was quicker. He lifted the butt of his weapon and smashed it into Ezra's face, leaving him sprawled on the ground. "Take her," he hissed, kicking at Ezra to push his body back inside the door. The last thing she saw was the blood smeared across his face.

The guards dragged her down a long, dark corridor. They'd looked at the Kronos device and shrugged when she'd pleaded to bring it with her – neither of them realized how important it was.

It was clear they were underground. What surprised Ash most was the warmth. Somehow, the Corinezians were managing to keep this place warm. But didn't that mean the ground above shouldn't be covered with snow?

She gulped. Just how far underground were they?

Twice they stopped at large security doors with more guards. Twice, there were short conversations before she was dragged on through.

"Don't talk," said one of the guards as he jerked her alongside him. Eventually a large steel door in front of her opened and she sucked in a breath.

It was a large oval room. It looked centuries old. The seating was arranged on different levels, with all seats facing a central grand-looking chair against one wall.

There were people scattered around the room, several on their feet, shouting.

It only took a few moments to realize that this was some kind of government. One of the men was arguing his point angrily. "Bomb them, finish them off. They would do it to us if they'd half a chance. It's time that they realize we have no empathy for them."

His words were directed towards a woman. Ash screwed up her face a little, trying to get a better look. The woman seemed far away, or maybe it was just that she was tiny. She was sitting on the central chair. It was higher than all the rest. And the more Ash looked at it, the more it reminded her of a throne from a childhood storybook.

Time felt as if it was slipping away from her and Ash automatically took a step forward, causing the guard to clamp an iron-like grip on her shoulder.

The woman had white hair. It must be long, because it was coiled in an elaborate braid around her head. Her skin was wrinkled and pale. Her bone structure was clear, and even though she was bundled in furs and blankets, Ash could tell how thin she was underneath it all. From just the way that the skin hung on her face it was clear that any fat reserves were long since gone.

The woman fixed sharp eyes on the man who was shouting, narrowing her gaze. Ash held her breath. Somehow she could tell this diminutive woman was someone to be reckoned with.

Her booming voice completely surprised Ash.

"Take your seat, Barock. Your opinion is noted." She paused a second before adding dismissively, "But completely unworthy."

Another man who was also on his feet took up the argument: "It is time. We have them. They have ruined our world. They have killed our children. Our revenge is due."

As he kept talking, Ash noticed others. Around the top edge of the room were men and women. Most of them were bundled up in clothes that looked as if they'd seen better days. But what struck her most was their faces. Every single one of them was thinner than the people back on her own planet. Their cheeks hollow, their complexions pale. It seemed it wasn't only their leader who was short of food.

Ash glanced at the guard next to her. He was bigger. He was bulkier. Presumably those involved in potential combat were given the lion's share of food on Corinez.

She turned to face him. "Is that Aurora?"

"I told you to be quiet." His lips barely moved.

Someone seated in front of them turned around. "Who interrupts our session?"

The guard's grip on her shoulder tightened. She couldn't help but let out an involuntary yelp.

Simultaneously, all faces in the room turned towards them. "I told you to shut up," the guard muttered as he steered her down the steps towards the centre of the room.

The room wasn't cold, but the prickling sensation on Ash's skin felt icy. She could sense the way they were all looking at her. *Intruder. Alien. Enemy.*

They didn't even know who she was. Yet.

Aurora Damocles kept her steely gaze on Ash the whole way down the steps. The guard sighed as he reached her, giving the briefest nod of his head. Ash noted it. He was giving Aurora her place, but he wasn't that sold on it. Interesting. And perhaps dangerous.

"We captured her and two others near the Reiss Fountain. One fighter had crash-landed, the other was intact. We've retrieved it."

"And?"

Aurora's voice was chilly, making it very clear the guard hadn't gotten to the point he should have.

The guard gritted his teeth. "Then this one demanded to speak to you." He gave Ash a sideways look. "She asked for you by name."

Aurora Damocles pushed herself to her feet, her body already physically shaking. Every footstep was a challenge as she made her way down the few steps to meet Ash.

"Name?" The word was like a command.

"Ash Yang."

"You're a pilot from the Star Corporation."

It wasn't a question. "Y…yes. I mean, no."

Aurora tilted her head and looked at Ash. "So which is it? Yes or no?"

Those eyes. They seemed to undo all Ash's defences. Those eyes had seen more murder, lives lost, and a greater struggle for daily existence than Ash ever had. Those eyes told Ash if she messed this up, she was dead. This wasn't some sweet, loving grandmother. This was a woman who was tired of this world. Tired of fighting for every morsel of food. Tired of constantly having to fight not only against three other planets, but also against the hostile environment of her own. Her body looked like a skeleton merely covered in skin. A body with no life left in it.

This wasn't the time to be coy.

"It's a no. I'm Ash Yang. I'm originally from Astoria. I went to the Star Corporation Academy. I tried to train as a pilot. But I didn't make it. Instead, I was sent elsewhere."

"Your point?"

"I'm the Guardian."

Ash's eyes were fixed firmly on Aurora's face. She could see others on either side look at each other blankly. But Aurora wasn't blank.

The change was gradual. Her jaw tightened, a tic forming at the base of one cheek, and another at the edge of her eye. Like she was trying to hold the fury in.

Ash could almost see a countdown ticking in Aurora's mind. Before she could open her mouth to speak further, Aurora had reached under her clothes and pulled out a large hooked dagger. As she moved towards Ash she limped, one leg slightly dragging, pain etched across her face.

Ash automatically stepped backwards, straight into the chest of one of the guards. She spoke quickly. "I came to return something that I think was stolen from your planet."

The last word had barely left Ash's mouth before the

dagger was under her chin. She wanted to gulp. She wanted to swallow. But she was pretty sure the tip of it had already pierced her skin. Talking or moving in any way would not be wise.

Aurora's large blue eyes widened. It was like she'd still been acting on Ash's first words when she'd heard the second.

Her other frail hand reached forward and grabbed Ash's hair with surprising strength. "You stole from us?"

Ash didn't speak. She couldn't. Not right now. The guard to her right looked completely confused. His eyes were darting to others round about. It seemed that Aurora was acting out of character. Great.

Ash's head was yanked again and the dagger repositioned just underneath her eye. "You dare set foot on Corinez?"

A trickle of cold sweat ran down her spine. The plan to win friends, create a good impression and find peace was really not going well.

"I had to," she said in a voice that only Aurora could hear. "I had to right the wrong that I think has been done."

Aurora pushed her sideways with such fury that Ash landed with a thud on the floor, the breath whisked from her lungs. She started to cough and choke.

"How dare you come to Corinez? You've murdered most of my people. You've stolen our land. You left us with a legacy that would watch us wither and die. And you dare to set foot here again?"

Ash was trying to catch her breath. She was doing her

The legs of her flight suit were dry. She put her hand back on the lump – as if holding it could protect it – and winced again as she looked up.

Trik was sitting on the other side of the small room, his legs stretched out in front of him and his arms folded over his chest. He looked angry.

Ezra was sitting immediately opposite her. His head was sagged on one of his hands; his eyes met hers.

"How do you feel?" he asked.

"Like I want to be sick on my shoes."

He gave a half-hearted smile. "You always seem to be sick around me."

She squeezed her eyes shut for a moment as she straightened up. Every movement was causing pain. "I take it one of them hit me. How long was I out?"

Trik answered. "We have no idea. They pulled us out of the snow. Got a machine to drag the fighter underground, then threw us in here."

"They have the fighter?"

Ezra and Trik exchanged a glance.

"What?"

Ezra sighed. "Trik's ship was unsalvageable, blown to pieces. Ours? They'll probably be able to download all the files."

The words struck fear into her heart. "It wasn't locked up?"

Any pilot had a manual plug on their belt they connected up to the fighter with. It meant the craft would know their

371

best to keep her head. But all her own feelings of anger and resentment were threatening to surface.

She pushed herself to her feet. This time, when she spoke, she made sure others could hear.

"I came here today because I thought I should, and could, do something to stop the war between our planets."

Ash kept her voice steady and ignored the catcalls and shouts of scorn from the rings of chairs around her.

She put her hand to her chest. "Yes, I'm from Astoria. Do you think I wanted to come here? Do you think I wanted to set foot on this hideous planet? You killed my sister. You bombed our village and destroyed the school. The school where my sister was learning. My mother and father died soon after. So you made me an orphan." She held out her hands. "You all did. You wiped out my family."

Ash put her hand to her chest again.

"I know what it feels like to hate you all. I know what it feels like to spend years of my life dreaming of ways to kill every living person on this planet. In fact, I made it my mission to do just that, to learn how to be a fighter pilot, so I could spend the rest of my days doing to you all what you had done to my family." She turned to face Aurora. "And do you know what? It seemed like the best job in the world to me. It was what I wanted more than anything else in this galaxy."

Ash couldn't hide the venom in her voice and she didn't want to. She wanted them all to hear it. She wanted them all to know how much she'd hated them. She wanted them to know what her intentions had been.

Ash stopped for a few moments as the people in the room looked at her in disbelief. She was as good as signing her death warrant. There were a few murmurs, a few mutters of "Kill her", among some of the people crowded together.

She kept her voice steady. "You might be pleased to know I didn't make it as a fighter pilot. I was allocated another role – one that I didn't even know existed. The role of the Guardian."

"Get to the point," the guard next to her growled.

She nodded. "Somewhere, far away from here, is a place called the Library. The Library holds artefacts from different planets across the universe. Artefacts that have been taken away from a planet, usually to stop some kind of war. On most occasions, these artefacts are eventually returned. While they're in the Library they're looked after by the Guardian. The Guardian has the power to transport to any world in the universe."

Ash took a long breath.

"I'm not the first Guardian. There have been many before me. But not all of them have conducted themselves in the way that they should have. If I'm right, the Kronos device was stolen from your planet by one of my predecessors. An Anterrean. Not by anyone from Astoria, or from Vallus, or from Hakora."

Murmurs started around her.

"I'm here to give it back. I'm here to help. There's been so much hatred between our planets. So many deaths. And while I told you I'd stored up a lot of hate myself, I realize now that was wrong. I didn't understand what had caused the war between our planets, and I'm embarrassed to admit that I accepted we were at war without asking questions. It's time for this to stop. And I hope I can help make that happen."

For a moment there was a booming silence in the room. An air of complete disbelief.

Aurora let out a snort. She started to turn away. "Kill her," she barked at one of the guards.

But the guard hesitated. It seemed he didn't want to follow orders blindly.

Ash felt a wave of panic grip her. "Do you want to stay like this? Do you want your planet permanently covered in ice?" she yelled. "You're fighting a war that has no merit. No real reason behind it. It's time to stop. It's time to think. It's time to put your people first."

Aurora whipped back around, a gleam of pure fury in her eyes. "You think I haven't spent my life putting my people first? How dare you come to my planet and talk to me like this!"

The guard was holding Ash, but his grip wasn't firm. He was looking at her in a half-bewildered, half-*what-should-I-do* kind of way.

Ash straightened her back. "I have to dare," she said calmly and clearly. "I have to dare, because this war isn't right. This war could be stopped. And it's my job to do that."

She held up the Kronos device.

"This is what you need. This is what you need to bring your planet back from the ice age. I've brought it to you today as an offering of peace."

She pulled back the brown sacking and held the Kronos device out. The crystal in the middle looked a little dull in this room, but the device itself was clearly more technologically advanced than this civilization now appeared to be. It seemed that putting a planet into an ice age had reprioritized things. Living and surviving had taken precedence over everything else.

Aurora looked at Ash in disgust. "You. You fool. For a Guardian, you're not exactly the brightest, are you? Now I have it, I can kill you." She leaned a little closer. "And I will. You, and your friends."

More guards appeared through the same door Ash had entered by, pulling Trik and Ezra with them at gunpoint. They were pushed down the stairs to the middle of the room, next to her, then roughly thrown to their knees.

She wanted to close her eyes, twist her bangle and just get out of there. But Ash would never do that. She would never leave her friends to a fate that she'd created for them.

Her heart was racing in her chest, her skin prickled and her mouth was drier than it had ever felt before. Sheer fear could have the weirdest effect on the body. But she tried her best to push it all aside. The last thing she needed to do was act like she didn't have a plan. Even though every single tiny element of control had long since slipped through her fingers.

Ash tried to keep a slightly confident tone in her voice. "And what use would that be? The Kronos device was stolen long before any of us was born. The knowledge of how to use and maintain it has long since been lost. Kill me, and you'll spend the rest of your life trying to work out how to save your planet – even though the key component is right in front of you."

Aurora's eyes narrowed again. Ash was taking a gamble – a gamble that Aurora didn't have a single clue where the machinery that controlled all this was, or how it worked.

She'd never prayed so hard that knowledge hadn't been passed down a family line for generations. If it had? She was probably taking her last breaths right now.

"I know how to use it, and I can show you. Because I came here as a friend, Aurora. No matter what you think. But only so long as you call off the attack on the space station right now, and you agree to let my friends go unharmed."

It was clear that Aurora was suspicious. "How can you know how an ancient device works? Have you lived for thousands of years?" Her tone was mocking.

Ash shook her head. "Of course I haven't. But I saw the schematics on another planet – another planet that had been terraformed, transformed from an ice age into a place with a mild climate and fertile lands. If it can happen there, it can happen here. After all, it's happened here before."

Part of her wanted to be angry with Aurora – angry with her threats and behaviour. But as she breathed in again, Ash caught a glimpse of something in Aurora's eyes. An age of sadness. A weariness that had been long since earned. All of a sudden, she just looked like a tired old woman. Someone who needed an arm around her. Someone who needed someone else to take the permanent weight off her shoulders.

"Let me help, Aurora. Let me try. Give me a chance. Give *this* a chance. For your planet, and for the others. What would it feel like to wake up one day and know we weren't at war?" She gave her head a little shake. "I don't know, because I've never lived that life. But I'm not afraid to tell you that I want it. Call off your fighters. You have nothing to lose, and everything to gain."

Ash couldn't catch an easy breath. Maybe it was being underground. Or maybe it was the tight feeling of hope across her chest. She dared to look sideways at her friends on the ground. Both of them were looking right at her.

There was so much emotion on their faces. Hope. Grief. Maybe a tiny glimmer of admiration. Nothing else mattered more than this moment. Had Ash done enough? She could only hope and pray.

One of the men who'd been arguing with Aurora earlier cleared his throat. "I think this is something we should vote on."

"Agreed," said a man in a low voice next to him, who hadn't quite raised his head.

Aurora gave the tiniest sway and Ash turned her head to the guard nearest her. He moved smoothly, taking a few quick steps and sliding a hand behind Aurora. "What are your wishes?" he said in a voice barely above a whisper.

It was then that Ash noticed. They had the same eyes. The same nose. They must be related somehow. She could see the respect in the guard's eyes towards Aurora. The protectiveness.

Family. Aurora still had family. Ash didn't. Tears threatened in her eyes. She wouldn't cry here. She just wouldn't.

Aurora turned her head. "Let them vote." There was something new in the way she said the words. An element of relief.

A man to her left stood up. "We vote. If you wish to continue with the immediate attack on the other planets in the solar system…" He paused as if he wanted to add in his own dialogue, then pressed his lips together and gave an almost imperceptible shake of his head. "Then raise your right hand and vote yes. If you wish the attack to stop, and the chance to see if this" – he gestured to the Kronos device – "mechanism can make a change to our planet, then raise your left hand and vote no."

The vote was silent. Ash stood with her heart in her mouth as each person in the Corinez parliament raised a right hand for yes, or a left hand for no.

She was counting, counting on her fingers, then in her head.

To begin with it almost seemed like a tit-for-tat vote. One yes, then one no. Nerves were getting the better of her. She moved over to where the Kronos device had been laid. She ran her hand lightly over the centre, where the stone was set. This object could mean the difference between life and death for this planet. For lots of plants, animals and people, it already had been.

Things had to change. They just had to.

"Stop," she said suddenly.

She didn't want to wait for a vote. She didn't want this to come down to a decision that could be made by one person.

She said it again, this time more loudly. "Stop!" She held up her hand until she was sure she had the attention in the room.

Trik and Ezra shot her a look as if she was crazy.

And likely she was. But she was sure about what she had to do.

She picked up the device. "Don't vote. You don't need to. I'm going to give this to you anyway. I'm going to take it now and try to make it work. Your planet and your people have waited long enough for this. I want things to change. I want *all* our lives to change. And I'm going to start here, and I'm going to start now."

She turned back to Aurora and the guard.

"I assume there must be machinery far beneath the surface of the planet. The Kronos device works with the tectonic plates. There will be technology, computer systems. Maybe things you've ignored for centuries. Can you take me there?"

There was an exchange of glances. Aurora spoke first. "We're not even entirely sure where to start. No one has been in the rooms far beneath us for many years. There was no need, no point. No one understood the technology there, or how to work it."

A sneaky little feeling of dread started to creep in. But Ash pushed it away.

"But you know where the rooms are, and you can still access them?"

Aurora nodded.

"Then send me down with your guard. Let me see if I can make things work."

There was a few moments' hesitation, then Aurora turned to the guard. It seemed that she was willing to give Ash a chance. A chance to earn the trust of the people of Corinez, with no guarantees in return.

"Take her down, Isaac, take her down and see if there's anything that can be done."

He looked nervous, torn at the thought of leaving Aurora on her own. But he guided her back to her central seat and then picked up the Kronos device. "Follow me."

He moved at such a pace that Ash struggled to keep up. His strides were long and determined. Up the stairs and out of the parliament chamber, along an endless corridor, and then down another few that were darker and colder than the rest. There were cobwebs, scuttling noises, and finally, a set of ancient-looking elevators. Isaac flicked a switch, and there was the longest wait before some lights flickered on around them.

He glanced at Ash. "Power. What little we have, we use

carefully. In all my life, I can't ever remember the power being on here."

Ash cringed as the doors slid slowly open with a horrible hissing sound. Chunks of metal and rust littered the floor.

She stepped inside. The air was old and fetid. The tang of ancient metal and oil filled the small space. Isaac pressed a button and there was a jerk, then a grinding noise as the doors closed and the elevator started to move downwards.

Down, down, down. The lights flickered on and off, giving the sensation that at any moment the power would short out completely and the two of them would be left here, stranded, for ever.

There was a thud as the lift ground to a halt and the doors took their time opening again. This time when they stepped out, lights flickered on as they walked.

The walls down here were smooth and shiny metal. Like they belonged in a different time and place. Isaac paused at a few doors, raising a hand to let them slide open, before looking inside and shaking his head.

Now it was just the two of them, he gave her a half-hearted smile. "I've never been down here before. It's all just legend to me. It's some kind of weird computer thing, isn't it?"

Ash nodded and then gulped. At one point this place must have been a hive of activity with a whole array of people who knew and understood the technology surrounding the Kronos device. All of them now lost.

She started checking some of the doors on the opposite

side of the corridor from Isaac. Could she really do this?

Isaac broke into her thoughts. "Wait. Could this be it?" he said as he stood back from a door he'd just opened. He gestured for her to go inside.

As soon as she stepped in, lights came on and computer screens flickered to life. She sent a little prayer up. This place must consume a whole host of energy. Would Corinez actually have enough for her to do what was needed?

As the room was illuminated, Ash realized there was a window at the end, separating this room from the next.

She moved closer, her heart leaping as she recognized the equipment beyond. It was the same as she'd seen on the screens in the high-security room on U62. The plans she'd tried her best to memorize.

She pushed open the door to the glass room and stepped inside. The lights in here were sickeningly bright compared to all the rest. Isaac stared in bewilderment, moving slowly past the elaborate machinery in front of them both. He stopped at a few points, as if he was trying to work out what each part did.

There was an intricate array of metal filaments to one side that Ash didn't recognize. But she ignored them, moving across to parts that did look more familiar.

The machine itself was huge, filling the room completely – bigger than two star-fighters put together. An elaborate network of computer screens, both metal and glass, were distinguishable. Silver, bronze and gold glinted at different parts of the machine. Ash ran her hands along it. Her heart was buzzing almost as much as her skin at touching such an engineering marvel.

Her brain wanted to understand every element, every molecule of this machine and how it worked. But she knew that could easily take a lifetime, if not more. The truth was she had the information she needed. She'd seen the plans and formulas in Aldus Dexter's control room. She knew how to make this work.

"Here," she said, stopping in front of a glass panel installed in the side of the machine. "This is where the Kronos device goes."

Isaac was at her shoulder, looking down at the spot in the mechanism where there was a space shaped exactly like the Kronos device. His brow furrowed. "What? It just slots in there?"

Her heart started fluttering at a rapid pace. "It just slots in there," she repeated with assurance. What she didn't know was if a machine that had lain dormant for five hundred years would actually work again.

After a moment, he nudged her. "Well, go on then."

This was it. This was the moment that everything else rested on. A moment that could change the lives of all the people around her.

She tipped the Kronos device up on one side, guiding it into place until it could settle just above its destination point. Her hands were shaking.

"Want a hand?" asked Isaac.

She could sense that he wanted this just as much as

she did. And she shouldn't do this herself. A Guardian shouldn't change the path of a planet alone, it was only right that she do it with someone who lived there. "I'd love a hand," she said.

Isaac's arms slid in next to hers, holding the Kronos device carefully. "Ready?"

She nodded.

They counted together: "One, two, three." Then they pushed the device into place. It gave a satisfying click. And they both stood, waiting.

The waiting continued. Ash turned to Isaac, not sure what to say, just as a little whirr sounded somewhere.

They both froze, watching. It was like each piece of the machine came to life slowly; jolting, twisting, moving. Noises started to amplify around them. The filament strands to her right illuminated in a rainbow of colours. Digital screens appeared in the air around her, causing Isaac to jump back in alarm.

She smiled and shook her head. "It's fine. It's part of the machine."

He held out his hand shakily, near to one.

Her eyes skimmed over it. "Temperature," she said. "It's scanning the planet, I think." She turned to another, as pictures appeared automatically on the screen. "This one seems to be mapping the current positions of the tectonic plates." Another seemed to be doing mass calculations, as dozens of formulas and numbers streamed past.

A gentle hiss came from the left-hand side, where the

movements of the machinery had started to grow bigger.

"Think we should be in here?" asked Isaac as he grabbed her hand and pulled her to the glass door.

They closed it behind them just as a whole host of laser beams lit up the room. Red, green, yellow, blue – they were all connecting up different parts of the overall device. There was a rumble – a deep rumble, not from the glass room, but from the earth around them.

Ash watched as the crystal in the Kronos device lit up. It had always looked a slightly dull, pale green to her, but now it lit up the whole room with dazzling white light.

Every computer screen in their room sparked into life, with data scrolling across machines – much like the hovering screens inside. The overhead lights stopped flickering.

Isaac moved over to a central display, obviously trying to make sense of what he was seeing.

Ash joined him and looked at the diagram displayed. "Oh." Her hand went to her mouth as tiny pieces of the puzzle started to slot into place in her mind. She pointed at one part. "The Kronos device is self-generating for power. That's what those other connections are."

Isaac was shaking his head. "But what does it actually do?"

She waved her hand across the screen, watching as one diagram after another filled their view. "I'm not actually sure," she admitted. "But look. Here. It's something to do with tectonic plates. Something to do with stopping the continual collision of them at certain points across the planet. That's what caused this ice age, and it looks like the Kronos device has a way of stopping that happening."

She found another screen and keyed in a few figures, then gulped and turned around.

"I think this is the original programme. I think this can predict how long it will take to move the planet out of the ice age."

Isaac watched the numbers calculate on the screen. When they finally stopped scrolling, he took a deep breath. "Is that years?"

"I think so."

It was a long time. The changes would be gradual, over many, many years. The Kronos device was not a quick fix. But it would bring Corinez to life again.

She waited for Isaac's reaction. He was standing side-on and she didn't have a clear view of his face. Was he angry? Had he expected the flick of a switch and for everything to become green again? She had no idea what the expectations of the people on Corinez were – there had been no time for those conversations.

Isaac turned around to face her. "So, that number, that's when Corinez will be officially out of its ice age?"

She gave a slow, careful nod, still waiting for his thoughts.

After a few seconds he extended his hand out towards her. "The people of Corinez thank you, Guardian. You've given us hope. A reason to start planning again." He held out his other hand as his lips quirked into a smile. "And power, and a whole lot of new learning today."

Relief flooded through Ash as she clasped his hand in hers. "It's not new learning, it's relearning. Someone here knew all this to begin with. It just got lost along the way." She paused as she met his grey eyes. "Can we go stop a war now?"

His face broke into a wide smile. "Let's go stop a war."

CHAPTER THIRTY-FOUR

Everyone was celebrating.

The people of Corinez had been stunned. The story about the Kronos device had obviously seemed like some kind of fairy tale, lost in the mists of their past.

The reality was startling. There had been a few distant grumblings about the length of time things would take to change, but there was an overwhelming agreement to stop the current attacks. After five hundred years, the population of Corinez finally had hope for the future, and were willing to concentrate on that, rather than continuing with old, destructive grudges.

The moment where Isaac had thrown his arms around Aurora and whispered, "It's over," had brought tears to Ash's eyes and a cheer from around the room that housed the government of Corinez.

The hug lasted a long time. When Aurora finally leaned back and looked at Ash, she gave a gentle conciliatory nod.

"Give me the names of the leaders of the other planets," she said hoarsely. "I think it's time we all talked."

Ash, Trik and Ezra were given back their fighter and allowed to travel in a somewhat cramped style back to the Star Corporation Academy. After a two-minute argument, Trik agreed to pilot. Ash was exhausted and exhilarated at the same time. She wasn't sure how well she could concentrate.

The journey seemed longer on the way back, and as they approached the space station they all caught their breath.

"Oh my," breathed Ash.

Parts of the station were missing. They'd already known about the medical bay, but other areas had taken serious damage too. One of the Academy training rooms was partially destroyed. Through the protective force field, they could see desks still in place – obviously welded to the floor.

"I'm surprised the station still exists at all," said Ezra.

Trik's voice was tight. "But we need this place. We need this place so badly. Even if we aren't at war with Corinez in the future, there's always the threat from other solar systems. We have to be prepared. We have to help save the station."

They nodded in agreement as Trik landed the ship in the battered docking bay. As they left the fighter, the atmosphere was odd. There were only a few people doing their duties. There was a feeling of everyone still being in a dazed state following the last attack.

Ash made her way to the control room. This time the

door wasn't secured, it was lying open. There were only a few staff, and Commander Trinley was sitting at one of the consoles. She stood as soon as Ash walked in. The look of desolation on her face filled Ash with fear.

Ash swallowed. Her mouth had never felt so dry.

"How bad is it?" she asked.

Commander Trinley blinked, and in that second, Ash could see a world of hurt.

"Forty lost, sixty-seven injured on the station. Damage to major systems, emergency repairs underway." She took a breath and continued. "Twenty-five fighters lost. Another twenty need serious repairs."

"Commander Anand and Commander Clay?" Their absence from the control room was conspicuous – just like it had been before.

Commander Trinley's voice dropped to almost a whisper. "Commander Clay died at the start of the attack. Commander Anand is injured." The woman looked exhausted, but she straightened her shoulders. "Give me a report." She paused for a few moments. "Please tell me this was all worth it."

Ash's voice shook. "I think it's over. I think it's all over."

The few heads in the room turned towards her. She blinked at the enormity of her words before continuing.

"The Kronos device has been returned to Corinez. Activation appears to have been successful. But it will be years before Corinez comes out of their current ice age. Aurora Damocles is their leader. She understands the device wasn't stolen by any of the neighbouring planets and she's agreed to discuss a temporary ceasefire. I need to arrange a meeting with the leaders of the other planets."

The control room was silent. Ash thought she might have heard a grain of sand if it dropped.

"Lin," Commander Trinley said sharply. "Get the leaders on comm." She turned back to Ash, "Do you have a way to contact Aurora Damocles?"

Ash nodded and handed the transmission codes over to Lin.

A few minutes later she was sitting next to Commander Trinley in a small undamaged room on the space station.

She breathed deeply, sliding her hands under her thighs to stop them shaking. She wasn't Ash Yang from the dusty village on Astoria any more. She couldn't let herself think like that. She was here as Guardian of the Library. A role she still had to decide if she would keep.

Lin's voice came over the comm. "All leaders available."

The screen lit up in four squares and the leaders of each of the four planets of the solar system appeared. Each person would be able to see all the people they were talking to.

Ash was so conscious that none of the other leaders had ever seen Aurora before, and likewise she'd never had contact with any of these people before. Aurora looked proud, dressed in a purple cloak with her white hair braided and pinned neatly around her head. She gave Ash the briefest of nods.

Commander Trinley started. "Thank you for joining us. I am hopeful that today marks a momentous day in our history."

She nodded to Ash, who stared at the faces on the screen. This was her moment. The moment when she could stop the war that had been the only way of life she'd ever known.

She tilted her chin upwards and spoke from the heart. "I am delighted you all agreed to this conference. I am the Guardian of the Library at the End of the Universe, and I'd like to tell you all a story that should explain how we ended up in the middle of a war that none of us are responsible for…"

Four hours later, their solar system was still a long way from complete peace but a temporary ceasefire had been agreed. That would have to do for now. The lines of communication were open for the first time in centuries. It was a good start.

Ash spent the next few hours doing anything she could to help her colleagues on the space station. Emergency repairs were prioritized, including work on the shields. There might not be any more direct attacks expected, but space debris drifted carelessly and could still cause significant damage.

Eventually Ash and her friends gathered in the room that had been set up as a temporary medical bay. Arona was still groggy from her head injury, and the rest of them sat around her bed.

"What now?" asked Castille.

"Now, we hope the peace lasts," said Ezra. "And in the meantime, we help rebuild."

Trik gave a short laugh. "You really think that peace can happen here? And what about us? We're fighter pilots. What use are we in peacetime?"

He looked genuinely annoyed and Ash couldn't quite work out if he was angry or still just overwhelmed by everything.

"They'll always need pilots," said Arona from her bed. "We just need to find a new place to fit."

There was a temporary silence as all eyes turned to Ash. She waited for one of them to ask the question. Ezra cracked first. "And what about you? What are you going to do?"

Ash bit her bottom lip. "The only thing I *can* do. I'm going to go back to the Library and make my decision about what happens next."

"What *does* happen next?" asked Trik.

Ash met his gaze. "Truth? I know what I have to do. I just need to have the courage to do it."

"We believe in you, Ash," Ezra said quietly.

"No," said Arona as she pushed herself up into a sitting position. "Don't say that." She gave a soft smile. "We believe in you, Guardian." She gave a salute and added, "Fly true and may the stars protect you."

The rest stood and all turned towards her. "Fly true and may the stars protect you," they said in unison.

Tears filled Ash's eyes. She repeated the words back in a breaking voice. "F...fly true and may the stars protect you."

Then she nodded her head, and pressed the bangle on her wrist.

CHAPTER THIRTY-FIVE

The silence of the Library felt eerie. Especially after the chaos she'd just left. Some things had been picked up. Some things were still scattered on the floor. Several of the rows had been pushed back into place.

"Orius?" Ash spoke warily, not sure where he might be.

She walked a few of the rows. The gold spear of Agillas, from U756 – the one that had killed Helios, and been tossed to the floor during the attack – was back in its rightful place. The crown from Agrean, gold set with blue coraporamine, was back sitting on a perch, just not behind the usual glass.

Her hand touched a remarkably undamaged large blue-and-white platter. She smiled as she realized she didn't even know where it had come from. The museum tag flickered up beside her, but she didn't read it. Not yet. There was so much still to learn here.

There was a shimmer and Orius appeared beside her. There was something different about him. The deep furrows and lines on his face weren't quite so pronounced, but he still had an air of sadness about him. Her heart squeezed in her chest.

"You returned," he said, as if he hadn't expected her to come back.

"I've returned," she agreed, then took a few moments to look around some more. This was hard. Harder than she'd thought.

She couldn't believe how attached she'd become to this place – and that when she'd thought it might be destroyed in the attack, it had turned things around for her. Made her feel again.

She thought about the last few months. Everything she'd been through. The devastation at not making the grade as a pilot. The confusion at ending up here. The bewilderment at anyone in the universe thinking she should be the Guardian. And everything that had come after. The learning, the knowledge, the decisions.

And it was time for the biggest in her life.

"Have you heard anything from U62?" she asked.

Orius nodded. "It seems that Aldus has been overthrown and imprisoned on U62. Once all the systems went down, the inhabitants started to realize exactly how much of a megalomaniac he was. It seems they objected to the way he'd handled both Humans and androids who weren't quite what he'd deemed perfect. He's somewhere in the salt mines." He met her gaze. "I can't foresee him causing any more problems in the future."

Ash paused for a moment, taking in what he'd just told her. In a way it was a relief. But it wasn't a solution.

"Things need to change, Orius," she said steadily.

"You're right," came the unexpected reply.

She spun around. "I am?"

He nodded. "Tell me what you want to change."

This was her opportunity, this was her chance. So why did Ash suddenly feel so afraid?

She thought about all she had done, and the people she had met. She thought about all the decisions she had made. Had they been the right ones? Often, she hadn't been sure. Even now, she still wasn't. But she knew in her heart that if she could turn the clock back, she wouldn't.

"I need to change how things are done. I need to be sure about staying here as Guardian. There is so much good that can happen here." She ran her finger along one of the cabinets. "But equally, there's room for so much error."

"Have you made an error, Ash?"

It was the first time he'd used her name today. It was almost like he could see inside her mind. She answered honestly. "I guess I'll never know. I'd like to think not, but that would be conceited. There's always the potential to make a wrong decision, and it would be wrong to be overconfident."

Orius gave a slow nod of his head. "What changes have you thought about?"

She swept out her arms. "About how things work. About the network of Friends across the universe. About how the wrong information" – she took a breath – "could be fatal – for me, or for others." She licked her lips. "I think it's time for an update on how things are done."

Orius sat down on a chair next to her. It was inlaid with bronze and had a plush red velvet seat. It wasn't a chair, Ash realized, it was a throne and he looked strangely comfortable there.

He tilted his head to one side. "Any ideas?"

Orius was being oddly amenable about all this. What was going on?

Ash gave a slow nod. "I think so. I've met a number of people who I think could be good in helping me make decisions." She looked around, parts of her insides twisting as she said the words out loud. Her intention wasn't to hurt Orius. "And I think, at times, I should invite them to be here with me."

She kneeled down next to his throne. "It's hard not to be influenced by my own prejudices, and my own feelings. It's hard to always act like I think the Guardian should. I've only seen a tiny part of this universe, Orius. There is so much more out there. I can't possibly expect to know or understand things I have no experience of. I think I need help."

Orius smiled and leaned over, his hand gently touching her hair. "Your words make me proud, Ash. Prouder than you can ever know. You've seen, you've understood. Change is needed, and you're right. The way the Library has worked hasn't changed in thousands of years. It's time. And you're just the person to do it." He nodded his head.

"Then you'll help?" She couldn't keep the anxiety out of her voice.

He shook his head. "Oh no."

"What?"

He stood up from the throne and he shimmered again, making her realize that something wasn't quite right. He gave a weak smile. "I won't be here to help you, Ash. Everything has a lifespan, even though it might not seem obvious at first. You were always going to be my last Guardian. And you've been the best decision I've ever made."

She stepped forward, her hand shaking as she lifted it to him. All of a sudden, he didn't seem quite so solid any more. The folds in his grey cloak weren't there. The lines on his face were less pronounced than ever.

"What do you mean? You...you're dying?"

Orius gave a gentle laugh. "How can I die? A hologram can't die. I've never been alive. My programming has just come to a natural end. You must have noticed that things have changed. It's why I've been able to touch you. It's why I flicker on occasion." He let out a sigh. "And shed a tear. I certainly wasn't programmed for that."

He held out both his hands. "For a moment I thought I was going to lose you, and the Library. But the truth is, you don't need me any more, Ash. You've found your true path. And it's here. It's always been here."

He looked around, his smile getting wider. "Your plans are good. The changes sound positive. And remember, if some don't work, you can rethink and try again."

His hand touched her cheek, and she felt it tickle her skin. A tear came quickly to her eye.

"I trust you, Ash, I held on for you – but you've got this. Go and do some good. You just prevented a war. You took a chance, you acted on instinct, even though it could have been your biggest sacrifice." He pressed one hand across his chest. "But you knew, you knew in your heart that if you offered everything freely, without any conditions, they would reciprocate."

The tears were flowing freely now. "But I could have been wrong," she said quickly. "I could have ruined everything."

Orius shook his head. He was beginning to disintegrate before her. "But you didn't. Your instincts are good. Trust yourself. Just like I trust you."

Ash was shaking. Of course holograms couldn't touch and be touched. Of course they couldn't cry. She should have realized something was wrong.

She held her breath. "Thank you," she whispered. "But how can I do this without you?"

Orius bowed his head. "I have faith in you, Ash Yang. I always have. The path is yours, Guardian. Take it." And he smiled as he disappeared before her eyes.

Ash's legs buckled underneath her and she fell to the ground, sobbing. She reached out into the air where Orius had just been. The emptiness of the Library seemed to surround her.

It took some time before she could finally catch her breath – before the tiny sounds of the Library started to penetrate again. Ticking noises, the rustling of papers and scrolls, tiny pieces of space debris touching the domed glass above her head.

She pulled herself up onto the throne that Orius had just vacated.

From this point, she could see just how much work there still was to do here. She wiped the tears from her face.

He had believed in her. The little orphan girl from the dusty village in Astoria. The girl who'd looked up to the stars, not to dream, but with the urge to fight. She sighed. Change was everywhere. Including in her.

Ash wanted to do this, and she wanted to do it right.

She stood up and dusted herself off. As she walked back up the stairs to the Proteus circle at the top, she started repeating to herself: "I am Ash. I am the Guardian of the Library at the End of the Universe."

Her bangle gave a tingle against her skin, and she smiled as a holographic diagram appeared in front of her face, showing an artefact and some details about a planet. She scanned them and gave a long slow nod. For this one she would take a Friend.

She lifted her hand and pulled up all the holographic screens, taking a few minutes to find what she was looking for.

There. The list of all the Friends, in all the planets in the universe. Thousands and thousands of individuals from countless galaxies who believed in the ethos of the Library. She nodded. She could think of a few friends of her own to add to this list.

She had this. *They* had this. But she also knew who to visit first.

She pressed the bangle and grinned as she emerged into a blue-tinged world. Columbia 764. The very first world she ever jumped to.

A figure with a familiar green face was sitting at a table nearby in a bustling marketplace. She looked confused.

"Guardian?"

Ash smiled and walked over. "Amara, can we chat?"

Amara nodded and shifted along the bench. "Sure." She had a half-smile on her face and it was clear she was wondering what was going on.

Ash slid in next to her and leaned her hands on the table. She grinned. "I need some help from a Friend…"